# Love
## Lifted
### Me

## Catherine Ritch Guess

## CRM BOOKS

CRM, P.O. Box 367
Paw Creek, NC 28130
www.ciridmus.com

**Publisher's Cataloging-in-Publication**
(*Provided by Quality Books, Inc.*)

Guess, Catherine Ritch.
    Love lifted me / Catherine Ritch Guess. --1st ed.
    p. cm. -- (Eagles wings trilogy)
    ISBN: 0-9713534-0-9

    1. Inspiration--Fiction. 2. Charlotte (N.C.)--
Fiction. 3. Christian fiction. 4. Domestic fiction.
I. Title.

PS3557.U34385L68 2001          813'.6
                QBI01-201124

Library of Congress Control Number: 2001118902

Printed in the United States of America

*To Glenn,*

*the inspiration that keeps me*
*a finely tuned instrument,*
*and*
*the only man who ever*
*moved a mountain for me*

# Acknowledgments

My deepest gratitude goes first to my parents, Elmer and Corene Ritch, for never squelching my creative dreams, no matter how far-fetched they seemed.

Secondly, to my in-laws and second set of parents, Forest and Betty Guess, for allowing many flowers to bloom through their interest in all my endeavors.

Thirdly, to Josh and Jamie for showing me the world through their eyes, for keeping me young (while making me gray!), and for continually giving me a new song to sing - you have been God's richest blessing. And to Glenn III, for adding yet another dimension to my life, my writing, and my blessings.

Lastly to Harriet McCachren and Jan Watson, whose daily help along the way enabled my vision to become a reality; to Sherri Brown and Luann Elliott, whose willingness to be my accomplices all over the world took them miles beyond the call of duty; to Gwen Abernethy, whose willingness to read my unproofed manuscripts took real courage and friendship; to Glenn Dedrick, who stretched my technological abilities *way* past their limit; to Pam and Robert at Plummer Graphics, who took the first step forward with me; to Jerry DeCeglio, who put my mental pictures on the cover; and to Kip Burke, my editor, whose encouraging words gave me the confidence to take that final step and never look back.

To each and every one of you, *THANKS!*

# PROLOGUE

She rounded the curve and caught a glimpse of the oversized deck on the back of her house. The walk she had taken to escape the thoughts of him suddenly failed its purpose as she visualized him standing there, leaning over the rail, flicking the ashes from his cigarette into the flower bed below. As she walked closer, as if drawn by a magnet, she could see him sitting on the corner of the rails, boots propped up against the huge, round redwood picnic table where they had shared so many of his meals, all cooked on the gas grill right there on the deck. Images, one after another, flashed before her eyes, of *him* – sitting, standing, leaning – all in this space where they had spent more time together than anywhere.

Feeling no lack of energy from the walk, she briskly made her way up the stairs to the white wicker writing desk in the hall. As she speculated about how long it had been since she had written anyone, she began to meditate about the long-lost art of letter writing. Had he been anywhere else except where he was, they, too, would have missed out on the charm of this lost art. But getting his letter yesterday was intriguingly wonderful. It brought her an

1

excessive amount of joy and happiness and laughter. How many times had she read it since yesterday? There was something about the waiting, the anticipation of the arrival of the mail, and the mind's wondering, *Will there be something for me, especially for me?* Then the excitement of ripping open the envelope to find words of love, or assurance, or just anything. The words didn't matter, for they had been written for a particular person – *me*! It was the mounting up of the heart, the butterflies in the stomach, the incitement of anticipation. Nope, phone calls – and especially e-mail – just did not have the same effect of making use of one's mind, their imagination or creativity. Plus, the simple act of communication had gotten lost in the process.

Savoring the opportunity to participate in this lost art, she pulled out her finest engraved stationery and a pen, and proceeded to write, *Dear* _____. Her monogram on the letterhead took her to a time before him, a time when she defiantly changed back to her maiden name after a horrendous marriage, and dared *anyone* to again abuse her – physically, mentally, verbally, *or* otherwise.

This was *her* house, *her* belongings, *her* personalized stationery – all shouting *her* independence. Even the towels in the palatial master bath bore her first name, lest someone should come in *her* home and even vaguely consider invading her space and her privacy.

While she sat there daydreaming, the chiming of the grandfather clock in the downstairs foyer beckoned her back to the present. Eight chimes. Eight o'clock. It was exactly at this very hour five months ago tonight that she saw him leaning up against the building, one foot up on the metal garbage can, talking on his cell phone, wearing a jean jacket and a brown suede cowboy hat.

Why did all of this stand out so distinctly in her head? The memory was so vivid, it was like she was walking closer to him all over again. Closing her eyes, she let the hypnotic state that was sweeping her mind carry her entire body, her entire presence, back five months as she relived that evening. *That fateful evening...* She

2

heard the words trail off as she watched herself as in a dream – a dream that had been a reality.

What possessed her to even notice him at all? Her, the prim and proper minister of music who was only lowering herself for this one evening to come here and watch the local yokels do line dances. All this to hopefully find some dance steps that might be useful in choreographing her upcoming children's musical.

She loved the wide open spaces of the Wild West, so she thought the idea of Moses in a western setting had been clever at first. But tonight as she drove here, she realized that she wished she had been going to the Trail Dust in Dallas, the Rawhide out in Scottsdale, or one of her favorite night spots in Fort Worth or on the Riverwalk of San Antonio. Somewhere in what was the *real* 'out west' to a citified East Coast girl, rather than some redneck imitation of a dance hall. However, this was as close as she could get in the vicinity of Charlotte, North Carolina, so she decided to make the best of it for one evening.

It had been a good thing no one could see her rummaging through her closet this afternoon trying to find the only pair of jeans (and they were black instead of blue!) that she owned, and one of her western shirts to get her through the evening. She knew there would be no one there she would be interested in, despite the fact that she had just recently vowed to go out and meet some new people. This hang-out was not her style, so she did not even entertain the prospect of "making an acquaintance"!

Her friends, who were the line dance instructors here and were also mutual friends of his, had told her he might be here. However, the thought of him did not register with her. She knew he was a good deal younger than herself, but more than that, she figured he must have some real problems because she knew that only five weeks ago, he had attempted suicide.

It was a hush-hush situation, but she had been in the church office when one of the other ministers was called down to the scene. *Poor guy,* she remembered thinking. *And right here at Christmas. This must be just terrible for his family and son. What a way to spend the holidays.*

She recalled her conversation with the secretary as the minister on call walked out the door. "There are so many desperate people who attempt or actually commit suicide during the holiday season. Seems they just can't handle the loneliness. There's probably not one person who can honestly say that at some time they've wondered whether their family would be better off without them, but then their love for their family was too great to think about doing something foolish. Or they were just too proud to become one of the statistics."

"Is he divorced?" the secretary asked.

"I don't know. I didn't even realize he was separated. All I know of him is that he was quite a wild character as a teenager, he had a 'far out' wedding when he was only eighteen, he has an adorable son who looks just like him, and that my son thinks he looks just like Chuck Norris, only

4

shorter!" Both women chuckled as she continued, "and that he had serious back surgery last October, so I thought he just came down and stayed with his parents during that period so he could be near the doctors during his recovery. I didn't know he was here for good."

Her flashback fast forwarded a couple of weeks as she remembered seeing him walk into the hospital to see Kevin on the day that Chelsea died. She was leaving and had just walked down the hall to speak to grieving parents who were about to lose their daughter when she saw him enter the room. Her mind wondered how he could even show his face here after pulling that incredulous suicide stunt at their house only a couple of weeks ago. Here, where Chelsea lay on her deathbed, and her children and family were trying to get past the holiday season.

But another side of her had thought, *How wonderful for this guy to come here in what must be a terribly awkward situation for him and speak to his buddy who is about to lose his wife. This is not a place where you usually see guys get together!* As she pondered over the hurt and pain that he must be feeling inside, causing his episode two weeks before, her thoughts quickly came to a close as she rushed off to direct one of her many holiday handbell concerts. *This one will be in honor of Chelsea*, she noted as she exited the hospital.

The twangs of the country music, as she'd opened the door of the Wildlife on that fateful night, promptly drew her thoughts back to where she was and why she was there. *Totally not my style,* she mused as she walked on into the building where she found a place beside the far wall. *Yes, this is a perfect spot to observe everybody who comes in, and watch the dance steps carefully.* Thank God, she had brought her younger teenage son to help her learn some new moves and invent some of their own. *There's no way I want to dance with any of these guys*, she concluded as she hugged the wall.

Then he sauntered in. She watched as he made his way across the dance floor, coming straight toward their group of mutual friends. Although she tried not to stare, his movement (which suggested a totally different character from what she expected) grabbed her eyes, causing her to look straight at him. Here was a person who needed a friend, someone to talk to, someone to accept him – whether they understood him or not. Just someone that would not look down at, or talk down to, him.

Once again, her thoughts wandered as a memory from the past came flooding through her mind, reminding her of when her older son was three years old. He had been pushed into Kulaski Lake, the lake at a spiritual retreat center, while playing. The lady who was supposed to be watching him had become heavily engaged in a conversation, and did not even notice that he had floated quite a distance across the lake, already going under a couple of times as he drifted farther from the shore.

It was this guy's uncle who happened to be walking around the lake with a friend and jokingly questioned which one of our kids had gone swimming in the lake, knowing full well that swimming was not permitted and that *surely* one of our group would not have been so lackadaisical as to let a child dive right in. But then he noticed it was a young child, and that he was drowning. So this man, giant that he was, jumped into the lake – clothes, shoes and all – and rescued her child.

She had never forgotten that rescue. And furthermore, it hit her now that just as this man had saved her son's life, perhaps she could return the favor to his family by saving this guy from whatever was troubling him. *Yes,* she decided, *she owed it to his family.*

The chiming of the clock, signaling that an entire hour had passed and night had fallen, woke her from her trance. Putting the pen back on the desk, no words written, she wandered back out onto the deck. She felt as if she heard their moon calling out to her. So many incredible signs had occurred in that exact spot over the past five months that she was almost afraid to go out, leery that what she would see might be a little *too* freaky, yet so curious about why she felt this gravitational pull to their spot that she *had* to open the door, *had* to see whatever sign of their love was out there.

She looked up at the spot they had shared and her eyes were filled with astonishment. Had she not encountered numerous signs right here previously, almost a daily occurrence, the sight before her eyes would have been utterly beyond belief. But she stared at the moon, with the clouds in the shape of a cross behind it. The moon was squarely in the center of the crossbar, casting light on the entire image. Should she rub her eyes and do a double take? No, she knew after all the many clear visions they had experienced together in this spot that she was accurate in what she saw. But, as if still not sure whether to trust her eyes, she called her younger son out onto the deck and asked him what he saw in the clouds.

"A cross. That's really cool, Mom!" He jumped right back into the video games with his friends as if the image in the sky was nothing out of the ordinary. But then, after their many episodes together, it wasn't. They had watched sunsets and stars and skies all over the world together, and it had always been as if God was giving his mom her own laser light show.

She grinned, thinking about what a special gift this son had been for her, looking back up at the clouds. As if the cross were not enough, the clouds were shifting their shapes until they formed a butterfly. Had she not just called this man in her life her butterfly? How many times of late had she referred to him as a butterfly, a new creation, a beautiful creature springing forth from its cocoon, its trapped world. Even four days ago, as he turned himself in, she saw a butterfly, a gorgeously colored specimen, lying on the landing going from the courtroom downstairs to the jail. And then yesterday, when she stopped to get batteries and a lighter to take to visit him, there was one on the sidewalk in front of the glass facade of the store. All of this proved to her that God agreed with her perception of him as a butterfly. But to see it in the clouds, on this very night, this five-month anniversary of their close encounter with each other!

She lowered her head and thanked God for all the signals that this was okay, that this love was real and that He had sent it down to her. The age difference was no longer an issue. In fact, she rarely remembered that she was older. His background of worldliness had given him a worn look that evened out their appearances. Given the fact that she looked much younger than she was, no one would have guessed that she was close to a decade older than he.

No longer did she feel guilty for being twice divorced, nor that she should be miserable and lonely for the rest of her duration on this earth. Rather, she immensely enjoyed this new lease on life that had virtually fallen in her lap.

Her eyes drifted back up to the sky, and to her amazement, the moon and the clouds were gone, completely vanished. The light that had been so brilliant during the past hour had disappeared. She looked all around as if the moon was playing hide-and-seek up in the heavens, but she realized how foolish she was. Once again, she had been privy to her own sky show here at The Moses House, the name her younger son christened their house when they moved here.

Chuckling at how blessed she was to walk so closely with Him, she wondered if God would still talk to her through the clouds after she moved from The Moses House. But her snicker turned to laughter as she thought about the fact that she was now going on to the Promised Land. Higher ground, so the signs would just get more spectacular.

The hammock invited her to another of their spots beneath the trees. Here, in the back yard, they had swayed many evenings while watching the stars twinkle and listening to the evening sounds. A plane flew over, making its ascent from take-off. How she longed to be on that plane with him, going anywhere, yet nowhere in particular. She wanted to show him all the places she had been, and to share their beauty and fascination with him. For she knew he could sense all of the awe and majesty of the world's natural wonders in the same way she had.

They had such a bond between them. No one could possibly understand it, for they did not even comprehend it themselves. But they both perceived its power, its uniqueness, and had learned better than to try to dismiss it.

She waited for a few minutes to make sure the moon would not reappear, but it seemed to be gone for the evening. It was a good thing, because she would have stayed right here, as if frozen in place, watching the changing shapes of the clouds for hours, and then retiring to the hammock to rest in the wee morning hours. But instead, she raced up the stairs, back to the writing desk to resume the chore she had first set upon.

This time the words flowed freely as the pen swept across the paper, turning the blank sheet into a volcano of words. Yes, it was too bad their letter writing would soon end and she would go back to the mundane communication line known as the telephone.

# *1*

S hane Sievers was not the least bit excited about his plans for the evening. But he knew that if he went out with any of his cronies, he would be subjected to his old addictions before he had even been gone for fifteen minutes. And he had reluctantly realized, after the suicide attempt, that his life had hit rock bottom. He didn't care to spend the rest of his life where he was, *like* he was. So he made up his mind to give up all the drugs on his own. Sure, he had quit the habit on three other occasions, but he kept on dealing them. This time, he was going to give it *all* up, *for good*! He knew that most people couldn't make this kind of a change after twenty-plus years, but then he was stronger than most people. Otherwise, he wouldn't still be alive now. *Shane Sievers is a survivor!* he thought confidently – the first time he had been confident in the almost three years since his accident.

He had started working this past week for a construction contractor, who just happened to be a line-dancing instructor. Even knowing only a bit of Shane's past, it didn't take long for his boss to realize that this guy needed a social outlet. "Why don't you come out to The Wildlife with me and the Missus this Saturday night? There's a live country band, and there's always a few single chicks to dance with."

"I'll think about it," was Shane's reply, not wanting to be impolite to his boss the first week. He really had no intention of going out with a bunch of people who were almost old enough to be retired. *God, they're nearly my parents' ages!*

But as the weekend drew closer, Shane realized that it was either go to the dance hall or sit at home with his parents. The only reason he was even in their house was because his girlfriend had been sent to prison for habitual DUIs, which was in fact a bad rap. However, she didn't have the money to get a decent attorney who could get her off the charge she was taking for her look-alike sister. So, he had lost his live-in lover and his free place to stay to boot. And his girlfriend before her had her teenage daughter, the daughter's boyfriend, and the daughter's baby by someone else, living in the trailer with her and a younger teenage daughter.

On Friday, Shane decided he'd better accept the offer to go out with his boss, not wanting to sit home on a Saturday night. *Surely I can stand it for a few hours,* he grimaced.

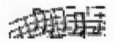

Saturday night came and he went out with his boss and three other couples to eat at the fish camp before going to The Wildlife. *The fun's already started,* he thought apprehensively as he sat there savoring his Coke, all the while dreaming of caressing a long-necked bottle. *I gave up a perfectly wonderful lifestyle for this?* But he knew inside that he really did want to change his ways and give his son a normal life. *He deserves that,* Shane would tell himself every time he got in what he considered to be an unbearable situation.

They drove up at the Wildlife and Shane already regretted his decision to come. He was used to places with a lot more life and noise going on, even on the outside. But here were couples and families going in. He didn't see one single female that wasn't with a group of friends or had kids with her. Not one person that caught his eye. He opted to stand outside and smoke for a while before going in, so he graciously excused himself from his party.

Once outside, Shane used his cellular phone to call up every buddy he had, trying to find one who could come and rescue him from this evening of torture. All he got were answering machines and voice mails. *Damn!* He stood outside, smoking a couple more cigarettes and trying to convince himself that he might as well make the best of the evening, when he heard the band inside tuning up.

*God, I can't believe I'm spending a Saturday evening at a place where they don't even serve beer. Some Wildlife this is — somebody needs to rename the place!* But he had been so desperate to get out of his parents' house for the evening that Shane would have gone anywhere. He flicked the cigarette butt out across the parking lot and turned to go in the door.

*Let's just hope the band is decent. I'd hate for the entire evening to be a waste!*

After last night's first choreography session with the kids, Christina Cache had been invited to go to The Wildlife with the instructors. Bob and Shirley were great dancers, and tonight would be the first chance she had to actually spend any time with them. She knew they taught line-dancing classes, and had invited her to be a part of their Saturday night group before, but she had never broken down and spent her one free evening of the week with a gang of Western wanna-be's screaming "Yee-haw."

However, they had been such a fun couple and pleasant

company last night that she and Noah decided to give up one evening to spend with them. Besides, they had no plans and being on their feet last night had unwound both of them. Christina longed for the exercise, and Noah just liked being up and moving, since it was a little too cold for skateboarding. The two of them decided it would be a new adventure, as well as giving Christina some helpful hints for her next upcoming musical project.

*Exercise, work, good company – at least the entire evening won't be a waste.*

The line dance instructor asked Christina to dance one of the slow dances with him. She really did not want to, but she was so appreciative of the fact that Bob and Shirley were going to help her choir kids with choreography that she gave in for one dance. At least she knew him, that he was married, and would cause her no harm, so she trusted him.

She could not believe how awkward she felt in his arms. Her – Miss Rhythm. The one with the dancing trophy at home from the New Year's Dance at the Sugar Bowl a few years back. Christina had done great last night, but then they had only worked on line dances and she did not have to be held in anyone's arms. The closest she had been to another male was during the Cotton-Eyed Joe, and she managed that easily because she did not have to look at her partner, or be face to face with him.

*What a joke!*

Christina Cache, the person with all the natural talent who had choreographed numerous dance routines and had always been the Queen of the dance floor. And now, here she was, petrified, just like a block of wood, in his arms.

As if she did not already know how clearly her loss of grace showed, her partner leaned in and whispered, "You can get a little closer. I'm not going to bite you." Christina wanted the dance floor to open up and swallow her right then and there. She knew exactly why she was so uncomfortable in Bob's arms, but how could she explain that to him – at least in one evening? So she tried to act a little less cumbersome, wishing that she had stayed, sitting in her corner, sipping her Sundrop Slushy. Too bad they didn't serve White Zinfandel or Kahlua. She might have overcome part of the problem!

*Or rum. Then I could be all over the dance floor!*

She danced all of the line dances after the first break, determined not to let the entire evening be a waste. Noah was a great partner, and he even got her up for one of the fast-paced partner-changing dances, but only after he promised to find her every time they had to get a partner. Luckily, the few times he could not get to her, Christina arranged to grab an older gent who could barely move, or else she slid out of the circle until time to change partners again. It got to be a game to her, and she actually enjoyed the playfulness of it.

There were a couple of times that Shane's eyes caught hers, but she always moved a little faster to get to another partner, afraid for him to see and feel her awkwardness at being here. Christina did not like to do things unless she could do them well, and she did not want to be totally embarrassed in front of him. Yet, she had to think of some way to talk to him.

They both retreated to the table at the second break, and she discovered she was glad for Shane's company. It was amazing they found subjects to talk about that both had experienced. Christina could not believe her good fortune, even though she was more than a little surprised that she had something in common with this reputedly rowdy redneck.

*Thank you, God, for giving me the ability to be able to talk to anyone, anywhere, anyplace.* Once again, Christina was grateful for the gift of gab. It had come in handy on more than one occasion.

By the time the band started back up, Christina found herself wishing that she could dance with Shane. There was a strength about him that she liked, that made her want to be in his arms. But she was still fearful of being a flop, especially to him. She could sense his worldliness, no more than they had talked, and she felt she would be able to talk to him more if she did not chase him away at first. So she made it clear that she wanted to stay in her corner when the band's third set started with a slow dance.

He sat there with her, still talking about everything, yet nothing. Since they had gone through some of the same experiences, although from different angles, Christina found it extremely easy to converse with him. Yet she found Shane most amusing with all of his stories and antics. Before long, she realized how much fun she was really having. That is, until the dance instructors came over and told him they were going to be leaving shortly.

Shane looked over at Christina, glad for what he had found there, and grabbed her hand, pulling her up out of her chair, saying, "You're not getting out of here without one dance with me!"

She did not even have time to balk before he had her out on the floor and had pulled her into his arms. *Okay, body, relax. Let your feet glide. Don't let him know how afraid you are for someone to touch you. And for God's sake, do not let him see the fear in your eyes if he looks at you.*

Luckily, her prayer worked, but only somewhat. She was still filled with trembling at the thought of being in a man's arms, and she was terrified that he might look at her face. Yet, she really liked the way she seemed to fit in his arms, as if they were a match. Christina could not help but notice that she enjoyed this. Perhaps she was only getting a little more used to the idea, but she was nonetheless afraid that Shane would take her awkwardness as not liking him or his company, or just plain naiveté. Whatever, she

16

hoped that he would not be too put off by her.

Shane liked having Christina in his arms. He liked the smell of her perfume. It was a far cry from that of the bar sluts to which he was accustomed. He tried his best to look into her face, but it was as if her eyes dodged him. She definitely intrigued him, and he fully intended to see what made her tick. *Why was a woman like her in a dive like this?* There was just something about her that would not turn him loose, and he knew that he had to know her, to find her. The attraction could not be denied, and he was determined to find a way to get to her.

*Shane Sievers, you're really out of line. This chick has class. She's not even going to glance at someone like you. There's way too much difference between the two of you.*

She was startled, both by surprise and confusion, that she hated to see him leave, and almost offered to take him home if he wanted to stay a little longer, but she decided against it. *Christina Cache, you must be fooling yourself.*

# 2

The next Saturday came and Shane was like a man on a mission. He had spotted a slender blonde there the week before, so he intended to go home with her. The hellion was way long overdue for having a female, since he got little opportunity to get out and away from under his parents' roof. He could care less about the dancing, but a guy in need would do just about anything to get what he wanted.

Shane wished that they would have eaten out again before they got to The Wildlife. He could have used a couple of beers to settle his anticipation. When they got there, he stayed outside again for a while, checking out any new prospects. *Who knows, something better might come along!*

When it was about time for the band to start, he decided to go on in and find a place to sit where he could keep an eye on things. He had made up his mind that this was going to be a great evening. There would be more than just dancing tonight!

Dinner got off schedule due to Christina going over all of her new dances again. She had made Noah's favorite, beef stroganoff – a bribe to get a fourteen-year-old to give up his Saturday evening to go dancing with his mom and her friends. No, actually, she knew that Noah enjoyed this as much as she did. He had gotten a real charge out of twirling around what to him were "old ladies" last week. And he was such a natural-born charmer that they all fell in love with him, wishing he were twenty or thirty years older. Besides, he had inherited his mother's rhythm when it came to dancing. Inwardly, Christina figured Noah was so glad to see his mom this excited about going out and having a life again, that he was willing to do anything. She knew he had seen the pain and hurt in her over the past, especially the last three years, and it was during that time that she indeed realized how close they had become to each other. He had transformed into the anchor that held her from going over the edge.

Noah, the younger of her two sons, had invited three friends to go with them, so Christina was not going to be able to count on him for her dancing partner this evening. Yet she was ecstatic that he had peers joining them. As much as she loved having him with her, she did not want to cramp his style, or have him feel responsible for her. She hoped that the dance instructor would be able to introduce her to someone that she could stand for at least one evening.

Christina had been waiting for this night all week. She had rented videos at the library, and even bought a couple of her own just so she would not be a wall flower this evening. Even the mundane chores of mopping and vacuuming had been enhanced by line dance steps this past week. And she had topped it all off by shopping for new jeans and boot shoes. No one loved being on their feet more than she, and tonight, she intended to keep the dance floor hot.

19

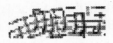

This night, he got to watch her make her entrance, just in time for the dance to start. She looked so much different this evening as she walked across the floor. Their eyes met and she smiled. Shane froze for an instant at the strange awareness he felt when he saw that smile – something he had never felt before. It was clear to him as he gazed at her that she had a way about her – a way that made those around her feel better, about themselves and the things around them. He could already feel the inner change in himself, glad for Christina's presence there.

As the music started for the first Paul Jones dance, his eyes raced around the room, looking for his blonde again, but he couldn't find her. He turned to ask Christina if she would like to dance, just in time to see her going out onto the dance floor with a friend of his who he had invited to come and see his catch, and check out the other babes. Shane watched her closely as she glided across the floor. Was this the same person who had seemed so frightened in his arms only one week ago?

Shane figured that perhaps it was him. She was not about to lower herself to be in his class, yet, here she was, dancing and laughing and talking with his buddy. He refused to let his friend be one up on him, so he walked around the circle of dancers, planning to grab her when they switched partners. The couples separated and just as it was time to find a new partner, Noah's friend grabbed Christina's waist and reeled her away.

He decided to forget about her as he was grabbed by a female looking for a partner. As they kicked up their heels, his eyes searched for Christina, determined to get her on the next go round. The couples split again, and Shane timed his movements carefully to meet her at the right second, only to see Noah cut in front of him and whisk her off again.

That did it. What Shane Sievers wanted, he got, and he would dance with her – NEXT! He watched her on the arms of her son, her head tossed back in laughter, as they both enjoyed the vitality of the evening. Her auburn hair was incredibly thick and styled so that it, too, danced with every movement of her head. No wonder everyone was in a rush to get to her. She was fun. You could easily see the joy and happiness exuding from her. This person who had made such an effort to avoid his eyes last week was setting the tone for everyone on the floor.

What had happened to her, or had he just missed it last week? No, he was an observant person, so he was sure he had not missed anything before. *I did find the blonde, didn't I?*

When he heard the music getting to the point where the guys turned loose of their gals to look for a new partner, he moved quickly to where she and Noah were. Christina was almost jolted right off her feet as Shane literally grabbed her away from Noah. They did not even get a chance to speak to each other because the music was winding down, Shane was so proud of himself at finally getting her, and Christina was still in shock at having been so rigorously knocked off her feet.

The music stopped, and Bob and Shirley moved quickly to Christina's side, welcoming her back, along with Noah and his friends. They chatted all the way back to the tables, inviting Shane to join in their conversation. The next dance was a slow one, so Shane smoked his cigarette, listening to their group make small talk, all the while checking to see if his quest had yet arrived. When he still did not see her, he looked forward to the music getting back to the fast-paced line dances so that he could have Christina to himself.

However, when the rhythm picked up, she was out on the floor, not only joining in the dances she had watched last week, but teaching their friends all the new ones she had learned during the past week. *God, what a ball of energy. It would take an army to keep up with her ... or one REAL man.* Shane Sievers loved a good challenge, only he liked it more when there was some money lying on it. But even *he* knew better than to make Christina the object of a gamble.

Shane's friend wandered over to ask about the blonde, hoping she had a friend. A little embarrassed to admit she wasn't there, Shane suggested that his friend check out all the other bait. He had already made up his mind that if he got up, it would be to dance with Christina. Already, he missed her sitting there with him, talking to him, and giving him her undivided attention, like last week. If the only way he could talk to her would be to dance, then so be it. He longed for her understanding face and comforting voice. Shane made up his mind that the entire evening would not be a loss.

When she walked back over to the table to gulp down some water, Shane formally introduced her to his friend, boastful that he knew a dame of this caliber. "Mickey, this is Christina Cache. She's the ... " he paused, wondering how shocked his friend would be if he found out this interesting creature worked in a church, much less was a minister!

Both Mickey and Christina stared at Shane. Christina, sensing the problem, extended her hand to Mickey.

"Hi, Mickey. I'm Christina, a musician friend of Shane's. You know, one of those weirdoes." She grinned, and winked at Shane, trying to save him from an embarrassing moment, for which he was both amused *and* grateful.

Mickey returned the handshake.

"Hi, Christina. I'm Mickey. Would you like to dance?" Mickey turned and looked at Shane with a 'Thanks, Pal' grin, then back at Christina. "Again?"

"I'd love to!" she retorted as she heard the band begin *Jailhouse Rock.*

Shane watched as she was gone again. Was he going to have to chase her all evening? *No!* Surely a slow dance would come next, and Christina would be his. He was a man on a mission tonight, but his mission had become to get this lady's attention. His thoughts stopped.

*A lady? Since when does Shane Sievers spend time with* ladies?

He gathered himself enough to decide that he missed Christina's company, and he would get her full attention before the evening concluded. Watching her move to the Fifties music made him even more driven to be with her. She obviously felt *all* the music, the hip-hop, the country line dances, and the slow numbers. It was like it was a part of her, that her body flowed with the music. Shane realized he was staring at her, so he lit up a cigarette, hoping that neither she, nor his friend, had noticed.

Shane had no need to worry. Christina had been oblivious to everything and everyone around her, simply enjoying being out, being herself, and getting out some of the nervous energy that had been penned up inside her these past years. To her, this was therapy. It was definitely the best stress relief she had experienced in quite some time.

And he certainly didn't have to worry about Mickey noticing his stares, either. That poor guy had been so absolutely overwhelmed when Christina told him about her *real* occupation that he almost dropped her in the floor on one of the spins during the dance!

Christina always loved seeing that reaction from people who were not too acquainted with the spiritual world. They didn't seem to compute that people of "the cloth" were *real* people, and could be *defrocked,* as she laughingly put it.

She didn't miss the opportunity to invite him to church the next morning, telling him that, "If Shane can stand it, so can you. It won't kill you. He's living proof!" to which they both laughed. Mickey didn't respond, but she would have taken bets that he would show up just to see what kind of church would hire a minister like her.

Shane was right. The disco ball came on, signaling a slow dance – the last one before the break. He saw Christina drop Mickey's hand and walk back toward the table. Before she had time to sit down, Shane clasped her hand, and asked her to dance, not giving her time to refuse. He led her to the middle of the floor, just so he could feel alone with her without everyone watching them. As she turned in to place her hand on his shoulder, he realized how much he liked the feel of her in his arms.

"I thought I never would get to dance with you," Shane said in an almost reprimanding voice.

"You didn't ask," Christina replied with a serious smile.

He looked into her eyes. She didn't look at the floor when he gazed at her this time. Those eyes told the real story behind this person. The pain and anguish Shane had caught a glimpse of last week were still noticeable, as much as before, yet the joy that was written not only on her face, but all over Christina's entire body, kept one from seeing that hurt.

*What a mask she wears.* Yet he could see everything inside her. Her love, her peace, her devotion, all of her emotions, everything, just by looking into those eyes, for he felt he could see all the way down to the very core of her soul. Shane had never seen eyes like those before. He knew nothing about Christina before last week except that she was the best organist he'd ever heard and that she had worked in a church, the one where he grew up, for a very long time. In fact, they had only spoken once that he could remember during all those years. And that was due to the fact that Noah wanted to meet the guy who resembled Chuck Norris! Now he felt as if he had known her for years – many years.

The music ended without either of them speaking another word. The lights came back up and the band dispersed for the first of their breaks. Christina did not notice that they were holding hands until they reached the table and she started to sit down. A little embarrassed, she dropped her hand, and made her way to the water fountain. Why had she not even noticed her hand in his? Had she just felt that comfortable with him?

Christina had hoped to get another chance to talk with Shane, to make him feel worthy and accepted. But he was her *job*, and tonight, she was here for her own pleasure. The business could come during the breaks. Dance time was hers, and she refused to share it with anyone, especially someone connected with her job. She had made a personal vow to give up her "All Business, No Pleasure" philosophy of the past few years.

Shane and Mickey went outside to talk about going out later, maybe to look for another blonde, and have a few beers. That sounded like a great idea to Shane, and he looked forward to living a little. But Mickey had found a dance partner, so he wasn't quite ready to leave yet.

They went back in and sat down across the table from Christina. Shane was surprised that she was able to start up a dialogue with Mickey, not knowing him. Yet she had done the same with him last week. He watched her face and expressions as she carried on this conversation, to the extent that when they questioned him about something, Mickey had to repeat the question. Shane had never met anyone who was so intent not only in talking, but in listening, as well. She possessed an uncommon charm in that area he had never encountered. He felt drawn to her, and he could tell Mickey did, too.

*Just my luck! I find a decent dame, and someone has to be here to horn in on my time.* Shane found himself resenting the fact that he'd ever invited Mickey to come to The Wildlife.

Christina was relieved that Shane had a friend here. She was truly glad for the opportunity to talk to him, but she did not want to seem unduly interested in him. Besides, after last week, she felt a little *too* drawn to him, and she had to be sure to keep her distance. One of the first lessons she had learned in seminary was to keep a safe distance from parishioners, especially those of the opposite sex. That had always been particularly challenging for her because of her natural caring for others, and her ability to relate to males so easily. She also knew that depression tended to draw people to someone who showed the least bit of concern, and not knowing his social status at present, she had to be doubly careful not to let him get the wrong idea.

*Why am I even wondering about all of this A guy like him wouldn't be interested in someone like me even if I were all over him!*

She got her logical brain back in gear, and found some trivial subject to discuss with the two of them. *Why can't the music hurry and start?* Christina found herself a little uncomfortable all of a sudden, although she couldn't quite put her finger on the reason why. She was used to being in control of every situation in which she found herself, but there was something here that she found uncanny, and she was more than a little anxious to leave it.

Shane was once again intrigued by her ability to wrap Mickey, a rough sort who had probably never entered the door of a church in his life, into their discussion. However, he had to admit that he was grateful Mickey had found his own dance partner. *Why can't the music hurry and start?* Shane found himself wanting Christina all to himself again, like last week. *Why couldn't we just sit here and talk?* She had a way of mesmerizing the people around her. He had never met anyone with so much charisma and he found it more than a little unnerving. But he was a tough guy, and he could handle anything or anybody, especially a broad. So he intended to

26

get her out on the dance floor the minute the music started. She was his until Mickey and he left for a better offer.

The first music of the next set turned out to be another Paul Jones, one of the dances where couples changed partners. He grabbed her hand and said, "C'mon. You're not gonna just sit here."

Christina was bewildered at his audaciousness, but pleasantly fascinated by his command of her. She was not used to a man treating her exactly like this, but she liked it. And Shane was such a wonderful dancer that she found it difficult to believe he had never done this before last Saturday night. When the whistle signaled them to look for a new partner, Christina hated to leave him.

*Damn it, I'll probably lose her again!* But Shane took advantage of the situation to check out any other interesting prospects that might have come in during the intermission. He grabbed a partner, but immediately looked to see who had gotten Christina.

*Mickey! What's he doing with her?* Shane kept a close eye on the situation to make sure they separated at the blow of the next whistle. He had gotten familiar enough with the music to get to Christina just in time to grab her before some other guy.

When it came time to switch partners a fourth round, Shane found Noah and told him to go dance with his mother. He was taking no chances on his friend getting too close to Christina. She was too good for a roughneck like Mickey. *Who am I trying to fool Mickey ain't jack compared to me!* Regardless, Shane intended to protect her from getting herself involved with the wrong crowd.

Shane was glad to see that Noah passed his mom off to his high-school friend on the last round. *Good kid. I like that guy,* he thought, relieved at Noah's perception and solution to the matter. *Takes good care of his mother.*

The next few dances were all line dances, so Shane went back to the table for another cigarette. He knew Christina would not find someone else to dance with until the next slow dance. But, when the lights went down, and the disco ball came on, he saw her briskly making her way back to the table.

*Why does she run and hide every time she has to be close to someone?*

He gave her enough time to get her water, but then asked if she'd like to dance. Christina was taken aback, especially after the way he had gotten her out to the dance floor earlier.

*This guy really can be a gentleman!*

Christina had intended to sit this one out, afraid that some guy might actually look at her, and she would be tempted to gaze back into his eyes. Her mask, that impenetrable shield, hid all of her feelings except the happy ones, and she refused to let anyone see what was hidden deep within her. But she was so touched by the tenderness in Shane's voice that she accepted his offer. They met at the end of the table, where he led her to the dance floor and then took her into his arms. She still kept her distance, but he could feel that some of her uneasiness was gone.

Shane led her, making sure not to get closer than she would allow, and kept her far enough away from the other couples that he could look into her eyes. Those eyes, those beautiful clear blue eyes that told a story, and he was sure could see the same in his own eyes.

Christina could feel herself enjoying this a little differently from all the other dances. Afraid to get caught in an awkward moment, she asked, "How did you learn to dance so well?"

"I have no idea. I told you I'd never danced before last week, and I only came here for something to do."

"But, you have perfect rhythm, and your lead is so easy to follow."

"It must be because you are so easy to dance with. It's kinda like you just fit in my arms and there's no effort."

Christina had to admit she loved dancing with Shane. There was no effort, for it seemed their bodies flowed together and each anticipated the next move of the other. As the music ended, she said jokingly, "Then I guess you'll just have to be my own personal dance partner!"

As the lights came up, the music swiftly moved to a fast number. Noah caught his mom on the way back to the table, yelling excitedly, "C'mon, Mom. Let's show these old geezers how to really move!"

Noah twirled and spun Christina from one end of the floor to the other. She was surprised that she wasn't too dizzy to stand up, much less dance. But they were both having so much fun, giggling incessantly all the while, that every eye in the place was on them. Christina was so proud of her son. She rightly beamed inside that her son had so much natural ability and talent, and even more, that he wasn't ashamed to be out in front of hundreds of people dancing with his mother. And not only that he was doing it, but he was having a great time doing it.

Their love for each other exuberated as people watched them controlling the dance floor. The people around them realized that they were not watching two good dancers, but a display of love that was completely uncommon for a mom and an adolescent. They should typically have been at each other's throats, and certainly not out together on a Saturday night. The truth of the matter was that Noah not only showed the people how to move, but gave them a more important lesson of the power of his mother's love, for he, too, possessed that same love. Little did he or his mom realize what a gift they were giving everyone there that evening.

As Shane watched Noah and Christina, he realized that he, like the rest of the crowd, was spellbound. *Her perfume, she smelled so good. Her thick hair, her sleek neck, that smile that pulled you into her world, her happiness. Just what was it with her?*

A red flag signaled him to watch out – getting too close could be dangerous. Yet, Shane Sievers had never run from danger. In fact, trouble intrigued him, especially this kind. He decided the only trouble here was some person who worked in a church.

Christina Cache was supposed to be some Bible-thumpin' Holy Roller. Yet here she was, moving so freely around the dance floor that he could not take his eyes off her. He had forgotten the blonde, or anybody else, for that matter.

Right now, this creature was like a puzzle, a mystery. The quest was his. Shane had to keep Christina away from the other guys. *He* would be the one to see through her mask, to crack her shell, to solve this mystery.

Christina tried once again to retreat to the table. She couldn't help but catch Shane's eye. His look pulled her right into his stare. *What is inside him that hurts so badly? Why would he want to take his own life?* That last dance with him had made her want to spend more time with him. She wanted to discover what he was hiding, to find an opening into his shell, so that she could worm her way into his life. More than anything, she hoped he would realize that he could trust her. She desperately wanted to reach him, to talk to him, to comfort him, to help him overcome whatever was so deeply masked inside that thick crust she could already tell he had built around himself.

Mickey walked over to the table and put his hand on Shane's shoulder. "Ya ready to go?"

Shane looked up to answer, but before he could open his mouth, he heard another voice join into the conversation.

"I can take you home, if you'd like to stay a little longer," Christina interjected.

Shane's eyes went from Mickey's to Christina's. As badly as he wanted to go out and find some real action on a Saturday night, he couldn't believe the opportunity that had just presented itself. That smile was all over her face, along with an embarrassed look that perhaps she had suddenly been too imprudent. He would probably have gone on with Mickey, but the apparent chagrin on her face aroused his curiosity. Maybe this was his opportunity to figure out what was going on with her. Besides, when had he ever

30

had a chance to be with someone like her before? At least it would be a new experience.

"I think I'll stay for a while. Go on and I'll catch you another time."

Christina felt her heart jump when she heard his words, although she wasn't sure why. Was it that she wanted to selfishly keep her newfound dance partner for a little longer, or did a job opportunity present itself? She had no idea of the answer, but it was a sure conclusion that for whatever reason, she was glad for the outcome.

They spent the rest of the evening, what was left of it, talking, each unleashing just enough of themselves to let the other get a slight glimpse inside, all the while trying to look for more than the other was willing to give.

The last dance was always a slow one. This time, Shane simply reached for Christina's hand and gently pulled her toward the middle of the floor. They were one of the few couples still left, so it felt as if they had the entire place to themselves. Their talking stopped as both of them concentrated solely on the music, and the pleasure of each other's company. For that brief instant, each of them forgot who they were and how vast their differences, as they became joined through the music and the mood created by the shimmering disco ball in the dim lights of an almost-empty room.

As the music ended, and the house lights began to come up, they caught each other's eyes for a moment, hands still clasped. Shane looked down at Christina and said clearly, yet so softly, "Thank you." She was stunned by his genteel manners, this man who appeared to be such a tough guy.

They walked back to the table to gather their things, then to the car without a word.

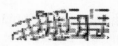

The ride home was nothing out of the ordinary for Noah and Christina. Laughter started the minute they got in the car. Noah's friends joined right into their merriment, and before long, had pulled Shane into the conversation. All of a sudden, it dawned on Shane that none of them seemed to think anything about the fact that she was taking some guy home.

*Does she pick up guys everywhere she goes, or is she just this friendly to everyone?* Shane realized that he didn't want either option to be right.

His next realization was even more startling. *They don't seem to care that I was an outlaw, a drug addict of over twenty years, an alcoholic. That I've spent my entire adult life living wild. That I'm near the pure definition of an outcast, and a far cry from their refined lifestyle. They don't even seem to notice. I wonder what they'd think if they knew about that thing a couple of months ago. Would that make a difference?*

Again he thought about his two previous questions, and this time he liked an affirmative answer to them even less. *She's too good for the likes of me. She shouldn't be spending her time with bad boys like me. She's in a whole different league.*

When they reached his house, Shane looked at her, not knowing quite how to end the evening. All he could think to do was mumble, "Thanks for the ride home."

"You're welcome. See you, *and Mickey,* at church tomorrow!" And she was gone.

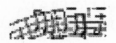

Shane had gotten so caught up in their conversation that he completely forgot his disappointment that the slender blonde did not show up, and his mission for the evening had gone south. He had gone there to get one thing, but, for the first time in his life, he felt a smug satisfaction that he had gotten something more – yet, he was just not exactly sure what.

Christina dropped off Noah's friends, then she and Noah laughed a few more minutes about the evening. If nothing else, The Wildlife was the epitome of places to go people-watching. They saw all sorts of people, all there for different reasons. But for the two of them, it had proven to be an excellent source of entertainment. They vowed to go back the next weekend for Valentine's Day. The dance hall was expected to be packed, and Christina felt sure there would be so much activity that she could actually get through that dreadful appointed day for lovers without all the blues and pain of the past.

She decided that she would definitely have to put in an appearance the next morning in Shane's Sunday School class. Christina had to know if he would even speak to her outside that social setting, especially in front of people he knew. *Or more crucial, people who know him. But then, why wouldn't he speak to me? After all, I am a minister. How much harm could I do?* She chuckled. To him, that was probably worse than the devil, himself.

It was no surprise when Christina walked into the class the next morning and saw Mickey seated beside Shane. They both turned and nodded at her, but not wanting to seem too interested in them, she only said hello and promptly found a seat beside Paul

Howell, her best friend's husband.

Christina had made a point to wear her brand-new outfit because it matched her vitality, and she wanted to make sure she was noticed. Her idea worked because as Shane and Mickey turned to look at her, they really didn't have a chance to strike a conversation with her. It was unusual for her to appear there on Sundays with all of her other responsibilities, so this room full of her closest friends took advantage of the opportunity to rib her and pull her into their chatter.

"I don't know many people who dress to match their vehicle," came one of the remarks. Her new purple outfit had been noticed and was a hit.

"Yeah, well you know what they say about purple people," she laughingly retorted.

The conversation continued back and forth from one person to another as members of the class wandered in, got their coffee and made their ways to empty seats. Shane could not believe how her entry had livened up the place. It was like everyone else not only accepted it, but expected it and joined into the hilarity that accompanied Christina. Her charisma was at work again. Everyone made a point of greeting her and drawing from her enthusiasm for life.

He looked at Mickey, and his friend could already read the thoughts going through Shane's mind. But Mickey figured he had as much right to enjoy her company as anyone, so he whispered over to Shane, "I think I'll ask her out next weekend."

Mickey knew that his comment would get a rise out of Shane, but he wasn't prepared for the daggers that appeared in his friend's eyes. He could see that his friend already had ideas of seeing her at the Valentine Dance next weekend at The Wildlife.

Christina exited early, along with her following of choir members, so neither Mickey nor Shane got a chance to talk to her, or even say good-bye. She couldn't help but wonder whether they had even noticed her, but after the lively start to the class, surely they had no choice.

Shirley stopped by the choir loft to speak to Christina after church and suggested that the singles group go to The Wildlife the next weekend for the Valentine Dance. Christina agreed with her that it was an excellent idea, simply because she knew Shane fell in that group and she was genuinely concerned for his welfare. She knew what a toll loneliness could take, and she did not want him to make the same mistake twice.

To her, Valentine's Day was the hardest of all days, since it signified lovers, but Christina wondered if the male psyche even picked up on that. Her cup overflowed with love, so she had found it a most difficult task not to share that emotion with someone. Sure, she had the boys and her parents, but that was different. She loved doing heartfelt niceties for others, and the one thing she missed most since her break-up with the boys' father was having someone to shower with all of her affection.

There had never been any emotion in her last marriage, so that made the chore of watching lovers even harder for her. Yes, she would go to the Valentine's Dance because she had no intention of spending that day alone this year. It did not matter to Christina that she would be spending it with hundreds of other people, she just would *not* be by herself!

Besides, there was a growing number of singles in the congregation, so this would be a good ministry for her. She certainly had empathy with them – probably more than for any other group in the church. It looked like a good project for Christina to take care of tomorrow.

The next morning was no different from her usual Monday. Christina fought the traffic to get Noah to school, rushing to get back to the church. There were several things that demanded her attention that day, since she needed to put in an appearance at the Duke Hospital tomorrow – a trip she dreaded, but that was part of her job description. Her first item on the agenda, though, was to write a letter to all of the singles about the dance next weekend. It would be so much fun that they would forget being alone.

She finished the letter promptly, got the copies in the outgoing mail, and went over to the choir room to practice and prepare for Wednesday's marathon of rehearsals. Christina couldn't believe her eyes when she saw Bob and Shane doing some repair work right beside her office. She felt her heart jump, but refused to acknowledge it.

Not wanting to look aroused, she chirped, "How are my favorite dancing partners?"

Bob was quick to answer, "I've got my radio going and we're just getting ready to take a break. Why don't you play us some good old country music?"

Christina got a charge from that question. She knew that her colleagues would frown upon that, probably because they were unable to comply with the request, but she sat down at the piano and ripped out *Down Yonder*, then went into a medley of Hank Williams' tunes.

The look of shock on Shane's face was no surprise. He hadn't heard music like that in this place since his own wedding reception, and she had already guessed that he had no idea she knew any country music, much less was capable of just sitting down and playing it.

It was Bob who broke the silence by asking her where she learned to play like that. Still watching the amazement in Shane's eyes, she continued to impress him with her "I'm more country than you" background. She had already surmised that he thought she was probably a snobby, spoiled city girl. This was Christina's chance to let him know she was a real person, just like him. Here was the in she needed to get closer to him and find a way to minister to his apparent distress.

This time it was Shane who questioned her. "Where did you learn to play that kind of music?"

"My mom's whole family is musical. Every time we got together when I was a child, there was a hoe-down. Everybody played something, even if it was the spoons or a washtub! I grew up going to gospel singings and the Grand Ole Opry on Saturday nights, and then the operas and ballets on Sunday afternoons, so I learned to appreciate and play every kind of music."

Christina loved the delight she saw making its way into Shane's eyes, so she continued.

"We always had a piano in my home, and my mother played a lot. By the time I was four, I would come home from church and play the hymns I'd heard that day while she was getting lunch on the table. And then when we went to Saturday-night Martha White country shows, I would come home and play the songs I liked, in the dark after my parents went to bed." Grinning, she added, "As if my parents couldn't hear me through the wall next to their bedroom."

She could tell she had made her point, and not wanting to appear *too* good, Christina asked Bob to show her the Sway, a slow dance that she had observed a couple doing the past Saturday.

Glad to oblige, Bob showed her the steps, then took her hands and did the dance with her. It was the most graceful of the western dances Christina had seen, and she had enough style and flair to really make it look beautiful.

Shane couldn't take his eyes off her as she literally flowed across the floor in Bob's arms. Here she was, off her pedestal, and in his world. He looked around, wondering what he'd done to deserve this, but glad he'd made the decision to come back to church, even if it was only after the constant badgering of his parents.

*So there are rewards in coming here, after all.*

Christina finished her dance lesson, and told Bob of Shirley's idea about the Valentine Dance. He was thrilled to hear that so many of their acquaintances would be there next weekend. She looked at Shane.

"I hope you'll come. Your letter is already in the mail."

"Oh, I'm planning on it."

He couldn't believe his good fortune. Shane had already hoped to meet her there again next Saturday, but now he didn't even have to wait all week to see if she'd show up. There was no doubt in his mind. Christina was going to be all his next Saturday night.

*Man, this place really* does *have its rewards!*

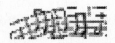

Christina literally waltzed away, grateful that her Father had chosen to smile on her in this manner. Not only had she found a way to let Shane know she could be on his communication level, she had a dance partner lined up for the Valentine Dance.

*I won't have to spend Valentine's Day by myself, after all!*

Now, even tomorrow's trip to Durham to visit her ex-father-in-law was not going to seem so torturous. It was not him she dreaded seeing, but Christina was afraid of what coming eye-to-eye with his son would do to her. She had been able to avoid him for two entire weeks, but the thought of meeting face-to-face with him sent chills down her spine. The hurt was still too present.

The next morning came too soon. Ever since Christina had gone to The Wildlife the first time, she had been hooked. It was just like being at the Trail Dust. *Well, almost.* There were no steaks, nor nearly as many good-looking guys, but the dancing sure was fun. Christina had practiced the steps so much that she was even dancing in her sleep. She found it hard to wait until the next weekend, and was already counting down the days until she could be on the dance floor again.

*Thank God my denomination does not have the commandment, "Thou shalt not dance." I would certainly be a fallen angel!*

There were still a few last-minute things Christina had to do before heading out of town. She threw on some old baggy clothes and rushed to the church, knowing no one would be there this early. Then she would come back and get ready for the day's ordeal.

Christina loved the serenity of the sanctuary when she entered it at these odd hours. It was just like she had God all to herself in His holy temple. She knelt at the altar briefly to ask His blessings not only for her safe journey for the day, but most of all, for strength not to become the object of abuse as she had so many times in the past.

Then, she hurriedly made her way to the office to finish the preparations for rehearsals on all the upcoming Lenten and Easter services. When the door opened a few minutes later, Christina yelled to whom she assumed was the secretary, "You're awfully early today."

She saw the faces of Bob and Shane peek around the door, as she heard Bob's cheerful voice.

"Yeah, I need to get in the other building. We didn't quite finish our job yesterday."

Christina realized how horrible she must look. She had literally jumped out of bed, thrown on old clothes, and made a path here. And now, to her dismay, here was her future dance partner looking at her, amusingly. Grabbing her keys, she led them to their destination as quickly as she could.

Not wanting to show how flustered she really was by being caught this unsightly, she said, "You know, I don't let most people see me before I get my shower in the morning."

Shane dared not miss this opportunity as he fired back, "Would you rather us have seen you *in* the shower?"

Both of the men laughed heartily, and Christina knew she had no choice but to join them. They had all gotten pretty relaxed with each other yesterday, and were able to joke easily about the verbal trap she had set for herself. But she was gratified when Bob changed the subject.

"I thought you were going to Winston-Salem today."

"No, I'm going to Durham to Duke Hospital to visit my ex-father-in-law."

"Why are you even going up there? I wouldn't bother to do that if I were you. Not in this case."

"I really don't want to, either, but since my ex is still in the choir, I feel obligated. I have to look at it as if he were any other choir member, and I certainly would do this for one of them."

Bob looked at Christina, almost in disbelief at her strength and ability to handle such a trying situation with that kind of outlook. "Well, you're a better person than I am."

*How many times have I heard that?*

"No, it's just part of my job, and every job has its hassles."

"You need to be careful. And you don't need to go by yourself. Don't you have someone that can ride up there with you?"

"I wouldn't dare ask someone to go with me! They probably

would not be able to stand my mood on the way there." She paused. "Or back."

Her words said everything about the fears that surrounded this trip.

Shane had listened carefully to this exchange of words between Christina and Bob, watching her face the whole while. He looked at her eyes, demanding that hers met his and said with a concern to which she was unaccustomed, "Call me when you get home."

Christina could not believe her ears. Nor her eyes. She was so touched by the expression both in Shane's voice and his face that she stood there speechless, completely forgetting how horrible she must look to these guys. This was a far cry from his humor only a few seconds ago.

When she finally regained her consciousness of the present conversation, Christina answered calmly, "Oh, no. It'll be too late."

His uneasiness for her continued. "You don't need to be on the road by yourself that long, coming in that late, especially after dealing with that unpleasant of a situation."

Shane was beginning to understand much of the reason for that mask he had encountered at The Wildlife. He had seen the fear in Christina's eyes when she talked about her ex, and he wanted to reach out to her, to hold her, and tell her she would be alright. But even he felt the urge to hear from her when she returned, to know that she actually was alright.

Bob added to the joint regard for her. "He's right. You do need to call someone and let them know you got back safely. It's just too much for you to be out like that by yourself."

Christina smiled appreciatively. "I'm used to being out by myself. I don't come home lots of mornings until two or three in the morning." She didn't bother to tell them she had nothing better to do and simply could not stand the thought of going home to an empty house when Noah was at his dad's house.

The secretary ended the seriousness of the moment by delivering a message to Christina. She looked at Bob and Shane, greeting them warmly, then got on with the business of her appearance.

"Abigail called. She said for you to come and get her when you get ready to leave. She's going with you."

Christina looked at her, surprised.

"What about her ..."

Before Christina had time to finish, the secretary gave her the answer to the obvious question. "She's already lined up babysitters for the kids, and she'll be waiting for you. We've all agreed on this. You are *not* going to Durham by yourself."

*Great! Now I have an entire flock of babysitters!!*

But as much as she hated to admit it, Christina was relieved that she would not have to make this trek alone, and Abigail was the one person she would allow to see the moods that the trip might evoke from her.

Abigail had been more than a best friend to Christina ever since she returned to this job. They had endured much together, for many reasons, and they had become more like sisters than friends. The fact that this self-proclaimed sister had made this arrangement to accompany her today was nothing out of the ordinary. It was just the way they did things for each other.

Christina looked back at Bob and Shane. "See, I'll be fine. But thanks for the offer to call. I really do appreciate your concern."

Shane looked at her, with understanding and empathy she hadn't experienced in a long time, especially from a male. "The offer to call still stands."

"No, I'll be okay."

She retreated into her choir room to finish up her tasks, and gathered the work she had planned to take with her. Abigail and she could use their time together to plan the music for their next handbell concert. As she made her exit, she looked back at Shane, and offered, "You mentioned that you like oysters. You're welcome to go with me sometime to eat seafood, if you like."

Before Christina could pray that she hadn't been too forward with her invitation, Shane answered, "I'd love to. When are you going?"

"Probably Thursday."

Bob piped in. "We're going to my beach house early tomorrow morning to do some work. I don't know when we'll get back."

Not wanting to discourage the open invitation, Shane added, "But I'll call you as soon as we get back."

Christina jotted down her phone number and handed it to him. As she walked past him toward the door, he took a piece of her hair between his fingers and said gently, "I like the natural look."

She smiled demurely, trying to hide her blush, and made her exit as quickly as possible. A long trip awaited her, and now she had something, *or someone*, else to think about on the way.

The three-hour ride to Durham proved to be a profitable experience for Christina. They outlined the children's musical and luncheon, and also planned possible future projects for the singles, depending on the success of the Valentine's Dance, which Abigail saw as a fantastic idea. She was personally glad that Christina had found an outlet for herself, not giving in to the sheltered life of her past three years. By the time they reached Duke Hospital, Christina felt pleased that she had done a good morning's work.

She longed for one more bit of information from Abigail, but she timed her inquiry very carefully, waiting until they were in the hallway just before the patients' rooms. Knowing that her best friend had grown up with Shane, Christina risked rebuke from her by firing one last request. She had no intention of telling Abigail why she had an interest in this person, and her job allowed her the privilege of asking about members of the congregation in order to better minister to them.

"Abigail, tell me everything you know about Shane Sievers."

Without even a pause to think, Abigail answered, "He's got the biggest heart of anyone I've ever met."

Her answer, although short, told Christina everything she needed to know. Shane was not *all* bad, and the briefness of her reply told Christina that her best friend had no suspicion as to the reason for her question.

The nurses' station was just around the corner, so Christina went in for the visit while Abigail sat in the waiting area. Abigail had been so excited that her friend had been talking about going out and getting a life lately, she had bought her a card as a joke to give to someone on Valentine's Day for next year, trusting that by next February, Christina would have found a perfect companion. She knew what a dreaded occasion this had been for Christina in the past, but Abigail fully believed that "someone perfect" would walk into her friend's life soon. Besides, she had been checking into single groups all over Charlotte trying to find just the right pool for Christina to go looking for a social life. She also had enough foresight to know that this visit would greatly depress her best friend, though Christina would never show it, or even admit it.

Christina's hospital visit did accomplish one thing. It made her totally aware of exactly how desperately she both wanted and needed out of that relationship from the past. She realized that she would have probably been a basket case on the way home if there hadn't been another item of interest in the back of her mind. As badly as she wanted to be alone to cry, or do whatever necessary to rid herself of the hurtful feelings that accompanied her visit, it was probably better that Abigail was with her.

However, had she been alone, she could have pondered over Shane, his past and his problems, all the way home. As it was, Christina was grateful that she was able to think in more than one track at a time. For as she and Abigail talked about everything under the sun, and planned future music programs, her mind was also thinking of ways to reform this "bad guy" she had met.

The minute they left the hospital, Christina looked for a place to get a drink. "You know me better than anybody, so you can appreciate this, but right this minute, I sure do wish I was a heavy drinker. You could drive home!"

Christina was right, for Abigail understood every word of this. She had never seen her hurting friend enjoy liquid spirits, even after the notorious dinner party. So Christina's encounter with Tom, her ex, really had stirred up some deeply harbored feelings.

Abigail thought back to just over three years ago. She had invited nineteen couples to her house for a festive evening, still enjoying the Christmas spirit, and preparing for a new year of dreams and goals. Everyone had spent a gala evening together, strengthening friendships, and admiring everyone's new clothes that had been found under the tree during the past week. Abigail had put out only her finest china, crystal and silver for the occasion. It had been a night to remember, and she was feeling that it was worth all the hard work that served as a prelude to the event.

As everyone settled in around the den fireplace for after-dinner coffee, Tom spoke over the social conversation.

"If I could get everyone's attention, I have an announcement to make."

Everyone, including Christina, took a seat to hear this great proclamation, thinking that a new musical or some such was in the making. However, everyone, *especially* Christina, sat dumbfounded when he finished with, "Things are just not working out between Christina and myself, so I am moving out."

The guests all waited for him to laugh, or say it was a joke. But after a few seconds of deafening silence, people realized he was serious in his statement that held no more emotion than if he had stated, "I'll have another cup of coffee."

Abigail burst into tears and rushed out the door onto her side porch, with Paul right behind her, trying to console her. Other guests decided to excuse themselves as Christina, still too shocked to react, sat on the sofa beside Tom until only Rachel Stockton remained in the room with them.

Rachel's husband had died unexpectedly that past summer, so she knew the jolt and the loneliness that came from being suddenly alone. She had only come for the evening to help Abigail with serving, not wanting to feel awkward as a single amidst all the couples. But as it turned out, she was the only one of the dinner crowd who was able to compose herself enough to even acknowledge the coldness of this remark, much less address it. She moved to the hearth, directly across from Tom and Christina, trying to convince him that he had no idea how fortunate he was, and that he was making the biggest mistake of his life.

But as she spoke persuasively with him, Christina's mind thought forward to a possible future of peace and contentment that she had not known in years. He was finally doing the one thing she had desired to do for so long, but could not do to her sons or her family. Tom was actually taking the problem, the horrible living nightmare, out of her life.

Now as Christina and Abigail chatted over sodas, they both thought back over that night, and the events that followed. At first, she hated the repercussions of being divorced, *again*, and threatened to quit her church job, feeling unworthy. But due to the support of many people, including her first husband and his wife, Christina continued to work in the arena which she loved so much, and became even more successful.

She had gotten Matt through high school, as she promised, and moved on the very day of his graduation to her beloved Moses House. Christina had battled the loneliness and the hurt, and she and Noah had made a wonderful life for themselves. That is, except for this yearning that Abigail could sense more and more on Christina's part. She missed the company, the companionship, of another adult. Abigail decided to give Christina the card as soon as they got in the car.

"Here, I thought you might get a kick out of this. And by next year, maybe you will even have someone to give it to!"

Christina proceeded to open the envelope to see a guy dressed in boots and a cowboy hat on the front of a comical card. She could hardly believe her eyes. They both laughed hysterically at the humor contained on the inside of the card, but Christina knew that Abigail had no idea as to how funny this really was. *Do I dare tell her what's going on?*

After a few seconds of weighing the consequences, Christina spoke. "Abigail, I met Shane Sievers at The Wildlife a couple of weekends ago, and then again this past Saturday. It has given me a chance to talk to him. I just wonder what is going on with him, and I wish there was something I could do to help."

Abigail listened to the compassion in her voice. She was aware of Christina's affection for the underdog. Only she knew of all the numerous cases of persons who had stayed in Christina's home during the past few years. In fact, she had dubbed her friend's house "The Cache Home for Wayward Kids." Although she had taken in mostly children and youth, there were a few instances of adults. And without any spoken words, Abigail knew that Shane Sievers had become Christina's latest project. She knew that Christina's mind was probably already made up about trying to help Shane, but, within the caregiver's careful statement, she heard a plea for input and discussion before she gave in totally to the situation. This counselor of a friend also knew Christina well enough to know that no matter what she heard in the next few minutes, she would privately care and pray for Shane, accepting him as she did everyone else – her equal.

"I'll never forget looking into Shane's eyes the last time we had communion. I had to hold the chalice, and as he walked past, I routinely looked in his eyes and uttered, 'The blood of Christ given for you.' Shane had tears in his eyes. He did not try to hide them, nor did he try to wipe them. There was such hurt inside those eyes. I have never seen such a pained expression in anyone's eyes. It was almost haunting. Yet, I smiled at him, and he smiled back. That was the most touching communion experience I have ever had."

Christina thought back to recall the date of the last communion service. January 3rd. Only a couple of weeks after his suicide attempt. She was surprised that he ventured out that soon, much less to a church service. *But what better place for him to come,* she reasoned. Then it dawned on her – the same day as Chelsea's death – the same day he came to console Kevin.

Their discussion centered around Shane for the next hour or so, until Christina decided she had exposed enough of her private life. *Oh well, if nothing else, Shane was good for something. At least he kept me from dwelling on the hospital visit, and spoiling the rest of my day.*

Abigail saw the honest concern in her friend's face. *This is good for her. It gives her an outlet for her caregiving nature, and something to take her mind off the horrible situation with Tom.* She knew Shane well enough to know that even though he had taken many wrong paths and gotten lots of bad breaks, he was a good person. He would not harm Christina. And she had watched this angel of mercy in action enough to know that perhaps she was just the person to reach out to him. *Perhaps one is exactly what the other needs at this point in their lives.*

The rest of the ride home was spent on solving the problems of the world, as per two cronies. Abigail had originally planned to invite Christina over for dinner, then invite her to spend the night, afraid for her to be at home alone with the thoughts that today had dredged up from the past. But they laughed so much that Abigail trusted Christina was okay to spend the evening alone by the time they got back to Charlotte. She did still invite Christina to stay for dinner, and both Paul and Abigail noticed the difference from what they had feared in her attitude following today's events.

This was a day of bonding that they had both needed. It had been a long time since Christina had allowed herself out of the proverbial shell she had built around herself in her attempt to block the past from seeping into her present life. And it had been an even longer time since Abigail had seen Christina's eyes have the least bit of a glimmer in them.

# 3

Christina was grateful for the uneventfulness of the next two days. It gave her a chance to finish her plans for the Mardi Gras service, something totally new to her congregation, and she could not wait for it to happen. Most of her church family misunderstood the religious significance of that particular day of celebration, and as a natural-born educator of sorts, she could not wait to open a whole new door for those worshippers. She was well aware of the fact that many of the parishioners would consider Mardi Gras a sacrilegious celebration, but they trusted her enough to at least give it a try.

Thursdays were routinely her day to catch up after the rat race of Wednesday rehearsals, and the rush of Mondays and Tuesdays spent getting everything ready for the varied choirs. It was Christina's custom to go to a favorite seafood house in her previous hometown on Thursday evenings. She could relax all by herself, without feeling guilty for being separated from Noah. The food was wonderful, and even affordable. After all she had been through during the past several years, Christina saw this as her private treat to herself. She had paid her dues, *plus some*, and she had no qualms about the one evening she went out on the town.

This particular Thursday was most welcome. Christina was exhausted after all the happenings, especially Tuesday's hospital visit, and the tedious planning of the week. There had been no rest for the weary since over three weeks ago, and by five o'clock that afternoon, she was ready to hit the door running. The half mile to her house from the church took the usual two minutes, from parking lot to garage. She walked in the front door and started upstairs to change clothes just in time to catch the phone.

"Hello."

"Hello yourself."

Christina listened carefully to the voice, but it was unrecognizable to her. She hated to be rude, but living alone as a single female had taught her to be extremely cautious. Wondering about the best way to identify the caller, she asked, "Who's calling, please?"

"It's Shane." He was audibly disappointed that she didn't catch his voice, for which Christina was embarrassed. "I just got back from the beach and I was wondering if you were still going out to eat seafood this evening."

"Yes, as a matter of fact, I ..."

"I'd love to go with you, if the offer still stands."

"Of course it does. What time would you like to eat?"

"What time do you like to eat?"

"I try to go early to avoid the crowd. I am not one to stand in long lines."

"How about six-thirty? I need to get ready, since I just walked in the door."

"That's perfect."

Christina didn't bother to tell Shane that she would have been ready in five minutes, and that after six o'clock, the crowd had already hit. But it didn't seem to matter. Nor did she bother to inform him that this was customarily her evening all to herself. She didn't mind sharing it with him. It would be neutral ground, away from the church, and she felt that he might talk to her a little more freely off her professional turf.

Instead of simply changing clothes as she had planned, Christina went to the oversized walk-in closet to find a dressy casual outfit. She jumped in the shower, washed her hair, and put on fresh make-up, trying to look nice, but without giving the appearance that she had gone to any trouble.

After she had gotten dressed and strolled past the mirror in the hallway, Christina decided the look was all wrong. She hadn't worn jeans since college, except to the dance for the past two weekends, but tonight was the start of a new era. No longer was she plagued by the rules and regulations of the past. The dress slacks were traded for her new jeans, and the wool blazer was swapped for a comfortable sweater.

Christina walked back to the bathroom of mirrors, this time actually stopping to look at herself, at least from her neck down. She was still too tormented by the verbal abuse of the past to look at her face. But as she stood looking at the new image of herself, she was pleased. She turned from one side to the other, a feminine habit she had long since forgotten, admiring the fact that her diet and exercise of the past month was showing some dividends. *Christina Cache, you do still have a shape, and not such a bad one at that!*

She bounded down the steps, actually excited that she had someone to share the evening with her, even though he was a part of her job. Christina sensed an exhilaration in her step that had been absent for many years. She caught one last glimpse of herself in the hall mirror on the way out the door.

*I am woman – hear me roar!* And she jumped in the purple Blazer, ready for her first evening out with an adult male, besides Tom, in nearly thirteen years. It mattered not that he was her job. *He's over eighteen, and he can carry on a conversation.*

Backing out the driveway, she noticed Matt's red sports car, which she had just picked up at the garage that day. It hadn't been driven in nearly a year, since the time that Matt lost his license.

*That's it!* she thought as she wheeled back into the driveway. *I bought this car, I paid almost $600.00 to have it fixed today, so I'm taking it out on the town this evening.*

She loved the sound of the engine as she started the car. *I deserve this treat!* Christina hit the gas pedal, and zoomed out the driveway. She put the car in gear, and cruised down the street of her development. As she turned onto the main road, Christina put her foot down on the gas, letting the car run wide open. *Besides, somebody needs to check and make sure they got everything fixed properly!*

Shane hung up the phone. He had rushed all day helping Bob, hoping to get home in time to catch Christina before she left. His heart breathed a sigh of relief when she answered after the third ring.

He had no idea why he was so determined to be with her this evening, nor, stranger, why he asked his mom to press his best chambray shirt. That request even got a rise out of her.

"Where are you going this evening?" It was more like an accusation than a question.

"Out to eat with some of the Sunday School class."

*That isn't a lie. She is a part of the Sunday School class. At least, she was a large part of it this past Sunday!*

Shane looked at the clock after he was dressed. Six o'clock. *Now what am I going to do for the next thirty minutes in this prison ward until she comes?*

A look out the window supplied his answer as he saw his

neighbor turning in the driveway across the street. Shane nodded his head, and grinned satisfactorily. *I've got just enough time to go over and visit Mickey. And to tell him that I am going out this evening with Christina Cache.*

He almost felt bad about gloating over the fact that he was going out with her, since Mickey had told him earlier in the week that he, himself, would like to ask Christina out. But, typically male, he didn't feel badly enough not to let it be known that he had gotten there first. It seemed that Shane always got the girl, especially the one that Mickey wanted, and he just couldn't pass up the chance to keep that reputation.

Shane walked across the street, shared a beer with Mickey, and watched the grimace as he broke the news. But, as disappointed as Mickey was, he secretly hoped that maybe Christina would be the person to make Shane forget the one obstacle that was *always* bad news – especially where his friend was concerned.

Mickey had watched Shane's life go from bad to "so bad that it couldn't get any worse" during the course of the past year, all because of one person. Carla. He knew that she couldn't do anything to Shane that he didn't allow to happen, but Mickey couldn't stand the fact that she had him so tightly caught up in her web that he seemed hopelessly trapped.

Her collect calls from prison had gotten so out of hand that Shane already owed Mickey a couple of hundred dollars, not to mention the ones that came to Shane's parents. Shane even had to borrow money for the last book of stamps he bought so that he could write her every day. And Mickey knew that it was because of her that his friend had tried to end his life back before Christmas. Carla's surname even symbolized stress and tension, and she certainly *did* have that effect on Shane.

At one time, Mickey had wanted to go out with her, but after seeing the bad influence she had been on Shane, now he saw her as no more than an easy piece, as did his dad. Shane tried to take up for her, and see the good in her, but Mickey had seen that Carla had turned into such an alcoholic, that her 'nice side' had completely disappeared, except for the few minutes each week when she was not drinking.

Mickey was aware that Shane had placed her name on the church's prayer list, and hoped that she'd come out of prison a different person. Yet Mickey also knew that Shane was still seeing another girlfriend from the past during Carla's absence. "There's nothing wrong with double-dipping," was the reply Mickey got every time he questioned Shane about his romantic affairs.

As he watched Shane strut back across the street in that cowboy stroll, he couldn't help but wonder if this guy really cared about Christina, or if she was just a toy until Carla's release. His first impression of Christina was of an angel, and from what he had seen of her effect on everyone else this past Sunday, through both her music and her personality, she certainly fit that description. As much as he would have liked to have been taking her out this evening instead of Shane, he secretly hoped that she could turn the direction of his friend's life. And even more, he hoped that Shane would not manipulate Christina as he had all the other people in his past.

Walking home, Shane almost felt embarrassed for taking his friend's beer and his girl, but his thoughts turned instantly to Christina. Even though Carla had just called him at Mickey's house, she was not here, so he might as well not sit and waste away.

*An evening out. It doesn't matter that she's a minister, and probably doesn't drink. At least I can get out of the house for a few hours and have someone to talk to. The last few weeks have been a bummer. I'm due one. Besides, I'll have her all to myself, and maybe I can pry a little farther into that secret she keeps buried inside.*

55

The forty-minute ride to the fish camp was endless chatter about NASCAR racing, rooster fights, and wrestling, all subjects which were completely foreign to Christina – not to mention the embellishment with four-letter words. She had spent the ninety minutes after he called wondering what the two of them could possibly find to discuss for an entire evening, without the interruptions of anyone else, or music to break the silence. They were only halfway to their destination, and now, as she heard about Shane's hobbies from the past, and his interests, Christina was sure that she had made a mistake by inviting him to join her for dinner.

*He's spent most of his life in places that I've spent mine trying to avoid!*

She listened to a couple more minutes of talk, and was sure that the evening would be a flop. Christina was already calculating how long it would take to get there, eat and get back home. She hated watching TV, but perhaps if they hurried, she could get back in time to watch one of the three television shows she liked. There was no way she was going to let her Thursday get by without something to give her that 'Calgon, take me away' moment!

*I asked him to eat dinner with me! Christina, you have NEVER invited anyone to be your guest. Of course, you never HAD to before. I wonder what kind of female he thinks I am. My generation does not go around asking guys out. This is most definitely not my style.*

The more Shane talked, the more differences Christina discovered about them – until an old country tune that they both recognized came on the radio.

She felt the shock ripple through her as he spouted, "I love that song. It really gets to me every time I hear it."

Shane proceeded to sing every word of the song that brought back familiar memories to her as she listened to both him and the radio. Christina nearly had to pull the car to the side of the interstate to regain her composure. Did she dare tell him that she had written that song? Or that she and Matt had flown to Nashville years ago when the song was recorded?

She opted to let that minute detail ride for the moment. It was not her type of music, and Christina preferred that most people did not know that she had seven recorded hits. Besides, the songs had come at a low point in her life, after the breakdown of her first marriage. A 'cry in your beer' time. And even though she was not a beer drinker, she had cried plenty of tears about the divorce, and the embarrassment she must have caused her family. However, the money from the songs did turn the tears into smiles for a short while and kept her sons from starving.

What shocked Christina most about his statement was the fact that this song, like most of the ones she had written, was filled with deep meaning, and did not fit the typical genre of country songs. And it did have reference to a spiritual belief, so after the conversation she had encountered with him thus far, she was surprised that a redneck with Shane's past could share in her inner feelings, the ones expressed in the lyrics. However, she was most gratified that her music had spoken to him. It renewed a spark in her that possibly she could speak to others through her creativity. And since she had not been able to join in the evening's conversation heretofore, she at least finished singing the song with him, catching him off guard, also, that she knew the words.

She couldn't help but laugh inside as she watched his questioning eyes. *If you only knew!*

Christina was relieved when she saw the restaurant sign just ahead. At least then, she could busy herself eating and not feel like she was being rude by not joining in the conversation. However, as she looked at the expression on his face while she parked the car, and he finished yet another story, she saw a look of ease in his face. Some of the tension was gone. Shane was starting to trust her. He was opening up to her, and she began to wonder if he had ever done that with anyone else.

Once inside, Christina ordered shrimp and scallops. He ordered oysters and scallops. Shane was the first person she had ever been with who liked scallops as much as she did. They spent the time waiting for their order discussing their favorite foods. She was amazed that although she had traveled around the world, and acquired a taste for various cuisines, he had quite an appreciation of different types of food, and obviously culinary skills to prepare them.

One of the things Christina liked about this particular restaurant was its promptness in preparing orders. True to form, their food was there within only a few short minutes. *Great, these minutes passed quickly. Maybe the evening won't drag too much after all.* Shane started to dig in, but he stopped in place as Christina asked if he minded if she blessed her food.

"No, of course not. And while you're at it, you'd better bless mine, too. I need all the help I can get."

She couldn't help but snicker inside. After the "Amen," they both enjoyed the tastes of a southern-style fish camp. Christina hoped he liked the food, since she had suggested the restaurant. Tom had always complained about coming here, but then he complained about anything she wanted to do, insinuating it was not quite good enough for him.

"Here, try an oyster."

"No, thank you. I used to love oysters, but they made me sick every time I ate them when I was pregnant with Matt, so I gave them up back then."

"Well, that was then, and this is now. Have one."

Shane poked one of the oysters in his plate with his fork, and handed it to her. Christina sat there, looking at him, then down at the fork, and back to Shane. She realized her reluctance when he asked, "What's the matter? Afraid I've got something that's gonna kill you?"

She was so used to the germ-conscious ideas of Tom that she was literally in shock. Christina's second husband would not even kiss her because of germs, and here was some guy she barely knew handing her an oyster off his fork. *With which he has already eaten!*

Christina laughed again inside as she ate the oyster and enjoyed every bite of it. As they continued to eat, Shane continued to rattle off stories, omitting no details. The more he talked, the more she saw the differences between the two of them turning into similarities. Their lifestyles, their pasts, their interests, everything. And, as they sat talking, it was like they had both come to a common crossroads, although from totally opposite directions.

Shane was without a doubt the master storyteller. Christina couldn't help but wonder, as she took in every word, whether he was just spinning off yarns enhanced with exaggeration, or if he was just plain full of it! *Or has this guy really lived all this stuff?* She watched his antics as he recited tale after tale. The way he tossed his head, or tilted it from one side to the other, and the way he held his cigarette, or the direction in which he blew puffs of smoke all became well-marked indications of how accurate the stories were.

Like most spinners of yarns, he was able to captivate his audience, which at this time was comprised of only one person. Shane had most definitely learned to play to his listeners, a talent of storytellers. *Or manipulators! Be careful, Christina.* But as she both watched and listened to his stories very carefully, evaluating any and every movement, waiting for any slip-up that would give away his game, she speculated that it would have been virtually impossible for him to make up all the details, the way he reeled them off, one after another.

*This guy's been through just as much as I have. That's hard to believe!* For the first time in her life, Christina Cache had met someone who was as much an extremist as herself.

While he excused himself for a few minutes, she sat there reflecting over what she had feared only a couple of hours ago would be a bomb of a night. It had turned out to be an outstanding evening. Not only had she been able to get Shane to talk to her, Christina had actually enjoyed his company. She had watched his eyes come alive and dance as she exchanged stories with him, allowing him to see the many paths she had traveled to get where she was, also. It was obvious that he was more than a little impressed with her background, her knowledge of an endless variety of subjects, and most of all, her common sense.

And as he got more comfortable with her, the language which she found so repulsive began to dissipate into thin air. It was as if Shane sensed that Christina did not need his wealth of – or in her case, lack of – vocabulary to enhance his stories, or hold her attention. After all, she was not his typical babe, nor did she fit into his usual mold of captivated listeners.

Christina smiled. In one evening, she had found out more about this guy than she had her last husband in the ten years of their marriage. It was like she and Shane had made the same journeys, like there was a link somewhere between them.

*If there were such a thing as reincarnation, I would swear I've known this man before. Those eyes. I recognize those eyes. That voice. I have heard that voice. Those stories. I could listen to his stories all night. It's like I have known him my entire life. There is an extraordinary charisma about him. He could have such a positive influence on people, especially people who are traveling the same wrong paths as he has.*

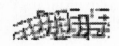

She knew that she was taking a big risk, and that the timing might not be right, but she felt compelled to ask him one last question before they left and while she could still look into his eyes to see the real truth. When Shane returned to the table, Christina looked him squarely in the eyes, as she shot the words that hit him as if they had come straight out of a cannon.

"Do you ever wonder if maybe God has something He wants you to do?"

It took a few minutes for the smoke to clear, but Shane survived the shocking blow. He looked blankly at her, clearly startled, at first, but then his eyes and face melted into an expression she had not seen from him, as his stare turned to compassion. How did this person – this high-class, artsy, *unique* female – pry inside him to challenge him with the one question that kept surfacing his thoughts, more and more frequently, as of late? *Shane Sievers, you really are slipping!*

"Yeah, I do. I've wondered about that on several occasions, especially after I had an accident with a dump truck. But I'm half-way afraid that if I do it, He'll kill me off, 'cause then He won't need me any longer!"

They both laughed aloud. Christina watched his expression, trying to figure out whether Shane was serious or not. Serious about thinking that perhaps there was a destined mission for him in life. Serious about whether he really thought his life would not escape the obstacles if he actually did follow his predestined sacred path. Serious about any of his countless stories. Serious about anything.

The couple had finished dinner and was ready to leave, but Christina had opened the floodgates with that one question. Those few words launched a whole new set of subjects, each turning into a deep discussion. And, more surprisingly, every topic that came up showed a common bond between them. Christina was shockingly amazed at his wealth of knowledge and common sense on every subject.

Shane laughed when she shared that thought with him. He winked teasingly at her and replied, "They call it common sense, but if it's so common, why don't more folks have it?"

She couldn't help but laugh at Shane's philosophical statements. This supposedly simple-minded, trouble-making redneck possessed seemingly more natural intelligence than any man Christina had ever known.

Her next question seemed mild after the original proposal that started this avalanche of soul-searching inquests, but Christina kept going, hopeful that Shane was ready for her to pry even deeper into the chasm she had unearthed.

"Do you believe in angels?"

Without hesitation, Shane looked right into her eyes. "How else do you think I got this far in life?"

That look allowed Christina to see a new light in his being. It was like she was seeing down to the farthest depths of his soul, and Shane was no longer trying to stop her. Yet, at the same time, she had opened herself to the same discovery.

Neither of them had any idea how long they sat there staring at each other. But strange to both of them, their eyes carried on an entire conversation, bouncing unspoken words back and forth between them, allowing years of hidden secrets to come forth. It was like wisps of air at first, but the intensity of the silent discussion mounted until it was like clouds, shooting across the sky from the force of a strong wind, darting back and forth between them. Pandora's box had been opened for both Shane and Christina, leaving them exhausted from the mystical power that had unleashed the buried treasure within.

When their eyes had finally reached as far into the crevices of each other's souls as possible, Shane reached his hand across the table and took Christina's in his. She took the cigarette from his other hand, extinguished it in the ashtray, and took hold of that hand, also. The energy that had been dashing through their eyes now flowed tranquilly through their entire bodies with the peace and calm of an endless stream.

They realized that the eyes of everyone still in the restaurant were on them, and that the waitresses had circled nearby, watching their every move. Both slightly embarrassed, Shane pulled Christina's hands, leading her up from the table.

"I think it's time to leave now," he uttered simply, yet full of emotion.

She nodded, grabbing her purse and coat. Like a polished gentleman, Shane helped her into her coat, then led her outside and to the car where he opened the door for her. Christina was unable to speak. She had no idea what had just swept over her, but it was certainly not something she had ever encountered before.

Christina was used to leaving her mark on places she visited, but not quite in that fashion. It was the first time that anyone else had shared in her brightening of the atmosphere. And oddly enough, she liked it.

Several minutes into the drive home, Shane was the first to speak. "We sure got those people's attention, didn't we? They probably don't know what hit 'em." He was trying to break the wave of emotion, to insert humor into the air, afraid to admit that Shane Sievers had just been hit with something foreign to him, also.

Now that it was dark, Christina realized the headlights on Matt's sports car were not working properly. Shane volunteered to take a look them the next evening after work. She graciously accepted his offer, glad that she would get to see him again. But at the same time, she was delighted that something provided a non-threatening change of subjects.

Christina joined into the conversation this time, anxious to escape from whatever had just gone on between them. They listened to the radio on the way home and, by the time they got to Shane's house, were laughing heartily about the looks on people's faces who had watched them at the restaurant, both grateful that the air had cleared to a much lighter tone.

"Give me a call tomorrow after work. I'll be glad to fix the headlights."

"Oh, I almost forgot. I promised to take Matt and Noah to see a basketball game."

"Call me after the game. I'll still be up."

"But what about your parents?"

"Don't worry about them. I'm an adult. I have my own life to live."

"I don't know. It will be awfully ..."

Breaking her off, Shane kissed Christina lightly on the lips as he opened the door and said, "I'll be waiting for your call." He closed the door and was gone down the driveway, not giving her a chance to argue with him.

*I like his style!* Christina thought, shaking her head and smiling at his way of getting the last word. He certainly had a unique manner of taking control of things. It was hard for her to imagine that less than two months ago, he had tried to take his life.

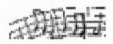

Christina lay back as she recounted the events of the day. All day, she had wondered what they could possibly find to discuss. A part of her wished that she had never had this brilliant idea. Yet, the rest of her had looked forward to an evening out with a member of the opposite sex and no kids. The fact of the matter was, it had not mattered what they talked about. Christina Cache had been out with a living, breathing, human being for the first time in three years. And she found herself giddily thrilled, even though she was trying to deny her excitement.

She could still see Shane's routine of movements as he told his stories. *Is there a pattern to how he cocks his head? Can the amount of truthfulness in his stories be measured in how he holds it?*

As she lay there, Christina had a brainstorm. He was the character she needed for her latest book idea. Shane Sievers had just become her final chapter. What a great love story! The heroine had become fed up with the high-class society life, and in her quest for reality, she had met a *real* man – a man who could treat her the way a woman wanted to be treated. He could pamper her, yet be strong enough to give her the security she so desired. The hero of her dreams was the total opposite of the city life she had just left. Her knight in shining armor had come charging in, only in cowboy boots and a jean jacket instead of chain mail.

*Of course, I will have to change my setting from Atlanta to Wyoming!*

Christina fell asleep outlining her latest novel idea in her head.

Shane stood outside smoking one last cigarette before going to bed. He could not get his mind to quit rambling over his past, and weighing the mistakes to see how he could make something good come out of them.

It was strange. He had spoken to several ministers and counselors lately, all of whom had turned him off with their holier-than-thou "you should do this" or "you need to do that" speeches. Christina had listened to him, and asked what he wanted to do. She found a way to make him think and evaluate life and what kind of future he wanted for himself, helping Shane find ways to make that life possible.

She challenged him, and he liked it. He was not used to being out with females who were that sharp, and she wasn't bad to look at, either. Shane dozed off, looking forward to his daily morning phone call from Carla, and dreaming about the angels that had gotten him this far in his life.

# 4

For the first time in years, Christina had looked forward to this special day. Three weeks ago, she was dreading it, as usual, but after the events of the past week, she was going to have a Valentine's Day to remember. The dance tonight would have been fun, regardless, but after the past two evenings with Shane, her anticipation was almost uncontrollable.

He had gone to visit his friend, Carla, in prison. It was the first Saturday he had been able to get a ride for the five-hour trip, and after all the time he had spent incarcerated, he felt sorry for her being there all alone, with no family in the area. Christina could understand that. She had watched enough of the loneliness from her experience with Matt.

One of the things that had drawn Christina so closely to Shane was that big heart Abigail had told her about. Abigail was certainly on target with that remembrance, for Christina saw right away that he had a heart as big as hers. She had always been the one to take up for the underdog and the outcast, and here he was doing the same thing. Shane had told Christina at the fish camp that he had placed Carla's name on the church prayer list, but it had not appeared in the weekly newsletter as of yet.

"I'll take care of that on Monday," she'd replied.

Christina was indeed touched that this 'bad guy' had the desire to place anyone on the prayer list. But since he had, it said to her that he believed in prayer, and that he was praying for Carla himself. *Or at least he wants the prayers of those he considers a little closer to The Man.* Whatever the reason, at least his request showed that Shane truly had a spiritual faith, no matter how strong or shallow it was. To her, that was a major hurdle he had crossed on the way to this sacred path she saw opening before him.

She was even more impressed that he would spend ten hours just to bring an hour or two of joy to someone of Carla's status. But then, her status was probably all he had been used to during the past twenty years of his life. Christina thought it was the most wonderful blessing in the whole world that Shane had been given the opportunity to climb out of the bottomless pit he had dug for himself, and was going to reach a summit to which he could help others who, also, were in the depths of earthly hell.

*And to think that God has chosen me to watch this miracle!* Christina wondered what she had done to deserve this special blessing. She knew that she didn't deserve it, anymore than anyone deserved the unconditional love He offered, but she accepted it graciously, just as she did His Love.

As she lay in bed thinking about what to wear this evening, she thanked her Maker as she did everyday, just for being alive, and having so many rich blessings, most especially her talents, her friends and her family. She laughed. Most people would think she was crazy for counting her blessings, which would have seemed like nightmares to anyone else. But she just could not see any reason to do otherwise. *After all, You DID give me the strength to withstand all these obstacles that fall in my path.*

Christina thought of Matt. Yes, life for her and her sons had been hell for the past three years, and it had really taken its toll on her older son. Even with the threat of not knowing whether he would even be able to function by himself again, she thanked God for this most precious son everyday. For if He did not feel she could handle it, He would have never given her the burden. The experience gleaned from Matt's situation over these last years had made her undeniably stronger, and had kept her so busy that she did not have time to dwell on how bad things actually were. It had been her life.

And most importantly, Christina knew that no matter what Matt had done or ever could do, she would love him with all of her heart and her soul, for he *was* the child God had given her. Her parents had given her the greatest gift possible, and that was true love. Love that was founded from above. Christina knew that because of that love, she could deal with *anything*, despite its difficulty.

The doorbell drew her back to the present, as she grabbed her robe and rushed down the spiral stairs, trying not to awaken Matt and Noah. Gray stood there, as debonair as possible for a four-year-old, holding a yellow rose, and reaching up to hug her with outstretched arms.

"What a terrific way to start my day!" she shrieked with joy. She jerked up the child and swung him around, taking the flower he offered.

Abigail enjoyed having Christina as her third child's godmother, simply because of such displays of affection. As much as she hated that her son's godparents were divorced, she was overjoyed that Tom was no longer in her best friend's life to spoil this day.

The look in Christina's face was just as glowing this morning as it had been last night when she and Shane had come over to Abigail's to fix Matt's headlights. Abigail had noticed a sparkle in her friend that she had never seen before. And the look on Shane's face was a far cry from the desperation she had noticed at that communion service a few weeks back, or even in Sunday school over the past month.

69

Abigail secretly wondered if something were going on between the two of them – something of which even they were unaware. She had mentioned her suspicion to Paul last night when they went to bed, but he stopped her hypothesis in mid-air.

"Christina's got more sense than that. Shane's a pretty rough customer, from what I've heard. You know Christina. This is nothing more than her reaching out to another soul in need."

Abigail envisioned Christina in all her formal gowns, gracing the most elegant of social circles, and Shane in his jeans and boots. Even she had to laugh at her ridiculous notion. And then she and Paul howled with laughter at the thought of Christina in her sequins and diamonds walking into The Plaza on Fifth Avenue with Shane and his western attire.

"Yes, I'm sure you're right," Abigail chuckled. "You *are* the one with the psychology degree!" But as she rolled over to go to sleep, her stomach told her otherwise.

Still holding onto Gray, Christina invited Abigail and Paul to go dancing with her.

"I still don't see why the two of you can't come this evening. You'd have a blast, if doing nothing but watching everyone else. You don't even have to get on the dance floor to have a good time!"

"You single people are going to have too much fun to be with an old married couple. We don't need to be in the way. Besides, we're going with you next weekend when you take all the choir kids and their families. I'm not sure I should push my luck by trying to get Paul out dancing two weekends in a row."

Christina did appreciate Abigail's dilemma there. Paul worked constantly. Even when Shane and she had gone to fix the headlights last night, he was still outside changing the oil in his car. He made lots of sacrifices so that Abigail could be a stay-at-home mom like her own mother had been. It was only one small part of the changing family role that her friend refused to accept. *But then, if more*

70

*people felt the same as Paul and Abigail, there wouldn't be the breakdown of families suffered by today's society.*

She thought of her own situation. Inwardly, Christina almost wished that she were staying at home this evening with Noah, while Matt took his date out for a special Valentine's Day. Or that her childhood dream of being in a wonderful marriage, cooking her husband's favorite dinner, topped off by a Red Velvet cake, and eating at a candlelit table, was what was really happening. But as it was, she was grateful that she was going to be out with a large group, *and Noah.*

Abigail looked at Christina's face. She could tell exactly what thoughts were going through her friend's mind. It was her who had watched how difficult the last three Valentine's Days had been for Christina, and she felt that her own prayer had been answered, just by seeing her going out this evening. She could not bear to see Christina go through another year like the last three – for the sake of either of them.

"I can't wait until next week to go, though. This place certainly has given you a new outlook on life!"

"Yes, it *is* fun to have a life again. I had forgotten how much I was missing!"

They hugged, and Gray gave Christina one last peck on the cheek before he and his mom left. Closing the door behind them, Christina felt slightly guilty that she wasn't keeping the children so that Paul and Abigail could go out for the evening they both needed and deserved. But Christina had been in the care-giving business long enough to know that she first had to take care of herself before she could take care of anyone else, and right now, it was her turn.

Noah shuffled into the kitchen as she was putting the rose in a vase.

Kidding, he asked, "Ah! Another flower from the yellow rose phantom?"

Christina glared at him, then burst into laughter. It had only

71

been three weeks since some strange guy visiting a relative in her neighborhood had left yellow roses on her doorstep three days in a row. To prevent embarrassment for his family, she stayed with Paul and Abigail until he went back home. But it had gotten to be a joke with her family and closest friends.

"No! They're from my favorite sweetheart. He may only be four years old, but he's the best one I've got."

"Oh, Mom. You know better than that. You've got two great men in your life – me and PaPa."

Even though he was joking, Noah was right. Had it not been for Mr. Cache and Noah, Christina did not know how she would have survived the past few years. There had been so many times that she wanted so desperately to get away from Tom, and all the problems of Matt's teenage years, that she had wondered what it would be like if she simply fell off the face of the earth. But every time she had that thought, she envisioned her parents and her sons, and she could not stand breaking their hearts like that.

Christina could not understand why Shane would have pulled such a stunt, but she clearly understood how he could think about it. And perhaps there was her answer. Could it have been possible that he was so strung out on drugs that he truly could not rationally think? She knew the answer to that, and suddenly felt a sickening pity for him that she had not experienced before.

Noah's bottomless pit of a stomach pulled her back to the kitchen in quick order. Today was their annual visit out for a breakfast of heart-shaped biscuits, and he had no intention of letting her forget it. She grabbed the keys and off they went for the start of a wonderful Valentine's Day together.

By the time they got back with their dozen biscuits and strawberry preserves, Matt was up and ready to eat with them. They sat at the table in the breakfast nook, with the shades open, looking out over Christina's bird sanctuary and natural area in the back yard. It was a beautiful day, feeling more like spring than the dead of winter, with cardinals and doves feeding amidst the crocus and daffodils. Christina offered the morning's blessing after Matt read the devotional. Both of the boys looked at their mother and noticed a change in her spirit. It had been a long time since she had seemed this excited. Her act had been a good one, but Noah had sensed her loneliness much more than Matt. Seeing her this vibrant was Noah's own private Valentine's Day present.

Noah reached on the kitchen counter and handed his mom a card.

Matt spoke first. "Read it now, Mom."

Christina opened the envelope to find the most sentimental card her sons had ever given her on Valentine's Day. She was struck by the fact that they had gotten a way to the store and bought the card themselves. What really brought her to tears, though, were the pictures her sons had drawn inside the card. There was a *Phantom of the Opera* mask from Matt, and a Grateful Dead Bear from Noah, along with a display of other shared symbols of enjoyment.

She could not believe it. It was only ten-thirty in the morning, and already the best Valentine's Day she had experienced in years. Christina set the card on the mantle, and they had a long relaxing breakfast, rehashing old memories and pleasantries, something they had not done in over three years.

The telephone rang just as she was getting out of the shower. Christina was already rushing, wanting to have time to look her best. She glanced at the clock to see it was already six o'clock as she picked up the receiver.

"Hey. Can you come and pick me up?" flew the question from

the other end.

Christina recognized the voice this time, as she laughed. "Are you making a habit of this?"

"Of what?"

"Catching me as I get out of the shower?" They both laughed since this made the second time Shane had caught Christina that way in one week. "Where are you?"

"Just off I-85 on Sugar Creek."

"How long will it take me to get there?"

"Ten minutes, if you hurry."

"Have you ever known me not to be in a hurry?"

"Or late!" came the answer.

"Okay, that's enough, or you can walk home."

"See you in a few."

They both loved the lightheartedness of their newly formed friendship. Humor and laughter came easily to them, as well as the ability to say anything without the other taking offense.

Christina threw on her make-up, not taking the time to make sure it was flawless, as she had planned, and an old pair of slacks and a sweater. She would come back and change after she took Shane home. *Ten minutes there, ten minutes back, drop him off, change, be at the church at seven o'clock. Yep! That's about par for my course. And he wonders why I'm late. It's because I'm always taking care of everyone else.*

She dodged last-minute card and flower shoppers, trying to bolt through the traffic. *Thank goodness, the dinner crowd hasn't hit yet.* Christina figured every restaurant, theater, and other public meeting place would be packed this evening. But she and her friends were going away from Charlotte, to a remote area. Hopefully, her entourage would not have to fight the multitude of lovers out basking in the serenade of the night air on their way to the dance.

She turned off the interstate, counting the two blocks to where she was to meet Shane. Christina saw him, sitting on the cement wall beside the sidewalk, bag in hand. She did not even have to guess what was inside the bag. Shane really enjoyed his beer, and it was not up to her to criticize, but if he was going to be with her, he was not going to need anything that would alter his naturally wonderful personality.

"Need a ride?" She pulled up to the curb and Shane got in the car.

"What took you so long?"

"Well, I did have to throw on some clothes. Besides, it looks like you had something to keep you company."

Shane reached into the bag for a bottle. Christina pulled the bag over to her, counting the bottles. She saw that three had already been emptied.

"Don't you think you've had enough before we go out? We *are* going to be with a church group. And how can you be my dance partner if you can't even stand up?"

Christina knew exactly how many beers Shane could have and still be sober. But she also knew he was an alcoholic, and the beer needed to go out the window with the drugs if he was going be able to break his addictive habits. And in the few days they had been together, she had already seen that more than two showed in his eyes, his face and his behavior, regardless of what he accepted or admitted. She had dealt with enough problems due to alcohol for one lifetime, and she did not intend to have any more attributed to it.

"You know I could still stand up even if I drank every one of these."

"Yes, I'm sure you could, but I wouldn't want to be with you if you did."

Shane just looked at her. He had never been with anyone, much less a female, who talked to him like that. She not only had morals, she had the guts to stand up for them. *How dare she tell me I can't drink my beer? Nobody talks to me that way.*

Christina knew what Shane was thinking, so she continued, "And I've been looking forward to this evening all week. I don't intend to let you or anyone else mess it up for me!" Although she had made her comment in a half-joking tone, they both knew she meant exactly what she had just said.

Shane sat there watching her as she made her way back to the interstate. *Has she just given me an ultimatum? I don't do ultimatums.* But he only glared at Christina, as if she had just made a perfect serve, knocking the ball into his court, impossible to hit back at her.

He did not like this game. Why weren't they shooting pool or darts, something to which he was accustomed? Here was this person, telling him he could have his beer or her. That was odd enough, but the clincher was that he wasn't even angry at her.

*I've just spent all day driving to see the best drinking companion I've ever had. My lover, my precious - that I got to hold and kiss for an hour - whose very presence made me want a beer the minute I saw her. And here is this person I barely know, telling me I can't finish the few I bought!*

Shane continued to glare at Christina. He had never met anyone exactly like her, and he did not quite know what to make of her. She asked him how his day had gone, only to find out he had to take his friend's car, without a license, for the day's trip. That is why he had no ride home. Both his parents and Mickey were already out for the evening, so he had called her, anxious to see her smiling face and feel touched by her dancing spirit. And now here she sat, already putting a damper on his evening.

*I'll show her*, he thought, figuring he would get out and tell her to go without him.

Christina again knew what thoughts must be running through his head, but she continued to talk about things having nothing to do with either the dance or the beer. She wondered if she would have to find a new dancing partner, but seemed unconcerned,

76

knowing that Noah would be there if she got in a bind, along with a few other single guys from the church.

The way she saw it, she had laid her cards on the table. He could either draw or call her bluff. There was only one thing different here for Shane. Christina did not bluff. And Shane was perceptive and intelligent enough to sense that, even if he had been coined "a dumb redneck." She had been with him long enough to surmise that he was just as smart as her, and his brain worked just as fast. Christina was gambling on him making the right choice, not so much for her sake, but for his own.

Shane opened the door as Christina pulled up to his driveway, ready to go out on his own for an evening of *real* fun. He looked back to let her have it, but said, "Pick me up in ten minutes."

Christina's smile was bigger than ever. She reached for the bag. "I'll hold onto these for you to make sure you're agile enough to be my dance partner." And with that, she drove off.

He stood there, looking behind her, madly excited by her spunk and boldness, and mad that he'd let a woman tell him what to do. *A minister at that. I have no use for ministers – well, not most of them.* Shane hurried into the house so quickly to shower and get changed that he didn't even smoke a cigarette. *Not that I haven't had enough today already.*

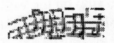

Noah caught Christina just as she was coming in the door. "Mom, my friends who went to The Wildlife last week are going again. Can I ride with them?"

Christina already knew the answer, but she looked at him with a questioning raised eyebrow, just to challenge his mind.

"*May* I *please* go with my friends?"

She laughed, and gave Noah a hug which he knew meant, "Sure. Go and have a good time." Christina had such a way with Noah that he did not even mind her grammatical corrections. He was intuitive enough to know that she figured he would need to know the difference someday, and she did it without nagging.

Noah grinned inside. His mom had climbed the ladder from being a small-community country girl to dining and dancing with the top crust of society. And she had done it all on her own. Christina's manners, grace and intelligence had helped to create the self-made person that she was, and as he stood there looking at her, he was more proud of her than usual. His insight told him that all she wanted was the same for him. So, because of her mild manner, Noah appreciated and respected her, knowing her wisdom would pay off for him down the road.

Christina hugged Noah even harder, once again realizing how blessed she was to have a son like him. Any other male teenager would have bucked at her correction, then huffed around until the mother and son wound up in a screaming match. But Noah changed two words, smiled, hugged his mom, and both went on looking forward to a memorable evening with friends. He had come into this world with a perception greater than most adults, and his wisdom had continued to grow with each passing year.

"Do you want something to eat before you go?"

"No, we're going to stop on the way."

They both heard the horn blow in the driveway. Christina gave Noah money for dinner and the dance, and they hugged again.

"See you there. Be careful. And have a good time."

"You, too, Mom!" he said with a knowing eye, as they stood looking at each other for a second.

Christina waved at his friends, and then ran up the stairs to get dressed. She threw on a black velvet top and jeans, her black boot shoes, and the silver-and-onyx earrings she had bought in New Mexico, ran the brush through her hair, giving her wedge style the fullness it needed, and dashed out the door. Shane's house was only a mile away, so she managed to make it back in fifteen minutes, not at all surprised to find him waiting at the driveway with his cigarette in hand.

"I knew you'd be late," he laughingly scolded her.

"I only wanted to give you time for a cigarette, since you did not get one when I dropped you off," she responded, smiling.

Shane was immediately sure that he had made the right decision. He could already feel the fun and energy radiating from her, and it made him instantly reciprocate with his own feelings.

Christina ran by the church to make sure everyone in the singles group knew how to get to The Wildlife, and to make sure they knew to look for Bob and Shirley when they got there. She told them to go on without her, that she needed to stop on the way for a second. *Okay, I've done my part of the job. Now it is MY evening.*

"Where's Noah?"

"He went on with his friends. They all had so much fun last weekend that they wanted to go back for the Valentine Dance tonight."

Shane gave Christina that wink she had seen Thursday evening, and grinned. "So I've got you all to myself?"

She couldn't help but laugh at his style. Shane was as much a joker as she was, and she really enjoyed having someone who could relate to her, without taking her too seriously. In Christina's line of work, that was generally a rarity.

"Yeah. You and four hundred other people," she answered, estimating the crowd expected at The Wildlife.

Christina pulled into a fast food joint on the way. "Hungry?"

"No, but you can pull into the convenience store down the road."

Christina smirked. "Sorry, but this is all you're going to get."

She knew that Shane was kidding, but he would not have turned down a trip to the store for a six-pack. This time he was calling her bluff, but Christina was not budging. And he felt comfortable with her, knowing she would not reprimand him for his desires. He actually enjoyed the fact that she was strong enough to stand up for what she believed.

Shane also caught one other hidden meaning in her statement, "this is all you're going to get." He was not a man who was used to being turned down, but here was one lady *(Yes, Shane, you said 'lady'!)* who would stand up to his whims. Maybe that was another reason he liked Christina's presence so much. He could be out with her and still feel he was being faithful to Carla. *After all, how far do even YOU expect to get with a minister!* He looked at her.

"I'll have a cheeseburger, fries and coke – if that's *all* you're going to let me have," and he gave her that wink again.

Christina loved that wink, for it said he was as full of himself as she was. He was terribly flirtatious, yet she felt no pressure from him, like with so many of the guys who had tried to hit on her. She felt totally comfortable with Shane, yet he was, by every definition of the word, 'the bad boy' that every girl's mother warned her about.

The parking lot was more crowded than they had expected. It seemed that the Valentine Dance *was* the big event of the year. They walked into the lobby, only to stand in line to pay the entrance fee. Even that was different from usual. Once inside the room, which was usually barren except for the rows of chairs and tables against the four walls, the decor almost transformed the gigantic rectangular room into a ballroom. The only thing that remained the same was the smoke that filled the air.

Christina had found it odd that as much trouble as she and

Noah had with allergies, they could even bear all the smoke, but so far, they had managed as long as they stayed away from the tables. That suited Christina just fine, for it gave her a legitimate excuse to stay on the dance floor, *as if I needed one.*

She mulled over the smoke factor for a few minutes, as Shane went outside to smoke. He made a point of not smoking in her face, but still his clothes smelled heavily of the lasting odor. Yet, it was as if she was immune to it. Since she could hardly stand to be around Matt or launder his clothes for the thickness created in the air by the lingering scent, this had become a puzzlement to her. Christina had never been able to be around smokers, but this guy who was practically a chain smoker did not have that effect on her. *What kind of supernatural aura does he possess?*

Her thoughts were interrupted by the flock of friends who had found her. They were all going on about what a great idea this was and making lots of small talk. Christina, who usually fit right into this, found it to be a terrible nuisance. *Is it because these people are my job?* That had never bothered her before in social spheres. Her job had always been an overwhelming part of her personal life, and she had never minded it before. But, tonight was so different.

*Why are you letting this bother you? Shane is your job, too. Are you going to let THAT keep you from having an enjoyable evening?* Christina was angry with herself for feeling this way about her friends. She was unaccustomed to this train of thought, and she did not like it at all.

"Why don't we get Shirley to show us some dance steps before the band starts the music?" was Christina's escape from the discomfort she was sensing.

That idea got great response as Shirley led them all out on the floor. "C'mon, Christina, you know all these dances. You can help me demonstrate them," the dance instructor yelled behind her.

Bob took Christina's hand and led her out in front of the group.

*Great, as usual, I am out in front of people! Why can't I just blend in like everyone else?* Christina still could not seem to shake this mood that had taken its claim on her, but as they started moving, she found herself able to get back into her own element. It was as if she fit in the pattern with everyone else and did not feel quite so in charge. Before long, she was fully into the dance routines and enjoying herself once again.

Shane saw the crowd of acquaintances arrive as he finished his cigarette. Either they had taken a longer route, or had stopped along the way, too. Their appearance made him a little uncomfortable, which struck him as strange, because normally, he had no problem being in crowds. The places where he usually hung out were full of mobs – literally – and it had never bothered him before.

Walking back to the building, Shane's mind ran rampant with questions, trying to explain his strange mood. *Is it because so many people recognize me? Is it because it is a church group? Is it because I am out, trying to have a good time, while Carla's locked up? Is it because I don't normally hang out in places where I can't have a bottle in my hand for security?*

He stopped dead in his tracks. *Or is it because I'm afraid they'll rob me of Christina and I'll have to fight for her attention all night? Or that one of these guys that she knows may wind up holding her in his arms the entire evening?*

Shane took a couple more steps before stomping his foot. *Get off it, pal. She works in a church, for God's sake. A church. She is NOT your type.*

He walked toward their table and spied her out on the floor.

Christina caught Shane's eye and motioned for him to join her.

"Why don't you come over and learn some of these line dances?"

Glad for the offer to be with her, Shane took off his jacket as Christina made room for him beside her in the line.

"You'll really enjoy these. They're fun!"

Shane laughed at her idea of fun on a lover's evening, but her exuberance made it fun for him, too. He watched her steps and followed them as closely as he could. His feet seemed awkward at first, but as Christina took his hand and walked him through the dances, he caught on quickly. Before long, they were showing the steps to others of the singles group.

After they had all the line dances under control, Christina asked Bob to do The Sway with her so that Shane could learn the movements.

"I love this dance," she called over her shoulder to Shane. "It's my favorite slow dance. I want you to learn to do it with me."

Bob did the basic steps with her a few times, then motioned for Shane to cut in. Shane took Christina's hands in his, and she walked him through the movements. Within a couple of minutes, they had it, and she got him to take her for a practice run around the perimeter of the dance floor.

Christina literally graced the floor with the smoothness of her movements. Even though he was supposed to be leading her, Shane found his job to be no problem because she seemed to float. *Is this the same person who was so stiff in my arms only two weeks ago?* She was so light on her feet, yet so precise with the rhythms. He could not take his eyes off her. Christina had turned into a beautiful work of art, and here she was, in his arms.

Shane thought of the woman he had seen in her last night. They stood in the Howell's back yard, working on Matt's car. He had planned to take out the headlights, replace them and be through in a matter of minutes. But Christina had insisted that he show her how, and allow her to do it.

"Pop-up lights are tricky," was Shane's reply. He did not want to spend all night on this chore.

But Christina's persistence won out. "Just show me how to take out one of the lights. If I can't take out the other one, and put in the new lights, then you can do it yourself."

Shane looked at her, sure that this city girl, who had tried to convince him that she was just as down-to-earth as he was, would be handing over the tools in less than two minutes.

"Fair enough."

He couldn't believe it when she not only knew the names of the tools and parts, but exactly how to use them. Christina did not mind in the least that she had grease all over her hands, and under her nails. Then, when she asked Abigail for the Goop so that she could wash her hands, Shane stood in amazement, watching her walk off after she slammed down the hood of the car.

Shane was shocked by her determination and self-will. Never had he been with anyone, much less a female, whom he allowed to watch him work. Yet Christina had stood beside him, looking over his shoulder, at his every move. Shane had figured it would take her all night, but after one time of showing her what to do, she took the tools, and within a matter of minutes, had the headlights replaced. He could not believe his eyes when she came back outside, flipped the switch and the lights worked perfectly.

That same woman who seemed so adept at working with tools, and had a common-sense knowledge of mechanical skills, was now ruling this dance floor with such ease that Shane had trouble understanding her.

*Okay, she's an awesome musician and a super dancer. She can talk to anyone about almost anything, and she listens like she's reaching inside my soul. She's obviously a mover and a shaker, with all those programs and tours she's done. And she can work on cars, and she's an all-star mom. Is there anything she CAN'T do?* Shane made it his personal project to find her weakness before the evening was over.

Christina loved the strength she felt in Shane's hands as he led her around the floor. The more she was with him, the harder she found it to believe he had given in to his weaknesses only a few weeks ago. He appeared to be a tower of solid stability, yet something had to have a hold on him to push him to that limit.

But she herself knew the downfall of one's limitations. That is why she refused to participate every time she reached hers, and looked for a detour to bypass her weaknesses. However, as hard as she tried, Christina was not always successful in her endeavors. It was her friends and family who had held her up in those times, helping her not to dwell on her failures, but rather her strengths.

*He has such innate intelligence and just plain know-how. He can take a car apart from bumper to bumper and put it back together again. He appreciates my music, and he possesses dramatic skills. He can cook. He can talk about practically anything, and he is a superb dancer, full of rhythm. Is there anything he CAN'T do?* Christina made it her personal duty, *not my job!,* to find out that overbearing weakness.

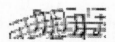

The people in their group watched as they took command of the floor, gliding around it as if they had been doing this all of their lives. Neither of them noticed the attention that had fallen on them until they got back to their starting point and their friends burst into wild applause. Shane and Christina just looked at each other, wondering why all the commotion.

They walked back over to the table, content that they had mastered enough dances to keep them busy for the evening. Both of them enjoyed the conversation that followed. It was as if they had a world of new things to tell each other, even though they had seen each other the last two nights and had the ride here to communicate any important items of interest.

When the band started, the lights dimmed, lower than usual it seemed. The music began with a rollicking, fast beat to get everyone up and moving. However, Christina and Shane continued to sit at the table, deep into conversation, uncovering more common bonds of experience. On the other two Saturdays, they had sat across from each other, but this evening, they had gotten there early enough to get two seats beside each other at the back of one of the tables against the wall. Not only did this give them the advantage of hearing each other clearly, it gave them a seclusion to look into each other's souls without being too obvious.

While the entire room full of people moved around in droves to the music, they had evolved into a world of their own, each for the first time finding another being who had trod their same path. Neither of them was conscious of how long they had been sitting there until Bob interrupted their aloofness.

"You two gonna sit here all night, or did you come to dance?"

Shane and Christina never lost their stare into each other's eyes, but changed expressions to let the other know it was time to get up. Without a word, Christina moved forward with Shane holding her hand and following her into the crowd. They were both relieved when the lights lowered more and the disco ball began to flash, signaling a slow dance.

Christina fell into his arms as the music started. Shane led her to the middle of the floor, away from the noise of the outside circle. They strolled in time to the music, continuing to look into each other's eyes, with a boisterous conversation going on through their senses. When the music stopped, they still stood there, their hands locked. The cue of the lights coming up broke their spell as Shane kissed Christina gently on the forehead, and whispered the words,

"Thank you."

The music changed tempos for a line dance. They were pulled into the singles group by a couple of Christina's friends who longed for her company. Still holding hands, they fell into line, but held onto each other's shoulders as they turned to different directions during the dance.

A partner change dance came next. Shane did his best to get back around to Christina every time the whistle blew to change partners. When he was not with her, he made sure she was with Noah, or else someone whom he trusted with her. He actually had gotten her all to himself this evening, and he had no intention of losing her.

Christina watched as Shane made his way outside to smoke. His gait told a story all its own. There were many years of heartache in each step, and she wondered when it all began. Looking into his most private thoughts had allowed her to see that along with all of the amazing and interesting stories from Thursday evening, there was an entire collection of other stories, just waiting to be told, yet they had never found the right audience.

*I am going to be that audience*, Christina decided as he disappeared out the door.

Shane stood outside, taking long, slow draws on his cigarette, trying to think what it would be like to be with Carla this evening, but his mind kept flashing to a new face, a face full of love and longing, longing and hope, hope and peace, peace and joy – joy, yet desire. A face that held expressions that he had never before encountered. There was something in the life of that face that he wanted in his own.

He went back inside only to find this creature that was captivating his thoughts surrounded by all her friends again. *I can't leave her alone for one minute!* Shane wondered if he had lost Christina for the evening, or if the next set of music would send her throng of followers in different directions.

As he walked toward the group, looking at her as if her body held the answer, Christina's eyes caught his. Those eyes that smiled at him, that sparkled as brightly as the stars in the sky. Those eyes that called to him, that invited him to come and rescue her. Those eyes were all it took for Shane to know what to do.

Christina felt the familiar hand slither around her waist as he announced, "C'mon. There's a couple of other dances you still need to show me."

She glanced at Shane curiously, her eyes questioning his sudden desire to be on his feet. And then Christina burst into laughter, realizing that he had read her thoughts.

"Thanks for the timely rescue," she said, smiling as she squeezed his upper arm gently.

Shane sensed a wave of pride in the fact that he could do anything of value for this classy dame. "Well, I wasn't *all* Mr. Nice Guy. I must admit that I selfishly wanted you all to myself."

"That's okay. I really just wanted to be with you, too."

Shane felt his chest rise several inches and his head enlarge at the realization that this glowing angel liked him well enough to want to spend time with him. He had already seen that Christina could be with anyone she chose. Her company was quite an ego boost for him.

*You have actually risen out of the dregs of your hellhole, MISTER Sievers.* Holding Christina's hand and looking into her caring face, he made a private commitment to himself not to go backwards.

The band started their second set of music. Shane held onto Christina's hand, not giving anyone a chance to grab her away from him. The music was a line dance, but he held onto her and made sure she stayed right beside him. When that song ended, he took her hand again to insure that she was his.

Noah had come in from the game room when he heard the music. He searched the room for his mom, wanting to make sure he did not need to rescue her from any undesirable partners.

"When is it my turn?" he asked.

Shane broke into the conversation. "Why don't you help me keep her occupied during this Paul Jones?"

"Sure!"

That was an easy request for Noah, for he loved the partner dances. He enjoyed swirling the older ladies and giving them an opportunity to see that all teenagers weren't drug addicts who didn't care about their elders. It was a treat for him to break their stereotypical ideas, and show them that *all* of his generation was *not* going "straight to hell in a handbasket."

The music started and Christina shook loose from Shane and moved in her clockwise order, while she watched her two male partners take off in their counterclockwise step. When the whistle signaled the guys to grab a partner, Shane appeared out of nowhere, whisking her away from the circle.

Christina laughed at his bold effort. He was turning into quite an impetuous character and she loved it. It had been a long time since she had felt wanted by anyone, and she had forgotten the thrill that went with that desire. She had longed to be needed for so long that she had given up on ever knowing that feeling again. However, she gathered that this was Shane's way of making her ease up from the horrors of her past. Whatever his reasoning, she loved the laughter that emitted from his playful antics.

Noah caught his mom on the next round. Christina spent every one of the changes with either Shane or her son. This pattern continued for the entire second set of music. By the time the band took their second and final break, she had gotten accustomed to having Shane on one side and Noah on the other for the line dances, and had found herself watching the two of them as they made their ways around the circle on partner dances, wondering which one of them would get to her on the next round.

Shane stood out during one of the partner dances, just to watch

Christina. She moved so easily across the floor that his eyes remained glued to her every movement. And when she danced with Noah, it was as if their energy and excitement took over the room. *She surely is an angel. NO teenage son could enjoy spending time and doing things with her the way he does, no matter what a great mom she is.*

He continued to watch the mother-son pair. The pride that shone in both of them was clearly obvious. They truly had a love for each other that was uncommon. Little did Shane know the deep dark shadows of the past few years that had drawn them so close, that had caused them to depend on each other for their very existence. And now that their lives were on an upward swing, the love that had developed between them continued to grow, and their bond was invincible.

Noah and Christina knew they were on the face of the earth because angels had saved them on many occasions. They loved life. They loved every breath of life because they both realized how precious it was to them. Thus, their zest showed in everything they did. Shane loved their display of affection and happiness, not only for each other, but for everyone and everything around them. And he saw that every time he was in their company.

*How could ANY idiot let her go?* Shane had seen Christina's former husband on several occasions, and sensed that they were not a match long before he ever met her, or knew anything about her. But now that he had spent even this minimal amount of time with her, and with his own past hellacious marriage, he could not imagine ever wanting to be away from this angelic creature, much less walking out on her.

He grabbed her as she moved toward him in the circle, and got back into the group of dancers. Christina loved the happiness she saw in his eyes. It was the first time she'd actually seen Shane's eyes dancing, and it gave his face – his whole *body* – an appearance of energy and anticipation that she hadn't seen. Until now.

She loved seeing him this way. He looked so alive, so vibrant. *This guy makes me feel glad to be alive, to be in his arms.* Shane had an effect on her that made even her carefree, yet wildfire spirit seem dormant, simply because his presence this evening had so enlightened her whole being. As they swayed around the circle to the last bars of music, Christina found herself hoping the evening would never end.

The others of their group left, going out for late dessert before returning home. Although Christina wondered if she should go and be their leader, she decided that these people were all adults who could make their own decisions. She did something totally out of the ordinary for her, and opted to do exactly what she wanted to do, which was stay and end this Valentine's Day with Shane.

Shane stayed on the floor for every single dance of the last set, not wanting to let go of her, or lose the scent of her perfume, nor the touch of her delicate hands. It seemed that the band played more slow songs during their last hour, and with each one, Shane and Christina found themselves more connected through their spirits until they were consummately meshed.

Even on the partner dances, Shane found it difficult to loosen his hold on her. He waited to see if she pulled away from him to be more a part of the crowd, or to check on Noah and his friends. But, Christina followed his lead and moved with him to every piece of music until finally he did not let go of her at all.

They spoke no words, but looked into each other's faces, exploring the longing that hid within. Christina saw a being who possessed the same emotions, the same care and concern, and the same thoughtfulness as herself. Yet, she also saw the same torment, the same pain, and the same search for something missing, all by which she was plagued.

As she continued to look past his eyes and listen to the horrible untold stories spoken only by Shane's soul, she heard a voice, as if coming from an abyss in the farthest reaches of her consciousness.

Even though Christina did not want to hear the message, she listened intently, carefully decoding every word of the warning. And then she responded and answered her own soul.

*I know I should be careful with this guy, but I have never been so comfortable with anyone in my life.*

By the last quarter hour, the oddly paired couple had become inseparable. Their eyes no longer held each other, but rather, Christina's head lay on Shane's shoulder. It was as if they were completely spent from the emotions that had surfaced during the course of the evening. There was an unexplainable trust between them that had somehow developed all on its own.

Something made a strange ripple go through Christina's body. *It must be the disco ball, or the dim lights, or the decorations. What I feel is nothing more than a romantic setting on a Valentine's night.*

However, as she looked around the room at the couples who had stayed for the duration, Christina saw that they were watching she and Shane. All eyes were on them. Obviously the other couples were not caught up in the same trance.

Shane held her closer, catching an ease in her step and her posture that had not been there before. He realized that he had been so transformed by Christina's presence that he had not gone outside, or stopped for a smoke, during the past hour. It was not like him to give up his cigarettes or beer for anyone, especially some dumb broad, and even worse, one who worked in a church.

Then he remembered something he had heard Christina quote on Thursday. *"Lonely people make dumb mistakes." Okay, Shane, she warned you. Be careful. You're not used to playing with angels. Fire, maybe, but definitely NOT angels!*

The band announced the last Paul Jones, to be followed by the final dance of the evening. Shane looked into Christina's eyes, determined not to let go of her. He had waited all of his life for his ship to come in, and now that it had, he refused to let it sail without

92

him.

Although the other gents and ladies split for the partner dance, Shane waltzed Christina into the middle of the circle. Neither of them were in the least embarrassed by what they were feeling, as they held tight to each other while the other people merrily strode from one partner to another. No longer did Christina see his eyes, searching the room for her, and walking through the circle to get to her. He kept her all to himself.

Christina loved the attention. It was something that had been void in her life for years. That is, void from someone special to her. Her talent and love for people brought her much unwarranted attention. But to have a man want her company, to hold onto her — that was different. It was a sensation she had completely forgotten. However, this evening's encounter with it quickly aroused her memory.

Then, as the lights dimmed and that romantically revolving ball lit the room with its slow turns, Shane pulled Christina in even closer to him. There was no struggle, no awkwardness. And as his eyes caught hers to again serenade her, everyone froze. Time stood still, and nothing, nor anyone, in the room mattered. It was as if they were the only two people there, surrounded by a mystical lake of fog sheltering them from any outsiders. Only them against the world, transforming it with the power of their bond. And not knowing why that bond existed, only that it was heaven-sent.

During the next couple of minutes as the music played, their souls became so akin that Christina heard and saw an entire opera in Shane's eyes. One so masterfully crafted that it could have been scored by Mozart himself. She saw the heart-wrenching pain, the outrageous comedy, the tension between the subordinate characters, and the struggle of bad against good, with the good winning, in this particular case.

The background music was no longer dominated by the twangs of stringed instruments, nor electronic keyboards, but rather the finest of orchestral instruments, played by the most skilled musicians.

Their lives had become an intricately woven tapestry, intertwining with each experience. The minor modes had lent themselves to the brightness of the major keys. And the notes of each instrument had become so harmoniously connected with each other that they boasted the perfection of sound. Christina and Shane became the characters of the paradisiacal leading roles in that opera.

Their movements became as precise, yet relaxed, as the classical music Christina heard playing behind them. Never had anyone loosed this theme within her nailed-shut psyche. The only thing she missed were the faint underlying dissonant chords that were the overture to the tragedy of a love triangle.

When the last notes of the final dance ended, they stood there, locked in each other's arms, still swaying as their souls continued to converse. They finally awakened from their dream sequence when they heard the band packing up and the janitor moving tables and sweeping, signaling that another Valentine's Day had passed.

Christina looked at her watch. 12:05. Valentine's Day was history. And what a memorable event it had been. She could not remember a year in her entire life when she had felt more captivated by Cupid's arrows. Not even the time in college when she had received five dozen roses from different admirers compared to the thrill of this evening.

Yet, as excited as she felt from the music and her company of the evening, she felt as if she were literally floating on the gentle breeze that blew in from outside. The temperature had dropped since their arrival, and Shane wrapped his coat around Christina's shoulders and held it to her tightly to keep her warm on the way to the car.

They found Noah waiting beside the Blazer. He had wanted to go on home rather than seeing the midnight movie with his friends. Christina and Shane still felt so encompassed by their own emotions that not even his presence broke their mood.

After they finally got onto the main highway, Shane turned on the radio, realizing that it was as if he had been kidnapped from within his own body. Christina was glad for the diversion, too, when she realized that their souls were still connected. Then, he reached over and took her right hand into his, still wanting to feel the unity that had developed between them.

It was Noah who finally broke the silence, sensing that both of these adults were a little uneasy by the strange link between them, yet not knowing exactly how to break it.

"Shane, you are the only person that I would let dance with my mother like that."

His comment caught both of them off guard. Although Christina was slightly embarrassed, wondering if her emotions had shown, Noah was grateful for Shane, for he had never known anyone who had shown so much respect for his mother. Shane was unsure how to respond, afraid his unwavering attention of Noah's mother might have upset her offspring. But rather, her sagacious son seemed genuinely proud and happy for both of them.

"Thank you."

Shane conceived that Noah was even more astute than he had first suspected. Not only did he feel an unsought closeness for the woman whose hand he held, but an inseparable bond to her son, too. He felt an unquenchable yearning for that same kind of relationship with his own son.

The ride home passed quickly as Shane continued to hold onto Christina's hand, unwilling to let go of what had transpired between them, and Noah and Shane talking about anything, everything and nothing, all the while developing a kinship through their mutual admiration for the woman who sat at the helm of their magical vessel.

When they pulled up to his driveway and said their good-byes, Shane reached over and gave Christina the most gentle kiss she had ever received. He started to pull away, but felt compelled to press his lips against hers once more before he exited.

*Even her kisses are angelic,* he whispered, as if talking to someone, though he knew that God was the only person listening. And then he did not even try to hide the huge grin that took over his face as he went inside, realizing that he actually had made that comment to Christina's "Man Upstairs."

# 5

Christina had loved going to church on Sundays. It was something she had done regularly from the time she was two weeks old. The only weeks she had missed in her forty-three years were the Sundays when she was sick, away on vacations, or giving birth to her two children. Even with that, she could have probably counted the times she had been absent from worship on her fingers and toes.

That being the case, Sundays had become the most routine act in her entire life. Not only was it a habit, it was a hobby. It was a part of her total being, a part which she enjoyed beyond description. Besides being a job she loved, it was one of the most fun aspects of her existence. Yet, the day after Valentine's Day found Christina awaiting the church service with more anticipation than she had ever known.

When she had dropped Shane off last night after the dance, he was quick to ask her, "See you in Sunday School class in the morning?"

"I wouldn't miss it."

"Good. I'll save you a seat." Shane paused for a second. "That is, if you will sit beside me."

He had made his statement with confidence, as if he fully expected an affirmative answer. But the truth was, Shane was a little apprehensive about Christina's willingness to let others know that she hung around with the likes of him.

"Of course. I'd be delighted to sit beside you. But make sure you sit near the back. Remember I have to leave early to get the choir ready."

"Sure thing." And with that, Shane had kissed her and hopped out of the car.

Christina was so impressed with Shane's decision to clean up his act. He was sincere in his effort to stay off the drugs, and it showed in his eyes and face. The problem was that he had taken his family and friends down so many dead-end roads before that they could not see it.

But with her, it was different. Shane had seen that Christina did not judge him nor condemn him, so there was an honesty factor that he shared with her that he had never known with anyone before. Not his wife, nor his lovers, nor his closest friends. In his previous line of work, he could not trust *anyone*.

Christina decided that what Shane needed most right now was a friend. Someone who would not criticize or judge, but just accept him. And to love him – just as he was. She did not want to change him. But she did want him to change himself, and that might take a little guidance, and a *lot* of encouragement from her.

She knew that one of her most beneficial talents had been the ability to reach out to people who seemed beyond help. Shane Sievers was a prime example. He had known plenty of ministers in the past, and only trusted three of them. And Christina was not too sure how much he even *trusted* them. Maybe *respected* was a better description. She highly suspected that for him, even that term might be stretching it a bit.

He was definitely a challenge waiting for someone, and she felt that she was just the person to handle it. Christina was anxious to get to work. She realized that here was a beautiful gem. An uncut diamond, still terribly in rough form and covered in the blackness of coal from years of being entombed. Shane was her find, and she felt honored to be the person to uncover his true worth.

*I have been given my next assignment.* Christina loved being selected for impossible missions. *Yes, Father, I do accept!*

She walked out onto her deck, looked up at the stars and moon still barely visible in the early morning sky, and prayed the words that she always used just before setting out to work with an outcast, as if they possessed the power of a magic potion.

*Lord, make me an instrument of Your peace.*

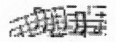

Always before, Shane agreed to go to church just to keep his parents off his back, but this morning, he got there first and made the coffee for the class. He was such a seasoned coffee drinker from his past alcohol addiction that he certainly had the right formula for that job. In fact, as people gathered, they all proclaimed that he be given the role permanently.

As if he was not already feeling chipper enough, their vote of confidence made him feel even better. He had marked two chairs on the front row. Shane knew Christina wanted to sit near the back, but he wanted to show off the fact that he was with her. It was not his usual good fortune to be with a dame like her, and he had to make the best of it.

Shane had brought both Carla and his other lover to worship before and sat near the back of the sanctuary. But Christina was different. She was loved and respected by everyone. She held a position. Being with her held its own credibility. Since this was a first for him, he was determined to milk it for all it was worth.

After several minutes, Shane watched the clock, wondering where she was. When everyone took their seats and the class began, he figured he had been stood up.

*Why did you think she would actually make a spectacle of herself by being seen with you?*

As he sat there reprimanding himself for being so vain, Shane heard the door open. He glanced around, and sure enough, it was Christina. Once again, he felt his emotions begin to swell. She glanced around the room, only to find him on the front row. He began to wonder if she would make her way through the crowd to get to him, but his eyes motioned to the empty chair beside him, and she quickly moved to fill it.

Both Shane and Christina could feel the eyes on them as they exchanged brief greetings. Christina was amused that she felt smugly proud to be sitting beside this roughneck in the midst of all the "holier than thous." She had always been one to rock the boat if she felt that so-called Christians needed a little shaking up, and this group was a bit overdue.

The lesson that day had to do with true happiness. It just so happened that Abigail was teaching the lesson that particular Sunday. She used Christina for an example on many Sundays, but today, she turned to Christina and asked her for a comment about finding happiness from others.

Christina did not even think before spitting out an answer. Her words came from personal experience, as well as seminary counseling classes.

"You can't be happy with anyone else if you're not happy with yourself."

Abigail and everyone else knew that Christina was referring to her ex. However, Shane sat there thinking about her comment. He realized that for the first time in years, he actually was feeling pretty good about himself. And now that he thought about it, he realized he was not getting as riled at every little thing that happened.

Up to now, he had always felt as if the whole world was against him, ganging up on him, but now – largely due to this newly found 'friend' – Shane saw that life could be fun and that he didn't need to be smashed in order to have a good time. He began to daydream about the mountains and the streams, and all the places he'd heard music while he had been out camping or fishing. For the first time in his adult life, he sensed a complete happiness that had been absent before.

He got his thoughts together and glanced over at the angel who had sent his mind soaring just in time to hear her whisper, "Bye. Have to go now." Shane spent the last few minutes there thinking about how different his life seemed now than it had even two months ago.

It was beginning to dawn on Shane that this one lone female had a lot to do with it. He really enjoyed the way he felt when he was with her. The way he felt about himself. The way he felt about her. The way he felt about life. The way he felt in general. It was all so good. So *right*.

The rebel redneck got a lot more out of the worship service than usual that day, but it was not from the words of the minister. He watched Christina as she moved from directing the handbell choir, to the children, and back to the choir loft with the adults. This woman was totally in control of everything she did. She was so different from *anyone* Shane had ever known. The other women in his life hadn't even been in control of themselves, much less anything else. But with Christina, it seemed that so much of what was going on around her hinged on her very presence. What was this secret gift she possessed?

*Yes sir, this creature is a shining star, and I intend to share in her light.*

He found that he couldn't even tear his eyes off Christina during the service. And when she glanced his way on a few occasions, Shane was even more determined to become an integral part of her life.

*I have to be with her. As soon as I've eaten lunch, I have to call her. I have to see her.*

Shane felt an excitement running through his veins that was totally uncommon to him. And every time she glanced his way, he sensed a tingle in his spine.

*This angel WILL be mine!*

He read the bulletin while the minister finished the sermon. His eyes caught the calendar for the afternoon. It listed choir after choir. Shane felt his conscience stop the words that almost slipped across his mind. Even Shane Sievers had more sense than to utter four-letter words in God's house, silently or not!

*She can't stay here all night.*

His eyes raced down the page. The last choir began at 6:30.

*Okay. It will be over at 7:30. She only lives half a mile away from the church. Maybe I can still see her, if I'm lucky.*

Shane smiled. His luck had been going pretty well lately. Was this glorious creature an angel, or his Lady Luck? Either way, he intended to keep her.

Christina walked in the door that evening at 7:35 p.m. She was exhausted after working for almost eleven hours that day. And she had danced so much last night that she was ready for an early date with the bed. She called Matt and Noah downstairs to eat dinner with her and then she planned to watch a TV show at eight before hitting the sack.

*Thank God the youth group had extra spaghetti at dinner!*

Even though the Sunday choir routine was rigorous, it sometimes held its rewards. Many nights the youth had leftovers from their dinner and she was able to grab three plates, keeping her at least from having to tackle the chore of fixing dinner when she got home.

They had just sat down and had their blessing when the phone rang. Christina glanced at the guys, who just sat there, wolfing down spaghetti.

*Why can't they still rush to the phone to see who can answer it first?* she chuckled to herself as she walked over to the phone.

"Hello."

"Mind if I come over for a while?" came the voice that was becoming more recognizable.

"No, come on over. The boys and I are eating dinner, so give us a few minutes."

"Great. I'll see you in a few."

Neither Matt nor Noah looked up from their plates. They were used to Abigail coming over on Sunday evenings to rehash all the exciting happenings of the week. It was sort of like the girls' catch-up party. Christina was glad she did not have to explain the phone call. All of a sudden it hit her that she had church members coming to her house all the time. It was always welcome to them. But she realized that Shane was not just *any* church member. It had been years since she had a gentleman caller, and the thought made her more than a little nervous. She had no idea where they would sit or what they would talk about.

Christina had no more than put the dishes away when she heard the doorbell. Thankfully, Matt and Noah had already parked themselves in front of the video games, so they paid no attention to who was at the door.

She opened the door to see Shane standing there in a black leather jacket. It made him look even more like the rebel he was. Christina loved his "rough-n-tough" appearance. It was so foreign to what she had grown accustomed. *He* was so foreign to what she had grown accustomed. Everything about him shouted that he was afraid of no one, and could handle anything or anybody.

*Then why did he pull that stunt back in December if he's so tough?*

"How did you get here?"

"I walked."

Christina felt even more privileged that he wanted to talk to her badly enough to walk almost a mile in his boots. She secretly wondered if this was completely professional, or if perhaps he had some personal interest. Knowing she was way off base, she motioned him in the door, trying to dissuade the flutters in her stomach that were reappearing from last night.

"Come in. Let's sit in here. Matt and Noah are playing in the den."

Shane had never been inside her home, and she hated to be so formal as to seat him in the formal living room with all the mahogany and marble of her Victorian furniture. Yet, it would serve to keep things from getting a little too relaxed. Even though she wanted him to feel comfortable and trust her enough to talk to her, Christina did not want to give this guy the wrong impression. *Nor yourself!*, she thought, remembering the disco ball dancing in the dim lights from last night.

She led him to the sofa, as she sat with her knees curled around in front of her so as to keep a safe distance from him, still allowing them to be able to turn in toward each other. Shane had originally intended just to come over and shoot the bull with her. But all afternoon, and especially on the walk here, he knew that he had to get something out in the open. Something he had mentioned to no one.

"I have to talk to you about something."

"Okay. Talk ahead."

Christina was glad Shane had something to say since, between being caught up in the lingering glow from last night's dance, but not wanting to compromise her professional composure, she was totally lost for conversation with him. The words that followed caught her a little off guard.

"Back in December..."

The minister could see him struggling as he searched for just the right words. All of the mounting thoughts and feelings that had been gnawing at her suddenly subsided as she watched his eyes very carefully. There were no tears, but massive amounts of emotion as Shane confessed his deepest, darkest secret.

She knew what was coming, but she didn't dare tell him that. Christina was fearful that he would feel betrayed if she already knew about his suicide attempt. Besides, she understood how therapeutic confession was for the soul. She hoped that Shane would tell her everything so that she could better help him.

"...I did something terribly stupid."

He paused. Christina wanted to tell him that everyone did, usually with great regularity. But she knew there would be plenty of opportunity for that later. Right now, she had to let him spew out his feelings, to get rid of the guilt and the anguish that accompanied a failed suicide attempt. She had already been around Shane long enough to know that if he had really wanted to succeed, he certainly knew enough about weapons to have done it. So, she felt inwardly that his effort was a desperate plea for attention, whether he was capable of admitting it or not.

"I tried to slit my wrists. Well, I did slit my wrists. Twice."

Christina had seen Shane's shirt sleeves rolled back before, and the scars on his wrists. The scars looked so fresh, she had assumed that was the method he used, and that the scars were the healing remnants of that desperate measure.

Sitting there, he was still wearing his black leather jacket. Christina had not taken it when he first walked in, not sure how long she wanted him to stay, afraid that her growing attraction for him might cloud the abilities of her calling. She was afraid that if she asked for it now, Shane would think she was trying to get a glimpse of the remainder of the wounds. But, feeling she could be of use to him, she wanted Shane to feel welcome. Knowing that the right moment would present itself to take the jacket, she decided to leave well enough alone.

His words became more labored and the pauses longer. Christina reached out and took his hand as if to say, "It's alright."

Shane's eyes looked deep into hers, as if to make sure he trusted her enough to continue. What he saw was such compassion that all of his fears vanished and he was able once again to speak. Christina made it so easy to talk, to just cut loose and say it. He'd never known that freedom with anybody.

"What made it so bad is that it has ruined my life with my son. It was at Christmas, and they took me to the psych hospital. One night in that loony bin was enough to make me realize that I didn't need that place, and I sure didn't want to be in that place."

Christina wasn't sure she agreed. If he had wanted to take his life, he obviously had a problem and needed help. Though, to be with him, he just didn't seem the type. Just as she had years of hell buried within her, so must he. She wanted so badly to take Shane in her arms and caress him like a small child, soothing his pain, and taking away the heartache.

But she knew she could not afford to do that. Not now. Not ever. She did not know him well enough. Christina had reached out to many strangers all over the world, yet she felt this peculiar apprehension of reaching out to a neighbor, someone in her own congregation.

*What's the matter with me? This guy needs someone, and I'm being so stand-offish that he probably thinks I don't even care.*

She could feel her emotions battling inside over what was the proper professional procedure, yet the true Christian one, not to mention her personal feelings. It was not like Christina to worry about what everyone else would think, especially when it meant reaching out to an outcast, someone who had no one. And clearly, this guy fit that billing.

A little saying that she once read flipped over and over in her mind. "A hug a day keeps the doctor away. Four hugs a day mends a hurt. Eight hugs a day keeps a person happy." It was apparent that this guy was long overdue on the hugs. Yet, Christina could still not bring herself to reach out to him. Not physically. She hurt for him. Her heart and her soul reached out to him so strongly that it seemed they were screaming at him. But she could not reach around him to give him that one hug, not now. She was crucifying herself inside, afraid that she was feeling this way more for her own self, rather than this hurting soul.

Shane continued to talk to her, more steadily now, not taking such deep breaths between phrases. It was clear that he wanted to rid himself of this haunting secret. Christina took in every word, analyzing each one for any clue that might give her an insight into the discord in the balance of his psyche.

However, the longer she listened to Shane's soul crying out from its farthest depths, the more Christina realized the profoundness of his trust for her. Whether there was anything personal to this or not, this guy truly had come to think of her as a minister, someone who held a hurting parishioner's inmost secrets sacred and confidential. He had ventured to take her on an odyssey that no one, *absolutely no one*, had ever traveled with him.

Her thoughts rambled back to her recent trip to Durham, putting her own emotions in danger, simply because Tom was a member of her flock, never minding the fact that she had once been married to him. Why, then, was it so difficult to take this man, who needed her worse than probably anyone in her entire ministry, in her arms as a hurting soul? Christina had been so caught up in trying to remain the evermore "on-my-pedestal" professional with Shane that she nearly lost sight of her call as a minister. What she was experiencing with him now went farther than any petty personal interest. Despite what closeness they may have felt in the past couple of weeks, and no matter that it was that closeness that had helped to bring him to this trust level with her, here was a broken spirit that needed mending.

*Did I not just this morning accept this mission? God, please forgive me for this grave oversight. I do promise that you can entrust me with this soul. And Lord, I come to you, begging your guidance to show me where to go from here, and how far to allow myself to go with this person.*

Christina was well aware of the fact that she tended to go way overboard when working with individuals who needed her attention. And although she had vowed in the past not to let herself get too close to anyone, she knew this case was going to test her compliance with that personal promise more than any other she would ever face. But she was a faithful servant, and she knew that this was a path she must trod. She had taken too many steps forward on it heretofore to back up now. Shane needed her, for many reasons, and she decided at that moment to be all of those things for him. *That is, as long as he is trying to move forward, too.*

She'd been in church work too long to expect Shane not to slip backwards from time to time. His path down that reverse road to success and happiness had taken over twenty years, and as optimistic as she was, Christina had enough experience *and* common sense to know that it was not going to be a short trek back, no matter *how* he rerouted his journey.

She now reached out both her hands to Shane, taking his in hers, a gesture which seemed to enable him to deplete all the leftover anxieties and regrets that stemmed from his suicide attempt. After nearly an hour of confession, the words stopped. When Christina felt confident that he had said all he wished, she twisted her legs around off the sofa so that she could lean close enough to give him the hug that she deemed necessary.

What Christina felt as he returned her embrace signaled her that she had made the right decision in reaching out to him. For she could feel the need in his body language that said how desperately he had needed someone who gave him the freedom to hurt, to confess, to ask forgiveness, to cry, and most of all, to be loved and accepted. She also had enough insight to perceive that Shane probably needed a cigarette right then as much as he did her hug, so she suggested that they move out to her deck.

Shane welcomed the chance for a smoke break, and appreciated her even more for being that considerate. Christina truly was a minister, *his* minister, even though his original intentions for the evening had been of a romantic nature.

As they stood on the deck, both leaning over the rail and looking up at the heavens, Shane flicking ashes out into the backyard, Christina told him how special this place was to her. The house, the natural area, the bird sanctuary – they were her temple to God. She had her own confession as she allowed him to see how much the stars and the moon spoke to her soul. Then, she invited Shane to pray with her, a custom that she followed every night on her deck, in all kinds of weather.

No date had ever prevailed upon him to pray with her, and had it been anyone other than Christina, Shane would have probably laughed to himself and gotten the heck out of Dodge as quickly as possible, thinking the entire evening was a flop, then sucked up his losses and gone home. But with this person, who seemed as natural as the clouds in the sky herself, it was not like a *preacher* going in for the kill. It was a part of her, a real part, a significant part, an inseparable integral part of her very existence. And for that, Shane not only accepted, but appreciated her offer.

As he listened to the words flow from her lips like well-versed poetry, not practiced, but rather a pouring out of her soul, Shane had to open his eyes to look into her face. Christina truly *was* an angel, as much a heavenly body as the stars before his eyes.

*She is MY angel.*

Shane looked up into the heavens where Christina prayed and said his own prayer to The Man, as his angel referred to Him. *O God, I don't know what I did to deserve her, but please let me keep her. I'll do anything you want me to, but let her be a part of my life.* He looked again at her expression, and realized how caught up he had become in her strength and power. Even more sure of the request he had just made, after reminding himself of his policy about being careful what he asked for, he glanced back up into the heavens and whispered, *Amen,* just in time to hear Christina finish her own prayer.

Knowing that she had to get up early the next morning to get Noah off to an overnight field trip, and Matt back to college, Shane decided he had better excuse himself. Christina offered to give him a ride back home, for which he was grateful and accepted, glad to have her to himself for just a few more minutes. While they were going back through the house, she asked if he would like to come over for dinner one evening during the next week and practice line dances.

*Maybe I'll get a chance to spend a social evening with her yet!* "I'd really enjoy that."

"How about tomorrow? Tomorrow is going to be my easiest day this next week."

"Great. What time?"

"Why don't you tell me what works for you?"

"I get off at five. How is six?"

"Fine, if you're sure that won't rush you."

Shane had no intention of admitting that as far as he was concerned, he couldn't wait to be with her again, and that he would have been there at 5:05, but he did not want Christina to think he was being forward. He was proudly amazed, himself, at his ability to control his desires with her. But like tonight, he saw that there was a lot more there than with your standard female, and he liked it so much that he was willing to wait for her, no matter how long it took. Shane did not even try to kiss her goodnight when she dropped him off, sensing that the evening had been the most sacred event of his entire life, and he dared not spoil the mood that she had created for him.

Besides, he would be with her in less than twenty-four hours, and he could spend the time he had planned for this evening with her then. Shane was becoming increasingly confident that Christina enjoyed his company as much as he did hers, and he was counting on spending a lot of time with her. This evening's experience had only whetted his appetite for getting to know her even better, making him ready to cast out his nets and pull her in, complete with all of her zest for life.

He lit up one last cigarette and slowly moved down the driveway, looking up into the sky and thanking God once again that such a beautiful creation had been sent his way, and pled for her to remain his own personal angel. Then Shane had a comical thought at what The Man Upstairs must be thinking since this hellion of a rebel had walked down the same driveway two evenings in a row, talking to Him. *Christina Cache, what IS this strange effect you have on me?*

Christina retired that evening counting down the hours until she would be able to see Shane again. She had thoroughly enjoyed all the time she had spent with him thus far. There was only going to be one slight difference on his next visit. *Tomorrow, he WILL NOT be my job!* Then she chuckled, remembering something she had overlooked all evening. *And tomorrow, I'll even take his jacket and ask him to sit down and stay a while!*

# 6

Christina had rushed around all afternoon after getting back from Matt's school, cleaning the house and cooking her most impressive meal. The videos and discs of music were ready and waiting for Shane's line-dancing lesson. At one point, she had even thought about lighting the candles on the dinner table, but decided against it, afraid of setting the wrong mood. She even opted to eat at the casual dining table, rather than the formal dining room where she usually received first-time dinner guests. However, after spending last night in the living room, she wanted the evening to be comfortable for both of them, and for her visitor to sense a more relaxed atmosphere. *Besides, did I not promise myself that this evening would be pleasure, NOT business?*

At exactly 5:55 p.m., the doorbell rang, just as Christina had expected it would. Shane was notoriously punctual, one more positive merit he had going for himself. She literally *skipped* down the steps, wearing jeans and a sweater, and very little make-up, a more casual appearance than usual – except for that unannounced morning he caught her at the church. The cheerful hostess opened the door just in time to see Bob's truck pulling away from her driveway.

"Bob says, 'Hi'," Shane said, smiling, while motioning down the street in the direction of the truck.

Christina nodded, waving out the front door. Keeping her plan from last night rolling, she asked, "May I take your jacket?"

"Don't know. Depends on where you're going to take it, and whether or not I'm going to be in it!"

She looked at him, shaking her head, laughing slowly at first, then bursting into a full-fledged fit of laugher. Christina could tell the evening was already headed for a "large" time, as Shane called it. *Thank goodness, I didn't do candles and the dining room.* Somehow, especially after that entrance, she could not imagine Shane ever being formal, socially or otherwise. There was something about his ideal of being so utterly laid back that she loved herself, and even envied, though she had always enjoyed dressing up and going out on the town.

Hanging the jacket in the foyer closet, she turned around and caught a glimpse of Shane walking toward the den. She loved the way he looked in his washed-out jeans, red-plaid flannel shirt, and boots. Even the sound of his boots on the parquet tile floor brought a musical countermelody into her home that was unfamiliar, yet most welcome, adding a fullness and a perfectly balanced blend to the melodies of love and joy and power that were already present. Christina was amazed at how good he looked. It was the first time she had ever seen him in anything besides the indigo blue Western-style jeans.

"You clean up pretty good, you know!"

"Glad you think so. But I have to warn you, this is 'bout as clean as it gets! If all my other jeans hadn't been in the washer, I wouldn't of worn these."

"But they suit you so well. I see a whole different person than on that first night I met you."

"I think that has more to do with *you* than the jeans," he said, winking at her.

Christina loved that look in his face, although it embarrassed her slightly, for she got the impression that he could gaze straight into her, seeing how much she really liked his company, and how much she was enjoying his visit already. She would have liked nothing better than to have lunged into his arms, wrapping her arms around his neck and telling him how glad she was that he was there. But she knew better than to let her guard down. Besides, she probably only felt that way because he had melted all of her glaciers with his incessant sense of humor.

Since she had been around Shane, she had laughed more with a man than she had her entire adult life. In fact, Christina did not recall laughing at all during the whole time she had been with Tom. His jokes were terribly forced, and he didn't even understand the importance of having a sense of humor most of the time. Everything always had to be so serious that no one even smiled around him, much less laughed, hardly even when he belted out with that bellowing roar that could be heard throughout a crowded theater, concert hall, or worse, a full sanctuary. That one that either embarrassed her and the boys, or else made them cackle hysterically at the sound of it.

Shane was so different. Not only was everything that came out of his mouth like a purebred part of him, it was as if he *expected* her to laugh when she was in his presence. And he seemed to really enjoy being able to put her in that happy state, like it was his plan, yet he made no effort at it whatsoever. Christina adored the way his quick wit took nearly everything she said and turned it around on her to make a joke. He didn't make fun of her, but rather, seemed to appreciate playing with her mind, as if with each of his whimsical remarks, he was drawn even closer to her.

That was something else that struck her as odd about him. She had never known anyone who could keep up with her mind. All her life, Christina had been so extremely creative and full of imagination that no one else could keep track of which turn her thoughts would take next. And, not only that, she was used to functioning in so many different tracks at the same time, that others just stood around mesmerized that she was able to accomplish so much so quickly.

And even though Abigail had gotten to the point that she could take care of lots of things for Christina at the church without being verbally instructed, and had learned to be the go-between, relaying messages that had not yet been given to her, she still had no idea of how her sister of a friend's mind functioned, just that it stayed in high gear all the time. So, for this intelligent redneck – *what an oxymoron!* – to be able to compute, organize, and spout off responses as hastily as she did, was difficult to comprehend. Shane was the first and only person who had ever done that. And Christina enjoyed suddenly having a "mind partner."

Christina was surprised when Shane walked on around the circular flow of her house, past the den sofa, and into her kitchen.

"What can I help you with?" he asked, looking around to see what still needed to be done.

Totally unused to that kind of offer, after Tom's W.C. Fields attitude: "Get out of my way, you bother me," Christina stopped in her tracks.

"Uh ... nothing, I think. It should be about ready." Then she looked at him with a raised brow. "Or did you just take it for granted that I was incapable of doing it myself?"

In his typical style, Shane put her mind at ease with an honest answer, yet in such a jovial manner, that once again, Christina laughed. "Oh, I knew you could handle it. I just know how late you always are, so I didn't expect to eat before eight!"

"Ooh," she groaned, but she knew he didn't mean it. Or, at least not all of it.

Shane pulled her to him, and hugged her. As their bodies met, they began to sway from side to side, a detail unnoticed by either party of the couple.

Pulling away slightly, Christina looked seriously into Shane's eyes. "I'm glad you came," scolding herself immediately for such a poor choice of words.

The rebel looked at her, and she could tell what remark was coming next, but Shane could tell she had already anticipated his smart-aleck answer, so he simply gazed back into her eyes and replied, "I'm glad you invited me."

His answer, combined with the expression on his face, struck a chord in Christina that had been silent for years. She leaned back towards Shane, with her head against his chest, as he took his hand and caressed her hair, still holding his other hand around her waist. The minute they locked in their embrace, their bodies began to sway again from side to side. Neither of them said a word, afraid they might wake up from the dream shaping before them, still gently moving with each other.

Suddenly, Christina stopped and bolted, back stiffened, and looked straight at Shane. His mind raced with thoughts wondering what he had done wrong. Had he offended her? Did she finally come to her senses and realize she was too good for the likes of him? Her stare seemed to be questioning him, but he could not find any clue of what her eyes were asking. Afraid that the evening he had visualized all day was about to end, he felt a strange twinge in the pit of his stomach.

*Shane Sievers, get hold of yourself. She's only a woman. There's plenty more where she came from.* And then, thinking of the angel she appeared to be, *No, there aren't.* Just about the time he knew she was going to ask him to leave, his ears heard her voice, and he was afraid to listen. But the words that floated delicately through the air assured him that his fears were unwarranted.

"Have you ever noticed how we never stand still when we hug?" she asked serenely, totally unaware of Shane's apprehension.

He was so dumbfounded by the way he had let himself nearly

panic over such a trivial matter that Shane could not even answer. His brain was trying to get back in gear with the rest of his body.

Christina mistook his silence as a negative reply, which prompted her next question. "Or is that the way you hug everyone?"

Shane was ready for her this time. "Nooo."

She stood there, still looking at him, as if unsure whether to believe him or not.

"You're the only person that's ever happened with." Christina looked as if she was still not positive until he finished the statement, "Maybe it's because we share the same rhythm of life."

Those words threw Christina into a tailspin. This guy was not a musician, he was not a philosopher, he was not a psychologist, he had *no* kind of higher education – except for parties on his sister's college campus – yet Shane had an insight that was so akin to her own, that it was alarming. Her face questioned him again, as if to say, "Where did those words come from?"

This time Shane saw what was brewing in the back of her mind. "What's the matter? You didn't think this dumb old redneck could think on that level?"

Christina blushed, ashamed that her reaction had been so easy to read. She did not want him to think that she thought he was stupid, which was the farthest thing from her mind. The right words simply would not come to her, and she was afraid that anything she might say at this point would make the situation worse.

Seeing him steadfastly waiting for a response from her, Christina finally blurted out, "That just seemed more like something I would say. And frankly, you don't look like the type to ...."

Shane broke her off. "To be so intuitive? To be able to express myself? To know anything about rhythm? *Especially* of life?"

She felt flustered that her words had insulted him and that she had ruined the evening until she saw the grin break across his face.

"Gotcha!" Shane blared out, pulling Christina closer to him again, not daring to let her know that she had done the same thing

117

to him only seconds before.

*Yeah, in a lot more ways than you know,* Christina thought. She knew the safest thing to do was drop the subject, for once again, he was keeping up with her at an uncanny rate.

The timer on the oven was a welcome sound, for Christina was still trying to find a way to escape the bewildering predicament she had just allowed herself to enter. But what she failed to realize was that watching her surprise and delight at having someone who could finally match her brain was one of the things that Shane loved about her.

"Let's eat," Christina offered excitedly. "I'm starving. I missed lunch because I was so busy getting ready for you," jokingly trying to impress Shane that she had gone to any length of trouble on his behalf.

But she knew the evening was still going strong when he came back with, "You mean it takes *that* much preparation just to put up with me?"

Christina only shook her head as she handed him a plate. Shane was so much fun that she could hardly wait to see what he would say next. She loved the brain games they played, and the way they had become completely comfortable with each other. He was totally unlike any male she had ever met. And, already totally enamored with him, her brain signaled her that this guy had just jumped camp from her professional tour of duty.

"I hope you don't mind if we just be casual and serve our plates from the stove. I didn't want to have too many dirty dishes so we could get on with the line dances."

"That's too bad. I was really looking forward to watching you wash the dishes!"

She continued to shake her head, staring at him in disbelief.

"Are you going to do that to me all night?" he asked.

"Do what?" she retaliated, not having the slightest clue of what he was talking about.

"Shake your head."

"Ohhh!"

Shane leaned over and kissed her, letting her know that he would stop the foolishness and enjoy a wonderful dinner with her, just like any other proper dinner guest. But Christina knew better than to accept that. That would have been too boring for him. It was obvious that he got a "large" kick out of challenging and teasing her, but she was not about to let him know that she loved it, too, for it meant he was completely attentive to her.

When they sat down, Shane immediately bowed his head, knowing what entailed the final step before dinner. Christina smiled as she lowered her head, thrilled that even this part of her life had already become a habit to him.

The grandfather clock in the foyer had just chimed its signal that it was 1:30 in the morning, but neither Shane nor Christina seemed to notice. They were both so totally caught up in each other that their feelings seemed to be like the aroma of incense which had permeated the room, and they were individually basking in the pleasurable lofts to which it had taken them. Had they not been so oblivious to what was transpiring between them, the hostess might have been prepared for what happened next.

But, all Christina could remember was hearing those three words escape her lips. She was breathtakingly startled. There had to be some way she could reach out and snatch the words back before he heard them. But before she got the opportunity to rescue the phrase out of the air, she heard Shane's voice, like it was off somewhere in the far distance, say, "I love you, too."

*Oh, my God! This can't be happening to me. I refuse to let myself be that vulnerable.*

Christina had earlier moved so that she was sitting on the floor in front of the sofa, where Shane was reclined, propped up on the pillows, with his feet dangling off the side. Her face had been resting on her crossed arms, on the edge of the sofa, so that their eyes were not too far apart, yet they were not touching. She felt as if she wanted to slither right down, and fade away underneath the sofa, but it was too late. The damage had already been done; the confession had already been made; there was nowhere for her to go but straight into his eyes to see what numbing effect this last minute had on him. Would she see there the same shock that was rippling through her own body?

But instead of giving her time to feel guilty or embarrassed for the unexpected words, Shane placed his left thumb and forefinger underneath Christina's chin, and gently raised her face so that she could, indeed, look into his eyes. She sensed a consciousness that she had never before seen or known in a male counterpart.

Sure, she remembered that she had loved her first husband, but the fire combined with the delicate sensitivity of what was going on between her and the man with her now created an aura to which both were unaccustomed. Now, instead of wanting to slither under the sofa, Christina wanted to melt in Shane's arms, a place she wanted to stay forever, as if he held the key to paradise.

She continued to watch that face, full of more compassion than she had ever experienced, and those eyes, which revealed the same words to her that his lips just had, until Shane's mouth was touching hers – it, too, expressing that his heart and body and soul felt the same love and longings and futuristic desires as did Christina's whole being.

Shane pulled her up until she was on her knees, and he leaned forward until their bodies were able to embrace and they could lock their arms around each other, as if both feared that if they let go, the ambience around them would vanish. These two creatures, both so individually full of love, had come together, unknowingly and unwarily, and now each sensed the power of an inner love that had been there all along, waiting to escape and be known, waiting for the perfect knight or damsel to come along on just the right evening, a night full of the moon's glow, and unleash, and then capture that love, sealing it in an unbreakable spell.

Christina felt like she was in a dream, her own fairy tale, and whatever it was, she found herself hoping she would never wake up from it. The beat of her heart had become so loud that to her it seemed like a tympani, being struck to its fullest dynamic level possible, during the finale of a great orchestral work. Shane took her hands and placed them against his heart, as if to let her know that he felt the same pounding, or that his heart said the same thing as his eyes and lips, as if it could talk to her right through his skin.

He held Christina with such a caress that she could tell he, too, was caught up in the surprise of the moment as he brushed his fingers through her full hair, and kissed her forehead and face ever so lightly, until she felt the tenderness of his lips against hers once again.

There was absolutely no fear in her, no thought that this devilish redneck only wanted to take advantage of her, use her, or throw himself on her. Instead, she recognized a trust that had been foreign to her in any other relationship, a trust that was borne out of a true love and understanding; possibly not a full understanding of the other person, but of the need to be loved for whom and what they were, someone who accepted them as is, rather than trying to take them and "fix them."

Shane saw in Christina not only the gifts that were so obvious to others, but her uttermost ability to love. A love to which he was totally unaccustomed, a love that had never existed, much less ever surfaced, with his paramours. He felt in Christina's eyes, mouth, and hands, a purity – a complete devotion to him – that broke down all the walls of hate and anger and bitterness that had become so tightly cemented in him over the years.

His eyes searched hers, and a part of him wanted to ask why she had done this to him. Yet, the part of him that was the *real* Shane, the part that had become intensely distorted to the point that it had become completely lost over the past few years, wanted to hold onto her forever, never letting go, knowing that she was the one catalyst he had ever experienced in his life that could share with him the power, the strength, and the wisdom he needed to pull himself out of the bottomless pit in which he had sunk.

When the air finally cleared enough that reality began to once again sink into this spellbound couple, Shane realized how badly he needed a cigarette – for many more reasons than just his normal nicotine fix. If his head and heart were still in the same flurry of motion after he returned from the chill night air, he would put some value in this potion with which Christina had showered him.

"You don't have to go outside, you know."

"Yes, I do. I know how bad the smoke bothers you, and I can't bear to see you go through that."

"Yes, and I can't stand to see you have to go out in the cold just to be able to smoke around me!"

"Yes, and I love you and I want to have you around for a long, long time!"

Christina did not have long to stand there, looking dumbfounded at the way Shane had taken control of the situation and put his foot down, before he reached out and pulled her to him. They clung to each other, their bodies swaying until the point that they began to dance a slow dance, moving in a small circle around the den.

Shane's need for a cigarette had been overcome by a feeling that he had waited for all of his life, yet had not known existed until just minutes ago. Christina could not believe that he had made the decision to hold her instead of a substance of habit that he had clung to for over twenty-five years. And what seemed even more shocking to her was the fact that he had not yet gone home to have his nightly beer. She had already learned enough about him to know that it was a natural part of his daily routine to have a few beers every day. That point bothered her, for she saw its effect on him, yet she was not about to judge him or lay down laws for him.

The last point was completely unnecessary, however, for Shane had already learned enough about Christina to know that her wonderfully exciting lifestyle was colorful enough without foul language or abusive substances. Usually, people like her turned him off immediately, but she was so different. She didn't condemn him, or try to lay a guilt trip on him. Christina didn't even say anything about it. She just didn't participate in those habits, and as he stood there looking at how she glowed in his arms, he even began to wonder how, and at what point, his life had become so shallow that the cigarettes, beer and drugs had taken over his existence.

Shane continued to lead her around the floor, picking up wisps of hair between his fingers, and kissing her head. Christina made him feel like he was on top of the world, a place he had never reached. And it was not a place he wanted to leave in the near future.

As comfortable as Christina felt with Shane, she did not want to let things get out of hand, even though she could already sense that he would never take her farther than she was willing to go. She found it hard to believe, even comical, that she trusted this man, *the* definition of a bad guy, more than several of the ministers with whom she had worked, and certainly more than any of the other guys she had considered dating lately. And even though this evening was completely social, and she refused to take her work home with her, she was determined to remember *who* she was, even though *what* she was did not matter at the moment. Her personal image meant more to her than her professional one.

Christina's cautiousness was what finally cut into the dance that had lasted several minutes without music, except for the rhythm that was going on between the beating of their hearts, and the melody playing in her head.

"Would you like something to drink?"

"Sure, and I think I will have that cigarette now."

"Okay, but not without this you won't."

She walked over to the kitchen, reached into the cabinet and pulled out the only ashtray she had in the house, a souvenir one from Alcatraz.

Following her closely, Shane burst into laughter. "Is there some message in this?" he asked with delight.

Christina had not really thought about it before, but even she could not resist the urge to howl at the outlaw using a prison souvenir. She proceeded to tell him about the book that she intended to write using Alcatraz as a setting.

"I love that place. It holds such an appeal for me. The minute I first walked up the steep incline, something grabbed me, and I knew there were endless stories inside that place. After all, look at all the movies that happen there. I'm not the only person that feels it."

Shane had jumped up on the counter at the sink, where it was caddycornered, joining the two outside walls, and sat there with his feet dangling, listening to Christina's creativeness take shape, dumping his ashes down the sink behind him rather than in the ashtray.

Her thought continued, "What I really want to do is to go there and stay a couple of nights and feel completely taken in by its inspiration. Can you imagine what those walls must have to say?"

He looked at her in wonderment of her brilliant imagination, and how incredibly sharp she must be, yet with a disbelief that a female of Christina's stature and background would tackle that assignment. "Yeah, and what about the ghosts? I'll bet they've got plenty to say, too!"

"Oh, you sound just like Noah. He says the place is haunted, and he refuses to go with me."

Shane looked at her, questioning in his own mind whether Christina was serious or whether she was just daydreaming aloud. The look in her eyes told him all he needed to know. Immediately, he knew that *his* woman was not going on a mission like that, not without him to protect her.

"Well, I'll go with you, and I ain't afraid of no ghosts!"

Christina laughed. It was the first time that this supposedly 'dumb redneck' had used incorrect grammar since the night they first went out to eat, and she knew that it was only to emphasize his point, but she found him most amusing.

"Well, I ain't afraid of no ghosts, either. Besides, remember that I take my own ghost with me."

"Huh?"

Shane had picked up on the fact that Christina was no ordinary individual from the first night they met, but this evening's confessionals had given him an insight to just what an amazingly different person she was. And so far, he had been able to keep up with her quickness of mind, simply because he realized that inside, in the part that lived on after death, they were almost *too* much alike. But this last comment caught him.

"My ghost, my Holy Ghost, my very own Ghost. I take Him with me everywhere I go," Christina said, completely matter-of-factly, as she handed him a glass of soda.

Shane stared at her, unable to move. The vision of loveliness standing before him truly was a heavenly creature, so full of mirth that it poured out on everything around her. He could literally picture her, walking through fields of daisies with this transparent apparition, floating along, so closely behind her that it was almost beside her, and her talking to him. The funny thing was that he could also envision the specter speaking back to Christina. And he knew that this illusion he imagined walking with her really *was* her

125

protector, harboring her from many of life's obstacles, yet carrying her – not just figuratively – through the ones she had to endure, which, he had found out thus far, were numerous.

All of a sudden, Shane saw precisely what it was that made Christina so utterly different from the other "clergy" and "church people" he had known, much less anyone else. Not only did she believe in her God, she truly *did* live in Him. She actually had a personal, *really personal*, relationship with that person, or being. He had not heard her confessing her salvation, or spouting off scriptures, or telling of her good works, but had simply watched her living - *really living* - her faith, in a gentle, indiscreet manner, making it more pronounced than if she had gotten on top of the steeple just down the road, and announced it over the loud speakers, pealing the bells to make everyone take notice.

The shudder he had felt down his spine as he imagined her seconds earlier with "her ghost" had turned to a breadth, a warmth, that, like everything else he experienced in her presence, was a new adventure for him. Even though it was hard to imagine some female, a minister at that, could teach him *anything* – a fact that had been unfathomable for him at first – Shane was beginning to look forward to all of his new realizations. It was just like being born all over again.

As he took the last draws on his cigarette, he examined the woman in front of him carefully. Shane felt that it was his turn to make a confession to Christina, but he didn't know quite what to say. Yet he sensed something inside compelling him to tell her what was eating at him.

"Christina, there's something about you that bothers me, that I find sorta disturbing."

"Only one thing?"

He smiled, but Christina could see that he wanted to go on with some haunting admission before he lost the momentum. "Ever since I met you, I've sensed this. But the longer I'm around you, it seems even more real to me. We've only been around each other for barely two weeks, and actually seeing each other for five days, but you seem to know me, not just know *about* me, my past and where I am now, but *me*. It is like you've always been with me, like we've spent eons together. And all the things about me that have frightened others don't even seem to matter to you. Like you already knew them about me, like you know *everything* in my background. I can't put my finger on it, and *that's* the part that really frustrates me." Shane stopped, looking at her, wanting her to clear all of it up for him.

Christina had no answer, except that she felt the same way. Nothing he told her surprised her. It really *was* like she already knew everything about him. And the way he seemed to understand exactly what she needed to hear and feel was unnerving, yet comforting, all at the same time. She had experienced that feeling with him ever since she first met him, too. But rather than get too bogged down in a discussion that had no answer or conclusion, she decided to make light of it.

"I *do* know you. I've met you in a past lifetime. *You* were the Sundance Kid," Christina blurted out with a straight face.

Shane's eyes widened, and Christina wondered if she had taken her merriment too far, afraid that he took her statement literally. The look of amazement on his face only seemed to intensify with each passing second.

Sensing that she needed to rectify the situation, Christina offered, "I'm sorry if ...."

"No, it's just ... well ... when I was in high school ..." Shane took another moment to compose himself. *What was it with her? Did she have to be so engrained in his very soul? How did she enter his esoteric world? Must she dare to trespass into his private territory, a place where no man, much less a woman, had ventured? There was no doubt about it, she had penetrated his space without him even knowing it, and right this minute, it seemed she was*

127

*playing this game of love unfairly.* He looked boldly into her eyes. "Christina, when I was in high school, there was me and my four closest friends. We had sort of a gang, you know, more of a joke than anything else, but my name was The Sundance Kid."

Christina wished that she could tell him to forget it, that it was just coincidence, but she could not. She had always been enamored with the tales of Butch Cassidy and The Sundance Kid, and in her mind, she pictured Shane as a modern-day Sundance. But now, the concern on his face still bothered her. She did not want to intimidate him for any reason.

So, to end the subject and move on, Christina interjected, clearly jesting this time, "That's okay. I was Etta."

"Who?" Shane asked, baffled.

"Etta Place. His woman. She was a classically trained musician." Christina did not bother to tell him that Etta left that profession to become a prostitute, from which Sundance rescued her, shortly after she entered that career.

"Great, so now you're telling me that I've loved you for a hundred years!" Shane retorted, getting into the game. *I am a fighter, and she can't win this easily!*

"Oh, no. That was just the *last* time we were here together!"

The twinkle in Christina's eye left Shane in a quandary as to whether she was really taunting him or not. She was laughing, but the way she got to him, the way she accepted him, the way she loved him, and most especially, the way she made him need and want her, spooked him.

It had always seemed that he was out of place, out of his time period, and now she had Shane questioning whether he actually had been here in another time and another place, all because of his unsettling emotions for her. But he was not about to let her know she had him in that state of confusion, although now she had intrigued him even more by her sense of challenging *his* mind. *No* female had ever been able to keep up with him in that area. The return of quips really had become a serious game to him now, and he intended to stick it out to the finish.

Seeing Shane lost in his own world, Christina called him back, "So, Sundance, after all those years, aren't you tired of me yet?"

"Nope. But I'll give you twenty-five more years to try to change my mind, and then you can ask me again!"

Ready to go back to a more comfortable setting, Shane hopped down, taking Christina's hand, and led her to the oversized chaise that was big enough for both of them. Since she obviously had pierced his clandestine past, and loved him anyway, his trust level for her reached a realm all its own. In fact, he had led such a dangerous life in years gone by that he learned to trust no one.

But in talking to Christina, it was like a cleansing. Even though he was still aware of his prior sins, they seemed to be vanishing one by one, or at least the guilt he had carried for them, as he acknowledged things to her that had never escaped his lips. Shane had no idea why once he opened his sequestered existence to her, it kept rolling out, gaining strength and momentum as it went, like an avalanche, snowballing all the while.

Neither of them bothered checking the time, as Shane sat there, rattling off experiences, one after another, never giving Christina time to respond. He watched her carefully as he went, sizing up any change of expression, to see if he had gone too far, if he had divulged more than a person of her background could handle. Yet, her expression never strayed from those caring eyes, coaxing him to let it all out, to empty his soul of all the bad memories, to purge out *all* the old, and make space for a whole new perspective of life, full of its own experiences. It appeared she was listening with her entire body, taking in every word he said, until he finally stopped, waiting to make sure his "hell of a past" had not frightened her away completely.

She didn't utter a word, waiting to see if there were any more confessions before the dam stopped itself up again. When he saw that she didn't ask him to leave, or make even the least derogatory comment, Shane took the final plunge, loving her so much that he felt he owed it to his angelic being to warn her what she was getting into, yet trusting her enough to never betray him, all the while aware that his next words could possibly jeopardize the most beautiful and meaningful relationship he had ever known. But, having weighed all the pros and cons, his love for Christina won out and he knew he *had* to make this one last revelation.

"Christina, there's one more thing . . . or actually, two more things that I have to tell you. I won't ever mention this again, and I'm not going to tell you more than what I feel you must know .... If I ever have to leave you, it'll be because I don't want to endanger you or your life. For a while, my drug dealings became so powerful that I was involved with the mob. From there, I just got even more involved until I had contacts in the Mexican drug cartel. There was a time that I had to be able to leave the country at any given time, if necessary. I'm not involved with that any more, but there are some things ... well ... what I'm saying is that I'll always protect you, even if I have to leave you in order to do that. Baby, I love you so much, and right now, having you beside me, it feels you've been here always. I never want anything to change that, but if that is what it takes to keep you safe ... well ...."

His pause was enough for Christina to let him know that she understood, and there was no need for further explanation. She had been sitting back in the chaise, and as Shane's words became more intense, he had propped himself up against one elbow, leaning closer to her, to search her eyes for mistrust, or rejection. While he groped for closing words, she pulled him in to her, so that he was directly in her face.

Shane looked at her, as far and as hard into her soul as he could, trying to decipher what to do next. He wanted her, he wanted all of her, for this was as close as he had ever been to *any* woman, in mind, body, *or* spirit, much less in *all* of them. Yet, he knew that part of her was off limits, and he wondered at this point if *all* of her was out of reach because of his mistakes from another time.

Everything inside him cried as he felt Christina's soft, tiny hands take his face in them, resting against his scraggly beard and worn skin. Cries of joy, cries of shame, cries of a long-awaited peace, cries of a soul burning in hell that had been released. As she leaned forward, her lips against his, the tears flowed freely down his cheeks, across her fingers, over their lips, christening their love for all eternity.

The next couple of hours turned into a more pleasurable recounting of tales from days gone by, a much needed break from the heavy-duty confessions of earlier. Shane enlightened Christina with wonderful tidbits of delightful stories of his childhood, dating back to his earliest memories, and then the events that led to the challenging paths of his youth and adult years.

She was thrilled at hearing the background of this child gone bad, and the personal perceptions of his life and the environment around him that had shaped the past twenty years of his life. Christina listened with delectation as Shane enchanted her, describing his grandmother's pies, his uncle's bumper crops, his own swimming ribbons and sports trophies, his tussling bouts with his sister, and the fondness he had for visiting his grandmothers in the summers. The more he talked, the more connected she felt to this person who had originally appeared to be in the farthest corner of the ring from her. And the more she realized that this renegade, who had been born, unwanted, to parents he did not know, literally fished out of a garbage dump, and raised by a couple who wanted to give him the best that life had to offer, had indeed been versed in many of the same joys as she herself.

It seemed that his entire life passed before him during that couple of hours that they sat holding hands, or wrapped in each other's arms, or Shane brushing Christina's bangs away from her forehead, or Christina massaging the sources of pain, untouched by his recent back surgery due to his bad accident. They never let go of each other, as though the vibes that ran through their fingertips also linked their brains. The conversation rambled on in a never-ending maze until Shane stood from the chaise to stretch.

"Christina, it's almost six in the morning! I've kept you up all night."

"It's okay. I knew it must be way over in the morning, but you had a lot of things that needed to get out, and I was afraid if you stopped, you might not be so free to talk the next time. Besides, do you have any idea how many all-nighters I've spent at the hospital, or with hurting souls?"

"So now, after I've spent all this time with you, you're telling me I'm not special?" Even though Shane had asked the question with a glint in his eye, Christina could see a lot of true concern behind it.

"Yes, of course, you're special. I've just spent an entire evening telling you exactly how special you are, but I just don't want you to feel bad on my behalf." Trying to think of a way to lightly alleviate his fears, without dismissing them as unimportant, Christina added, "Missing my beauty sleep does happen with some regularity." Then, realizing how horrid she must look after what little make-up she had even used last night, she pointed to her eyes, leaned into Shane's face, and said, "Can't you tell?"

"Oh, Christina," he sighed. Then really gazing at her, and actually seeing what she did look like first thing in the morning, after spending an entire evening with her, of sorts, a slight smile appeared on Shane's face. "Christina, you are *very* pretty. I like what I see when I look at you, and even more than that, you're such a beautiful person on the inside that I can hardly concentrate on just your outward appearance." Stopping to view *all* the loveliness he saw in her, he went on, "And I think waking up beside you every morning, seeing all of your beauty, would be ... well, let me put it this way, I'd like to be so blessed."

"Or cursed!"

"Like I told you before, I'll give you twenty-five years to change my mind." But then, Shane's face went back to the serious expression of before. "Hon, you must understand this. I don't want to be a part of your job. Yes, I know you give a lot of time to a lot of people, and I also know that you'll never stop doing that, nor do I want you to, but I don't want to just be one of those people."

"Shane, I'm glad you understand that dealing with people is not only part of my job, it is an inborn part of me, and whether you want me for twenty-five years, or one year, that will be a continual part of my life." Christina paused long enough to let him see the glimmer in her own eye, though, as she finished. "But, I'll let you in on a little secret. After you walked out the front door Sunday evening, I made a promise to myself that you were no longer part of my job."

The relief, combined with joy, written all over his face was a picture of Shane that Christina loved. He grabbed her, holding her tighter than usual, grateful that he really did feel like more to her than some other professional relationship.

When he finally lightened his grip on her, he looked down at her with a face that looked so young, so stress-free, so open, and so full of love that Shane did not even vaguely resemble the man she'd bumped into barely two weeks before. Christina wanted to comment on that fact, but was afraid it might bother him if she let him know that his bad-boy, redneck image was changing right before her very eyes. Besides, she secretly wondered if he appeared this good and markedly changed in two weeks, what would happen in the *next* two weeks. She decided to leave well enough alone and wait for a recheck at the end of the month.

"You don't happen to have any coffee around this place, do you?"

"Only if you can stand instant. I don't drink coffee."

"I can stand anything, as long as it's not decaf."

As Christina went to the pantry to find the coffee, she heard him yell after her, "How do you stay so wound up all the time if you don't drink coffee? You've got more energy than anyone I know."

"It's because I live on iced tea from the time I get up until the time I go to bed. We all have our vices, you know," Christina admitted, as she joined him back in the kitchen. "What can I fix you for breakfast?"

"You cooked last night. It's my turn." Shane was already looking in the refrigerator for what was available. "What would *you* like for breakfast? How about bacon and eggs?"

"That's great! I take it you've already found them in the fridge."

"Yep, how do you like your eggs?"

"Scrambled, well." She looked back over her shoulder at him. "I like *everything* well done. You know the saying: 'anything worth doing is worth doing well'!"

"I'll make a mental note!" Shane added, grinning broadly.

"The pots and..."

"I know."

"The plates are ..."

"I found them."

"The ..."

"I've got it all under control. You've got a big meeting this morning, and I've taken up enough of your time for one night. Go get ready and I'll have breakfast waiting for you when you get done." Shane kissed her lovingly on the cheek, popped her other cheek and sent her out of the kitchen.

Calling back over the banister, "Just yell if..."

"I got it. I'm good!"

Christina laughed back at him, "Yeah, I'm finding that out more and more all the time!"

She laid out her outfit, and jumped in the shower. Christina stood there, letting the water run over her, refreshing her skin to match the vibrancy she felt in her heart and her soul. Downstairs stood the worst hellion that had probably ever stepped foot in her home, he had stayed the night, and now he was rummaging through her cabinets, and she did not even lock the bathroom door behind herself.

*Am I crazy? Have I completely lost it? I tell this guy that I love him after hardly knowing him for two weeks. What I do know is unbelievable, and I should have red flags jumping out all over the place, calling me from every angle, especially after some of the things he told me this morning, and all I can do is love him even more. I'm not the least bit frightened, and in fact, cannot wait to spend even more time with him. Christina Cache, you have truly gone over the edge. The work, the stress, your teenage sons, Tom constantly in your face badgering you - yep! You have without a doubt gone over the edge, and as soon as you get to work this morning, they are going to call the men in the little white jackets!*

Christina dried off, laughing, at first to herself, then getting louder and louder until she was sure Shane must have heard her. *Girl, you ARE crazy! But, if it feels this good, BRING IT ON!!* She just hoped the so-called redneck downstairs didn't think she had lost it.

She got dressed, and ready for work, bounding down the stairs in a jaunt that was becoming more and more routine for Christina. *I guess even the steps can tell that something strange is going on here!*

When she reached the kitchen, Shane had the table set, and had lit the candles.

"Did you know that it's bad luck not to burn candles? You can blow them out now. I just thought they needed to at least get the wicks burned."

She did not bother to tell him how much those spiral candles had cost, figuring bad luck took precedence over expensive candles. "No. I think I'll leave them burning. I don't remember ever having a candlelight breakfast before."

"Well, get used to it, baby. I intend to give you a lot of things you've never had before," Shane said as he set a plate of food down in front of her.

Christina grasped his arm before he could turn to go back to the stove. "Shane, you have already given me more than you know."

He leaned down and kissed her forehead. "There's a lot more where that came from. Like I said, I'll give you twenty-five years to decide you don't like it." Shane grabbed his plate and sat down beside her. "Guess it's my turn, huh?"

She looked at him, unsure of what he meant.

"If I'm going to be a frequent guest here, I guess I'd better get used to saying the blessing, too."

His angel stared at him. Shane bowed his head and proceeded to say the blessing. Christina was so shell-shocked that she could not even pick up her fork.

He kept talking, waiting for her to recover. "What was so comical upstairs?"

"Nothing, except that I'm taking a trip to the funny farm today."

"Why? For falling in love with me?"

"Uh huh," Christina answered, teasing, yet serious at the same time.

"You probably need to."

Then they both dug into the most delicious breakfast Christina had tasted since her residency in The Moses House.

"Shane, this is wonderful. I think I'll keep you."

"For at least twenty-five years?"

"For at least twenty-five years."

Shane pulled her out of her chair and kissed her with all the love and emotion he had inside him. Christina wanted to lock the doors, bar the windows and dare anyone to ever come in and disturb them. But she knew she had a job, and he had a lot of doors to close behind him. They embraced for a few minutes, letting everything from the evening and early morning hours settle.

Christina looked at him. "Don't you need to call your mom?"

"And listen to her because I didn't come home. I *am* an adult."

"I know. But maybe you should have let her know where you were since you are living under your parents' roof presently."

"She knows where I am."

"Great. Now she'll wonder what you were doing here all night."

"No, she won't. She knows me!"

The minister looked at the man in front of her – the man she loved. "Shane, you're impossible."

"Yes, I am, and you'd better get used to it." He kissed Christina again while walking to the sink with the dishes. "It's as much a part of me as helping people is to you."

"I was afraid of that!" she smiled.

"Just drop me off on your way to church. I'll deal with the situation at home."

As the parent of a troubled son, Christina could not help but worry for Shane's parents. But, she also knew he was an adult and needed his space. She had to think of a way to help that situation and still stay out of the way, for all parties involved.

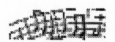

Christina pulled up to the Sievers' driveway in her typical rush for work. Shane reached over and kissed her one last time before getting out of the car. "So, what are we doing this evening?"

*Here's my chance,* she thought, knowing if she ever was going to approach the subject, she had better strike while the iron was hot. "We're going to sit down and *you* are going to make a list of what you need to do to get your life in order and start moving in a new direction."

"You don't waste time, do you, baby?"

"Absolutely not!" Christina grinned, as she waved and pulled off.

# 7

One of the few drudgeries for Christina in her work was the weekly staff meeting. She was a people person, and even though she knew the necessity of being in the same boat, a member of the same team, those meetings always tended to antagonize her. Most of the agenda really did not apply to her, so she always sat there, working on rehearsal schedules, plans for forthcoming events and programs, or any number of things to not only occupy, but make the most of her time.

Her outlook of this morning's meeting was no different, but as she sat there listening to the secretary read over the calendar for the week, Christina wondered if her face mirrored everything she was feeling inside. *Dear God, I hope not. The colors of my moods would look like a rainbow!*

The voices in the room became a distant blur as her mind wandered, thinking over all the conversation of last evening and this morning, feeling Shane's gentle touch and caress, tasting the delectable meal this strange man who spent the evening in her home had cooked for her, visualizing what he must look like sleeping this morning with his eyes puffy from lack of sleep and his hair all tussled, and looking forward to sitting with him again this evening, putting their collective instincts together and doing something constructive with their time.

All of a sudden, Christina prayed that she did not look like the cat that had swallowed the canary. *Have I missed anything? Did they ask me about something? How long have I been sitting here daydreaming?*

Just then, she heard the words that signaled to her that all was okay, the same words that were directed to her every week during the dreaded regimental ordeal.

"Christina, do you have anything for us today?"

Her initial reaction was to laugh with glee, shouting out her innermost thoughts, letting her love run wild and free, as wild and as free as was the reason for that love, as wild and free as Shane himself, and declaring to the entire world that she had completely lost her sanity and that she was in love with the most outrageous specimen of a male on the face of the earth. But Christina sat there, secure that her secret was safe, and reported on the upcoming Fat Tuesday service, Lenten services and special Easter music, all in the demeanor of the prim and proper individual that she was.

Once the meeting had been dismissed, she retreated into her office, finding ways to keep her busy and away from anyone who might interpret her blitheness for exactly what it was. Christina loved her work, and her enthusiasm was always on a high when she was being productive and had a slew of irons in the fire at once. She hoped that her bubbliness would be attributed to all she had going on with her work right now.

By lunch, she was feeling the repercussions of being an all-night listener. Since she did much of her work at home in her own space, Christina decided to take a nap for lunch and finish her tasks in the comfort of her den where she could lounge around and review everything that had transpired in the last twenty-four hours. Her life had taken a hundred-and-eighty degree turn overnight, and the rush had left her badly in need of a recharge.

Christina buzzed the secretary to tell her that she was going home for the afternoon should her presence be missed. "I've got plenty of work to do at home on the computer. Oh, and last night was an all-nighter – another hurting soul crying on my shoulder. I'm going to take a quick nap."

All-nighters were quite common for Christina, due to either her energetic, creative juices having their own schedule, or people knowing they could call on her at any hour, so her message was nothing out of the ordinary. What did strike the secretary as odd, however, was that the staff musician was going to relax, much less take a nap. Naps, to Christina, had previously been declared "wasted time."

"I'm glad to see that your age is finally letting you catch up with the rest of us!" was the reply she got from the other end of the phone.

*Yeah, and I'm glad you can't see my face right now*, Christina thought.

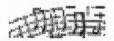

The afternoon nap was cut short by a phone call, requesting Christina's personal touch at the hospital. An emergency heart surgery on one of her biggest fans took precedence over her own needs, so the afternoon work had to wait, something else that was quite common with Christina.

As the afternoon progressed, she was glad for the diversion. Her newest found attraction was playing with her mind, directing all her thoughts to him. Christina hoped that she was not the only one suffering from that infirmity.

*Too bad they don't have something to cure this ailment*, she smiled as she darted into the Chaplains' area for a quick boost of energy, her usual cup of cranberry juice cocktail.

All of a sudden, it struck Christina as odd that she had not once given any credence to the fact that Shane might have changed his mind during the day. He might have come to his senses and realized that things were moving too fast, or that he really didn't want to change his lifestyle, simply because some persuasive female minister suggested that he do so. Or he might have been such a quick study that he learned all he needed to know in the course of one day, making his "twenty-five years" deal obsolete. But even with all of those thoughts blazing through her mind, she pushed to beat the rush traffic, confident that she would have plans for the evening.

Shane awoke to the feeling of holding his beloved. Only he did not know which was the real one, and which was the imitation. Carla had called every morning, afternoon, and evening since her incarceration, and he had looked forward to those calls just as much as she. But, this morning, he was so engrossed in a life of his own, he did not even think about her call.

However, now that he had come down partially from the high of the night before, the guilt of missing this morning's call was eating at him. Shane would be there to take her late afternoon call, but then he would have to listen to the round of non-stop questions about his whereabouts from earlier. His heart told him that Carla needed him; that her current illegal alien live-in was incapable of taking care of her. But, it also told him that for the first time in his life, he had hit the pinnacle of what he wanted in life, and he was not anxious to climb down from the summit he had now reached.

His short time with Christina had given him a new vision. It had started his mind turning, thinking of ways to get past the hell of before, and into a life where he could provide for himself, Shay, and Christina, and still take care of Carla, making sure she got her own life back on track.

Shane knew his ability to make excuses, so he would have one prepared by the time Carla called. He busied himself the rest of the afternoon by making a mental list of what he had to do to turn his life around, and charting a whole new existence for himself. *With Christina's help, this is going to be so much fun. SHE is so much fun.*

He was already counting down the hours until the fated phone call when he could escape safely, not letting Carla know that he had found someone to take her place in the forefront of his thoughts. Yet, still feeling slightly embarrassed and anguished with the large time he had last evening, he decided to sit down and write her a short letter before going to spend an enjoyable few hours with his newest love.

While he penned words of love and encouragement, he laughed to himself that he was actually looking forward to sitting down with a female and "making a list and checking it twice" for his evening's entertainment.

*That's a FIRST for you, Shane Sievers. You really HAVE lost your marbles. Maybe you should go check yourself back into that psych ward! You've got a good looking broad to yourself for the evening, and all you can think about is having her help you with some stupid list.*

Yet, somewhere, far back in the annals of his intuition, Shane heard little voices, *perhaps of elves!*, telling him that any presents that came from being a good little boy, and that twice-checked list, would be better than anything he had ever gotten from Santa Claus.

143

Shane called Christina as soon as he got off the phone with Carla. "Ready for that proposition you made me this morning?"

*Proposition?*, she thought. *That's a strange choice of words, and if I WERE in the habit of doing that, Shane Sievers, you are the LAST person I should be propositioning! Of course, I wouldn't come out feeling like a failure, 'cause you'd surely take me up on the offer!!*

Christina kept her unruly thoughts to herself as she answered, "Sure, if you think you can handle it."

The raucous rebel loved the way the sharp-witted female was able to throw things right back in his face, and not only challenge him, but practically dare him at the same time. Shane had thrived on dares his entire life, and he had a problem turning them down. *Too bad they're not all this much fun. Or this good for me!* Then, catching himself before he was out of control, *Shane, you didn't really say that. Since when do you worry about what's good for you. You've spent your last twenty years doing exactly what WASN'T good for you, and that was your sole ambition in life. Now some female wanders into your path for two weeks, and you are subconsciously considering what is good for you. Next you'll be worrying about your calorie intake and your cholesterol level. You'd better be checking out of here before it's too late!*

But as hard as he tried to convince himself otherwise, Shane could not, nor would not, miss his visit with the angel he had found. *I'm strong enough to throw off anything that comes flying at me that I don't want.* And so, confident that he was the strong one, he grabbed his leather jacket and strode off down the street for the ten-minute walk, taking in all the nicotine he would need for the next few hours.

Christina was ready and waiting for him when he got there. She had a purple legal pad and purple pen lying on the breakfast nook table, where they had shared their first candlelight meal only hours earlier. After their embrace and ritual of swaying that somehow seemed to connect their souls, they both set down, anxious to get Shane's new life on the road.

"Where do we start?" Christina asked, ready to write as fast as Shane could dictate.

"We start with you explaining to me why you have this rock sitting on the hearth in front of the fireplace. I've already been around you enough to know that you're unusual, but I've never seen a rock as an accent piece, especially with the word 'Clueless' carved in it."

"It's sort of a conversation piece," replied Christina, as she sat snickering.

"Well then, it works, because now we're having a conversation about it."

"Rachel, a very dear friend of mine, and Paul have always used the adjective 'clueless' to describe Tom. It really fit his personality. Abigail and Rachel were at a craft show last year, and found the rock. They bought it for me as a gag gift, and, well, we've all had a lot of fun with it."

Shane could tell by her hesitation that Christina did not really want to converse about the rock, conversation piece or not, so he dropped the subject. But he also made a mental note that one day, the rock would have to go.

Changing the unpleasant topic, he named off goal after goal while Christina wrote as fast as she could. She was amazed at all the problems Shane had in his life, all left hanging, while he continued to go on with some pseudo daily existence. There was no embarrassment as he rattled off one statement after another, a fact of trust that made the secretary of the evening most appreciative. When he finally stopped, they had compiled three pages of items that needed attention – some immediate, and some with more of a long-term range of direction.

"Shane, this is *great*! I am so proud of you. This took a lot of work. You must have thought about these all day."

"Yeah, when I wasn't thinking about you." Shane reached over to Christina and took the pen from her hand and laid it on the pad. "If you are so proud of me, how 'bout a little positive reinforcement?"

She giggled, already bursting with a desire to show him her affection for the progress he had made in one evening. After she sat on his knee and gave him a long kiss that told him how much his attitude and hard work meant to her, she leaned back away from him and asked the question that was forcing its way from her lips.

"Okay, Mr. Redneck. How do *you* know about positive reinforcement? Since when did *you* take Psychology of Education?"

"I'm not completely stupid," he retorted in his own defense.

"I'm not suggesting that you are. But positive reinforcement somehow does not appeal to me as the subject of choice at your local beer joint."

"Christina, contrary to popular belief, I have *not* spent my *entire* life guzzling beer, smoking joints, and sniffing coke." He glared at her, and Christina feared she had hit a raw nerve unintentionally. She began to wonder if she had been a little too frank with him. The rebel on whose lap she was parked had come so far in the two weeks she had known him that she certainly did not want to say or do something that would force him back to his prior undesirable behaviors. Besides, he was so much fun this way, she could not bear the thought of losing him back to his old ways. About the time she decided to change the subject, he added in a straight tone, "Only three-fourths of it!"

She knew her man was back. Still unsure about whether she had insulted him, Christina reached over and gave Shane another hug, one that said "I love you just the way you are. You are a wonderful person."

"Babe, you're the only person I know that can lie without opening their mouth! Besides, if you really think that, you're the only person in that minority."

"Do you constantly have to read my thoughts?"

"And why not? Don't you know the saying about 'what's good for the goose is good for the gander'? Is it fair for you to know everything I'm thinking if I can't do the same to you?"

Christina smiled lovingly at her guest. Before she got a chance to admit he had her, Shane beat her with the word that was on the tip of her tongue: "Touché."

Her blank stare told him that not only was he one up on her, he had also taken the word right out of her mouth. Shane tugged her closer to him, and held her there, not saying a word, but brushing her hair with one hand, and letting Christina know he would shelter her from any harm with the strength that radiated from the hand around her shoulder.

Shane finally loosened his grip on her to allow Christina just enough space that he could look into her face. He carefully looked past her eyes for the truth he was hoping to find as he asked her very simply, "Christina, what is it with us? How is it we seem to sense everything about each other – that we can even read each other's minds? What is our strange connection?" He paused, allowing her to see that this had apparently been eating at him for a while, but that he had just now gathered enough fervor to accept the answer.

She fronted him with eyes that wanted him to find the axiom for himself, a look that Shane was seeing more and more in her as his life unfolded, making his past openly susceptible to criticism, yet that got none. Christina directed her words with the same candor of his questions. "Do you *really* have to ask that?" He looked at her, not surprised by her return question, but still not speaking, as if hoping for more, so she continued, "Are you *really* looking for a verbal response, or are you simply trying to get the answer to exude itself from your own consciousness?"

Unpretentiously, Shane looked at her, yet with a resoluteness in his voice, and answered, "No, no, and I suppose so." Christina took his hands in hers and started to speak, but was interrupted. "Christina, you have to understand that I have loved other women, that I *really* loved them . . ." and she saw the thoughtful reflection in his eyes as his voice broke off, recognizing that his solicitations were coming more from a newly developed doubt of his current situation with Carla than it was for her. She had already surmised that there was much more there than he had been willing to share with her, and now, the discussion that he was having, more with himself than her, told Christina she was right. The counselor part of her chose not to speak, but let his thoughts run their course, so she stood up, pulled her own chair over to face him directly, still holding onto one of his hands, and positioned herself so that her eyes could continue to give him the attention and support he needed, rejoining the hand she had dropped.

Shane finished his sentence. "Or so I thought." His voice broke off again, and his eyes looked down at the floor for a moment, long enough for him to regain enough stamina to persevere. "Christina," his eyes caught hers again, "I have never met anyone like you, I have never felt this way about anyone else, and my entire being never got caught up in the love I had for a woman." He stopped, abruptly.

Christina sat quietly for a few seconds longer, letting the silence interfuse with the weight of his erupting disoriented emotions. She could see how difficult the conversation was, even for Shane's stalwartness, and she did not want to push ahead too soon.

Finally, after she felt the time lapse was sufficient, she cautiously threw out the final question. "Shane, I know that you understand what this feeling is, but do you know where it comes from?"

With the same seriousness in his eyes, he looked at her, emotionless, and replied, "Yes."

There was no doubt for Christina that therein lay a great deal of Shane's misgivings. It was apparent from his past marriage and varied assortment of lovers that there had never been an outside force or power at the center of a relationship. And now, on top of wondering where he was with the woman he had thought would be his next wife, because of some strange female who had literally dropped out of the sky into his life, there was an entity involved in Shane's life who was taking over his emotional life, as well as standing at the proverbial crossroads with him.

As much as she would liked to have continued working on his goals, Christina knew that right now there was another area of Shane's life that needed some profound soul searching. She also knew that as much as they enjoyed each other's company, this was one path he was going to have to travel alone. The minister knew that she had laid as much ground work as she could to influence him in his thoughts and decisions, and now it was up to him to look to The Omnipotent Being for the right answers. His answer to her last question assured Christina that Shane *did* recognize that Being's power in his life, so he would know where to turn. However, his background also told her that he had no idea how to go about starting this journey, so she took the liberty of throwing him out of the nest.

"Shane, I need a break. Why don't we go out on the deck?"

"Good idea. I could sure use a cigarette right now."

Christina stood, still holding Shane's hands, and led him outside. She loved the atrium doors that were right beside her breakfast nook. It made it most convenient to open up the house and feel the nature come inside with her. Not to mention the fact that when she needed to see the stars and the moon above, it only took two steps until she was joined with the heavenly bodies that brought her fulfillment, inspiration, and total peace of mind. And for the evenings when it was absolutely too frigid or wet, she could look out the bay window onto the deck and up to the sky above.

That window was unquestionably the spot that evoked the most emanation in her house. The only other point that came close was the ledge upstairs where the railing looked out over the vast foyer, living room and den, from twenty-two feet up above the ground floor, where Christina felt the majesty of a temple every time she stood leaning over it, looking past the house to the outdoors through the front bay windows that were fortified in sovereignty by the copper overhangs of the windows. But Christina knew that area of the house was off limits to her rogue for now, and that it was too formal for his tastes anyway. So the breakfast area, the den and the deck would have to serve as his special private area for now – that is, private inasmuch as she dared to share it with him.

It took nearly thirty minutes of silence and cigarettes before Christina felt that Shane was ready to go home and face the rest of the trial on his own. She had stood beside him on the deck, leaning over the rail as he lit cigarette after cigarette, flicking the ashes out into the cold, dark, night air. Their arms were against each other, and both took turns looking into the starlit sky, then back to the barren ground below. Both were in a state of prayer and quandary: Shane for what to do and where to go next, and Christina for guidance to help this newfound friend, yet at the same time, to stay out of his way.

Christina took her right palm and placed it against the left side of Shane's face. Her gentle touch and delicate fingers drew him back to the deck as he turned his head to look at her. She could see the tracks where the soft tears had flowed down his cheeks, as she wiped away the faint traces with the backside of her left hand. Shane reached up and clasped her hands, swallowing them up with his own thick, Herculean palms – those same hands that had broken many a jaw from the force of their fists. Yet they were hands that carried such warmth and depth of feeling that Christina completely forgot that she was harboring an outlaw on her deck. An outlaw who had smuggled anything illegal you could name, both in *and* out of the country, one who still faced numerous charges in several counties, and one whom the law officers had left alone for years, for fear that those same hands would tear them to shreds.

Although she knew any *normal* person would be terrified to be in this desperado's presence, much less have him holding onto them, Christina weltered in the love that flowed from those rough fingertips into her own extremities and through to every part of her body. She knew that in a few minutes Shane would be home, and she would be back here all alone, but that she would feel those hands protecting her all evening.

"Do you think we've done enough work for one night?" Christina asked, wishing that he would never have to leave her side.

"I think maybe we've done enough work for a *lifetime*." She could feel the grip tighten in his hands. "Christina, I'm not sure I can accomplish all the things you wrote down on that list."

"You can't. At least, not by yourself." Christina stepped closer in to him. "But you've got not one, but *two* people, helping you."

"I know that. I really *do* know that. But baby, I'm not used to having *anybody* in my corner, and it's a little bit of an adjustment."

"Well, Sundance, it's *not* just anybody, and *you* don't have to do *anything* to adjust. Just let The Man take care of it."

"Christina, you don't understand. Nobody has taken care of anything for me in over twenty years. I've been a loner, I've worked by myself, and I've trusted no one."

"Yes, and that's the whole point. It's about time you weren't a loner, that you let me stand by your side, and that you trusted me *and* God." Christina paused, thinking of one more item she had meant to drive home. "Oh, and for your information, some *thing,* some *body,* did take care of you for the last twenty years, not to mention the rest of your life, or you would not be standing here on this deck, in love with the greatest *thing* that you have ever met in that entire life!"

Shane scowled at her as he asked, "Do you *always* have to be so blunt?"

"Only when I have been given the strictest orders on good authority!"

He shook his head at Christina, unable to even think of an appropriate comeback.

She added, "And don't you go doing that to me all evening."

"What?"

"Shaking your head." They both laughed, remembering Shane's comment from the night before. This time it was Christina's turn. "Touché!"

"Yes, my dear. Now we're even. Take me home before I get behind, in this confused and dazed state you've got me in. The least you can do is play fair."

"Okay. But only if you promise to come back and finish where we left off this evening."

"It's a deal."

"Good. Let's shake on it."

"Fine." And Shane took that as an invitation to pick Christina up off her feet and shake her from side to side as hard as he could.

When he put her down, and she could stop the uncontrollable laughter he had started, she blared, "Shane Sievers, you most definitely *are* impossible."

"Yes, and I told you last night there's not a thing you can do to change that. But I'll still give you the twenty-five years to try!"

They kissed each other goodnight on the deck, then went inside to grab Christina's keys and his jacket, each in their own wonderland of thoughts and dreams.

# 8

The ringing of the phone woke Christina earlier than usual the next morning. She looked at the clock. Six-thirty. Wednesday was her day to sleep in, for once she got to the church, the rush never stopped. The choirs started the minute school was out and went on through the entire evening, with not even a break for dinner.

Most people would have hated her schedule, but for Christina, once she got on her roll, it was easier to keep going than to slow down, relax, and then try to get the momentum going again. The rush from one choir to the next only made her more excited and energetic as the day progressed. Of course, it took her at least two hours to settle down once she did walk out the door at the end of the evening, but she used Thursday to catch up and go out for her evening of peace and solitude.

So, to hear the phone now was a most unwelcome and rude awakening for her, literally. Christina's immediate reaction was to expect the worst: that one of her flock had a problem which needed her undivided attention. *Why must this only happen on Wednesdays? Why is it that every time one of the boys gets sick or*

153

has an accident, it must be a Wednesday? Or that someone has unexpected surgery? Or, or, or . . . Those MUST be some of Murphy's Laws!

"Hello," she answered groggily.

"Good morning, angel."

"Good morning." The sluggishness in her movement and speech disappeared the minute she heard the gruff, yet smooth, voice on the other end of the line, and the glower on her face turned into a pleasant smile.

"I woke you, didn't I?"

"Yes, but what better way to be wakened?"

Christina loved the laugh that came through the receiver. "I had to hear your voice this morning before I went off to work. I knew that you would be tied up all day and all night, and I didn't think I could get through the day without at least saying hello to you."

"I'm glad to hear your voice, too. This is my 'see how much I can cram into twenty-four hours' day,' and your phone call will give me an extra boost to get through it."

"What time will you get home?"

"Probably around 9:30, if I hurry."

"Well, hurry faster. I don't know if I can stand it that long without you."

"Yes sir, boss."

"Good, and make sure you don't forget who the boss is."

"Don't worry. I come from that old school that still likes to think that I have a man to take care of me. But don't ever go overboard, because I am just enough of a liberationist to enjoy my freedom and making decisions for myself."

"You got it. I gotta go. Bob just turned in the driveway. See you tonight."

"No, wait." But before Christina could catch Shane to tell him how zonked she was after hours of rehearsal, he had hung up the phone.

*Oh well. He'll call and find out what a pain I am when I finally get home and off my feet, and that will take care of that! I don't do company on Wednesdays after choir rehearsals.*

She laid the phone down on the bed beside her. *Yeah, and you didn't do Saturday evenings before that big Sunday work day, either, until some hunk of a redneck waltzed, literally waltzed, into your life a couple of weeks ago.* Regardless, Wednesday evenings were *hers*, and she had no intention of adjusting her lifestyle for him, or anyone else, for that matter.

Christina closed her eyes and tried to get in a few more winks before starting her day. But the thought of Shane needing to talk to her, to hear her voice, excited her to the point that it was useless to try to shut her eyes. She jumped out of bed with an unusual vigor for a Wednesday and got ready for her longest, hardest day of every week. She decided to go out and treat herself to a Western omelet, stuffed with green peppers, tomatoes and mushrooms, and then make sure things were together for next week's Fat Tuesday service.

She hit the shower with a dreadful thought. *Fat Tuesday is less than a week away, then a week from today is Ash Wednesday. Another service. My last two choirs will miss rehearsals. That means I'll really have to hustle tonight. We'll have to double up.* Then Christina thought about her saying, "God always takes care of fools and babies." *Thanks for the call, Shane. I needed that extra time today!*

By the time the last choir started, Christina was bushed, but she had timed herself so that she had just enough juice to make it through one more rehearsal. There was so much music to practice that she did not have time to think about how tired she was. But by 8:30, she started counting down the last thirty minutes. *It will take me FOREVER to unwind this evening.*

Ten minutes later, she was still her usual self, throwing pages out of the way that had fallen on the piano, or on her hands, trying to get the choir through their last two pieces without having to stop and wait on her to catch and reassemble music. She was grateful for the gift of memorization. Christina was so adept at making up the music as she went that her choir members had long since given up getting out of their chairs to retrieve the pages for her. They knew she could do just as well without them.

Just then, she caught the sound of footsteps outside the door, and heard the knob turn. She turned, expecting to see the minister, who had no doubt come to make an announcement about next week's services. But to her chagrin, the guest was Shane, who reached down and picked up the pages which were scattered all over the floor, organized them in the right order, and placed them back on the music rack, all while Christina kept playing, the choir kept singing, and no one ever missed a beat. The only thing any different was the fact that all eyes were on Christina, waiting to see what she was going to do, and wondering what this guy, who had rarely darkened the church door in over twenty years, was doing here.

*Why can't they watch the director like this all the time? Maybe I should put Shane on the payroll!*

She finished the last chord, gave the choir their release, looked at the visitor, and muttered very simply, "Thanks."

"You're welcome. I'll see you in a few minutes." Then Shane turned and walked out the door, shutting it behind him, and sat in the adjoining Multi-Purpose Room waiting for the choir's dismissal.

No one had uttered a word and every eye was still glued to her. Christina hoped that her face was not shouting out the thrill of seeing this unexpected stranger as loudly as her heart was. She tried to finish the rehearsal as if nothing out of the ordinary had happened, but she could not help but notice the smiles and the fact that everyone was still watching the director to see if anything changed in her demeanor.

After the last piece, the list of communal concerns was announced, and one of the members closed with a prayer. As he was finishing the oral plea to God, Christina added her own petition of thankfulness. *And Lord, thank you that I am so full of enthusiasm and elation during rehearsals. Maybe no one noticed that my heart skipped a few beats. Amen AND Amen.*

It was not Christina's imagination that the members disassembled more rapidly than usual. They didn't mull around like other nights, but rather exited quietly, whispering for the most part, instead of with the regular loud chatter. She wondered how many canaries it looked like she had swallowed from all the smirks that passed her.

*Christina, you're letting your mind run completely away with you. You're just paranoid. Everyone knows how many people come to you for counsel and advice, and you are the minister who always gets the underdogs. Get a grip!*

After everyone had left, Shane walked back into the choir room. "C'mon. I'm taking you to get something to eat."

She started to tell him that was unnecessary, that she was used to going home and crashing, nibbling on just enough to get her to sleep, but something stopped her. The guy had made an effort to take care of her, sensing her needs, and took the risk of humiliating himself in front of her closest friends to do it. How could she be that insensitive? *Besides, he probably needs a friend.* Then Christina caught herself in mid-thought. *Nope, he is NOT my job. If I go, it WILL be strictly pleasure.*

"I don't usually eat a meal after choir rehearsals. There's no time to work it off. Besides, I save that luxury for Thursday evenings."

"I know. But I told you that I'm going to give you a lot of firsts. You need to eat. How else are you going to be able to deal with somebody like me? I'm not easy to put up with, you know."

"You have been so far."

"Yeah, but I'm just trying to make a good impression. How am I doing?"

The grin that spread all over Shane's face turned Christina into a giggling teenage stereotype, for which she was embarrassed. But she couldn't help herself. She adored being with this guy, this guy who should have *never* been in her circle of friends.

"What the ...., let's go!"

Shane's grin turned into a full-fledged laugh. He hadn't been sure whether she would take him up on his offer or not, remembering what she had told him last week about Wednesdays. But this was one gamble he took with her, and won.

*I'm in,* he thought as they walked across the parking lot. *She likes me!* And Shane felt like an idiotic teenager who had a crush on some new girl in town.

The evening proved to be well worth their efforts. They laughed the entire time, closing down the restaurant, and hating to leave each other. As they prepared to leave the restaurant, Christina suggested that Shane play basketball with some of the other men in the church the next evening.

"What's the matter? You can't put up with me on your private Thursday evening for two weeks in a row?"

"No. You mentioned that you wanted to get some exercise, and I had just thought that if you would like to hit the baskets, I would stay home tomorrow evening and cook dinner for when you are finished."

"I'm invited for dinner *again* at your place? You got it. I'll do whatever it takes." There was a pause as the expression on his face changed. "Do you have *any* idea how long it has been since I shot

158

hoops?"

"Shane, these guys are all my age. You'll be fine."

"Christina, don't you *ever* do that again," he reprimanded her.

"Do what?" She had no idea what he meant.

"Talk about your age. I don't notice your age. You don't seem any older than me. I do *not* want you to make an issue of it. To me, it doesn't matter."

Christina looked at him, stunned. She had been so conscious of the age difference that it really embarrassed her to be out with him, yet she tried to deny that it mattered. However, Shane was so insistent, she decided not to argue with him, and take him at his word. His face told her that he would be unrelenting in the matter, so she figured she might as well drop it. But she didn't give it up without an enormous amount of relief. It had been the one stumbling block that she feared was in her way.

# 9

The next day became the one of reckoning for Christina. She had dealt with a growing emotion, and the worry that came with it, all week. Each day had become increasingly more pleasurable, yet, at the same time, had carried the mounting reverberations that she feared would come from the relationship between she and Shane.

Her fear came not from who or what Shane was, for everything about him – his appearance, his rebel style, his inborn love for others, his way of just taking care of things for her – represented all Christina wanted in a man. A real man. *Her* real man.

There was still the way he carried himself that she saw becoming more confident with each passing day, and some of his gruff mannerisms that she noticed changing. But those were things that she observed as points of growth for *him* – not the least of which was his faith journey. Shane's spiritual life was taking a whole new direction, one in which she loved being included. He had openly admitted his shortcomings and was tackling them with his inner beliefs, which were becoming stronger through Christina's challenging questions and words of wisdom.

That aspect, more than any other, drew her to him like a magnet. It showed that Shane was more interested in seeking his own inner strength and happiness, and chasing his passions, than his ego and what others thought of him. In Christina's eyes, that point made him the strongest man she had ever met. To her, it made him a disciple. It made her want to keep him. For an entire lifetime. For all eternity.

During the change in him, Christina also felt a change in herself. One that she liked. It was a change that made her feel even better about her faith than she ever had. A change that made her work even more productive. A change that allowed her to stop and smell the roses, and enjoy life to subliminal reaches she had not known before. And, for once, a change that allowed her to truly be herself and forget doing everything just to please others. Her own happiness had become a valid issue.

However, the big concern for Christina was still prevalent. She was a minister. She was supposed to be an example to all of the children and youth with whom she worked. She was in charge of much of the worship each week. She was expected to be a shining light to the community. She was supposed to be able to carry herself above the human frailties of the rest of her congregation. She was not supposed to be swayed by human desires. And she was supposed to walk a step ahead of everyone else in her flock. To be their leader.

But here she was, the person who was supposed to be their tower of strength, divorced – *not once, but twice*! – falling madly in love with one whom the church would look at as unlovable. An outcast. Someone who was not worthy of her affection. Yet, someone whom her ultimate Boss had chosen for her. And as aware as she was of the repercussions, who was Christina Cache to turn away and run from the task God had set before her? She knew the story of Jonah!

The one thing that bothered Christina more than any other about all of her questioning was a fact that was too strong to be ignored. She knew that people would raise their eyebrows. She knew there would be whispers all over the community. She knew people would question her scruples. She knew people would take a second look at her call to leadership and service. *And*, she knew that people would wonder about her emotional stability.

But Christina also knew what was in her heart and what God had given her, and she was willing to stand up to anybody on Shane's behalf. And the clincher: she was willing to give up everything she had lived and worked for, thirty years' worth, to be with him, to be his helpmate. She believed that strongly in him. That was a discussion she had not entered with Shane, nor did she intend to. Christina prayed that the issue would never get that far, and if it did, she fully intended to keep it to herself and fight the ensuing battle alone.

Yet, Christina was a sharp person. She knew churches and their gossips and hypocrites. She knew small communities. She knew exactly what was at stake. *But, I know myself. AND, I know my God.*

Her mind was made up. She got her purse and car keys, and called to let the secretary know she was leaving the office. It was time for an afternoon chat with Abigail. After tomorrow night, when over fifty people would see the love in their eyes, Christina Cache and Shane Sievers would become public knowledge. And Christina knew who would get the brunt of all the questions and comments. She felt it only fair to warn her best friend that she was about to become not only a target, but the bulls-eye.

As the proverbial comment went, *it was about to hit the fan!*

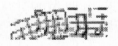

Abigail was out in her yard planting flowers when she saw Christina pull in the driveway. She was thrilled. They had hardly spoken since their trip to Durham, and Abigail wondered where her friend was keeping herself, knowing that she had a long list of upcoming programs, services and musicals. It was time for one of their afternoon front porch chats.

The winter had been extremely mild, and even a month away from spring, people were mowing lawns and landscaping their yards. Christina grabbed a gardening tool and set into helping with the impatiens. She was the world's worst with plants, so Abigail knew immediately that something was on her friend's mind.

They shared the usual chit-chat until Abigail's curiosity got the best of her.

"Okay, Christina, what's going on?"

"What do you mean?" Christina answered with a question. All of a sudden, her stomach feared that her secret was already out and she could feel the sickening waves beginning to roll.

"What brought you here this afternoon? I know you like me too much to mess up my flower beds with your not-so-green thumb!" Abigail paused, seeing no immediate answer, thus confirming her conclusion that there truly was a reason for the unannounced visit. "Besides, it's Thursday. You're usually closing up shop around this time so you can head off for your weekly seafood fix."

*Ah, she really doesn't know*, Christina thought as she inwardly breathed a sigh of relief. *And thanks, Abigail, for providing me with an opening to get into this confession.* "I'm not going to eat seafood this evening."

Knowing what a necessary part of Christina's week the Thursday ritual was, she feared something had gone awry to make her friend miss her therapeutic outing. "Nothing's wrong, is it?" Abigail asked with the deepest concern in her face.

Christina could hardly keep from laughing, knowing that the

real truth might evoke that very same pained expression from her best friend. "That all depends on your definition of 'wrong.' "

Abigail looked at her, puzzled, wondering what kind of perplexing problem Christina had walked into this time. The visitor decided to go ahead and spill the beans, for she could see the anxiety that the guessing game was causing her hostess. "I'm not going out to eat because I have invited someone over for dinner."

She saw the worry leave Abigail's face and excited curiosity take its place. "Who? Who, Christina? Is it someone I know?" Christina laughed at the fact that Abigail seemed more thrilled about the situation than she herself. And then Abigail started babbling off a list of eligible single guys she had been working on as a matchmaker. It was apparent that she was going to have to hurry and finish her disclosure before the gardener went into a tizzy. "Abigail, I have been seeing Shane Sievers."

"I knew it. I just *knew* it. I told Paul there was something going on when you came over and worked on Matt's car. Wait until I tell him that my woman's intuition won out over his degree in psychology!" Abigail replied in a bragging tone, recalling her bedtime chat with her husband on that particular evening.

Christina chuckled at the visual mental picture of Abigail telling Paul about her new love. He was such a staid individual that he would probably go into shock. But then, on second thought, she changed her mind. *Paul has been around me for five years now. There is nothing I can do at this point to shock him any more than I already have.* She had always loved the way that Paul accepted her off-the-wall ideas, all the while jerkily shaking his head and laughing hysterically. *At least I'm good for laughs!* She was glad she could provide free entertainment for her friend's husband, as she thought about all the times that Paul had taken her crazy brainstorms and made them work in the musicals and programs.

"I met him at the Wildlife that first night I went with Bob and Shirley, the one after the kids' choreography session. He just came with them for something to do, and Noah and I went to try to get some ideas for the musical. We started talking and it was … there was this *attraction* from the very beginning. Neither of us jumped at it, yet we kept bumping into each other. The only reason I even talked to him was my concern that he needed a friend, someone who could accept his past and make him feel worthy in spite of it. You know me and the underdogs."

"Yes, I do. But obviously you don't feel about him the same as you do about your usual projects." And Abigail remembered her thought that Shane was going to be Christina's next mission endeavor on their trip to Durham.

"No, I don't. When I asked you about him that day we went to visit Tom's father, I knew he'd left me with a whetting to learn more about him. I went out to dinner with him the following Thursday, and what I expected to be a total bomb from the get-go turned into one of the most fabulous evenings of my life. Both of us got slapped upside the head, in a way of speaking."

"And then you came here the following night to fix the car?"

"Yes. And we've seen each other every day since then. In fact, we spent the entire evening talking Monday. I don't know what it is. It is like we can't seem to get enough of each other. Just in this short period of time, he's learned more about me than Tom did in an entire decade."

"Christina," Abigail said in a scolding tone, "Tom is not one to compare *anyone* to - *especially* Shane Sievers."

"I know. But he is so *very* different from what I've been with the past decade. He seems to *want* to know me, *everything* about me. My likes and my dislikes. My background and education. *And* about Matt and Noah. Noah is enthralled with him and his desire to turn himself around. He has fixed me breakfast, taken me to dinner after Wednesday's rehearsal, and you know how private I am with my mornings and my down time after rehearsals. I am *not* the person to be social then. Yet, he has me thinking from one time to the next about when I'll see him again. Oh, and best of all, we sat down and he made a list of his goals to get his life on the track he wants it." Christina continued to gush the events from the past couple of weeks. Finally she stopped, looking at Abigail, as if to derive some solution to the mystery from her.

Abigail looked the best friend she'd ever had squarely in the eyes. "Do you love him?"

Christina knew that she did not have to verbally answer those four words. The answer was written all over Abigail's face, reflected there from the glow in her own face and tears. Yet, she knew that this was only her first skirmish, and she sensed the incurring battles would be much tougher, so she had to get used to admitting her human weakness.

Amidst a flood of tears, Christina looked calmly at her friend and whispered, "Yes." Abigail hugged her, handed her the tissue box, from which she took one herself, and heard Christina say again, in a louder, more confident voice, "Yes." Then Christina's voice grew into a crescendo of fanfaring brass: "Yes, *yes, yes*, yes, YES!" She was no longer sitting, leaning on the porch rail, but standing in the center of the steps with her arms outstretched to the heavens, announcing her gift, not only to this community, but to the entire world, including its farthest galaxies - *and* to The One who had given her this gift.

Abigail could hardly contain her own emotions. They embraced for what seemed to be hours. It was like the resurrection in Christina, for which this friend had prayed so long, had happened right in front of her very eyes. She had stood on this same porch three years earlier, crying buckets of tears, bitter tears, after Tom's pronouncement of their shattered marriage.

And now, tears of rejoicing were streaming down both their faces as Christina admitted her love for Shane. A love she had no idea existed before five days ago, and a love she had given up on ever finding. But it was a love Abigail had never lost hope of for her friend, a love for which Abigail had prayed without ceasing for this sister God had given her.

They spent the next hour with Abigail telling Christina about the discussion she and Paul had on Wednesday when Shane had showed up at the choir rehearsal, and Paul reassuring Abigail that Matt's car was still in need of some repairs after having sat parked for a year. Abigail recalled Shane's youth and their years of growing up together and how they had actually liked each other once. She found pictures from the past and gave Christina an even keener insight into Shane's life, saying there had always been a deep goodness within him, one that got lost or sidetracked from everyone's memory once he went off on his rebellious tangent – a tangent that lasted for over twenty years.

The tears turned to outrageous laughter as the pair went back two decades, delving into the social events that shaped the lives of Abigail and Shane, and how the strong foundations that had been so firmly engrained in him were still there somehow, waiting for someone to excavate them from the years of crust piled on them.

Christina left Abigail's house still fearing the reactions of everyone the next evening, but satisfied that now her best friend would be armed and ready to tackle any flack that would arise from the obvious pronouncement awaiting to be made. She decided not to worry about the ensuing comments, for there was nothing she could do to ward them off, and she felt that the love growing between Shane and herself was the most pure emotion she had ever known in her entire life.

Her fear turned to an anxiousness, though, as Christina prepared to face the world, and especially her friends, with Shane by her side. She almost laughed aloud at the thought of all the socialites who, in just a few short hours, would be straining their necks to get a glimpse of the two of them. The laughter rang out as loudly as the outburst of tears a few minutes earlier.

*Let the head-spinning begin!*

Evening came and Christina fixed a scrumptious shrimp stir-fry dinner. She had told Shane to give her a call as soon as he finished the game. When the phone rang shortly after eight, she knew it was him.

"You can come and pick me up now." He sounded terribly out of breath.

"Are you okay?"

"Yeah, I'm just not used to running this hard."

Christina was worried that he would pass out before she drove the half-mile to the church gym. "Why don't you sit down until I get there?"

"Nah, I'm going outside for a cigarette."

"Oh yeah, that's *just* what you need. In fact, that's probably why you're completely out of breath now." She hated that she had made that statement the minute it came out of her mouth. But Shane sounded so horrible that it scared Christina. Already she had become so fond of their time together that she could not imagine life without him.

*I only hope he's still speaking to me by the time I get there.* Christina feared that her critical comment had ruined the evening before it even got started.

When she pulled up to the gym door, there was no sign of Shane. Figuring he was still around back smoking, Christina rounded the building. Just as she turned the back corner, she got a glimpse of him in her rear view mirror, coming out the side door with his boots, jeans and flannel shirt in hand.

"That was a quick smoke break," she noted as he opened the door and hopped in the car.

"I didn't have one. Someone I recently met informed me that cigarettes were bad for me."

Christina stopped the car and looked straight at him. Feeling guilty, she tried to offer an apology. "Shane, I should have never ..."

Before she could say another word, Shane covered her lips with his fingers. "Baby, I've never had anyone who cared about me like you do. I know you're not being critical. You only said what you did because you love me. I'm not so stupid that I don't see that. Besides, you're right. I do need to stop smoking — especially if I want to live around you for twenty-five years."

Touched past the point of tears, Christina could only bite her bottom lip. She reached over, put her arms around his neck, and kissed him long and hard, thinking what a sacrifice he was making, just to be in her company. No one had *ever* surrendered so much for her.

When they finally let go of each other, Shane smiled at her, his face glowing in the reflection of the street lamps that lined the parking lot. "That was better than any cigarette I ever had. Who needs those things when I've got you. And besides, you're a lot more fun, *and shapely*," he added, grinning with his eyes, "to hold onto."

"Do you always have to say just the right things?" Christina was growing more and more awestricken with his precision timing of words, words that literally made her melt, engulfed in his charms.

"I'm just being me."

Christina wanted to believe him. With all of her heart she wanted to believe him, but due to her past ten years, it was hard to imagine a man who could be that sensitive to her every whim and every need. She was with a man who had been with plenty of women and no doubt had lots of experience in saying exactly what it took to get him exactly what he wanted. *Girl, you'd better be careful. You've got a live one here.*

She decided there had been enough conversation in the parking lot, so she drove slowly to The Moses House, trying to give herself enough time to think over this guy who was too good to be true, *and* the warning from her conscience. Christina was trying her best to think of a word to describe him, but all that came to mind was a word that she remembered from the score of *The King and I:* "puzzlement." *Yes,* she agreed to herself, *Shane Sievers is most definitely a puzzlement.* She cautiously pulled into the driveway so that she did not scrape the bottom of Matt's car, and had one last thought. *But am I any better – or any different?* The minister deduced that she was probably just as much a puzzlement to her redneck outlaw rebel, deciding they were even. There was one last comment she wanted to make about him and the cigarettes, but determined it was in her best interest to save it until after dinner.

They walked in the front door, and Shane closed it behind him. Dropping his change of clothes on the floor, he grabbed Christina and kissed her again.

"I love you."

Totally confused about what brought that on, she asked for an explanation. "What was that for?"

"We made a pact Monday night that we would never greet each other, or leave each other, without a kiss or saying 'I love you'."

Christina did remember. They had talked about what kept love alive in marriages and relationships, and they had both agreed on that point, one that Christina's grandparents taught her early in life. It had worked in her first marriage until her first husband found something he liked better, but it never got off the ground with her second marriage. To Tom, it was all a bunch of hogwash, and he refused to buy into it. She always used to silently scoff, bitterly thinking, "How can you like something if you never try it?" And as many times as she suggested they try it, Tom found just as many excuses or opportunities to walk away, leaving her in torment.

170

Once again, she was hit upside the head with the bold realization that underneath the cover, she and Shane were both products of their childhood examples of love, and the ability and ways to express that love. Christina felt more in love with her hoodlum every time she was with him. It was like God was not only offering His approval, but that He was throwing her *huge* messages of why it was okay. She already knew that when she went outside tonight for her final prayers of the day, she and The Man were going to have a serious discussion about that very thing.

Christina kissed Shane again lightly, and said, "I love you, too," more satisfied with her emotional state than she had been in years. She knew Shane had to be starving, so she added, "I'm going to get your dinner on the table."

"Do you mind if I take a quick shower? I'll be out by the time you have the food up."

She was not used to sharing her facilities with strange men, yet it seemed she knew more about this guy than any other man she had ever known, and her education of him was expanding greatly by the minute. And after all, Shane had gone to get all hot and sweaty at her suggestion that he get some exercise, notwithstanding the fact that Christina really just wanted him to get to be a part of her circle of friends. There had been an ulterior motive of letting them see the Shane that she knew.

"Sure, that's fine. Use the boys' bathroom at the top of the stairs. There's towels in their linen closet. Help yourself."

By the time she had served the plates and poured the drinks, Shane appeared, coming around the corner. The sound of his boots on the hardwood parquet floor in the foyer announced that he was ready to eat. Christina was becoming affably accustomed to that sound, one that was completely exclusive to Shane, at least in her realm of suitors, which, she had as yet failed to mention to him, had been many. For the time being, it was safe to let him assume she had been a wallflower, rather than the person who had never been without a date – that is, until her divorce from Tom. That had cured her for quite a while.

Shane came up behind her as she set his plate on the table and gently nibbled on the back of her neck. Not only did his words get next to her, his gentle, yet commanding, way of making Christina feel so divinely feminine made her limbs grow limp. There was no dispute that he possessed a gift for getting under her skin, yet she refused to let him know that, at least yet.

"It's a good thing that I'm a minister."

"Or maybe *not*!"

Christina could not help but laugh at Shane's honesty. As she turned to go get her own plate and join him, she heard his words follow her, "I'm sure glad *you* can laugh about this." She knew better than to turn back and look at him just then, for she was afraid there was no joking expression on his face.

The blessing was *indeed* a blessing as far as Christina was concerned. She needed something to break the tone of his last statement. There was no fear in her, at least of Shane, for even though he was honest, he was not pushy. That was actually an asset, as she saw it. It made it far easier to trust him than the guys who were so suave and debonair, yet the minute they got you alone, they were unstoppable – another reason she had put off going out with other guys lately. But she knew how much she was going to have to restrain herself, and for now, she did not want to have to deal with that.

Dinner was full of their usual jovial laughter. As Christina put the plates away, Shane went out on the deck for his after dinner smoke. The time had come to finish the conversation from before. She joined him just as he put out the butt in the ashtray.

"Shane, about earlier,"

"You don't owe me an explanation. I'm fine with what you said."

"This is no apology – I believe you. I saw that you were fine, and that makes me love you even more. It's like we can say anything to each other without either of us taking offense. I truly feel like we have a special love, a love from above, or that wouldn't come so easily to us. But I know that within the past two months, you have sworn off drugs completely, and I really do believe that you can lick that habit by yourself. I've never known *anyone* that I thought could handle that kind of tolerance on their own, but I've already seen that you're not alone in this struggle, and that you know it, too. You know how much I despise the alcohol, and one day I'll share the reason behind that, but for now, I know that you've cut back a great deal, almost completely, just to please me. And now it's like your cigarettes are all you have left. As much as I'd *love* to see you give up that addiction, also, it's like the only thing you have to ward off the temper that you used to have. I've seen you growing into a much calmer, stronger individual just in the two weeks we have been together. But I almost feel like you need to cut back gradually on the smoking because I'm afraid it'll be *too* much, even for you – and I do think you're the staunchest survivor I know besides myself – to stop suddenly on everything. The need may get to be too great, and you may find yourself giving in to one of the other habits. For now, I feel like the cigarettes are the lesser of the evils. Maybe you can just smoke one or two less each day. I would love to see you give them up eventually, only for yourself and your own health, but for now, I wonder if you still might need them to cope from time to time. And I don't want you to feel like a failure if you have to turn back to them."

"Christina, now *you're* too much. I accept what you just said. But I *do* want to quit so that I don't endanger you and your well-being."

"I'll tell you what. I'll make another deal with you – that is, if you promise not to shake on it."

"Aw, come on, that was the best part."

She tilted her head sideways just a little and smiled at him, warning him, with her expression, not to try that stunt again. "If it ever bothers me, I'll tell you. How's that?"

"Okay, if you really think you can stand it."

"You don't smoke in my house or car, so it isn't so bad. If you ever see me having bronchial spasms, you'll know to get me to the hospital quick."

"Christina, that's not funny. I don't think I could stand knowing I had done that to you."

"And I'm not kidding. Really, if it starts to affect me, I *will* let you know."

"While we're on the honesty trip, I have to apologize for the remark I made earlier."

"No, please don't."

Shane took her hand and looked into her eyes. "I let you bare your soul to me, now it's my turn." Christina knew he was right, so she nodded her head. "I know that your job keeps you on guard, even though I believe you when you say I am not 'your job.' After our talk Tuesday evening, I've thought long and hard about our relationship and how it is we came about being together – two totally mismatched people from the most extreme opposites of the pole." He rubbed his other hand down her hair, as if touching her gave him a courage more potent than his own. "Christina, I do know that God has joined us, and that *He* is calling the shots here. I trust *you* enough to trust in that, even if I couldn't have seen it for myself. I may say things or insinuate things, simply because of my joking," and his eyes glanced down for a second, "and not-so-joking, nature." His eyes met hers again. "But, baby, I do love you, and I would never want you to do something you would later regret," and she felt him squeeze her hands, "or that I would regret. I respect your job, and who you are, and what you are. There is no way I ever want to jeopardize your position because of our relationship."

"Oh, Shane." Now it was Christina's turn to let the tears flow.

She did not want him to see her cry, yet she could not help herself. Here stood the most gallant, sincere, tender-hearted man – all rolled up into one – that she had ever known. As Rachel was fond of calling it, this man *was* "the total package."

Shane held her tight, letting her cry all she wanted, still stroking her hair. He sensed this was the first time in years that she had cried on anyone's shoulder. "Baby, you can *always* cry on my shoulder, anytime you need to. And I've got *real big shoulders* – big enough to handle anything *you'll* ever need."

Christina held her head back and looked at him. "Do you have any idea how long –"

"Yes, I do," Shane cut her off, and laid her head back against her shoulder. "Let it out, baby. Let it all out."

Her strong nature stopped the tears before too long, but the cry healed a lot of lingering wounds. Christina felt more married to the outcast standing on her deck than she had to either of her former husbands. The magnetism between them was indescribable, and she imagined what it would really be like to spend a quarter century with someone as caring and sensitive as this man, whom the rest of the community, with what they thought was good reason, depicted as unlovable.

Shane wanted to finish their project from earlier in the week, because tomorrow night was going to be an evening he was looking forward to with dire pleasure. He was going to be Christina's date in front of all the people who entrusted their children to her each week. As he saw it, Shane Sievers was about to have his first coming-out party. The thought of all the shocked faces suited his cockiness to no end.

"Christina, where's that list we started Tuesday? I'd like to get that out of the way so that I can think of nothing tomorrow evening except holding onto you in front of half of Elmwood. You're not gonna chicken out on me, are you?"

"I was about to ask you the same question."

"Ha. There's no way in – there's no *way* I would miss tomorrow evening. All those people who grew up with me are going to get the shock of their lives."

"Yeah, I don't know which is going to be worse for them – wondering what I see in you, or what you see in me."

"Maybe they'll get a double-whammy. It's about time *something* got their attention, they're all so into themselves."

"That's not quite fair."

"And that's easy for you to say. You're not the one who they wish would just go away. None of those people want to be bothered with the likes of me."

"Shane, that's not true. You just don't know them."

"Christina, I'm the one who grew up here. I'm the one who went to school with those people, for twelve years, thirteen if you count kindergarten. And yet, Abigail Howell is the only one of 'em who's even spoken to me, much less given me the time of day, since I've been back. One Sunday, she asked how things were going, and I could see that she really listened, she paid attention. Not one of those other hypocrites has even said 'hello.' Do you have any idea how hard it is to face that every Sunday when you're trying to get your life back together? Not only do I have to deal with my own shortcomings and my fight against the addictions, but I have to go into what seems like a jungle of enemies who would just as soon I fell off the face of the earth. Christina, I'm tellin' ya, they just don't want to be bothered with the likes of me."

She could hear the dialect regressing to the dropped endings of his past. This was not the Shane that had wormed his way into her world, and she indeed could see just how easy it would be for him to leap backwards. There was no visible support from his family – probably because they were burned out on trying to help him, or even believe in him – from all the years of broken dreams. And now, Christina saw exactly how absent the support was from the very group of which it should have been coming. Her beloved saw

176

her closest friends, the people who were like family to her, as nothing more than a bunch of empty-hearted do-gooders. And as much as she wanted to defend them, she saw how right he seemed from his standpoint.

"Shane, I'm so sorry. I wish there were something I could do to change all that for you. But it's just because they don't know you. Once they've been around you like I have, it will be different. Trust me."

He started to interject something into her statement, however, she cut him off this time.

"And before you start debating the issue, you're exactly right. It *should not* be this way, but it is. I can't help what has happened in the past. But I certainly can have an effect on the present and the future."

Shane was not interested in her help, yet he was not ungrateful. He wanted to do it on his own, to be accepted for his own steps forward. Yet, society doomed him to pay his dues, *and then some.*

*So be it. I'll pay their damn dues. And I will be just as good as they are. I can out talk any of them on most any subject, and with just as much intellect.*

Reading his thoughts, Christina edged her way into them. "Shane, you *can* do this on your own, and I applaud your efforts and desires. Just don't be too proud. You must remember these people have never been there, they've never done that, like we have – you with your own mistakes, and me with Matt's. But, *please*, don't start being judgmental. You'll be no better than they are. And you know the old saying . . ."

This time, Shane did interrupt. "'Two wrongs don't make a right.'"

"See, I knew you'd understand."

"I never said I understood. I just read your mind."

"Yes, but at least you listened. That means you must have given *some* credibility to what I was saying."

"I listened. I didn't say I agreed."

"That doesn't matter. At least, not yet. For now, just take it all in, and think about it. You can come up with your own conclusions."

He didn't tell her so, but as badly as he *did not* want to admit it, Shane knew that Christina was right. It was just that his entire life, he had taken offense at any wrongful look or action people had directed at him. He had shot what he got right back at them. And now, she was expecting him to not only excuse them, but also forgive them.

"Shane, sorry, but I *do* know what you are thinking. Please look at it this way. Just think about all the things you have gotten away with during your adulthood. Sometimes we *all* need a little forgiveness, a little oversight."

The hellion was ready to get off that subject. He knew they had agreed that they disagreed on some points, yet they still felt completely drawn to each other.

Christina leapt forward, like a little girl in her innocence, during the brief pause. "Shane, do you realize that we have just nonverbally agreed that we disagree. Yet, neither of us got upset, and our love is stronger than ever."

"Christina," he belted back, "do you realize who you're talking to?"

"Oh," she said, still with that naive look in her face and the unpretentious tone in her voice.

Then they both chuckled as Shane wrapped Christina's waist with his stocky arms and pulled her to him.

"Baby, I do love you. You are the closest to heaven that I'll ever get."

"Nope, you're wrong. I'm going to *take* you there!"

"Oh, baby," he murmured, "promises, promises!"

They both burst into laughter again as each of them thought of how wonderful it would be to take their love to the ultimate limits, at the same time thinking about the two connotations of heaven in

*LOVE LIFTED ME*

Christina's statement.

She stood there, silently still for a short while, enjoying the luxury of having a man understand her needs and wishes for the first time in years. Christina had shared that kind of love to an extent with her first husband, yet, here was a man, who, more than that gift in itself (and who she knew many women had never experienced), understood and appreciated her – her values and her vows that went with the territory of her job – so well that he did not even offer to overstep her unspoken boundaries.

Christina wondered to herself whether he would still be that way if she were not as strong as she were. But before he had a chance to prove himself completely human, she directed her thoughts to another area.

"Shane, why don't we finish that list you started earlier this week?"

"That's a good idea. You must be reading my mind."

She grinned sheepishly and looked down, knowing that he was playing with her again, yet hoping that he could not read her mind. Shane took Christina's hand in his and kissed it as they walked back inside. He had called her an angel on a couple of occasions, but his treatment of her really made her feel like one. Her entire being was swept with a newness of love, stronger than she had felt even just a few short days ago. Did she dare tell him that she was falling in love with him all over again?

Abigail and Christina, in their countless hours of girl talk, had commented on that subject numerous times - about all the little things that made one's heart melt and their body quiver with a fresh awakening of just how deep their love for another was. And her hellion, who unconsciously had made her admit her love for him three days ago, was already doing that to her.

*What would it be like to spend an entire life with this man? Would he always possess this supernatural ability to do all the right things at just the right time? Would he continue to do such small insignificant gestures, those little things that make my heart go awhirl? How is it that bad boys do this to good girls?*

They were standing beside her built-in desk that joined the breakfast nook and den when Shane spoke to her. "I know I'm ugly, but you don't have to stare."

Christina caught herself and wondered how long she had been that way. Starting to sputter all over herself, Shane took the opportunity to finish his statement, letting her know that he was daydreaming, too. "And why exactly is it that good girls do this to bad boys?" he asked with a raised eyebrow and a smirk.

Both of them resisted the urge to grab each other, knowing that if they did, the work they had come in to tackle would remain on the desk and they would spend the rest of the evening talking and holding on to one another. Christina grabbed the pad and pen and put them on the table, suggesting that Shane read over his goals while she went to the refrigerator and fixed them something to drink.

His eyes followed her as he sat down at the table with the paper in front of him. Shane wanted to read what was there, but his mind had ideas of its own. *What would it be like to spend an entire life with a woman like this? Would she always be an angel? Would she keep taking such good care of me, and let me do the same for her? Would she always have this effect on me, making me WANT to strive to do all the right things?*

When Christina's eyes were directly in front of his, she mumbled, "No fair staring if I can't!" They both laughed, knowing they had each been had.

They went over Shane's list of goals one by one, with Christina challenging each with how he was going to set about correcting the problems, or facing the issues. She tossed ideas back and forth with him, and suggested approaches that would get people's attention, letting them know he was serious about changing his ways, but made sure he came up with the final solutions himself.

By the time they had gone over every single detail on the list, he questioned her about his ability to really attain the proposed goals.

"Christina, do you *really* think I can do all this? I mean – well, I *know* I can *do* it, but *look* at me, and look at my *life*. Do you think that I could ever really have a life that isn't smeared by my past? You know how people are, and you know how this small community is. Everybody here is kin to somebody else."

"Except me."

"Yeah, but they're *all* your family!"

"Yes, they may be my 'family' of friends, but look at it this way. You're adopted, and you're not *really* related to any of them, either. That puts us in the same boat. They've accepted me, and taken me in as one of their own. I've made it here." Shane looked at her, but she wasn't sure he was buying into her idea. "And besides, you know the old saying, 'It's not *what* you know, but *who* you know.' "

"I *do not* want to depend on anyone to pull me through this, Christina. I have to do it on my own."

"You *will* be doing it on your own. Don't you realize that I got where I am because of *Who* I know? And it is the same *One* who knows you!"

"I understand what you're saying, baby, but I've been so damned independent all my life."

Christina cut him off, "And so have I! Don't think I am not the most stubborn, bull-headed Taurus you have ever seen, but even *I* know that *everybody needs somebody sometime*. And that is a lesson that I just recently learned, and am still struggling with, but I had to go to graduate school and take counseling classes on how to help others to finally get it drilled into me that the two basic needs in life are 'Number one, to need someone, and number two, to be needed.'" Continuing her argument, "It's the truth, Shane. For years I refused help from anyone, always being the one to 'Do unto others.' But I never allowed them to 'do unto me,' so I wasn't really living out the rule. It's finally dawned on me after more years than you've been alive that people only want to give back a part of what I've been giving them all this time, and by not allowing them to do that, I am cheating them out of the opportunity to fulfill one of their basic needs."

"Girl, you drive a hard bargain, don't you?"

"Only when I have to, and only when I have it on the highest authority. Now, please, don't ever make me do that again. I don't like it." Christina reached over and kissed him, hoping she had not gone too far overboard for Shane. She was sure he was not used to having a woman put her foot down like that. "I like it better when you are the boss."

Shane pulled her into his lap, and kissed her again. "I guess God figured that I had so much to fix that I might just need my own private angel to pull me along."

"Nope, I'll never pull you along, just walk beside you, hand in hand." She paused, seeing that he was genuinely touched by her sincerity, and that he had bought fully into her idea this time, so she added, "Exactly what I want you to do with me." There was just enough of a pause to allow her thought to sink in before she added the finishing thought, "with Him holding onto both our hands."

He pulled her over against his shoulder and leaned his head down on hers. "Christina, will I ever be good enough to have you?"

"You already are. But you and I both know that you will feel a lot better about us once you get your life moving in the right direction. I will never let you pull me back, but I will come and meet you, so that your journey will be easier and more fun."

"Christina, all these things you've told me about how my life is going to be if I manage to beat all of these problems seems like a whole new identity – like the witness protection program."

"Well, I guess you could put it that way because you *do* have to be a witness. Only this way, you get to keep the good things from your past!"

Unfortunately, the solemn look in Shane's eyes told her that there really were no good things for him to keep from his past. Christina felt bad about her choice of words, hoping she did not make him feel worse. Shane sensed her apprehension.

"How about if I just take you and Shay into my new existence? You're the only two things that I want to keep anyway."

"Speaking of Shay, how would you like it if I took you to see him on Saturday?"

"Are you serious?"

"Am I ever *not* serious with you?" They both looked as if they were about to burst into hysteria. "On second thought, don't answer that!" Christina gave Shane one of her simple squeezes on the arm. "I thought that if you weren't busy, maybe we could drive up to the mountains to see him. I love the mountains, and with all of the work I have been doing to get ready for Fat Tuesday and Lent, I could use the break."

"Oh, Christina. Nothing would make me happier. But it's not exactly across the street."

"I know that, but you need to see him and Shay needs to see you doing so well."

"If you're sure you really don't mind, I'll call his mom tomorrow."

"Of course I don't mind or I would have never mentioned it."

"Baby, you really *are* an angel."

"No. I'm a mom who loves my kids and couldn't stand it if I couldn't see them."

Shane reached over and kissed Christina's forehead. "You know all of those firsts I told you I was going to give you? Well, you're getting quite a track record of your own firsts."

"Why? Just because I give you lots of things that your other women never gave you? Maybe it will make up for what I can't give you."

"You give me everything I need."

Christina secretly knew that Shane would have never spent as much time as he had with her on anyone else without getting some sort of gratification. But, she also knew that for the first time in his life, he was seeing another side of love, the side that really made it grow stronger. She hoped that it would be enough to satisfy his bad boy appetite for the present.

"We've got to get some rest if we're going to steal the dance floor tomorrow night."

Shane chuckled, shaking his head at her. "Baby, we're going to steal the whole show the minute people see us together tomorrow night."

"You're really not going to chicken out on me?"

"Noooo!"

Christina reached up on her tiptoes to kiss him, giggling. "I love it when you say that."

"You're the only woman I've ever known who liked for me to tell her 'No.'"

"It's not the word, it's the way you say it. I love the way you hold out the 'ooo'. That country drawl and that pitch in your voice just tears me up. It has a musical quality to it – one that is *most* appealing."

"If I tell you *no* everyday, will you love me forever?"

"If I tell *you* no everyday, will you love *me* forever?"

"Ohhhh, nooooo, baby!"

They grabbed each other, hugging and twisting wildly, like two people who had gotten a chance at love again, having missed out on it the first time around. Shane loved holding her, feeling her energy and innocence, and Christina loved the security she felt when those strong hands touched her, and he wrapped his arms around her. Yet, in an unspoken truce, both of them knew that was all they could have for now.

# *10*

The day could not go fast enough for Christina. She had laid her clothes out during the morning. Shane came over first thing and they went out for omelets before running errands and getting set materials and costume pieces for her upcoming musical.

Although her first husband had been helpful with moving sets for her when she had done productions in the past, this was the first time she had actually had a 'partner in crime' as far as being a hands-on part of her work. Christina was amazed not only at Shane's interest in her musical, but his intuitiveness about ideas for the sets and props, as well as the character developments for each of the cast members.

After spending the best part of the day rushing all over Charlotte to home improvement stores and back-street thrift shops, they took their collection of goods back to the church and then Shane offered to make tacos for Christina and Noah for dinner. While he stood in her kitchen preparing a Mexican feast for them, she could not help but notice how natural he looked there. She loved watching the care he put into doing things for her and pampering her in his own small way, which to her, was the greatest thing any guy had ever done for her.

Christina thought back to all the resorts and the gourmet restaurants she had visited in the past, and how insignificant they seemed compared to this guy, supposedly a "creature from hell" who made her feel so wonderful with the things he did to help her. Every time she commented on it, Shane's reply was the same.

"TNT."

Afraid to seem stupid, Christina let it slide the first few times. But this time, curiosity had the best of her.

"What do you mean, TNT?"

Shane flashed Christina the smile that she loved. "I wondered how long it was going to take you to ask about that."

"Well, I guessed it was something that you figured I was supposed to know, and I didn't want to admit my sheltered existence by asking questions."

He looked at her with his devilish grin and Christina knew what was coming. Shane had a way of joking with her without making fun of her, and, in fact, causing her tremendous laughter. She could tell by his face that an uproar was on its way.

Shane laid the spoon on the counter and wheeled around to catch Christina by her waist and pull her to him, wrapping his other arm around her, too, as she came in contact with him. He looked straight into her face, his eyes still sparkling with that 'I've got you now' expression.

"Christina Cache, you are the most *unsheltered* person that I've ever met, even in *my* hellacious life. And will you quit being afraid to ask me questions? You're the brightest person I know and there is no way I would ever think that you're stupid."

With that, he tugged at her waist a little tighter. He loved the shy, naive smile she gave him when he did that. To anyone who did not know her whole background from the past twenty years, they might accept her coyness. But he knew better, and could see right through her. Yet he loved that face. It was the same as it was in the high school and college pictures he had seen hanging in the collage of her family pictures. Shane could tell by those pictures that Christina had never been alone in her life, at least when it came to capturing guys' attention. There was just something about that look that attracted him, and he knew he was not the first person to be caught up in it.

"T'ain't nothing to it."

"What?" Christina questioned, trying to pull back from her waist and catch a clue in his eyes as to what Shane was talking about.

"TNT. T'ain't Nothing To it."

Christina smiled. "Okay, I get it."

"One night, looking for something to do while we were sitting around wasting away an evening, an old buddy and I came up with several abbreviations to shorten common expressions we had."

"Like OFW?" another abridgement she had heard him utter several times.

Shane winced and said, "Kinda," sheepishly, knowing Christina's next question.

"What does that mean?"

"Oh well."

"Oh well? What does the extra letter stand for?"

"Never mind!"

Christina reared her head back in laughter, as Shane joined her outburst. She had known the missing word, but was curious as to whether he would tell her. His dialect had cleaned up considerably since their first meeting, and she wondered if his clever contractions would also apply to that respect he gave her. Knowing she had caught him in his game was quite a boost for her.

Shane gave her a kiss and whispered, "I love you," as he went back to catering for her. Christina leaned against the counter beside him, thinking about what an odd sort this guy was. He had so much to offer, yet appeared to be the person who had never been anywhere or done anything worthwhile. She mused at his attentiveness to her every whim, and wondered how many females had gotten that kind of attention, unusual for most males, from him in the past. It was hard for Christina to imagine him being married to the woman she perceived his ex-wife to be when he was so sensitive and so intelligent in every circumstance they had encountered.

While Shane got the taco shells ready, Christina set the picnic table on the deck. It was still briskly cool outside, but the sun was warm and they had already made a habit in the brief time of his visits to retreat to that place of solitude. Noah was out skateboarding and came home just long enough to ask if they would be offended if he ate his tacos on the way back to his friend's house.

Christina longed for Noah's company, but lately, it had become easier for her to let go of him since she had found someone with whom to occupy her time. Noah's presence never bothered either her or Shane, but they had spent such a pleasant morning together that they both relished the thought of continuing to enjoy the mood of the day.

Once they had finished eating, Christina proceeded to ask Shane about a subject which she had secretly been debating all morning. They literally stared into each other's eyes all the time, so she had no trouble catching his attention. And she saw no other way to approach it than to just come right out with it.

"Shane, why don't you help me direct the children's musical?"

He gulped down his drink, trying not to spit it all over her face. "Say what?"

"Why don't you be the co-director of my musical with the children and youth? You were involved in the dramas in high school, and you obviously have a natural sense for what it is all about."

Obviously caught off guard, Shane's reply came almost as if in defense of himself. "Christina, I've never directed a play in my life, and I have *certainly* never worked with children. Who in their right mind is going to let *me* loose in the church with their kids?"

Christina could not help but howl at his response. There was a point to what he said, but she had been around Shane long enough to see his inborn dramatic skills, and she also had the foresight to know that he needed something to keep him busy and from resorting back to his old friends and bad habits. It was a way of calling him to task.

Inwardly, she knew her job and her reputation could be in jeopardy if he blew the assignment, since minors were involved, *and* since they were in a church setting, but she had learned enough about him to know that he would not hurt anyone, *that is, unless they are trying to kill him,* and that he had one of the deepest and most sincere faiths of anyone she knew. It had just gotten sidetracked and waylaid. To her, the suggestion was like killing a lot of birds with one stone.

Before she went on with the conversation, she questioned herself one last time. *Do I really trust this guy and believe in him enough to stake my entire career and reputation on him?*

But one look at him, in those eyes that could not hide his big heart from her, gave Christina the answer she needed.

"Do you *not* think you could handle it? Have you ever been unable to do anything you put your mind to?"

Christina knew that Shane had a reputation to uphold and that her challenge was a dare to him – one that he could not, nor would not, resist.

"Sure, I can do it."

"Good. Then it's settled. We're going on a retreat in the mountains next weekend to work on the musical and you can go along and help chaperone."

"What?" he blurted, knowing he had been caught in a trap, but not about to give in to a conniving female. There was no way

Shane Sievers was going to appear to be beaten.

"We're leaving next Friday afternoon right after school. I'll pick you up at work around lunchtime so that you can get ready. We can even stop and pick up Shay on the way if he wants to be in the musical."

Shane sat there, staring at her. She had done it to him again, just like last week when she had conned him out of his beers before the Valentine dance. He was completely baffled by Christina, but he had already fallen so hard for her that there was no way he could be upset. Rather, he enjoyed being spellbound by her ingenuousness. And even more than that, he got a kick, a long-needed kick, out of being the companion of a woman of her class. It reminded him that once upon a time, he did have a little class himself.

Before he got too ripped up about Christina's clever way of involving him, Shane reminded himself of the other single guy who was going as a chaperone. He had heard it rumored that this guy had his eyes on Christina, and Shane had gotten just close enough to her to know that there was no way somebody was going to get his girl. Still reluctant to admit he had been had, Shane pretended to himself that this was just what he had planned. It was his own sly way of keeping an eye on her.

He was already looking forward to the glares that were sure to come later this evening – especially after Christina had told him about yesterday's confession to Abigail. The acceptance of him by Christina's best friend gave him enough courage to feel he had actually passed the pre-test and was ready to face the drove of Christina's closest acquaintances that evening. Besides, he still carried enough of the bad boy "in your face" attitude to throw it at them if they looked at him the wrong way.

They spent the rest of the afternoon reminiscing over the events of the past week, events that had brought them so close together that they felt inseparable. Neither of them could believe that they knew nothing of the other less than a month ago. And as they both thanked God for bringing them together, the bond between them grew even stronger.

Christina had been right about one thing. The glares hit and her ears started burning the second she drove into the church parking lot with Shane. She had wondered earlier whether the heat would be a little too much for her, but like Shane, she was enjoying the look of surprise on everyone's faces. Not one person said a word to her about it, but she caught the glances going back and forth from one set of parents to another. Both Shane and Christina wanted to laugh aloud, but they knew the best was yet to come.

Her anxiety about the rumors that were sure to start had been relieved by the comfort she felt in Shane's presence, not to mention the strength she had gotten from their time together all day. Abigail came over and hugged Christina while whispering in her ear, "This is going to be great. Paul is surprised, but thrilled for you. We can't wait to see how the evening progresses." Then she joined their hands, winking at Christina and squeezing Shane's hand.

"Tell Paul he has to save a dance for me."

"Sure." Abigail caught the puzzled look in Shane's eye, and decided to add to the predicament, flinging her next comment to him. "I always let her borrow my husband anytime she needs a man."

The two females were struggling to hold it together while watching the confused look on Shane's face. Their innocence made him wonder even more about what kind of relationship the threesome had.

"Don't worry, she's only playing mind games with you,"

Christina said, not wanting him to get too alarmed. "But she really does let me borrow her husband when I need something done around the house or at church."

"Well, I guess he's going to have to find something else to do with all his free time, 'cause I intend to take care of that from now on," Shane declared, wanting to alleviate any situation that might get out of hand with his woman.

Abigail winked back at them over her shoulder as she walked away, looking like the cat who had eaten the canary.

"What does she know?" Shane asked, trying to make some semblance of heads or tails out of what had just transpired between the three of them.

"Only that I'm madly and hopelessly in love with you."

"Oh yeah? Does she also know that I love you, too?"

"No, but I hope she's fixing to find out!"

Shane wanted to shower his lady with kisses from head to toe, but he decided that this was not the place to do it. *But if I did, I'll bet it would leave little to the imagination, and they'd all figure out what's going on here. Of course, with their small judgmental minds, they'd get the wrong idea. Funny, they all think they know Christina so well, and I'll bet I know more about her than anyone here, with the exception of Abigail.* He stood there eyeing his catch, *and maybe Paul,* he thought, still wondering about how much there was to the comments between Christina and Abigail. He made a mental note to check with his girl on that matter after the dance.

No longer was Christina worried about all the sideways whispers, but was impatient to be swirling around the dance floor in Shane's arms, drifting into his soul via his eyes. She loved her man, *truly* loved him, and she had heard enough of the choir moms complain about their own personal situations to know that she had a blessing that most of them did not, so she thanked God privately, signaling everyone that it was time to go. *The head spinning has just begun!*

In their rush of the morning, Christina had forgotten to fill the car's tank, so she had to stop for gas on the way. Instead of going on, every car in their convoy pulled into the station behind her. Shane jumped out and filled the car while she went in to pay.

Touched by the nicety, one of the mothers looked at her spouse and the couple riding with them, and said in a cooing manner, "Look, he's pumping her gas."

Her husband glared at her, taken aback by the naive sound in her voice.

"Well, if you ask me, I'll bet he's pumping more than her gas."

She retorted back at him, ashamed by her husband's insinuation, "This is Christina Cache I'm talking about."

"Yeah, and this is Shane Sievers *I'm* talking about!"

The evening was more wonderful than either Shane or Christina had imagined. Not only did they catch the attention of all her friends, but they stole the dance floor for the evening. Bob and Shirley had a blast with all of the kids, but even they were amazed at how their newly found dance couple took center stage.

Bob grabbed Christina at one of the partner change dances. "Have you guys been practicing?"

"Sure thing. Every single night," was Christina's reply.

He wanted to ask if there was something besides dancing going on between them, but he saw the answer to that question in Shane's eyes as he passed by Christina while they were dancing. And, as if he had not caught on to the emotions between the two, Shirley told him to watch the couple during the slow dances.

Even with both of them consciously making an effort *not* to be conspicuous, everyone saw the love that bounced from one to the other as they moved across the floor together. Shane was especially pleased that the one single guy he was worried about moving in on his girl did not even ask her for one dance. *Wait 'till next weekend's retreat. He'll really get the big fat picture!* The rebel meant for everyone to know that Christina belonged to him by then, and that he intended to keep it that way.

The kids and their parents all left shortly after ten, so Shane had Christina all to himself for the last two hours. He held onto her the entire time, only letting go for a couple of smoke breaks. Every time he danced with her, she felt even better in his arms, and it was getting more obvious to him that he wanted to feel her there forever. Even during the smoke breaks, he had quit checking out the other merchandise, and was wishing that he could take his angel home and hold onto her all night.

When the dance was finally over, and the couple was on their way home, Shane asked Christina to stop at the store. She looked at him, smiling, for his frequent requests of stopping to buy a single beer – an improvement from the 6-pack or 12-pack previously – had dwindled down to only an occasional stop. As much as she hated his request, he had gone through a major battle that evening, and had come out victorious, letting everyone see the love, the pure love, in their hearts for each other. And after all, he *was* a grown man.

To Christina's surprise, instead of the beer she expected to see, Shane came out with a rose and a card that read, "I love you." She had no idea how to respond. It was *not* what she expected from a redneck.

While she sat there staring back and forth from him to the flower, she heard Noah's voice of wisdom from the back seat, "Mom, I think this deserves a kiss."

"Thank you, son, " added Shane.

Christina glanced at Noah, with a tear in her eye, and back to Shane. She leaned over to kiss him on the cheek, but he turned his head so that his lips pressed against hers. Her hands found his face and reiterated the fact that she loved him and his loving gestures, through her slender, delicate fingers. Shane had never liked anyone being that close to him, holding onto him in that manner, due to his past, but with Christina, it was the most tender, gentle, loving feeling he had ever experienced. Her fingers spoke to him and made him come alive, just as they brought music out of any instrument she touched.

The drive home was a quiet one. Everyone seemed to be reminiscing about some subject. Christina's mind was floating on air, thinking about the rose, the evening of truths, where their love would go from there, or if it would. Shane's mind was wrestling with the fact that he was less than two feet away from the most spectacular creation he had ever beheld, yet his heart was supposed to belong to another. Noah was concentrating on the fact that this redneck from the underworld had just called him "son," a word that he'd detested coming from the lips of his step-father. Yet, from this man, it held a reassuring quality, especially after they had spent an entire morning together this past week after one of Matt's explosive episodes. The trust and respect that reached from one person to the other inside the vehicle was immeasurable, and it took center stage for the ride home as each thought of how they fit in the scope of things with the other two.

As Christina turned into the community of Elmwood, Shane broke the silence. "Christina, I know we both need to get to sleep with the trip to see Shay tomorrow, but could we go to your house and talk for awhile?"

"Sure," responded Christina, sensing that something heavy was on his mind.

Noah, who was close to sleep in his thoughts, chimed in, "Oh, Mom. I almost forgot. May I spend the day and night with Chris tomorrow? His mom said it was okay, and that she would make sure we got to church on time Sunday."

"Are you sure it's alright with Mrs. Kirkpatrick? Shane and I are leaving first thing in the morning and I won't get an opportunity to call her."

"It's fine, Mom. If I need you, I'll call on the cell phone."

As much as Christina hated the telephone, her cell phone had become nearly as indispensable as the microwave. "Sure, that will be fine. Just make sure you don't get hurt on that skateboard while I'm gone. And you call me the minute you get to Chris' house so that I know you got there safely. That way I can double check this with his mom."

"You got it," and Noah raced up the stairs, giving her a big hug and telling her he loved her. He stopped halfway up the stairs and looked back at Shane, who had followed Christina into the house. "Shane, you're an okay guy. I hope you have a great time with your own son tomorrow."

"Thanks, Noah. You're an okay guy, too. I wouldn't mind it if my own son turned out to be just like you."

They both nodded their heads in acceptance as Noah bounded the rest of the way up the stairs and disappeared for the evening. Christina busied herself getting drinks while Shane made his way to the den sofa.

"Would you rather go out on the deck?"

Shane, knowing how much Christina loved her deck, and the privacy it offered at anytime of the day or night, needed the shelter of the closed quarters within the walls of her house – at least, for the time being. "Not just yet."

Christina sensed that Shane was really bothered by something, and she hoped the excitement of having to face so many people in one evening did not panic him. She knew he needed to talk, to get something off his chest, otherwise they would both be getting rest for the trip tomorrow.

"What's wrong?" she asked as she handed him a glass.

He motioned for her to sit beside him. "Christina, I haven't seen Shay since . . ." he broke off in silence and looked at the floor. She placed her drink down, and reached out and took his empty hand between hers. His eyes made their way back up to hers. Christina knew the words that were wanting to come out, yet she had to let him say them himself, to admit his weakness so that he could get past it. Her warm, caring smile alerted him that she knew the rest of the sentence so that he felt comfortable enough to again speak. "I haven't seen Shay since the day ..." Another period of silence, and a glance at the floor followed. She took his glass and placed it on the floor beside hers, and took his other hand in hers. "The day they hauled me off to the hospital. What am I going to say to him? How is he going to react to me?"

Christina had no answers to his questions. She knew Shay from last year's summer Bible school, but she didn't know much about him. They had been attracted to each other from the beginning, yet she had no idea as to why. Now, having met his father and learning all about their past, she wondered if she had subconsciously sensed that the child needed a positive role model, which she had tried to be to him.

"Shane, this is one of those times that you are going to have to trust that child, yourself, and most especially, the Almighty. Everything will be fine ... I know it."

"How can you be so assured when you say that?"

"Because I have faith."

"I have faith, too, but I'm not used to God, or anyone, being on my side."

"Maybe that's because you haven't asked Him, or *let* Him, be on your side."

"I sure do hope you are right. As excited as I am to see that little fellow, I am scared he's not going to want to see me ever again."

"From everything you've told me about him, if he is as much like you as you say he is, that's impossible."

Shane looked at Christina, already feeling better with her encouragement. He picked up his glass, and pulled her up with his free hand. "Why don't we go out for that talk on the deck now?"

Christina listened as Shane recited every detail about Shay, from the time he was born to the day they had last seen each other. To hear him speak, she wondered even more how he could have tried a stunt like that when he had such a precious child who needed him so desperately.

Yet she had seen enough people on drugs and alcohol who had lost all sense of reasonable thinking, that she knew the answer. And she had gathered that his friends were no source of strength or comfort. In fact, far from it. She had heard some of his stories about Carla, and she knew that situation was as volatile as they came. But once again, Shane was an adult and Christina had to use as much discretion as possible where she was concerned.

The serious conversation turned to a comical one as they retold the events from earlier in the evening, watching people's faces as they made a remarkable dance team, and catching all the comments about what a cute couple they made.

"I would love to have been with them when they got back to the church, and all the gossip started," Christina laughed.

"You'll get to hear it all soon enough," he replied, knowing that Abigail would give her the full scoop.

They laughed and talked until Christina went inside to get a jacket. She saw the clock as she passed back through the den, and couldn't believe her eyes.

"Shane, did you have any idea that it was after 5:00?"

"No! You should have been in bed hours ago."

"So should you. Grab your coat and at least get a couple of hours rest before we leave."

He pulled her to him before they took off. "I don't know where the time goes when we're together, but there never seems to be enough."

"Me, either. Your mom is not going to believe that you spent *two* nights at my house in one week."

"Ah, she's used to me showing up at all hours of the night, or not coming home at all."

"But not with *me*!"

"Maybe she'd better get used to it since there's nowhere I'd rather be."

Christina dropped him off, and rushed back home to jump in bed for a ninety-minute snooze.

# 11

She could not believe how refreshed and exhilarated she felt when the alarm clock rang and she jumped in the shower. *I had forgotten how good love felt!*, she thought as she let the water wake her entire body with its energizing sensation. Christina was amazed that she was actually looking forward to seeing Shane again, less than two hours from when she had left him, and drive for over three hours to see a child she barely knew, just to drive back for three more hours.

*What is wrong with me? I could be spending a relaxing day at home. No kids, no work, no nothing. Just a long deserved day to chill before the rat race of the next seven weeks. But what am I doing? Shuffling around before seven o'clock on a Saturday morning, trying to decide which earrings to wear to match my outfit so that I can look my best for some guy I met less than a month ago.*

Christina took one last look at herself to make sure it was not obvious that she had been up all night with some nearly strange man, and that every hair was exactly in place. She liked what she was seeing in the mirror more and more, and she was now actually taking time to look at herself. *At herself.* The image in the mirror was a pleasant one. *Christina, you know you love this, and wouldn't have it any other way.* There was a slight pause in her step as she went to look in on Noah. *On second thought, maybe there is one slight change I would make,* feeling very naughty, but not guilty, for being human.

Noah was still sleeping soundly. She wrote him a note, taped it to his door, then went downstairs to lay out breakfast for him, wondering if he would even touch it before he bolted out the door on his skateboard for a day of fun and play. He still made her sun rise and set, after the past few years, and she hated to think that in only four years, he would be gone and she would be all alone.

*Let's not go there today,* Christina reprimanded herself, as she thought how they were both going out for a day of fun and play.

Shane lay down for a few minutes, but he found it impossible to sleep. He was so excited at the prospect of seeing his son again that there was no way he could shut his eyes.

One of his agenda items for the last week had been to get custody of his son and give the child the home that he deserved. His mind settled on Christina and Noah, and what a swell relationship they had. It had taken years for him to get to his present point, but he was determined to make that same kind of life for himself and his own son.

*The child needs a mother. A good mother. Someone who can love him and guide him and encourage him . . . and keep his father in line.* Shane chuckled to himself. He only knew of one person who fit that bill, and he fully intended to see how she and his son related to each other today.

It was his intention to see how things went during the course of the day, after taking Christina's advice from the wee hours of the morning. Depending on whether he and his son got along as well as usual, he was going to ask the child if he would like to live with him all the time. If the answer was affirmative, he was going to get about the task of making that a reality for the two of them.

*Shane Sievers. You must be out of your head. That is the hardest thing to accomplish on the list and that's the one you want to start with. But then, on the other hand, it will take longer to accomplish, so maybe it's a good thing to do first.*

He couldn't wait to tell Christina his idea. It was funny how she had become his sounding board for everything that went through his head. How much Shane had come to depend on her in the last three weeks. He stopped to think. Yes, it had been exactly three weeks today.

Shane had gotten up and headed for the shower, but his last thought stopped him. *You've let a woman get this close to you in three weeks. Shane, you really HAVE lost your mind.* But he went on about the business of getting ready as he thought how the ideal life would be to live out west with Christina, Shay, and Noah, and have horses and a truck. *God, what a life!* He turned on the water. *But who are you kidding anyway?*

The ride to Shay's house was no less than their usual jovial time together. They stopped for breakfast, getting the attention of everyone in the place, then walked next door to a convenience store where Shane found Christina a purple pen. Their life was so exciting, yet so full of nothing more than small trivial things. It was just *who* the two of them were and where they had been that seemed to set them apart from everyone else and every other couple. But for whatever reason, they loved what had happened, and was continuing to happen between them.

It was obvious to both of them that the time away from Charlotte and their friends only proved to draw them even closer to each other. Although they were both a little shaken by how fast they were moving, neither of them minded it, nor tried to change the direction of their relationship.

By the time they reached Shay's house, both of their faces were hurting from laughter. Christina wondered if Shay would even remember her, and Shane wondered if his son would still want him for a father. He got out of the Blazer and sauntered to the front door in his usual manner, only to have the door jerk open just as he got to the top step.

A young boy came bounding out the door and jumped into his father's arms. Even if she would have had to leave at that precise moment, the drive there and back would have been worth it to see that sight. Christina felt tears in her eyes, and she quickly wiped them away before either of the guys saw her mushy sentimentality.

She heard Shane tell someone at the door an approximate time that they would return, then he started down the steps and toward the Blazer, still holding Shay in his arms. The child looked around to see where they were going, and yelled excitedly, "It's Christina!"

"You two know each other?"

"Sure we do," the child blabbed as Christina nodded her head. "We had a thing for each other last summer at the church. We kinda took a special liking to each other. Besides, she's only the prettiest girl in the whole church. In fact, she may be the prettiest girl I've ever met." Shay stopped, then added, jokingly, "Besides my girl friend, that is!"

Shane scrutinized Christina. "Do you have that effect on *every* male you meet?"

"Nope, just those whose last name is Sievers!" Then she started to laugh, with Shay joining in behind her.

Shane wanted to join their party of laughter, but he was afraid there was more to his question than she admitted. It showed in the way her eyes met people, in that irresistible smile that looked so innocent, yet reeled you in like you were nothing, and her inability to meet a stranger. He suddenly found that combination a bit unsettling as he wondered how he was going to make this mare, as free as the wind, his for keeps. It made him want to brand her, even more, for his own.

Christina looked at the rutted steep drive behind her. "How am I supposed to get out of here?"

"Just back up," both guys offered at the same time.

She sized up the drive she'd just nervously come up. *They actually expect me to back down this narrow path that crooks down a mountain?*

"What's the matter? Can't you handle it?" Shay called from the back seat.

"Would you like for me to drive?" Shane questioned.

That was it. The two of them were *not* going to get the best of her. She could keep up with the best of them, and she intended to let those two know it. Christina took one last look at the drive, and made her way cautiously down the steep grade. She got to the bottom of the drive, headed the Blazer toward the way they had come in and asked, "Now where?" very proud that she had not just gone over the side of the mountain, while giving a silent prayer of thanks.

Shane's mouth was curled up in a huge grin, knowing full well what had just gone through Christina's mind. "We're going to the mall in Asheville, have some lunch, and then go to a movie. How does that sound, buddy?"

"Great!" Shay said, bouncing in the seat as if he had never had that much fun in one day. "I just want to ask Christina one question. Why didn't you get a *purple* Blazer?"

She looked at Shane with a twisted mouth and shook her head. "Well, you *were* right about one thing. The boy is *just like you!*" to which they all laughed.

The day was a great success and in Shane's words, everyone had a "large" time. They walked through the mall, all holding hands, with Shane in the middle joining the three of them. Next they laughed over lunch until Christina was afraid they would get thrown out of the restaurant; and sat in the movie, sharing popcorn and linked together. She had no idea the last time she had enjoyed a Saturday that much, and was pleased at how they accepted her so heartily into their trio. Shane could not believe how much fun he had with his son. They had not had time like this together since he could remember. Shay was ecstatic. He had never seen his dad so excited, or looking so well. It was obvious that Christina was good for him, and he took every opportunity to bring that point across during the day.

When they were on their way back to Shay's house, Shane asked him if he would like to be in the musical with his friends from the church, adding that he was going to help with it.

"Sure, that sounds like lots of fun. But how did Christina talk you into doing that?"

"I had a little help," Christina answered before Shane had time to find an answer.

"You must have. I can't believe anyone talked Dad into something like that."

"Let's just say an angel was involved," Shane winked at Christina.

"I know there was an angel involved if Christina had anything to do with it. Hey, Dad! There's a song that reminds me of Christina and I've been trying to think of it all day."

Christina could hardly wait to hear his next sentence, expecting another smart-aleck comment.

"You know the one. It says something about some angel wearing a choir robe."

"Yeah, I know. And you're right, son. I think about her every time I hear that song."

"Okay, guys. Fill me in. I'm not a big country music fan."

"You don't listen to country music? What's wrong with you? I know they say everybody has one fault, but I've already found two that you have. Of course, I'm sure they're the *only* two. You're too beautiful to have any more."

She looked at Shane and smiled. "Maybe I need to keep him around for my ego." Then she turned toward Shay. "Okay, I don't listen to country music. What's my other fault?"

"You drive a Chevrolet."

"And what am I supposed to drive?"

"A Ford! What else?"

Christina sighed and shook her head.

"He has a point, you know," Shane added in defense of his son.

"Am I ever going to be able to stand being with the two of you?" Christina joked.

"You'd better. I don't ever intend to get rid of you."

"And I don't intend to let him," she heard from the back seat.

She had reached the driveway and made the climb once again. Christina stopped the car and looked at the two male passengers. It was clear that they had both enjoyed her company just as much as she had theirs. Shane opened his door and then Shay's. Christina got out and hugged the child. He responded as though he would never let go. She was touched beyond words, recognizing how badly he needed her love and acceptance. *He really is like his dad.*

206

Shane walked very slowly to the door with his son, and Christina knew that he was asking whether the boy would like to come and live with him if he could arrange it. She could tell from the child's hug and yelp what the answer was.

Now they had both accused her of being an angel, and she felt like, to them, she probably was. Christina could not help but feel a thrill inside her each time she helped Shane over a hurdle. Hurdles which became higher and more frequent with each passing day. She was aware that the day had gone much smoother because of her presence, and she was thankful that she had given her day to allow Shane the privilege of holding, and being with, his son. The small things in life, just like that day, were the bonuses that came with her job, and although Shane had far surpassed any part of her job, the reward of doing something for another person was still there. She was also aware that if Shane ever did get his son – and she was sure he would, simply because he had put his mind to it and it was a challenge – it would take more help from God than she'd ever witnessed. Her prayers started then, knowing how many prayers Shane's first goal was going to take. She couldn't help but wonder if he had any idea how much divine intervention his task was going to need. However, she knew his mind was made up, and she intended to hang in there with him to the bitter end.

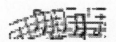

Both of them were excited on the way back to Charlotte. But it was Shane who could not get over how well the day had gone.

"Did I not tell you there was no reason to worry? The Man had it all under control."

Shane, who had been holding her right hand the entire time, brought it up to his lips and kissed it. "Thank you. Thank you for everything. I don't know when the next time I'd have seen him woulda been. And things wouldn't have gone like they did today if you hadn't been there."

"Yes, they would have."

"No, Christina. For one thing, you kept me settled on the trip there, and for another, you took off any edge that might have been there, either with Shay or his mom's family. They respect who you are and what you do. I needed you."

"It's okay to need someone," she said, reminding him of the incident with Matt during the past week and Noah's time with him.

When they made the turn at Little Switzerland, Shane told Christina to pull in a driveway and stop the car.

"Where are we going?"

"Come on, you'll see."

Shane took Christina's hand and led her into a restaurant that looked more like a bar, gave the waitress an order for a beer and an iced tea as they went by the counter, and headed out onto the patio with his lady in tow. He started to sit down, but Christina was mesmerized. She looked out over the most spectacular scenic sight she had ever beheld in her home continent.

"Oh, Shane, it's beautiful!"

"Thought you'd like it."

"No wonder they call it Little Switzerland. I've never been here before."

"I didn't exactly think you'd been here before. It doesn't remind me of your usual hangout."

She looked at him, smiling. "Did you plan this?"

"Yeah," he answered, rather sheepishly. "I thought you deserved a reward after giving up your day for an ornery old redneck. The sun will go down behind the mountains in about thirty minutes, and they have superb potato skins and fried 'shrooms here."

Christina kissed him, holding onto him tightly while looking at the mountains that surrounded them in a 360-degree panorama. She could not take her eyes off the sight that stretched for miles out in front of her in every direction.Even the chill of the February air on top of the mountain did not chase her away from that outdoor spot. They were clinging to each other, and swaying from side to side, as she oohed and aahed.

Shane was glad that he had thought to do this last night. He had prayed for the weather to be perfect, and it was far beyond his expectations for a typically cold, wintry day. *Okay, God, did You do this for me or for her?* It didn't matter, though, as long as it brought joy to his angel. For the first time in a long while, he got the feeling that maybe God *was* listening to him. That day certainly had proven to be a great starting example for a new lifestyle. They both stood there, hanging over the rail and praying their own petitions of thanks as the sun slowly made its way to the horizon, making the view even more breathtaking.

The waitress signaled Shane that their order was ready, but he asked her to keep it warm until the sun went down. She could see that there was something special going on between the two of them. They were not the usual beer guzzlers who came through the restaurant. Touched by the glow on their faces, she gladly complied with his wishes. Shane felt honored that he was able to give such a rare gift to his beautiful lady. *My beautiful lady*. He stared at her profile as she watched the last rays of the sun. Shane could not decide which was more beautiful, Christina or the sunset.

Several people had made their way into the restaurant while the couple had been on the patio, but neither Shane nor Christina noticed them. He reached down to kiss her, and they stood there, on the deck that reached out over the mountains, embraced for what seemed to her an eternity. She did not want him to let go, not now, not tomorrow, not ever.

No man had ever planned a more terrific surprise for her. Once again, she fell in love with the bad boy. Their kiss said everything between them. Finally, when the darkness began to set in, Shane led her to the corner table which the waitress had saved for them. They could still look at the few lights that showed over the sides of the mountains while enjoying a delectable meal. Christina could not believe the food was so delicious in such an out-of-the-way bar.

"Shane, please bring me here again. I would love to sit here and write all day."

"I don't have a problem with that as long as you let me drink what I want."

"Oh, you! Just don't drink any of that rot-gut beer."

"You got it." Shane sighed, saluted her, and laughed at the fact that after twenty years of drinking cheap beer, this dame had him asking for the imported stuff, or ales that had a lower alcohol content, or even sodas.

They sat there for over two hours, overwhelmed by the events of the day and the picturesque evening, making it a day to remember for both of them. As badly as they would liked to have closed the joint down, as had become a custom for them, Shane and Christina were both aware of the fact that they had been up practically the whole night before, and that she had a full day of responsibilities the morrow.

"I guess we'd better get going," he said, as he pulled her chair even closer to his.

"Shane, thank you for making this one of the most memorable days of my life. I love you." And their lips met again, as they disregarded the bar full of patrons, now alive with the nightlife

When they reached the car, Shane let her take one last look over the cycloramic view, then hugged her as he whispered in her ear, "Christina, you are the most wonderful thing that ever happened to me. I would be dead right now if it weren't for you."

Her right hand rubbed across his scruffy beard, as she stood there looking up at him in the dim moonlight. "And you're the best thing that ever happened to me."

"Baby, I'm going to have you one day – in *every* way."

"I hope you really truly mean that."

"I do."

They both were startled at his last two words and the sincerity with which he said them. His response came out so naturally that neither of them caught the significance of those two small words, only consisting of three letters, until they had hit the air. Christina eyed him to see if he had caught them, too, as Shane gazed in her face to see if she caught them. Both were aware that they were thinking the same thing, yet neither said a word, but instead, clung to each other in a long, assuring embrace that promised that one day they would take their "I do's."

# *12*

Sundays were becoming Shane's favorite day of the week. He didn't have to wait all day to see his heavenly creature. People watched very closely as she walked into the class for the third Sunday in a row to see how she was greeted by her newest friend. They glanced at each other and occasionally his knee hit her leg, but they were careful to keep everyone in suspense as to what was really going on.

As soon as the service was over, Shane was waiting downstairs at the choir room door. "How about lunch?"

"Great. But I need to check with Noah to make sure he has no plans."

About the time they saw Noah making his way to the choir room, Tom was on his way out. It seemed that everyone had put two and two together except him. He gave the teenager his usual pat on the head, insulting him terribly, and asked if he would like to eat lunch.

Before Noah could worm his way into an excuse, he heard a familiar gruff voice in the background. "Sorry, Bub, but he's got plans."

"Okay, maybe another time," replied Tom, still clueless as to what was going on.

Noah looked at Shane, and grinned from ear to ear. "Shane Sievers, you just stood right in the church building and told a bold-faced lie."

"I did not lie. You do have plans. You're going with your mother and me to eat lunch."

"Maybe so, but you're not one bit sorry!"

Shane knew Noah had him on that one, and they all howled as they left the building.

"What do you want for lunch, m'lady?"

"Do you like Chinese?"

"Love it."

Noah butted in at that point. "How about House of China?"

"That's our favorite restaurant," Christina explained. "Is it okay with you?"

"Perfectly fine, as long as you're going to be there," Shane answered as he lifted her hand and kissed it.

As they were getting in the car, Christina looked at Shane, who had already grabbed her hand. "We need a song. A song just for us."

Shane had never had a song before, at least not one to symbolize a relationship with a female, but he liked the thought and figured it went with the territory. "I know just the one."

"What is it?"

"I'll let you hear it. It plays on the radio all the time. I'm sure you've heard ..." Remembering their conversation from yesterday, he retreated. "I'll let you know when it comes on," Shane declared as he changed her radio station, and they both smiled at his realization.

He flipped the buttons back and forth from one country station to another until, just as she parked the car in front of the restaurant, the song came on. It was so beautiful that even Noah stayed put and listened to the words that the outcast thought described him and his mom. *The words fit the pair to a tee*, Noah thought as he listened intently to a female crooning about love and heaven and angels.

Christina pulled Shane toward her when the song was over. "It's perfect," she murmured, trying to hold back tears.

"I thought you'd like it."

"How did you come up with it so quickly?" she asked, as they were all getting out of the car.

Shane was not quite sure whether to share his secret or not, but decided there was no use hiding it. She would see straight through him anyway. "I think of us every time I hear it."

"So you do think of me when we're not together?" Christina queried, delighted that she already had an answer to the question.

"Sometimes, but don't tell anybody. I'd hate for anyone to get the wrong idea."

"As if they haven't already!"

Abigail loved what she saw between one of her oldest friends, and a relatively new friend – albeit the new one was her best friend – for they were so obviously connected, in mind, body, and spirit. Yet she feared how the small community of Elmwood would respond once word leaked out.

She didn't have long to wait. That evening, only two nights after the outing at the Wildlife, the three combined families decided to get together for a Sunday night ice cream bash, since ice cream was the thing Paul was giving up for Lent. The phone rang just as Paul was digging the containers of frozen concoctions out of the freezer.

Christina could tell by the panic-stricken look on Abigail's face, and the way she headed for the laundry room with the cordless phone, that the call concerned she and the "new man in her life." She immediately turned around from the way Shane was holding her to look into his eyes.

"That call is about us."

"How can you tell?"

"I've known Abigail very well for five years now, and this is the first time I've ever seen her leave the room with the phone. She knows my obligations to keep quiet as a minister, so if I ever feel uncomfortable with a conversation, *I* leave the room. Besides, did you see the fear in her eyes as she turned away? Somebody's making a stink, and no doubt, one of the choir members has called her to find out exactly what is going on and how serious it is."

Shane looked at her, struggling to find the right words to say, wanting to calm her fears, but he knew from what he saw in her face, and the closeness he knew she shared with Abigail, that Christina was right in her assumption.

Paul and the two of them chatted about lots of trivial things, but the conversation always got back to the question of why Christina couldn't have a life, too, and why she was not trusted in her choice of partners. Abigail's call took almost an hour, and by the time she had gotten back to the party, Christina had made up her mind that she was *not* going to work in a place so judgmental in its views.

Abigail heard Christina as she rounded the corner. "I refuse to work in a place that is so critical."

Shane was trying to think of a solution, since *he* was the problem. "Baby, this is about me. *Me*. Not you."

"And that's the whole problem. It just isn't fair. How can they condemn someone they don't even know?"

If Abigail and Paul had any prior doubts about Shane's suitability for Christina, his behavior and attitude toward all of the uproar that had just started alleviated all their fears. They were amazed at the gentleness and true concern in how he dealt with their mutual friend. He spoke to her softly and lovingly, yet when the time came, he put his foot down and she listened.

Paul and Abigail served the ice cream so that the evening would not be a total flop for their guests, and by the time the last bite was eaten, it truly had turned into a party. Laughter abounded as Shane and Abigail recalled old times, and Paul and Christina sat in hysterics listening to the two of them tell every funny thing that had ever happened in Elmwood during their lifetimes.

Abigail put her threesome to bed, and Noah went downstairs to play on the computer, and the team of friends went back to the subject at hand.

"Since I seem to be the source of the uproar, I'd like to put a stop to this. I'm going to meet with the minister in the morning and get all of this out in the open. Christina, you love your job and those people love you. Their concern here is not *about* you, but *for* you. They want to know what the bad boy from hell is planning to do with their fair maiden. And frankly, can you blame them? I refuse to let you leave a good job on my account. There is absolutely no reason why you can't keep working as you always have, and we can still see each other."

The married couple respected his responsibility, and his forwardness in taking the weight off Christina's shoulders. His openness to the issue made them see how deeply he truly did care for her and her well being. Paul could tell from the look in Abigail's eyes that she agreed wholeheartedly with Shane's decision.

"Do you want me to go with you?" Christina asked.

"No, this is between them and me. It is about time I faced up to some of the garbage I've caused in my lifetime, and the reason people don't trust me. You just be in your office when it's over in case I lose my temper."

Paul and Abigail also knew Shane's reputation for losing

control, and even though they were impressed with what they saw from him now, and the positive change he had obviously made in Christina's life, they both feared what could happen. And no more than Christina. She knew that Shane had a short wick, and one wrong word could set him off. He already had little use for the hypocrites in that small community. Before the party ended, the four of them joined hands and prayed for a positive outcome of tomorrow's confrontation.

"Why do I feel like it's going to be high noon at the OK Corral?" Christina laughed, trying to make herself feel better.

The problem now was that all four of them had the same apprehension. They made a pact to have dinner together the next evening to discuss what happened.

"Why do I feel like this is such a big secret? I'm in love. Why can't everyone see what Shane does for me and how he makes me feel?"

Shane kissed her forehead gently as they walked out the door, "It's going to be alright, Baby. Remember what you told me about my visit with Shay? Let God handle it."

Christina stared at Shane in disbelief. Not only had he been taking in every word she had said, he was now feeding it right back to her. Paul and Abigail looked at each other, knowing inside that the bad boy of the bunch was turning into a respectable man right in front of their eyes, and that both he and Christina had found a prize in each other.

# *13*

Monday morning found Christina busily at work in her office trying to get ready for the Fat Tuesday service the next evening. She checked and rechecked her lists, trying to keep herself from thinking about the worst-case scenarios that could happen before lunch. The secretary had already been alerted to expect a call from Shane, and requested to please schedule a morning appointment for him if at all possible.

Christina's extension rang. She heard the familiar, pleasant voice on the other end say, "It's done. He's coming in at ten."

"Thanks. You're a true friend."

The secretary did not ask questions or make comments, but she was sincerely concerned for Christina. She had tried, in her own way, to warn the music guru that she needed to be careful with Shane. Christina hadn't bothered to fill in anyone, besides Abigail, on the closeness of her relationship with the guy whom everyone seemed to fear was dangerous to her. Although the trusted co-worker knew better than anyone how adept Christina was of handling problem after problem, she feared Shane Sievers was more than even she should tackle.

At 9:40, Christina heard the familiar footsteps heading toward her office, just as she had expected. Shane's face appeared at the doorway.

"Good morning, Angel."

"Good morning. I'm afraid you really *do* need an angel this morning."

Shane took a couple of steps to face her. "I *do* have an angel, and I'm going to keep her," he said, kissing Christina's forehead. "Relax. Nothing is going to happen. That is, unless our Reverend Elwood Jenkins tells me I can't see you anymore, or that I'm not good enough for you. Then you might hear glass breaking and see blood flying."

"That's what I'm afraid of," Christina blared back at Shane, not kidding just as much as he was kidding.

They spent the next ten minutes locked in an embrace, drawing strength from each other, each a different kind of strength. As the clock drew nearer to the appointed hour, they both felt a little calmer.

"I'd love to be a fly on the wall when you walk in. I'll bet Elwood is already shaking in his shoes at the thought of the bad boy coming to visit. He's heard *all* the horror stories, I'm sure."

"Not to mention that he was totally mortified at the scene of my attempted suicide."

"Face it, Shane. A lot of ministers don't know how to deal with certain situations because they haven't lived through them. Life and all its crap cannot exactly be summed up in Counseling 101."

"Yeah, I know, but you'd at least think they could accept a sinner."

"It's not that he doesn't accept the sinner. He's just scared to death of him!" she surmised, as they both laughed at the visual image of the senior minister wondering what was going to happen before the morning was over.

"Is he scared to death of his wife, too? And how about those three daughters who look like the most exciting part of their day is getting on the school bus? Is he afraid of them, too?" He scanned Christina's face carefully to make sure she was not taking offense at his humor. Seeing nothing more than a half frown, half smile, he continued. "I got it. That's why he stays shut up in that office all day and night hiding behind that desk. He's afraid to go home and face the four females in his house. Why, to look at him, I'd bet their dog is even female."

"That's enough," she tried to scold. But even Christina could not help but smirk at the image of her chief-of-staff, so squatty that he could barely fit into his office chair, slithering down behind his desk and hiding as he cautiously peered over the top of his glasses, unable to look into the eyes of someone as lowly, yet fearsome as Shane Sievers.

"Yeah, I guess you're right. You should fit right in 'cause I've got friends in low places, too," she joked, referring to the height of Elwood rather than his social status.

The bad boy hugged his angel a little harder, glad that she could keep the air between them light-hearted even when he knew she feared a storm. "I guess it's about time to get this show on the road."

"You have to come back and tell me everything that happened."

"Don't worry. I will."

"Yeah, if they don't lock you up first!"

"If I start to get too PO'ed, I'll just think about your smiling face."

"Yes, and my patience. Take my patience with you."

Shane smiled, nodded, and started out the door.

"Wait," yelled Christina, as she ran behind him. She took off the angel pin that Shane had bought and placed on her shoulder Friday while they were gathering items for the Fat Tuesday service and musical, and handed it to him. "Take this angel with you. It is *our* angel."

"What more could I need?" Shane responded, and kissed Christina one last time.

She watched him saunter out the door, a confidence in his stride. Christina knew the goodness wrapped inside her man. But she also saw the many tightly packed layers of grudges and bad attitudes that overlaid all that goodness. From the moment she met Shane, she had heard countless stories of him being "PO'ed" at someone or something. And even though she had helped him get a handle on that, and had watched him learn to accept things objectively rather than so personally, this morning's meeting had her worried.

Shane expected everyone to be as sharp as he was, and she had tried to warn him that was not the case. At least, not most of the time. The rebel was surprisingly quick and intelligent, and people did not realize they had met their match when he walked into a situation. Christina knew that he had become extremely defensive of her, and she knew that this morning's talk could prove volatile enough to throw him over the edge.

Try as hard as she could, Christina's efforts to work were of no avail. She could not stop praying, as she stood there, visualizing every thing in her senior minister's office – every piece of furniture, every knick-knack, every book. *Dear God, please let it look that same way tomorrow!* And for once, she found herself looking forward to the Tuesday morning staff meeting, just so she could take inventory.

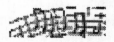

Elwood Jenkins dreaded Mondays as a rule, but that particular day had gotten off to a good start, or so he thought. As soon as he walked into the building, though, he was handed a piece of paper that notified him of the 10 a.m. appointment with Shane Sievers. He looked at his watch. *Maybe I've got time to cancel. Maybe I'll get an emergency call with one of the members at the hospital. Maybe one of my daughters will get sick at school. Maybe...*

He was interrupted by a firm knock at the door. The clergyman quickly walked over to the door to be greeted by the familiar well-built man. His black leather jacket and sunglasses did not help to nullify the big and bad dude image of the guy standing face to face with him.

"Good morning, Shane. How nice to see you."

*Great! I have little use for most ministers anyway, and this one has to start off with a lie!* "How's it going?"

*It was going fairly well for a Monday until I got here and found out that I was starting off the week by having a confrontation with you.* "Fine, just fine. Won't you come in and sit down? Can I get you a cup of coffee?"

"No, thank you. I don't reckon this is exactly a social visit."

Neither of the men were aware that in addition to the Holy Spirit who always hung out around the place, there were three other spirits. Paul and Abigail, as well as Christina, were all there in absentia, holding the place up by their non-stop prayers. As badly as they wanted the meeting to turn out with Shane and Christina still seeing each other, their main concern was that there were no headlines of a minister being booted out his window into the church parking lot.

"So what brings you here today, Shane?"

*You can't be that dumb.* "You know that as well as I do. I'm sure you know that Christina and I are seeing each other and some people have got their noses outta joint over it."

"Ah, well ... It has come to my attention that she's been a counselor to you."

"Well, I hate to bust your bubble, but she ain't no counselor to me." Shane watched as Rev. Jenkins nearly spewed the coffee he had just put in his mouth all over his desk, and started clearing his throat. *One for me.*

Christina's boss put down the coffee cup and leaned forward. "What do you mean, she isn't counseling you?"

"I mean that I am not her job."

"D-Do you mean to tell me that there is some … well, romantic interest here?"

Shane loved the look of trepidation on the face in front of him, disapproving of what its mind was hearing, but afraid to say too much about it. He smiled. "You could say that." *Two for me.*

"If she's not your counselor, what exactly would you call her?" the holy man asked as he inched in even closer.

The hellion sat and thought for a split second. "Well, for lack of a better term, *at the moment*, I'd say she's my significant other." Shane watched as the expression on the face opposite him melted, like an ice cube that had been placed on a hot surface. *Three for me.*

Once Elwood got himself halfway composed again, after hemming and hawing for a minute or so, he gave Shane a lecture about Christina's position as a minister of the church and what that entailed. Then he began to question Shane, and had the conversation involved anyone besides his angel, the rebel would have reached across the desk and laid the inquisitor out cold in the floor.

"Did Christina inform you that as a minister, she must remain completely faithful to her husband?"

"Yep."

"And did she also tell you that as long as she is single, she must remain celibate?"

"Yes." Shane was furious by this point, knowing that the line of questioning was completely out of order, breaking Christina's trust. It was a good thing for the man seated across from him that he had promised her that there would be no bloodshed or broken bones.

223

He decided that it was time for the ludicrous inquisition to stop, so Shane took it upon himself to get to the business of why he was there. Scooting his chair forward, laying his arm across the desk and leaning face to face with her superior officer, all the while remembering Christina's warning to watch his language, he began, "Listen here, ah, *sir*. Christina is over twenty-one and she is no one's slave. Not yours or anybody else's. Her personal life is her own business as long as she doesn't overstep her boundaries – the way you've done here this morning. And the way I understand it, *God* is her boss, and *He* is the only one who can judge her. Now if anybody has a problem with that, they can go directly to her, or even better, they can come see me." *Four for me.*

Shane started to excuse himself, but he was wound up, and secretly, he had to admit that this kind of beat down was far better than his usual fistfight, so he kept the ball rolling. "And furthermore, I have raised my share o' hell in the past, and then some. Probably more than all the people in this congregation put together. That is, unless they want to start spreading unfounded rumors and gossip all over this community about the best person that has ever set foot in this church. Thanks to Christina, I have set goals for myself, and I am turning my life around. It's my understanding that once I repent from all those sins of the past, I get to start with a clean slate. One as clean as yours, or hers, or anybody else's who professes to be a believer. Now if that's wrong, then I've been lied to by all the ministers I've ever heard in the pulpit." He stood and walked toward the door. *Five for me.*

Just as Shane was heading out the door, he turned, put his sunglasses back on, and leaned with one hand up against the door frame. "Oh, and by the way, bud, she's doing a damned good job of keeping those vows," and he turned, walked out, and gently closed the door behind him. *K-O'ed in the sixth round!*

He stopped just long enough in the secretary's office to speak, and to hear his opponent buzz her and say that he was leaving for the morning. Shane leaned over her desk, winked at her, and said softly, "Has to go home and change his pants!"

The secretary howled at Shane's playful bluntness. *You can't help but like him,* she thought as he strolled out of the building toward Christina's office. *No wonder Christina enjoys being around him.*

It seemed like it had been an eternity when Christina heard the sound of Shane's boots against the tile floor. His steps were slower than usual, causing her blood pressure to skyrocket. She glanced at her watch. *Only twenty minutes? Perhaps they didn't even get to meet.* However, she feared the worst, moving out into the hallway to meet him. He grabbed her, hugging her with even more intensity than usual.

"What happened?" she asked, craning her neck back from his grip to see his face. "Are you alright?"

"I'm fine."

"Is *he* alright?"

"He will be. I'm not sure he knows what hit him yet."

Christina gulped. "You *hit* him?"

Shane could not help but laugh at her reactions. "No, baby. Not actually. At least, not with my fist."

She was not getting any calmer. "Please tell me you didn't kick him or throw him through the window."

"No, no, no. Nothing like that. I did *not* throw anything or anybody and there is no blood on anything. I followed your instructions carefully, and I did not even use but one word that you would have disapproved of. And that was only when he asked me about your vows of celibacy."

Christina's fear turned to immediate anger. "He did *what*? No, surely he didn't ask you that." But Shane's expression and the nod of his head told her that he was telling the truth. "Why that ... how *dare* he?" And she jerked around and stormed toward the door, ready to hit the man herself.

Shane ran behind her. "Whoa, Nellie. If I can't hit him, you certainly can't. Wouldn't that give the old biddies in Elmwood something to talk about?" He pulled her to him, rubbing her back and trying to console her. "Besides, he's already left for the morning. I told the secretary that he probably had to go home and change."

At that, Christina's anger left as she burst into laughter, with Shane joining her. They stood in the choir room, holding onto each other and swaying, while he gave her a play-by-play recount of the meeting, and their faces were sufficiently in pain from all the laughter.

"C'mon. Lunch is on me. You've already done a full day's work."

"Does that mean I deserve a beer?"

Christina rolled her eyes at him as she grabbed her purse. "Shane Sievers, did I ever tell you that I love you?"

"I think so, but why don't you tell me again so I can be sure," and he kissed her as she went by, while Christina grabbed Shane's hand, swirled him around and pulled him along behind her.

That evening Shane asked her to go with him to Mickey's house. He wanted to tell his buddy about the day's meeting. Christina was honored that she was asked to go along, and though she had a hundred other things to do for tomorrow night's service, she agreed to go. Especially when Shane offered to help her after the visit.

Mickey was gratified that Christina bothered to show up at his house, figuring he wasn't good enough for a personal visit. He was even more grateful that he had a soft drink in the fridge to offer her instead of a beer.

It was pretty obvious that the couple had a sure thing going, especially when they got ready to leave and Mickey asked if Shane wouldn't like to stay and have a beer.

"Nah, thanks anyway, but I promised to go to the church and help Christina."

"Boy, you *must* be hooked. You sure are spending a lot of time down at that church lately."

"It kinda goes with the territory."

Christina gave Shane one of her arm squeezes to let him know she appreciated his sacrifice. Mickey caught the look between them and knew that his wish of a couple of weeks ago might actually become a reality. He caught Shane as they were going out the door and whispered so that Christina would not hear.

"Man, did you know that chick is in love with you?"

"Not just in love. Head over heels." He had made a point of saying his reply loudly enough for Christina to hear.

She just turned and gave the two cronies the familiar smirk that Shane loved so much. Mickey saw exactly why it was so easy for his buddy to give up the nothing life that he'd had to be with a female like her. *She's got it all,* he thought to himself as he watched them back out the driveway. *Too bad I'm such a nice guy and let Shane have her.* But he also knew that to see his friend straighten up and be that happy was worth it. And he walked back inside, opened up another beer, grabbed a slice of lime, and sat back down to his movie.

227

# 14

The next day moved quickly due to the Fat Tuesday service. Christina was so busy making sure she had memorized every detail that she didn't even get time to join in the Cajun dinner, for which she and Shane had carefully done taste tests and shopped in the wee hours of the morning the two days before.

Totally into her zone of rehearsing the anthems in her head, she did not catch the sound of footsteps in the building until he had walked in the choir room. It was not until she heard the cat whistle that she was even aware of his presence.

"Whew, baby, look at you!"

"Do you like it?"

"Like it? I'm glad I'm the one taking you home after this is over." Shane hugged her, then held her back at arm's length to get a good look at the woman before him.

"I'm sure all the costumes are going to get a lot of attention – not all of it good. But this is meant to be a festive occasion, and I told the choir to dress as such."

"Well, I'm sure no one is going to look as good as you."

"Thanks," Christina smiled shyly, looking again in the mirror at the black velvet slacks and the sequined top of gold, green and purple on a black silk background, trying to decide on whether it had achieved her own seal of approval. "I bought this top in Dallas during my last semester at SMU. It was sort of a self-congratulations present, but I've never found the right occasion to wear it. I don't go out on the town like I used to." She glared accusingly at Shane. "My present company isn't into Broadway productions and symphony concerts."

"If you're going to look that good, I might could get used to them."

"I'll tell you what. I'll wear my long, slinky black skirt with the slit up to my thigh, and we'll get you a Western tuxedo."

"I didn't say *would,* I said *might*," Shane retreated.

They both laughed and hugged again, loving every minute of their jovial conversation. Christina was grateful that her cowboy had managed to come in and relieve her pre-program stress. She was in the habit of being by herself, going through the music and all the details, double checking everything in her mind. Never had she allowed *anyone* to interrupt her process of getting into her zone. But, like everything he did, Shane sauntered in, took her in his arms, made her laugh, all the while taking away any jitters or anxiousness that may have been present. She *loved* his style, and proceeded to tell him so.

"Shane, where have you *been* all of my life?"

"You really don't want to know! They're not places that I think we want to discuss. Especially not here, *or now!*"

Christina was rolling in laughter again. They could hear the outside doors opening and voices coming toward them. He reached over and quickly stole a kiss.

"I love you, baby. Good luck. I know everything's going to be great." Shane started to exit just as the first choristers reached the door. He looked back at Christina, winked, and added, "I've got it on good authority!"

Other choir members began to dawdle in, making their usual clamor, plus some, interjecting approvals of the many brightly colored outfits each of them had worn for the evening's celebration. Everyone was involved in the conversation, also commenting on the scrumptuous meal they had just enjoyed, and catching up on the events of the week since Sunday when they had last seen one another.

One of the biggest topics of discussion was what everyone was giving up for the next forty days in observation of Lent. Christina heard the usual array of answers – chocolate, desserts, fries, etc. However, the clattering ruckus was brought to a halt when one of the men jeered at her, loudly enough for all in the entire room to hear, "Hey Christina, what are *you* giving up this year for Lent?"

Although the question was meant as a joke, since everyone knew that she had given up *everything* meaningful to her, *not by choice*, during the course of the past three years, the hand was turned when she glanced off in Shane's direction and said smugly, "I'm giving up giving up."

No one spoke another word, wondering whether she was serious or not, as she proceeded to give directions for the evening's service. They were used to Christina's quick wit, and her way of kidding about areas of her life that were extremely painful – too painful, in fact, to handle. But the tone in her voice and the expression on her face as she threw that particular answer back at them gave her flock the clear understanding that Shane Sievers had indeed become a very real presence in her life. And from all indications in her mood, her work, and her body language, it was an extremely positive presence.

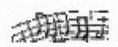

Even Christina wondered if Shane would show up for the Ash Wednesday service, afraid that it might be a little too somber and reflective for him. But just as she played the last phrase of the prelude, she caught sight of a familiar amble sashaying down one of the side aisles. She glanced at Abigail and flashed her a gratifying smile, receiving one in return from her friend.

No one knew more than Abigail how meaningful Shane's presence was to Christina, especially on that particular evening. The woman who always seemed to be in high gear was the one who thrived on the Ash Wednesday and Maundy Thursday services. *I'm sure it comes from her depth of faith, and her ability to look into the blackest darkness and see the light.* She had noticed years ago that it was those services that inspired Christina the most and strengthened her closeness to her Father. *As it should be!*, thought Abigail.

When the service concluded and Shane walked up to the choir loft, Christina could not help but stare at the ashen cross on his forehead. She relived the same eerie feeling as of the previous evening, when after the Fat Tuesday service, he dug the hole for her to place the oversized cross in the front lawn of the church for Lent. On previous years, it had taken two men to carry the huge wooden structure from the storage building, across the parking lot, past the sanctuary, and to the corner of the property. But when Shane single-handedly picked up the cross and carried it on his back, Christina shuddered at the image she saw. An outcast, hated by many, scorned by most, slowly making his way up a path, carrying an object that had symbolized a death for the sins of the world – she realized even more so that *this* man, like the one two thousand years before, was no ordinary man.

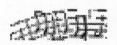

231

For the second Thursday in a row, Christina missed her weekly evening out on the town, savoring the peace and quiet as much she would have the scallops. But it was the only day this week she had time to tie up all the loose ends before tomorrow's weekend retreat with the kids. No one besides Abigail was aware of the fact that Shane was going to be one of the chaperones, so she was looking forward to an instant replay of last weekend's stares when they had arrived together, ready to go to the Wildlife.

Shane's construction job depended largely on the weather, so she was secretly glad that she awoke to a steady rain. It meant they could spend the day together while she was getting all of her work done. *What a hard-knock life!* she hummed, knowing that in addition to making her job a lot easier, he would provide endless entertainment.

Although she was excited about having his constant presence for the next three days, especially since they had not missed a day of seeing each other during the past three weeks, she was more than a little apprehensive about how he would manage being surrounded by children and youth all weekend. After all, they were most definitely a far cry from his usual crowd. *But then, his usual crowd HAS changed quite drastically over the past three weeks.*

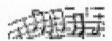

Friday afternoon came, and in his usual fashion, Shane took over the tedious chores of packing the vans and gathering supplies for Christina. No one uttered a word about his presence, but the stares were priceless. She could hardly wait until they all saw his leadership and creative ability over the course of the weekend. Finally, her rebel was going to get a chance to be seen as she saw him.

While everyone else stopped for dinner, they went to the drive-thru and headed on so that they could get Shay, and pick up the keys for all the rooms at the retreat center. Their five-minute lead was just enough time to allow Shane to jot down all the room assignments, and have maps and keys waiting for everyone as they arrived.

Christina set up the rehearsal room and by the time Shane had given out all the room assignments, helped unload all the vans, and get everyone settled, she was ready to begin the first work session. Her cohort came in, supervised the mothers in setting up the snack tables, and made sure that all the kids participated and gave their best effort. He even took the lead characters aside and coached them in understanding their roles. All she had to do was tend to the business of the music.

Mothers sat and watched carefully as Shane and Noah helped Christina teach the choreography. It wasn't long before the co-director had all the other parents involved, and the rehearsal turned into an unforgettable parent-child bonding experience. After the evening's devotion, everyone realized this was no ordinary rehearsal weekend, and that they were all going to return home enriched.

The leader retired to her room zonked after a full day, ready to hit the sack. But she had no more than closed the door behind her when she heard a rap across the room. Christina turned to see another door. She turned the deadbolt, and Shane threw open the door from the other side.

"What are you doing?" she shrilled with delight.

"Two of the rooms adjoined, and I *had* to make sure I assigned them to two occupants who wouldn't cause a disturbance!" Shane said with a wink.

"You...."

"What?"

"You are *totally* impossible!"

"I'd only disappoint you if I were any less!" Shane hugged

233

Christina with all his might, then grabbed her coat off the bed and pulled her toward the door. "C'mon. I've found a place that you just *have* to see."

She didn't even have time to object before he was reeling her down the hall and out of the building with his hand over her mouth, trying to keep her from laughing so they would not arouse the other parents and kids. Within a short distance, Shane stopped Christina beside a babbling brook, noisily gushing water over rocks and broken limbs. The moon was full, high overhead, with an abundance of stars dancing across the sky.

"Oh, Shane. How did you find this?"

"There are *some* benefits to smoking," he said, as he reached down and gave Christina a kiss.

Once again, the man whom everyone feared would take Christina down the 'wrong' path had led her to a spot of divine inspiration, which, in turn, sent the couple into a profound theological discussion. They both adored the challenge that came from being with the other, and the appreciation each had for God's handiwork. It was several hours later before they returned to their rooms, neither of them tired from the time they had managed to sneak into their schedule.

When they got back to the building, Christina remembered that all outside doors were locked at midnight.

"Not to worry," Shane replied, pulling open a door beside a snack room.

"Okay, Shane, I know you've probably broken every law there is to break, and I'm sure I probably don't want to know, but how did you manage this?"

"It's all legit. I met the security guard first thing, shared a smoke with him, and got him to leave this door ajar so that I could have a smoke break in the middle of the night."

Christina shook her head at him.

"See, I told you that smoking had its benefits!"

She gave Shane a squeeze on the arm.

"Oh, baby, wasn't your surprise worth more than that?" And the former outlaw reached down and kissed his angel, releasing emotions that had never surfaced, as he realized that this woman, by involving him in her world, had given his life purpose and meaning. When she looked into his eyes again, the expression was totally changed. "Christina, you'll never have *any* idea what you have done for me. I wouldn't be here, *or anywhere*, right now if it had not been for you."

"You're wrong about that. You had already made the decision to get your life on the right track, and were making moves in that direction. I really had nothing to do with the fact that you have changed."

"Christina, without you, I would have either OD'ed or successfully committed suicide by now. At best, I would be out on the streets somewhere," holding to his claim that she had single-handedly saved his life.

"Shane, you were strong enough to lick your past, to 'beat the hell out of it,' in your words. God only allowed me to *watch* that change, which to me is one of my greatest blessings. It gives me the strength to carry on, and the hope that one day Matt will make the same positive change."

But, whichever way it was, they both knew that their meeting was not simply chance, and that they had a wonderful life out in front of them – overseen, of course, by Christina's Boss.

Arm in arm, they made their way up the stairs. Neither uttered another word, but Shane dropped Christina off at her room with a gentle kiss that made her float on air, and then went to his own room. She tiptoed to the adjoining door that had been left open earlier, closed and locked it, and stood leaning, with her back against it, as she dreamed of the man who was only steps away from her, the man she wanted to be beside her.

Christina could already hear tongues wagging the minute the mothers got home with their endless list of amazing feats, and telephoned their friends to tell them how Shane had single-handedly taken charge of the retreat, handling the trivial problems, supervising, managing crowd control, and keeping her focused, able to do her best quality work. She never even had to ask for a drink or snack because he had already taken care of it for her. He had her music on the right pages before she announced the next selection for each rehearsal. It was clear that Shane possessed some magical trait that sensed Christina's needs even before she did.

Everyone noticed not only how chipper she appeared, but the healthy glow on her face, as well. And they had gained a tremendous amount of respect for the man, who not only created a successful experience for their children, but had made such a difference in their beloved Christina's appearance, behavior, and work. There was no doubt as to how important they were to each other.

She was bursting with pride at the way he had both controlled *and* represented himself over the weekend. All of the kids, not to mention the adult chaperones, had seen a side of him that they had never known existed – all of them, that was, except Abigail.

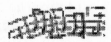

Noah opted to go home on the van rather than going with Christina and Shane to take Shay home. Christina was looking forward to a ride home alone with Shane, glad for her son's perception of her needs. The twosome had a great time reminiscing the events of the retreat, and Shay's opportunity to make new friends and be involved in a project alongside his dad. The child had no idea that his father possessed any dramatic talent, much less the ability to organize and run things. He, too, felt a great sense of pride in his father.

Still on an emotional high after they dropped Shay off, Christina wondered aloud why Noah chose not to ride with them.

"Christina, that's a sharp kid you've got there. I think I may have the answer to your question."

Shane reached in his pocket and took out a small piece of paper. Christina recognized it as being from the envelope like everyone got at the retreat. Each person had written a comment about all the other participants and slipped them into envelopes, each with a different person's name on it. The "gift raps," as she had called them, had been distributed and read just prior to the final benediction. She had been pleasantly gratified that Shane had gotten an entire envelope of accolades, all denoting acceptance from the children, youth and adult chaperones.

A slight chill ran through her as she wondered whether Noah had written something which had offended Shane, thus being the reason he had hidden it away in his pocket, not sharing it with her earlier. *But that's not at all like Noah,* she reasoned with herself as Shane handed her the paper. *Has Noah become jealous of our time together?* Christina was almost afraid to read it, but she turned on the interior light and gazed down at her son's barely legible scribbling, reading the words, *Future Step-dad.* She read the words again, shocked at her son's forwardness, yet pleasantly surprised at his approval of her relationship with this man. Yet, at the same time, she didn't want Shane to feel insulted or uncomfortable by the words her son had penned.

"I'm sorry," was all she could muster, trying to find other appropriate words.

"For what? I took it as a genuine compliment. In fact, I don't know that I have ever been judged so highly."

She was grateful that Noah's message did not complicate matters between the two of them. Christina was even more touched when he reached over and took her hand, squeezing it lovingly, and watched her profile as she made her way down the mountain. When she had driven a few more miles, Shane piped up, "Take a right down here. There's a special place that I want to take you."

Christina knew that had any other man given her that direction, she would have probably ignored them, especially if he had half of Shane's reputation. But instead of arguing, or asking questions, she did as she was told. She thought of the view from Little Switzerland last weekend, and his delight in sharing that with her. There was no doubt that she should trust him.

Yet, as they turned down road after road, finally winding down dirt paths, Christina began to wonder if she had been a little too trusting. Then, Shane began to tell her about a place where he used to go camping.

"I hope no one's there right now," he ended.

Christina almost laughed aloud. *Here we are in the dead of winter and this guy hopes no one is out on this mountain in the middle of nowhere, camped out for the evening!* But as she glanced over at Shane, it dawned on her that this man loved and worshipped God's natural wonders just as much as she, and that a little cold air was not going to stop him from enjoying anything that earth had to offer. *Besides, one of my first impressions of this guy reminded me of Grizzly Adams. And what is it he always says to me, 'Did you forget who you're talking to?'*

She was well aware of whom she was talking to – the man who had killed a bear in his backyard once when it tried to attack him, the man who had faced warlords and drug lords. *Nope, it would be nothing to find him out here on an evening like this.*

Shane gave her one last direction. "Turn to your left at that opening."

The space was so small that Christina was not even sure she

could get in it. But as she got past the initial opening, the headlights shone on a beautiful spot of clearing that rounded itself into a circular paradise.

"Wait here," Shane said as he got out and walked around to Christina's side of the vehicle. He opened her door, took her hand, and told her to close her eyes. The gentleness in his touch as he led her forward several yards made her want to melt in his arms. When they stopped, he wrapped his arm around her back. "Look up."

Christina opened her eyes to behold the most starlit sky she had ever seen. She had never seen anything comparable to the skies of Australia and New Zealand, that is, until that moment. There were so many stars, the sky seemed almost white. It was like they could have touched and made a blanket of light over the earth. Tears rushed down her cheeks.

"Oh, Shane. It's gorgeous."

"I thought you might like it. It's called Sugar Cove. Listen. Hear the music of the stream?"

She concentrated on the sound of the night. All she could hear was the rippling of water hitting over rocks in the stream. But, most of all, she was mesmerized by the fact that, to Shane, it was the sound of music.

He took her hand and led her to the edge of the bank. "Listen to the low bass notes right here. As the water moves its way downstream, the pitches get higher. It makes its own melody as it travels, always something new, as nature changes its path."

Speechless at his insight, Christina hugged him, still watching the ripples under the starlight. No one had ever given her the gifts that he had, gifts that were priceless treasures, yet had cost not a cent. Every breath in her body told her that she wanted to stay there forever, exactly as they were at that precise moment, with Shane standing behind her, holding her close to him with his hands clasped around her waist, sheltering her from the cold, with both their bodies swaying to the rhythm of the stream. That was the first time she had even noticed the least bit of chill in the air. The scenery surrounding her was so awesome that outer stimuli were completely unnoticeable.

They stood, picking out constellations, with Shane promising to bring her back there on a camping weekend. Neither of them wanted to leave, but they both knew it was still quite a ride home, and Christina did not want Noah to worry about her. Shane opened her door, then held her for a couple more minutes. He loved the vision he saw looking up at him as much as she loved seeing him so tough and rugged in his black leather jacket. The attraction became so unbearable between them that he let go of her, and walked around to his own side.

She backed out of the close space and retraced her tracks to get them on the main road. Christina once again thanked Shane for sharing another of his special places with her. "I cannot wait to show you some of my favorite places, too."

"There's one small difference, Miss World Traveler."

"What's that?"

"Most of your favorite places are on the other side of the world, and cost a whole lot more to get to, not to mention the time it will take to get there."

"It won't take so long if we fly."

"Christina, do you realize that I have never flown in my life?"

"*You* have never flown? Shane Sievers, I cannot imagine anything that you've not tried at least *once* in your life!"

"Yeah, it is pretty remarkable, isn't it?"

"Shane, I *have* to take you on an airplane. You will *love* it."

"I'm sure I would."

"Great, then it's settled. Where would you like to go?"

"I don't know. I've never really thought about it."

"Well, start thinking. I've got some frequent flyer points that I need to use. We can go anywhere you'd like."

"Baby, that's like letting a kid loose in the candy store."

"Yeah. And your point is?"

Shane could not help but laugh at Christina's persistence. He knew that going somewhere with her would be a blast for anyone. His only problem was to decide where to go first. *Every man should be so lucky*, he speculated, as he thanked God for placing such a woman in his life.

"Christina, there is one more place that I would like to take you."

"If it's anywhere nearly as beautiful as the last two places, I can't wait."

"You will have to wait for awhile. I have never taken *anyone* there. It is where I intend to get married the next time. And I only want us and the minister. Mickey and Abigail can be witnesses, and, of course, Shay and Noah can come if they want. It is a secluded spot on the side of a mountain that I found once when I needed to get away. The view is absolutely more spectacular than anything I have ever seen."

For the second time that evening, Christina found herself without words. After the past two weekends of spending so much time with Shane, there was no doubt in her mind that she would love spending the rest of her life with him. In less than a month, he had completely taken over every part of her being. And she loved every minute of it. But more than that, she felt a fulfillment, knowing that he wanted her in the same way.

# *15*

The phone rang to awaken Christina to a perfectly gorgeous day. It was Shane's first day out from under his parent's roof. He had moved into Ron Kershaw's basement, another good strategy on the part of Christina. Ron, a former minister of Shane's (one of the two he actually liked), and his wife were always taking in people who needed a fresh start. Both of them were anxious to help Shane, having known him since his troubled teenage years.

Christina's friends had finally come around to the point of seeing how great the couple was for each other, and *everyone* was glad to lend a helping hand to keep Shane moving in the forward direction in which he was headed. Thus, she coaxed two of her choir buddies into helping Shane move his necessary items to the Kershaw's. Ron and his wife were perfect for Shane. Their lifestyle was very relaxed and laid back, and although their guest was allowed his own space in their downstairs apartment, they invited him upstairs every morning and evening for coffee. Ron was a superb source for positive stimulation of Shane's thoughts. He was able to challenge the rebel's mind just as much as Christina.

Both Shane and Christina realized that this was his first step to moving on to the rest of the goals on his list. He was now, at least partially, out on his own. Like any other adult, after being out from under his parents' roof for nearly twenty years, it was hard to fit in there again, so this was the logical initial step toward freedom and acceptance of personal responsibility.

"Good morning."

"Good morning, Baby. Did you sleep well?"

"I certainly did, since I had dreams of being with you all day."

"Then why aren't you here making that dream come true? What's taking you so long?"

She laughed. Christina loved the fact that Shane loved being with her as much as she did him. And what's more, he was not ashamed of that fact that he cared so deeply for her and wanted to spend every waking moment with her. She had never met a man who was able to express his feelings so openly and so naturally. It was a rare gift, and Christina was thankful that she was the recipient of his expressions, especially after the emotionless state she had been trapped in during the past decade.

What seemed strange to her was the fact that Shane had admitted this was not his usual character. He had never been able to relate to another individual the way he did with her. As she pondered their situation on many occasions – daily, in fact – Christina had come to the conclusion that it was not that Shane had changed, but only her receptiveness to his feelings that allowed him to express himself.

That heart of gold he possessed had shown her the compassion he had for so many others during the course of the past month, both through his stories and Christina's own time with him. He loved being a friend to man, no matter how gruff he appeared. And she had learned, as she suspected many others had, that his bark was most definitely worse than his bite – or at least he didn't bite as often as everyone had feared.

Learning of his past, Christina knew that in prior times, he had to keep up a tight guard just to survive. And Shane had never been able to be up front with his wife because she could have been dangerous to him with her ever-running mouth. So, it was clear to see why he had been so private about everything.

Yet, Christina was not sure exactly why he chose to trust her – *except for those two basic needs*. Shane had obviously reached a point in his life where he desperately needed someone to whom he could unload a lot of past pain and strife. And even though she had never met any of his friends besides Mickey and one of his past lovers, Christina was sure there had never been anyone with her compassion and clear understanding, a person founded in God's love, in his life before. He was able to see and accept the gift of confidence that came under her professional auspices. Even though he was not her job, in this case she was grateful that it came in handy.

Christina did not care why he needed her companionship, she was just glad that he did. Her mornings had come to depend on hearing his voice to wake her, and seeing him before work to exchange hugs. This morning was no different.

"I'll take a shower and be right over."

"No. Come now. I can't wait to be with you and hold you."

Christina smiled again. She loved his impertinence. It was actually more of a need for her constant presence, and it made her feel even more special in his eyes.

"Okay. I'll be right there." Starting to hang up, she asked, "What is this strange power you have over me?"

"What is this strange power you have over *me*?" There was a brief pause while they both searched for an answer, then, "Just hurry up and get over here. I need you."

*Those magic words,* Christina thought as she hung up the phone and got dressed. *I'm so glad that he needs me as much as I do him. It would be terrible if this were a one-sided love affair.*

She didn't even think about which clothes to wear. Christina simply threw on the first T-shirt out of the drawer, and the first jeans she could reach in the closet. Her mind was lost in his last phrase to her. "I need you." The words kept playing over and over again until she pulled into his driveway.

Before she had a chance to ring the doorbell, Shane jerked the door open and hugged her with all his might. The vibrations that ran through her body as he held her so closely spoke loudly to Christina, telling her that there was no other man alive like this one. He held the keys to all the doors in her life. She took off her coat and laid it across the sofa as she sat with her feet tucked up under her.

Shane took one look at her, then blurted out, "That shirt has *got* to go."

"What?" she retreated, leaning back away from him, afraid that she had made a wrong decision in coming over to his place. She was no longer in her own safe haven, her own guarded territory. It was not like her to show up and get so comfortable in the home of some male.

Seeing the concern written all over her face, Shane could not help but cackle. "Baby, you should see your face. It's okay. I'm not ever going to attack you, or even take advantage of you." Then his devilish grin spread all over his face as he added, "That is, unless you *want* me to!"

Christina pursed her lips, gave him an evil eye, and told him, with her eyes, to get on with an explanation. She tried to look upset, but Shane saw straight through her, making him laugh even harder.

"But look at your shirt," he ordered.

"What about it?" she inquired, knowing she had not eaten, so she could not have spilled breakfast all over it, and trying to see what was so bothersome about her choice of dress.

"It says 'My next husband will be *normal*'?" he asked in a bewildered tone, reading the words printed on her shirt. "Christina, I am probably the most *abnormal* guy in the world!"

She chuckled at his response, not even thinking about the words on the shirt, yet taken aback by his suggestion that he would even be in the running for the next in line. "Oh, that. This only happens to be a shirt that Rachel gave me after the split with Tom. We needed something to laugh about at that point. Besides, the thought of me being able to survive spending all my time with some *normal* person was a joke in itself. What normal person could even stand the thought of me twenty-four hours a day?"

He listened, taking in her words thoughtfully. "Well, I'm glad you're not *too* serious about that statement."

Christina looked into his eyes, suspecting to see them still laughing, but instead, she saw a solemn straightforward expression that he was not prone to give her. "What gives you the idea that you would be the next one anyway?"

"What gives you the idea that I won't?" he flashed back at her, still unchanged in his serious expression. "Who better to take care of you?"

She didn't answer his question. Rather, she searched his face and his soul for a waiver in his responsiveness to the matter. For the first time since she had met him, Christina felt slightly threatened. Inside, there was nothing that she wanted any more than to be legally and officially tied to the character who sat across from her. But she had a no-hit record when it came to leaving guys once she sensed they were serious about her. She had failed to mention to him that she had gotten seven previous proposals, neither of them from her first two husbands. And she never bothered to see any of the suitors again after those fatal words.

But the point that really frightened Christina was her inward fear that she could not tell *this* man, "No." And she knew that she could run, but that she could never hide from him. He knew her too well. She was sure that he could track her to any part of the globe. Her gut feeling was that this was the only man on the face of the earth who truly *could* make her happy and totally satisfy her every longing. Yet her conscience still told her, "Beware!"

She sat there, sizing him up carefully. Gentle and sensitive. Genius and talented. Ornery and gruff. Witty and clever. But there was a missing link. A phrase of two descriptive adjectives that would not come to her. She could see the spaces in her mind. She could hear her brain trying to speak the words. But there was a blank that would not be filled. At least not right now.

Christina decided to drop the internal debate for the time being. She could finish that later, *without* his presence. "What are we doing today?"

Shane walked over to the table and picked up his musical score. "I've sketched out some sets for the play. Tell me what you think."

She leafed through the pages of rough drawings, drawn to scale, then looked back at him.

"Don't you like them?" he asked, taking her silence as a negative reaction.

The woman who had worked solo for thirty years shuffled through the papers again, shaking her head. "Like them? I *love* them. Shane, you've even got a collapsible rod that will really turn into a snake, pyrotechnic ideas for the burning bush, and chemical reactions for the river water turning into blood and back again."

"I've also got a killer idea for the parting of the waters, but I didn't have time to scribble those out this morning before you got here."

"You mean to tell me that you did all of this from the time you called me until I got here?"

"Well, I sat up with the script last night after I left your house, and then penciled out the sketches after I talked to you this morning." Shane still sensed a displeasure in her hesitation. "Christina, if they're not what you had in mind, please say so. It won't hurt my feelings. They're just my initial thoughts. We can fine tune them today. That way I can go ahead and get started with all the set construction."

She looked at him once more, trying to find the words to aptly express her surprise and appreciation of his talent. But, knowing she had to spend the day with him, Christina did not want her hellion to become too cocky. She was not up for the ridicule.

"Shane, these are *terrific*! Much better, in fact, than I had anticipated. Your talent is incredible, and I have *surely* met my match. This is going to be an *awesome* production – the best I have ever done. But there is one thing ..."

"What's that?" he asked, grabbing his pencil.

"Well, your idea about the parting waters. That's not so original. It was *already* a 'killer' plan!"

They smiled and hugged each other as they grabbed their jackets, the script, and the sketches, and took off to a "killer" breakfast.

# *16*

Two days later marked a four-week anniversary for the happy couple. A month was not long, yet much had transpired between the two of them in that short period. Both of them liked the direction in which their lives were moving, even though they each wondered if the magic would soon wear off and the other would go back to the path from which they had come. But for the time being, they were more than just content, sharing in the feelings that came so easily and naturally for them. They had decided to celebrate the next afternoon to mark the event.

It was a perfect Sunday afternoon. The weather was warm enough for people to be out in short sleeves. Shane had come over to Christina's house before church and started a Boston butt marinating so that he could cook his specialty on the grill for lunch. After church, he took off his jacket, rolled up his shirt sleeves and went into the kitchen to make his own recipe of sauce.

Noah watched the guy who had made his way into their lives, now standing in the kitchen of The Moses House as if he belonged there. Shane looked so natural being the man of the house. What amazed Christina's son most was the way the rebel seemed to *enjoy* taking care of things for them.

The child was especially appreciative for the gift this man had already given his mom – the gift of stopping to enjoy a leisurely afternoon. Noah had never seen his mother enjoy a Sunday afternoon in his entire life. There had always been rehearsals or meetings, any number of things to stress her and take her away from their family. To watch her sitting on the deck, in casual clothes with her feet propped up, sipping on an iced tea and chatting with Shane about mundane subjects, gave Noah a thrill he had never known.

Her son reveled in the fact that here stood a man who moved to the beat of his mother's drummer, a fact that, in itself, was quite a feat. Not only that, he was able to control Christina's free spirit without squelching it. In fact, the opposite, for Shane had shown her how to take time for herself, allowing her spirit to really roam and find fulfillment – an effort the Board of Ordained Ministry had made unsuccessfully her entire ministry. And he had taught her so much. He'd given this woman, who knew the world, a whole new perspective on life and its situations. The fact was, Noah, who had always thought of his mom as the most vibrant, compassionate and creative creature on the face of the earth, now saw in her an even greater sense of reaching out to others and using her imaginative ways in taking that to new heights. The redneck rebel who truly *did* seem to come from hell had met his match in a strong-willed female who had come from heaven and met him in the middle. What transpired with that union – the chemical chain reaction that erupted when their souls and wits met – was one that had made a change in both of them. In their own rights, Shane and Christina had been fighters before, but together, there was nothing that seemed out of their reach.

The teenager shook his head as he thought of the impact they could have on the world. He knew his mother was aware of her role in that Almighty plan, but he wondered if Shane even had a clue as to the dynamic task that lay before him. *Or, if he could* comprehend that, how he would go about the job of meeting the challenge. *Oh well,* reasoned Noah, *there's only one person out there who could help him through that, and he's got her right by his side.* The perceptive son also knew one other fact about his mother. *Now that he's got her, I just hope for his sake he knows how to keep her!*

Seeing the two of them together was such a welcome sight that the grateful son offered to clear away the dishes so that Shane and Christina could have the rest of the afternoon alone. Shane smoked his cigarette in silence, leaning over the rail, deep in thought. Not wanting to disturb him, Christina went inside to get a pad and pencil so she could write in the peaceful, quiet free time that was such a rarity for her.

As she came back out on the deck and started to sit down, Shane turned and grabbed her with a force to which she was unaccustomed from him. His hands caught her shoulders and wheeled her around until she was right in front of him, their bodies facing each other like a stand-off. Before Shane even spoke a word, she felt a fear for the words that were about to come as she saw the visible intensity in his eyes. She wondered what was wrong, and a tremble ran down her spine as she grew afraid that he was about to end their relationship. Christina had no idea how dependent she had become on him, nor how badly she wanted him until this very second. She did not even have time to utter a prayer before he opened his mouth.

"Christina, I *have* to talk to you. I am *very* angry with you."

She felt the walls within her innermost being come tumbling down. They had known each other for only a month. But that month had seemed like an eternity. Time had passed so slowly, giving them time to succor both the sweetness and the bitterness between their souls. Everything between them had turned to sweet nectar, just waiting to be devoured by the other.

And now, here Shane stood facing her, about to shatter her entire world. *How could one man have made this much of an impact on me in only a month? What IS this strange power he has over me?* Christina knew to expect the worse, for his eyes told all. Her mind began to race with reasons for his sudden change of heart about her. However, he abruptly ended all her thoughts as his husky voice began to speak, and he held onto her forearms, looking straight into her eyes.

"Christina, I have only known you for a month now. Four weeks. Four short weeks. And in those four weeks, you have *completely ruined* my reputation – one that took me years to build. *Years!* You just nonchalantly stroll into my life and it shatters, in ruins, to the ground." His serious expression changed to a grin that covered his entire face as he finished, shaking his head, "Yep, in four short weeks you've completely ruined my reputation."

"What ... no hells or damns? I really have made a change in you!"

They both lunged toward each other in unstoppable laughter, a laughter of joy and rejoicing. Even though Shane's threat was meant as a joke, they were both fully aware of the seriousness of his statement, and the weight that it carried.

When they were able to stop laughing and let go of each other for a second, he looked into her eyes again and said, "I told you that you ruined my reputation!"

"Well, I do hope that you're not *sorry*," she replied sternly, yet smiling because she knew the answer.

"Actually, no I'm not. It feels pretty good. In fact, *damn* good. I have *never* felt this good in my entire life."

"Hey, watch it now. There go those four-letter words again!"

"Sorry. I just couldn't resist. I didn't want you to get *too* much of a big head!"

And Shane pulled her into him again, giving her a hug full of adoration and love. Christina wanted to bask in that moment forever, for it said a world about their relationship. She was more than a companion, a female, a prospective lover. Much more. She was the *one* person who had ever made a difference in his life.

At that very instant, Christina was the happiest she had been in her entire life. Her fears of a few minutes ago had completely vanished, and she was feeling even stronger and more sure of their need for each other.

After the glow of his announcement wore down, Christina glared at Shane. "It's only fair, you know."

"What's only fair?" he asked, afraid of the answer he might get.

"Well, after all, you *have* completely deculturized me. Why shouldn't you be a changed person, too?"

Again, they held onto each other, even more aware of the power of the bond between them. Their hearts and souls truly had meshed. The feeling between them was without description, and they both realized the uniqueness of it, and the gift that they shared. They were not even able to explain exactly what they felt between them, except that it was, without a doubt, a blessing that could only have come from God. Thus, both of them expressed a gratefulness for the power of His divine intervention in their lives.

Shane stood leaning over the deck, cigarette in hand, again looking off into the distance. Christina could tell that he was battling with his thoughts, and she knew that whatever was controlling his mind had to do with a lot more than just her. He finally spoke, still looking into a place far away, "Christina, there really *is* one thing that bothers me about all this."

She could tell that he was entirely serious, and this was not like the conversation of a few minutes ago. "What is it?"

"It's just that ... well, I'm not complaining or anything, but ..." Shane turned his face toward her, then walked over to the chair beside her, sat down and took her hand. "Christina, I always thought that I would have a choice in who my life's partner was to be."

Christina hated the struggle he must be experiencing inside. She could hear from his words and his heart that he was perfectly content with their situation, but his head was still not used to a spiritual being, a Heavenly Father, making choices for him. And the rebellious side of Shane liked *that* no better than it had when his earthly father tried to tell him who he could spend his time with, or marry. She wanted him to be happy with her, and all of a sudden, she sensed and feared that she had become an obstacle to his freedom. As she opened her mouth to speak, he started again, trying to explain away his distress.

"I really do love you, baby. More than I've ever loved anyone. And I know that you are the best thing in life for me. This is all so new to me. I have never allowed anyone *completely* in my life, and now all of a sudden, there's a woman who seems to know more about me than I know myself, and I have feelings and sensations that I've *never* had before, and we are so connected in every way that I literally feel like you are attached to me at times. Christina, I'm not sure I can take all of this. I have never been happier, but this has all happened so fast, like my own thoughts and wishes don't even exist anymore, like they've been taken over by some 'thing' that I can't see, or even explain." Shane was holding her hand, trying to make sure she understood, when he did not even understand himself. He paused, looking at her, hoping she could make some sense of it for him.

Although she had no prophetic words for him, Christina tried to let him know this was a new experience for her, also. "Shane, I've been married twice. Twice I married someone whom I thought that I loved – that I loved with my whole being. And twice I've been divorced, knowing that God was not in those marriages, even though I thought I had made a wise decision both times. However, I would have stayed in the last marriage forever, knowing what a severe mistake it was, just to save face and protect my image. Had Tom not left, I would still be in that miserable, intolerable condition.

Having someone appear in my life, someone who it seems is supposed to be in everything I do, is quite abnormal for me, too. You must understand that even though I have *always* been close to God, He does not usually send me such astounding messages about whom I am supposed to be with, *or marry*. Otherwise, I wouldn't be twice-divorced. No offense, dearest, but if I had been going out to hunt a partner for myself, it would not have been you, anymore than you would have chosen me. It just seems pretty obvious to me that my Father did seem to choose us for each other, and I've got more sense than to argue with Him. Besides, I'm not unhappy with the choice He made for me."

"Christina, please don't think that I am, either. It's just that this is so far beyond me, my lifestyle, what I'm used to. I want you more than anything in the world, and I would love nothing better than to spend my entire life with you. But I do wish I could have had *some* small say in it. You know me. I'm not used to *anybody* telling me what to do."

She honestly did understand his dilemma – much better, in fact, than Shane himself. But Christina knew this was another of his battles that he was going to have to tackle for himself. Early into their relationship, she drew the line at making decisions for him.

They sat there holding hands, looking at each other, wondering which turn in their paths to take next. Neither of them wanted to lose what they had, yet Christina could tell that the struggle within the man who had changed her entire life revolved around another female – one who was conducive to his past lifestyle, one in whose presence he felt at home, and one who did not always expect him to be 'on his toes' or do his best. And one who could, *and would*, give him the one thing she could not.

Their trivial conversation turned to hopes and dreams for their futures, which ultimately wound up with them together. It seemed that no matter which path they wanted to take, or in which direction they wanted to venture, each realized the importance of the other for reaching that end. Their work, their personal lives, their interests – they *all* seemed to involve *both* Shane and Christina to be successful.

After a lengthy chat curing the problems of the world, or at least *their* world, Shane leaned back in the chair with his boots propped up on the rail, while Christina laid back in her chair, looking past the blue sky, daydreaming of nothing, yet everything. Noah watched as the two of them had retreated into their own worlds, yet were still connected by the holding of their hands.

It seemed a perfect sight. The one thing he had laughed about at Christina's projections for her old age was that she wanted a man with whom she could sit on the front porch and hold hands, reclined in their rockers, and sleep the afternoon away. The vision in front of him made him wonder if his mother had actually found that man. Noah chuckled to himself, glad for this period in his mom's life, no matter whether it lasted past tomorrow, or an eternity.

He went upstairs to get his skateboard, and as he started out the front door, he took one last look at the winsome couple. The words to a song he'd heard Shane singing along with the radio last night ran through his head.

As he ollied off the steps and made his way down the sidewalk, Noah sang about green grass, rocking chairs, peaceful rivers, and blessings of the Good Lord. And he hummed the finishing bars of the song, cruising down the street, with the wind blowing through his shoulder-length locks of blonde.

# 17

For the third weekend in a row, Shane got a chance to see his son. This time, Christina and Noah went to get the child so that they could be back on Friday in time to pick up Shane at work. Shay became the immediate center of attention as his father came out to greet him, whisked him up off his feet, and carried him inside the place to introduce his co-workers to the apple of his eye.

Watching the two of them embrace always touched her heart in a way that seeing her own children with their father never had. She knew that it was because this rebel who had somehow wandered into her life had missed years, literally years, with his son due to his habits of the past. And now, here stood a father, trying with everything inside him, to make up all of that lost time to a child who, in spite of Shane's past weaknesses, worshipped the ground on which his father walked.

Christina knew how desperately the child needed some quality time with his father, so after picking up a pizza on the way home, and eating dinner as a foursome, Christina and Noah left The Moses House, giving Shane and Shay an opportunity to play, talk, wrestle, or do whatever struck their fancy.

When they returned in a few hours, it was obvious her idea had been a success. The love and excitement in the eyes of both Shane and Shay told Christina that she had done the right thing by going after the child, no matter if it did take six hours out of her weekend. She began to see that God had brought an angel and a rebel together for a lot more reasons than one. They were both getting many opportunities to be instruments. The angel had no concept of how the rebel felt about their roles, but the satisfaction inside her, both for herself and for him, at being chosen to do God's work, gave her a warmth inside that far surpassed those glows she usually felt after knowing she had been part of a plan.

Shay came running to show her the new baseball cards and book that his dad had given him. Shane's face was covered with a smug, yet humble, smile that gave her all the thanks she needed for her efforts in this operation.

Knowing the child had never been to an amusement park, Christina used one of her many resources to get them free tickets for Carowinds, where they were going to spend the next day with the Howell's. She pulled the tickets out of her pocket, holding them up in front of the male duo.

"Look what I just happened to find."

Shay's eyes sparkled as he jerked the tickets from her hand and held them up in his dad's face. Shane looked at his female counterpart with his own eyes questioning, *How did you manage to pull that one off?* But then, looking at her smile, retreated with, *Never mind!* He walked around his son and placed his hand on her arm, reached down to kiss her appreciatively as he whispered in her ear, "Thank you, baby. You really are an angel."

She would have loved nothing better than to whisper back to him in a sultry voice, "You're welcome. You can thank me properly after you son goes to bed." But before her conscience even had time to reprimand her for her thoughts, Christina heard a small voice.

"Thanks, Christina. You really are an angel. Will you ride the first roller coaster with me?"

Rearing his head back in a raucous laugh, Noah answered for her. "Mom doesn't *do* roller coasters."

Shane pulled her body against his, looking straight down into her eyes. "She will with me." Her laughter diminished instantly as she returned the stare of the man who had the tiger hold on her. Seeing the apprehension in Christina's eyes, he ran his hand down her hair. "Do you think I'm going to let any thing happen to you, baby?"

Trust that Christina saw in his eyes was mirrored back to Shane as she replied, "No."

The look in her face and eyes was one that Shane had never seen, even on her. There was a love, a trust, a respect that told him she truly would give him twenty-five years to share with her. Realizing the light mood from Christina's entrance had been thrown into an ambience that neither of them was ready, or able, to face yet, he broke the seriousness. "So what's the problem, then?"

Christina answered him, appreciative of the fact that he had enough foresight to change the direction of their emotions, "Only that you'll have to hold onto me the entire time."

The playful sparkle was back in Shane's eyes. "Gladly, baby, gladly!" He hugged his son firmly, yet lovingly, as he added, "Maybe *I'm* the one who should be thanking her for the tickets," and grinned back at Christina.

Shay laughed, then pulled Christina, who was already holding onto Noah, into their hug. The foursome stood there, huddled in an embrace, but united more firmly by the love, respect and appreciation that radiated through all of them, each for the other. Neither of the adults wanted to stop the feeling in the room, but Shane, for the first time since he had known his angel, felt an uneasiness that alarmed him.

"I hate to break up this solemn party, but if we're going to get an early start in the morning, I'd better be leaving."

Noah, fully understanding the need for a father-son bond between the two guests, turned to Christina. "Mom, why does Shane have to leave? He doesn't get enough time with Shay as it is, and it seems unfair for them to have to be separated when they can be together."

Christina inwardly had the same regret, but she knew better than to question the situation. Shane became the authoritative figure, wishing to save his love from being placed in an awkward position. "Noah, I appreciate your concern, but this is a small community. Your mother has a reputation to uphold, and I don't intend to endanger it."

"But it's not like we don't have four bedrooms. And mother has always opened up her home to people in need. The choir is forevermore kidding her about her 'Home for Wayward Kids.'"

"Maybe so, but the key word in that statement is 'kids.' And I'm not quite a kid."

"Yes, but the other key word is 'wayward,' and I'll guarantee you that you'd certainly be the most wayward houseguest she'd ever had," argued the teenager.

Christina and Shane both howled at her son's quick wit and insight, knowing the boy had said more than a mouthful.

"Okay, I'll have to give you that one," Shane responded, still laughing.

"Yeah, Dad. Why do you have to go? I want you to stay here with me," Shay added.

Christina felt even more guilty, hearing the young son long for his father's presence. The tug at her heartstrings was nearly unbearable. Shane hated watching the struggle he saw going on inside her.

"Look guys. Christina is a lady. She is a minister. She is ..." Even the guy who had verbally manipulated his way through lots

260

of dangerous situations was at a loss for words.

Now it was Christina's turn to defuse the mounting conflict. "What he's trying to say is that people in the church would not understand if Shane stayed here. They would get the wrong idea, and the whole community would be bouncing with ugly rumors."

"That's their problem, Mom!"

It was obvious that Noah was not going to give up. His May birthday, the very day after his mother's, made him just as much of a stubborn bull-headed Taurus as she was.

"I've got a great idea." Christina's brief diversion had given Shane just enough time to come up with an alternate plan, one that he hoped would go over with the boys. "How about if we borrow a sleeping bag from Noah, son, and you can camp out on the floor beside the sofa where I sleep at my place?" he urged, remembering how much the young boy had loved their outdoor expeditions from years earlier.

None of them was overly excited about the idea, but it did satisfy the child enough, knowing that he would at least be with his dad. The foursome said their good-byes, excited about all the fun that awaited them the next day.

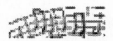

The minute he got Shay down for the night, Shane called Christina. "I'm sorry for the hounding you got before we left."

"Forget it. It really didn't bother me." But Christina stopped the statement, and thought for a minute. "No. That's not true. It bothers me terribly, Shane. Noah is right. He is *exactly* right. Were you anyone else, my door would be open to you. You would be right here, either sharing a spacious room with your son, or sleeping next door to him. But because of people and their small minds,

261

your son is sleeping in a sleeping bag on the floor, and you're on a sleeper sofa."

"Christina, don't do this to yourself. That is exactly why I called. This is exactly what I *don't* want you to do. Quit pounding yourself."

"But, it's just not fair."

As she took another breath to keep up her debate, Shane broke in.

"Baby, we're fine. Really. Shay looks at this as if he is camping out. I told him that as soon as it gets a little warmer, we'll be doing this outside in my tent. He was thrilled. Besides, we're guys – you know, the rough and tough sex."

"Look, tough guy, let's not bring sex into this."

Shane nearly died laughing, knowing the humiliation that was already spreading all over the face of the party on the other end. "Oh, but let's do," knowing he could not turn down that opportunity.

Christina was already laughing before he finished the words, knowing full well that she had left herself wide open for that one, and nothing she could do was going to stop his taunts. There was nothing she could do but to grin and bear it, which she admitted to Shane.

"Bear it? *Bare* it? Oh, baby. Now you're really talking. I'll be right over." Shane could just imagine his verbal opponent shaking her head, not knowing what to say next.

"Okay, Mr. Smarty. You win this round. Keep this up, and I won't ride *anything* with you tomorrow," figuring that would stop the game and shut him up.

"Yeah, right. You know you're looking forward to tomorrow just as much as I am. Remember, you've already told me that I have to hold onto you the entire time." Shane could hear the exasperated groan on the other end of the phone, knowing she was ready to give up and accept her loss. "Okay, baby, I'll stop. Besides, you need to get some sleep before in the morning. You're going to have a full day tomorrow."

"Great! I can hardly wait."

But Shane knew that she was the one teasing this time. He loved the way they were able to laugh and joke, even when inside, both of them knew their attraction was getting harder and harder to take as a laughing matter. The need, the love, and the desire between them was growing, and he wondered how much longer they could fight that battle. It would not be too much longer before it would be staring them in the face.

"Good night, sweetheart. Pleasant dreams. And I promise to play fair next time."

"Goodnight."

Shane could hear her sighing smile through the receiver. She truly *was* an angel to him. Christina was, hands down, the best thing that had *ever* happened to him. But he knew that he would never let her image be tarnished, especially on his account, even if that meant he had to give her up.

He lay down beside his son, thinking of what it would be like to have a family, *a real family*, with the closeness that he had shared with Christina and Noah only an hour ago. He thought of what it would be like for his son to have a mother, *a real mother*, who would hug him and praise him and spend time doing things with him and for him. He wondered what it would be like to have a wife, *a real wife*, who would give herself to him openly and completely, saving herself only for him. He dreamed of having a woman, *a real woman*, stand beside him, believing in him, holding his hand, helping him, strengthening him, encouraging him, smiling and laughing with him . . .

Christina sat down with Noah, who was still agitated by the

closed concepts of small-minded people. She tried to explain, without being critical or judgmental, in a way that would satisfy her son. *Bless his heart. He did have to be born with my open-mindedness.* She prayed for the right words to come to her that would not squelch his own wonderment and honesty about things.

"Noah, I'm so very grateful that you've inherited my sense of humanity. In my opinion, that is one of your greatest assets, although it will be the source of much criticism for you. I'm just thankful that you're even more strong-willed than I am, and that you don't care what others think, but only do what you feel, with your heart and soul, is right. You have more backbone than I do, and that's a good thing, although many would disagree with me."

"Mother, you have more backbone than anyone I know. You've *always* stood up for what you believed, and you've taught Matt and me to do the same. Why else do you think Matt has had so much trouble fitting in at times? It's just that he tends to worry about what others think, and I don't. I really *don't* give a flip about what people think of me."

She sighed, knowing this was tougher on both of them than she had thought. "Noah, you of all people know how much faith I have, and how much I believe in doing what is right. Most people, especially in this community, have not lived through the conflicts that you and I have, thus they cannot conceive the things that have shaped our thinking. But regardless of whether I agree with them, or they with me, they *do* pay my salary, and if I want to do my best job, I am somewhat ruled by their thoughts and beliefs."

"Then maybe it is time for you to get out of that line of work!"

Noah was merely voicing what Christina had been thinking much of the time herself lately. She'd felt farther and farther removed from the people and the job that she loved, not because she no longer cared, or that she even cared less, but because she could feel a prayer, a prayer she had prayed since she had been

Noah's age, being answered. A prayer that she could move outside the four walls of the church building. A prayer that she could reach out to others with whom the church folk refused to associate. A prayer that she could always be an instrument, even when her feeble hands could no longer make music. A prayer that she could follow in the path that was meant to be hers, and only hers. But a prayer that, in being answered, was going to pull her away from her family and friends whom she loved so dearly. A prayer that was going to change her entire line of work. A prayer that was going to change her direction. But a prayer that would certainly not leave her standing still, or spinning her wheels.

"I've been thinking that same thing lately, Noah."

The young man looked at his mother in amazement. Even though he fully meant the words he had just uttered, Noah knew how much Christina loved her job, her co-workers, and her friends that had been her family. He never suspected that there was any way she would leave her place of employment, much less her beloved profession.

Waiting for an explanation that did not come, Noah, almost fearfully, questioned, "What exactly do you mean, Mom?"

"I feel pulled in a very different direction, son. My job just isn't the same anymore. It isn't that I don't still love it. It just isn't enough anymore. There is something lacking. Something very significant. Something that I think I can identify, but that I am afraid to admit until I have the final word from the Lord."

Noah was always amused at the way his mom referred to God as if He were her big boss. But then, he always knew that to Christina, He *was* the Big Boss. Because he knew that so well, he was not even concerned about the words coming from his mother's lips.

Christina finished, "Something that makes my skin feel like it doesn't quite fit right anymore."

The teenager saw that his mother had her own personal battle

265

going on right now, and didn't need any more anguish from him, so he dropped the subject, praying that God would soon give Christina the answer for which she was waiting. He had long since learned from her not to pray for the specific outcome of that answer.

"We'd better get to bed, Mom. I can't *wait* to see you on all the rides tomorrow."

"Thanks!" she replied in her best 'I can hardly wait' voice.

She and Noah walked upstairs, silently, but arm in arm. Christina gave her son a goodnight hug and started to move on to her own room. Noah looked at the clothes on his bed that the two of them had found in his favorite thrift and consignment shops that evening while they were out shopping.

"Mom?"

"Yes, honey?"

"You know that joke you always hear as a child about how 'your mom dresses you funny'?"

"Yes."

"Well, you *do* know that they were thinking of you when they came up with that joke!"

Christina laughed uncontrollably, sitting down on Noah's bed and giving him a big hug. "Noah, what would I *ever* do without you?"

"Well, one thing's for sure. You *certainly* wouldn't have as much fun."

"No, I wouldn't," she muttered, as she walked out the door. Christina took a couple of steps back and added, "But you know you love dressing funny."

"Yes, I do! I can't *wait* to wear this cool fifties tuxedo to school next week. Now I just have to find some Buddy Holly glasses."

The proud mom grinned to herself. *Oh dear, a little TOO much of a chip off the old block!* Christina thought as she made her way around the circular hallway to her bedroom.

She lay in bed agonizing all the stomach churning that lay in store for her the next day. Her thoughts rambled with the tossing and turning that her own roller-coaster life had taken the past few years. Christina fell asleep lulled by the gentleness of the carousel horses, as she imagined what it would be like to have a man like Shane to walk with her, talk with her, laugh with her, hold her every night, listen to her dreams, share his own hopes . . .

The foursome met the Howells bright and early the next morning at the front entrance of the amusement park. Christina and Abigail talked the men into stopping for a photo shoot as they walked down the main thoroughfare. Considering there were three families in the picture, it turned out exceptionally well. Well enough that they bought three copies so that each of them could have one to remember the day.

Abigail was the first to notice that each of them had been holding on to another one of the group, so that they were all connected. She was so ecstatic at the thought that Christina finally had a mate and that all of their families were a unit, that her day was perfect from the word "go."

Even though the trip to Carowinds was intended to be a special treat for Shay, it was Christina, who had not ridden a roller coaster in over twenty years, who turned out to be the heroine of the day. With a little encouragement from Shane and Noah, she rode every ride there was to ride, and even chanced one roller coaster twice, backwards the second time.

Paul was the one to notice how inseparable Shane and Christina seemed to be. When they were not holding onto each other, their eyes followed each other, glued to every action. He had never seen her so contented or excited, nor him so active and involved.

Whatever had clicked and was going on between the two of them apparently worked, to the point that even *his* fears for his son's godmother were calmed. Abigail loved being able to say, "See, I told you so!"

On the way out of the gate, after hours of non-stop fun and excitement, with Christina carrying a stuffed animal which Shane had won for her, and Shay carrying a Tarheel basketball that Noah had won for him, everyone rehashed their favorite part of the day. Shane turned to Paul and Abigail, who were amazed he had gotten Christina to be an active participant on all the thrill-seeker rides, and jeered, "I had Christina turned every way but broke down like a shotgun!"

They all howled, as Christina rebuked, "Great, I can hardly wait to tell the choir *that* tomorrow! I'm sure that comment will get *plenty* of raised eyebrows."

On the way home, Shane instructed Christina to take an exit. "Why?"

"Just do it and don't ask questions."

She knew he could not be taking her anywhere too outrageous because Noah and Shay were with them. After following Shane's directions for nearly thirty minutes, Christina came to a narrow lane that appeared to lead to nowhere.

"Where are we going?" she finally asked, knowing they had to be on a dead-end street.

"Right here," Shane answered, as they rounded a curve saw a restaurant. "You missed your weekly seafood fix because of me, so I wanted to fix it."

"Shane," she whimpered, touched beyond words. "You didn't have to do this."

"I know I didn't have to, but God didn't *have* to throw you in my path, and you didn't *have* to listen to Him."

Christina chuckled and replied, "Oh yes I did. He *always* gets the last word!" with her eyes looking very pointedly at him.

"Is that a hint or a warning, angel?"

"Both!" The tone in her voice told him to drop it because he stood no chance in this match.

# *18*

At first, not many people paid any attention to Shane making his way to the Choir Room to meet Christina every Sunday after the service. But by the sixth week, heads were turning and eyes were questioning, especially when he became a presence before the service began, bringing in her music, or one of the children's choirs, or taking care of something else for her so that she could concentrate on the worship service. Then, when his seat in the sanctuary changed to the front side pew so that she could sit with him, the choir, as well as the entire congregation, knew this was more than a passing friendship.

Everyone had begun to notice the way they looked at each other. And for the life of them, they could not see any attraction there could possibly be between two such unlikely individuals, yet they could not deny the obvious love that the couple shared. Shane and Christina knew that in this small community, their every move would be the topic of gossip. But neither of them had anything to hide, and they enjoyed each other's company so thoroughly, that they were oblivious to the sideways glances and questioning comments. Besides, the fact remained that neither of them had ever been too overly concerned about another person's disapproval for what they believed was right, or was for a just cause.

What really surprised the couple was when little old ladies would walk past the two of them after a service and squeeze one of their arms, or take both their hands and shake or pat them, or hug them and say nothing. Christina's favorite occurrence was the one elderly lady who pulled her aside and whispered, "I understand."

Shane was blown away by the sudden acceptance he got from everyone, especially people who acted as though he had never even existed before. As badly as he hated that his newly found attention probably had more to do with Christina than himself, she continued to try to convince him that it *was* him, his efforts and his achievements. "You *are* doing this on your own," she would constantly remind him. For whatever reason, the rebel cowboy had to admit that the life he now enjoyed was incomparable to anything he had ever known. He liked the rewards that came with hanging around Christina. It made him *someone*.

"No, Shane. You make *yourself* someone. I don't do anything," the petite female would say, with a tone that told him the discussion was closed.

Each Sunday brought a new and different experience for the couple, even though one had spent practically her entire life in church, while the other had been running uncontrollably away from it for the past twenty years. The services only tended to bring them closer together as Christina found a way to involve Shane in each of them. His greatest gratification came unexpectedly, though, on the following Sunday.

Noah had outdone himself on a solo that morning and after the service, the choir members were congratulating him on his talent.

Christina had already noticed Tom loitering around the choir room, and she knew what was going to happen next. She already dreaded the humiliation for her son. As she stood looking down at the piano, pretending she was unaware of her ex's presence, she followed his every move out of the corner of her eye.

*That's it!* she told herself adamantly. *He will not lay a hand on my son again. I'm the one who married this guy and dragged him into my son's life. Now it is time for me to get him OUT of Noah's life.* Christina's mind was made up. She waited patiently, yet anxiously, like a bird preparing to swoop down upon its prey, watching carefully for exactly the right moment.

The teenager made his way toward the piano to see if his mom was ready to leave. Christina saw Tom follow the child's footsteps toward her direction. She was ready to make her move and take whatever abuse ensued as a result of her action. As she caught sight of Tom's hand raising up behind Noah's head, she heard a quiet but commanding voice begin to speak just as she saw an arm appear out of nowhere and grab Tom's hand in mid-air.

"The kid ain't a dog, so don't pat him on the head like he *is* when he's good, or kick him when he's bad," the voice rattled.

Christina caught the look of surprise on her son's face, accompanied by a beam of tremendous satisfaction. They had both been so intimidated by Tom that neither of them heard Shane's footsteps as he entered the room. She turned to see Tom's face in time to see him moving backwards toward the exit. All eyes were on him as he headed out the door, head bowed, and uttered, "I guess I'll be seeing you."

Not a word was spoken, but Shane turned and saw that Tom had left his music behind. Shane picked up the music and got as far as the choir room door when they heard footsteps coming back in the building. The rebel stopped at the door, reached out his hand and asked in a simple manner, "Forget something?"

Tom gingerly removed the music from Shane's hand and

retreated as quickly as possible with oversized steps without even a good-bye. The trio could barely hold their laughter until they heard the outside door shut.

Noah was the first to speak. "Thanks, Chucky baby, but you almost missed your cue."

"Huh?" Shane quizzed him.

"That was about too close for comfort."

"Didn't I promise you that he'd never pat you on the head again?"

"Yes."

"Did he pat you on the head?"

"No."

"So, what's the problem?" Shane teased, as he turned to Christina and gave her one of his winks.

Noah realized how wonderful this man's presence was in all of their lives. But he was not about to let Shane get too much of a big head, so he walked out the door, shaking his head. Christina and Shane followed him, the rebel's arm around his angel's shoulder.

"What was that you called me back there?" Shane forwarded to Noah.

"What? Chucky baby?"

"Yeah. Just exactly what is that supposed to mean?"

Christina had caught Noah's reference right off the bat, but she was going to let her son have the pleasure of clueing Shane in on its hidden meaning.

"Well, it's like this, Shane. Not only do you *look* like Chuck Norris, but you also come in and *kick it* like Chuck."

The mother was relieved for her son's choice, or lack, of words in his explanation. And she was also grateful for the fact that her hellion, who feared no mortal man, actually *had* strolled in and saved the day. Christina knew what could have happened had she confronted Tom, for she had been down that road too many times in the past. Now that it was obvious there was a man who not only cared about her and her son, but was willing to take care of them, she breathed a little easier knowing that one stress point of her life had finally been alleviated. The three of them all sensed that Tom was no longer a part of their life.

Christina slipped in the car and leaned over to kiss Shane. "Thanks!" she whispered.

"Baby, as long as I'm alive, no matter what we are to each other, *no one* is ever going to hurt you or lay a hand on you," and Shane glanced in the back seat at Noah, *"or your sons*, again." And for the first time in over a decade, she felt security.

Shane not only showed up for all the services, dinners and programs, but stayed until Christina had taken care of every detail afterwards. Everyone was not only surprised at his willingness to stand around and help her with the numerous mundane chores of pulling off the special programs, but at his expertise and ability to take charge and get the job done. No one expected what they were seeing out of the "dumb redneck."

On Easter Sunday, she had been asked to find two men to help children place flowers from their yards on a large cross constructed inside the sanctuary. Christina surmised that Shane and Mickey would be perfect for the job. She could see the disdain on Elwood's face at her suggestion, to which she replied, "They're perfect. Kind of like the two thieves."

No one could argue with her point, so on the biggest, most-attended Sunday of the year, the two outcasts stood at the front of the sanctuary, greeting everyone who came in the door, holding up every child, and setting center stage for the opening event of the service. And that was only after Shane brought breakfast for all of

Christina's choirs and brass musicians to start the day.

Shay had come to stay with Christina for the weekend and all of Easter break so that the father and son could have some *real* quality time together. They went out to an exotic restaurant every evening, only to be interrupted by Carla and her phone calls. Shane never bothered to tell her that they were in the middle of dinner and that he would get back to her, feeling bad about her constant badgering that came with a whining voice of insecurity. Christina hated the fact that they were never alone anymore, but knew she would have reacted the same way for a hurting friend, especially one who was not stable enough to handle any type of rejection.

When Friday came, they replayed the events of the past week: all the dinners with Noah and Shay, dyeing Easter eggs with Phantom masks, Grateful Dead bears, and psychedelic and tie-dyed colors, working the puzzles and playing with all the toys from the boys' Easter baskets, and, of course, all the marshmallow bunnies and coconut eggs. Christina thought back about Kevin coming over with his own children, then taking Shane out because he was so determined to find her an Easter present. No one had ever gone to so much trouble to find her the perfect gift. When she unwrapped the hummingbird feeder Shane brought her, Noah caught her tears on camera. They had even gotten pictures of their week as a family, something that was a first for both Shane and Christina.

They were sitting in the breakfast area, looking out into the backyard where Shay and Noah were swinging in the hammock. As Shane turned his head to speak to Christina, he got a glimpse of something that had bothered him from the first time he saw it, or rather, tripped over, on that first night they were practicing dance steps. He took her hands in his, and told her that it was time to lose the "Clueless" rock and its ghastly memories of Tom.

"Christina, I am ready to board our proverbial train and leave with you. *But,* you've *got* to throw that excess baggage off the back. It cannot go with us. And I cannot abide it."

She sat looking at him, knowing he was right. That rock seemed to have much of her life attached to it, thirteen years' worth, in fact. It was going to be difficult to part with it, especially since it had been a gift from Abigail and Rachel. Her mind visualized the Valentine's Day they had given it to her.

"Here," Rachel had said as Christina pulled it out of its brown paper bag wrapping, "you can hit it, kick it, even set a match to it, any time you have a bad memory of Tom."

When Christina saw the word "Clueless" engraved in the rock, she nearly dropped it from laughing so hard. The three of them had laughed, cried, and talked, way into the wee hours of the next morning – a special Valentine present they all knew was desperately needed to help her weather another lonely day for lovers.

*Yes, the Clueless rock has served its purpose. It is most definitely time to close that book and start another.*

"Okay, big boy. You've got yourself a deal. But what are we going to do with it?"

"How about we take it with us Sunday night, and after we take Shay home, we pitch it over the side of the mountain at Little Switzerland."

Christina thought for a moment. "I think that I would really like that. It seems the perfect spot for one life to end, and another to begin." She felt at ease with her decision, knowing Abigail and Rachel would not be upset that she was ridding herself of their gift, but excited that she was finally moving past it.

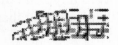

Shane spent the entire trip up the mountain writing on pieces of paper all of the scars he had seen and heard about from Christina, Matt and Noah of their treacherous years with Tom. He read each one aloud, then asked her if there were any that he had omitted. She listed the few that he had missed, struggling with the memory behind them. When all of the tortures had been named, he pulled out a roll of packaging tape strong enough to adhere to the stone's surface, and stuck the papers to it.

When they arrived at Little Switzerland, Shane had to lift the heavy rock into Christina's arms. He helped her raise it up far enough that she could give it a decent toss, then let go of her, allowing the victim to have the sole privilege of throwing the rock with the hell literally attached to it, out of her life. She mustered every ounce of gusto she could as she heaved the weighty object out into the night air. They heard it hit chunks of rock on the way down the mountain, then disintegrate into what sounded like hundreds of fragments, as it hit bottom.

He left her standing there alone until she finally moved again, allowing Christina time to cope with the ripples of all the aftershocks of emotions that accompanied her excruciating effort of release. Shane watched her silhouette under the night sky as she appeared to gain strength and composure with each second that passed. She truly was the strongest woman he had ever met, and as he continued to gaze upon her stoicism, her stance resembling a statue, undaunted by the *real* crushing blow that had just happened in her life, it dawned on him that he knew few males who could even compete with the tenacity of this creature.

*Good things truly do come in small packages*, he thought as he stepped quietly toward her. Christina looked over her shoulder, beckoning Shane with her eyes to join her. He placed his brawny hands on her shoulders, and she reached up and placed hers on top of his. The two of them continued to stand there, silent for a short while, until she finally turned to face him with a huge smile all over her face that broke into laughter. Laughter that took the place of tears as she jumped up into his arms. He caught her in mid-air as she clung to him, wrapping her arms securely around his neck with a force that indicated she would never let go.

They still uttered no words as the clash echoed through the hills, then through their minds, signaling them that a major barrier had finally been broken with that symbolic sacrifice. A sacrifice that should have been easy to make, but that had been one of the hardest to make in Christina's life.

When she finally reached up and kissed him, Shane whispered, "I'm so proud of you."

"I'm proud of me, too," she murmured, with the first tears of the evening. The tears were short-lived as Christina took Shane's hand and led him back to the Blazer, which at the moment felt more like a purple party wagon.

There was no place still open for the two of them to celebrate, but the victory that ran through their veins was celebration enough. Shane felt, for the first time, that Christina was his, *all his. Well, almost! At least, I don't have to worry about the Other Man.* Nothing could stop them now from the wonderful life she had been painting in his mind ever since the day they had met.

# 19

The next weekend proved to be one of the most memorable ones in the lives of both Shane and Christina, and also a turning point in their relationship. When he called her before he left to go to work on Friday, she informed him that she had a surprise for him when he got home.

While she was packing to go on their overnight excursion, Christina replayed her conversation with Abigail, from the day before, over and over, trying to convince herself that she was not making a mistake, or entering forbidden territory.

"Abigail, I want to take Shane to my hideaway in the mountains. He's working and trying so hard to correct all the mistakes of his life. For one thing, I think he deserves a reward for his efforts, and for another, I want to share my sacred spot with him. I want to see if it speaks to him the way it does to me. We've come remarkably far in the past few weeks, and before I can go any farther in this relationship, before I can continue in this path, I have to know whether or not his heart really beats like mine."

The trusted friend knew exactly what Christina meant with those words. How often had she heard her make reference to John

Wesley's words, "If your heart beats as my heart, give me your hand." Abigail also knew that to Christina, love took on a depth that was probably foreign to most people. And she knew that for her friend to truly know whether the fascination between herself and Shane was moving into that four-letter territory, she *had* to find out how close he was, or could become, to her God. Lastly, she knew that her beliefs, combined with an unsuccessful past of marriage sacraments, ruled the boundaries of any relationship.

Abigail had seen the love written in the eyes and all over the faces of both Shane and Christina, but she knew that each of them had come to the table with a lonely heart, a concern for unpremeditated foul play. But she had watched their love grow, and she had watched the one factor that had controlled that growth. It was her encouragement that sealed Christina's plan with approval.

"Christina, you know what's in your heart. No one else can answer that for you."

"Maybe not, but they can sure criticize without having all of the facts."

"This is your life. You're the *only* person who can know what's right or wrong for you."

"Again, you're right. But how many of those people would have left me in that life of misery with Tom, even if they'd known how bad and abusive it was for all of us?"

"Precisely my point," argued Abigail. "They weren't in your shoes, they had no clue as to what was going on, and they had no grounds on which to make a judgment."

"Right again. But if they find out that I've gone away for the weekend with Shane, they'll think they have *plenty* of grounds to judge."

"You cannot go through your entire life worrying about other people. Besides, that's not like you anyway."

"No, it isn't. And that's what bothers me about this whole thing. If I were going away for the weekend with you or Rachel, no one would say a word. And granted, Shane is *very* different from either of you, but the point is that I do not intend to abuse our friendship, or take it farther than it needs to go right now."

"Christina, you're both responsible adults. You both have minds and are *quite* capable of using them. You have to trust that you'll both make the right decisions about your behavior."

"I'm not worried about that." Christina hesitated, then got to the real root of the problem. "Abigail, do you want to know what really bothers me about this whole thing? If I were anybody else, or were in any other line of work, no one would care where I went, or with whom I went. In fact, they wouldn't even realize I was gone. *But*, simply because of who and what I am, they judge me differently from others. I know the commitment that goes with my calling. I've known that for thirty years now – in fact, longer, for I went into this career with my eyes wide open. And I also know how devout I am in that calling. *And*, I know that I *am not* like everybody else."

"Then go and have a good time, and don't think about it again. You've already answered your question, and *you* are the only one who needs an answer! He already knows what's in your heart."

As Christina threw her belongings into an overnight bag, it dawned on her exactly how excited she was. It had been years since she had gone on a trip with a friend. *A friend.* She had been on the usual choir trips and retreats, but to be away with one person – one single solitary person – was a treat in itself. She was beside herself with the attention Shane and she would be able to devote to each other. No children, no job, no nothing. Just themselves, the wide open space, and their Father.

That afternoon, when Paul dropped Shane off at Christina's

281

house, she was waiting in the driveway beside the Blazer.

"Hop in," she said, greeting him with a big hug and kiss as he got out of one vehicle and into another.

"What gives?" he asked, figuring she had plans for an exciting dinner.

"Here. Read this," she replied, handing him a small piece of paper folded in half.

Shane opened the note which read:

*To my Sundance,*

> *You are my sun and my moon and my stars. I am looking forward to a wonderful weekend with you. I love you.*

"Don't ask questions. Just sit back, relax and have a good time," she directed him as he turned to ask where they were going. And she reached into a cooler on the back floorboard and handed him a cold soda.

"What, no beer?" Shane asked, giving her a wink and a grin.

"I intend for you to give me your full undivided attention this weekend – *your uninfluenced undivided attention,*" to which she winked and grinned right back at him.

Her forthrightness about certain things that had always been ordinary to Shane only made him appreciate her even more. Christina went out of her way to please him, but she did it in such a manner that he realized it was even more of a sacrifice for her. Never did she condemn him for his bad habits, but neither did she tolerate them in her presence. The control that she had over him was so powerful that he never bothered trying to figure it out, knowing she was only a messenger for her Father.

"Where would you like to go?" she asked. Remembering their conversation from the prior weekend, she continued, "I thought you might like to have some small choice in the matter."

This time they both grinned at each other.

"You mean you practically kidnap me, and you don't even know where you're gonna take me?"

"Yes, I have a very good idea of where I'm going to take you at some point, but we can go anywhere you would like in the North Carolina mountains."

Shane drew his lips together, hard in thought, like a kid in a candy store who could only choose one item. "How about Waynesville?"

Christina slammed on the brakes. Shane looked back at the road, figuring an animal had run out in front of her to make her come to such a sudden halt. Seeing nothing in the road, he looked back at her to make sure she was okay.

"What is it, baby?"

"Shane, you really *must* be my soulmate. That is the very place that I wanted to go." She hesitated slightly, then added, "Have you ever heard of Kulaski Lake?"

"Sure have. I remember riding by it once when I was small, but I don't know anything about it."

"What a wonderful denominational member you are! It only happens to be our retreat center for the entire southeastern United States."

"Babe, I told you before. No one *ever* accused *me* of being a saint."

"And I *certainly* never suggested that you are a saint. It's just that I thought you might have heard of the place."

"Sorry." And indeed Shane was sorry. He regretted being quite that uninformed in Christina's view. There were few subjects in which he had been unable to match her, and he had amazed her repeatedly with his theological insights and reasoning, so the fact that he was unfamiliar with a place so sacred to his lady love embarrassed him slightly.

"Think nothing of it. It is so well hidden that most people don't even see it when they drive by its exit. In fact, there are people who live in Waynesville who are unaware there's such a secluded spot right in their backyard."

"Sounds like a neat place."

"It really is. But it is not quite up to the speed of your normal hang-outs. I'm not sure you would ..."

"Christina, would you *please* stop worrying about me fitting in your hang-outs. If I have a problem with them, I'll let you know."

"You promise?"

"Yes, I promise," as he sealed it with a kiss. "Besides, if you and I are going to be together as much as I suspect we are, I'd better get used to this Kulaski Lake."

"Oh, Shane. It really is beautiful. But, even more than that, it is so divinely inspiring. You cannot possibly go there without feeling God's presence. And at night when the huge cross lights up against the black sky with the moon in the background ..." she paused, trying to find the right words to describe the sight.

"I get the picture. If it's as beautiful as you say it is, I know I'll like it. But whether it is or not, I'm sure I'll like it simply because it's so much a part of you."

She was so touched by his sensitivity to the things that were important to her that all traces of guilt for spending a weekend with a male friend vanished. Christina had played all kinds of havoc with herself all week since she had the brainstorm to kidnap Shane and take him away. Secretly, she had hoped that they could make their way to Kulaski Lake, knowing that he would be caught up in its Spirit the same as everyone else who went there.

Now there was absolutely *no* regret on her part. It no longer mattered that Shane happened to be of another gender, nor that people – especially people in her congregation – would not understand the depth of their friendship.

Shane looked at Christina, suddenly amused. "Might I ask, just exactly what do you intend for me to wear this weekend? Or did my angel think that I wouldn't need any clothes?" His question was accompanied by the devilish smirk that she had been waiting for ever since he read the note. She knew he was kidding her, even as badly as she knew he wished he wasn't.

"It just so happens that while you went upstairs to get something to drink last night at the Kershaw's, I grabbed a couple of changes of clothes for you."

"So that's why I couldn't find all my clean clothes this morning. My angel has turned into a devil." Shane sized her up carefully, knowing that the next two days were going to be one of the best times of his entire life – both before *and* after this weekend. "Damn, I'm good!" he blurted out, reaching his arm up across the seat and taking hold of her shoulder.

"What brought on *that* sudden outburst?" Christina queried, eyeing Shane with a puzzled look.

"For one thing, I must have had *some* influence on you for you to be that sneaky. And for another thing, I must mean *a lot* to you for you to go traipsing off for a weekend alone with a member of the opposite sex."

Christina glanced at him, trying to be obscure. "Yes, on both counts." Then she changed her expression, giving him that all-knowing look and added, "But there will be *no more* of those four-letter words."

"Yes, ma'am!" he replied, saluting her. Then Shane leaned forward and to the left, making her look into his face. "And don't you ever forget who the boss is."

"I won't!" Christina added, broadly smiling, as she pointed upward with her right index finger. "Don't *you* ever forget who the Boss is!"

"Yes, ma'am," Shane replied, as if some of the air had been taken out of his balloon. Once again, the minister had him and he knew to give up this round of the smart games.

They listened to the radio for the next few minutes. Shane became lost in thought as he realized that his cell phone would probably ring any minute now, his daily afternoon call from Carla.

Since her release, her calls had become more frequent and more demanding, even though she was living with two other guys. He was not in the mood to deal with her badgering at the moment, even though he felt slightly sheepish about not being at home for her. She had become more reliant on him since her return, and even though Shane had tried to hint around at his relationship with Christina, he had never been able to come out and admit to her that he was in love with his angel.

Carla knew that some "angel of a person" had wandered into Shane's life, and that they were working on a few ideas together, but she had no idea that his thoughts and all of his time were spent with her, much less how dependent he had become on her. Just as she expected Shane to be at her every beckoning call, she suspected that he needed her the same. What Carla failed to realize was that once again, just like before she went to jail, she was sharing her man with another woman. The only difference was this woman had a secret weapon – one that even Shane himself could not elude.

Shane scolded himself for even thinking about Carla when he was on his way to a perfect weekend with an angel by his side. But his thoughts of pity for his old lover still tore at him. He knew she was emotionally unstable right now, and he feared throwing her backwards, even more than she had been at her incarceration, if he came clean with her. After all, he knew what addiction did to a person, how it made them think. However, he drew himself back to the present with words he had heard Rachel tell Christina when she was distraught over cruel things Tom had done to the boys: "He's not here. We're not going to talk about him."

He looked over at Christina and realized that she was the most beautiful creature he had ever beheld. She was nothing like his women of the past, and he suspected that if he searched the world over, he would not find another like her. At least one who accepted him the way she did, much less showed him the love that she did.

*Shane, if you let this jewel get away from you, you really don't deserve her. Play your cards right and you'll be the happiest man*

286

*on earth. A far cry from where you were only four months ago.*

Beginning to feel the pangs of hunger call out to him, he took Christina's hand in his. "Pull off at the first Morganton exit."

She started to ask why, but Christina was aware that Shane knew these mountains like the back of his hand. This was their weekend, and if her man wanted to stop in Morganton, so be it! The exit was only five miles away, so she watched the road carefully as he sang to her along with the radio.

Christina wondered where his mind had been the last few minutes, sensing that he was clearly off in his own world. But she decided better than to question him, sensing that she probably did not *want* to be a part of that world. She saw the exit sign just ahead, so she signaled and pulled off the interstate.

"Now what?" she asked, approaching the end of the ramp.

"Take a left, then give your right turn signal."

"What am I looking for?" she started to question, but then Christina pealed with delight.

"Hope you like it!" Shane smiled as she turned into the parking lot of the seafood restaurant. "In my opinion, it's the best in the western half of the state."

"I love you!" Christina remarked as she parked the Blazer and gave him a kiss.

"I love you, too, angel," he replied reflectively, as he wondered if he was strong enough to hold onto her.

The meal was more delicious than Christina's usual Thursday night fare. "Oh, Shane. This is wonderful. Thank you so much."

Shane stared into her excited face. It took so little to thrill her, even though she was in such a classy league all her own. He loved the exhilaration that had exploded all over her entire body, giving her a glow more brilliant than the sun's.

"No, Christina. Thank *you*. I have never had anyone to give me this kind of happiness."

"Just chalk up another first to me!" she squealed as she jerked his hand and pulled him out of the restaurant.

"Anxious to be alone with me, huh?" Shane teased.

"You and The Man," she whipped back at him, squeezing his forearm.

When they reached the car, Shane leaned up against it, pulling her to him, but keeping her far enough away that he could see her face. "Christina, I'm never going to get you all to myself, am I?" knowing the answer before he even asked.

"Nope," Christina said, smiling, yet with a very serious expression. She wondered if there was any regret in the answer that he heard, but that really did not matter. The minister had no intention of compromising for anyone, *not even Shane Sievers*, as much as she loved him.

Shane woke at his usual early hour the next morning. He turned on the coffeemaker in the room, then went to check on the woman in the adjoining room, hoping she had not locked the door from her side. Although he had spent the evening talking with her on two other occasions, he had never seen Christina sleeping. As he watched her gently breathing, he was completely taken aback by the glow that shone on her face even as she slept.

*My God, she is such a lovely creature.* Shane caught himself. *Lovely!* It wasn't a normal word in his vocabulary, especially when it came to females, but he could think of no other way to describe her. The beauty from inside her radiated on the outside as well. He stood by the door, still in a trance by the vision before him. *I wonder if she has any idea how truly beautiful she is.* But then, he answered his own question. She had been too scarred by the harshness of abuse in her former marriage to recognize her outward *or* inward appearance.

*There's peace written all over her face. It would be heaven to wake up beside her every morning.* And Shane thought of the struggle he had letting go of her last night. He had never wanted anyone anymore in his entire life, but he knew better than to force himself on Christina. Still eyeing her resting silhouette, he wondered if she sensed his longing for her. It was becoming more and more difficult for him to be around her, fearing the physical desire of passion would take over before too much longer.

As he saw the purity of her heart and her soul, Shane pledged to himself that he would never get in the way of her vows. *Those da… those ever-lovin' vows. God, why MUST You give me a gift like her, and then torture me by not letting me have her?* Then Christina's words, "Never ask God why," came roaring at him as if she had the ability to reprimand him even in her sleeping state. *Well, she is an angel. Why would I expect any less?* He shook his head and grinned at her as he walked over to the bed and sat down.

"Good morning, angel," he whispered in her ear while stroking her hair.

Christina heard the tenderness in Shane's voice as she opened her eyes and looked up at him. She did not *ever* remember being awakened like that. It was as if her fairy tale had come true, and her Prince Charming was sitting, looking at her. *Oh, please let the shoe fit!* she thought, staring into his eyes and replaying that voice, *in more ways than one!!*

"Good morning," she replied, grasping his hand.

Shane leaned down and kissed her so softly that she could barely feel his lips on hers. She was so engrossed by his sensitivity that all she could do was stare at him.

"Are you always this quiet in the mornings?" Shane questioned, taunting her, since she was not her usual wide-open self.

"No. Only when I am this much in love."

The sight of him, and the warmth of his touch, brought back her feelings from the evening before. There was no way she could let him know how badly she wanted him. She began to wonder if taking the risk of boosting his spiritual life was worth the torture she was inflicting upon herself. *God, why did I have to meet my Mr. Right when I can't even have him?* Catching herself, Christina immediately asked forgiveness for asking a question like that. The fact that her subconscious went in that direction alerted her that this guy was getting to her in a way that made her lose all her senses.

Leaning up, she wrapped her arms around his neck to hug him with the words, "I'll give you twenty-five years to start out my morning this way."

"No deal," he replied, shaking his head with a look of seriousness to which she was unaccustomed from him. She looked at him rather oddly, surprised at his response, which was precisely what Shane had anticipated. Knowing he now had her full attention, he finished what was on his mind more and more these days. "I intend to wake up holding onto you, kissing you and telling you how much I love you – *not* walk in from the room next door."

He loved the smile that spread its way over Christina's entire face. It was not even accompanied by the usual turn of her mouth which gave her an appearance of shyness. His angel took the comment exactly as he meant it, something that excited, yet slightly surprised him.

"I think I'd like that even better. But maybe you'd still better give me the twenty-five years to decide."

Shane felt his heart jump a few beats. "Now that *is* a deal!" he exclaimed, glad for her affirmative response. *Maybe this angel is not out of my reach, after all!*, secretly boasting to himself.

The couple's souls were laughing with delight as their lips met and their bodies embraced. Each of them was well aware that the passion they felt also raced through the other, as they both wanted more than they knew was possible.

She pulled the Blazer up the mountain to the cross, where they sat and talked. Talked about the present, talked about things to come, talked about everything – *except* the past. For the past mattered not to either of them. The past held all the experiences that had brought them to a common ground. Yet, the past was what they were leaving to start their new life. A life together. A life full of promise, a life full of love, a life that made each of them stronger.

Shane talked about things that were coming alive for the first time in his life. Things that had always been a part of him, but that had never really surfaced because he had never before sensed their power. Things that gave him a whole newness of life. Things that he felt he was supposed to do with that new life. Things that were his own special gifts and talents.

Christina suggested that Shane step out of the vehicle and go stand by the cross and look out over the lake and across the mountains. She sat in the Blazer taking notes on everything that was happening with him, with her, with them, with the entire episode. As she stared at him while writing, she could not help but notice his gorgeous long, flowing reddish-blonde locks that sparkled with streaks of gold as if the sun were always shining on them, illuminating him and his entire presence.

The vision before her struck her with a magnitude that would have been frightening had Christina not been so used to such supernatural experiences. But had Shane been dressed in a long robe rather than jeans and boots, he would have looked identical to the picture of Christ hanging in the entrance of the chapel just down the hill. It was a picture that most people missed, but she'd spent so much time there praying that she had taken in every window, every picture, every memorial plaque. She knew every scar and scratch on the altar rail. She had cried note after note on both the organ and piano in her attempts to flush her heart and soul of its many periods of pain and anguish. *And* she knew that picture which had spoken to her so many times after she had first spied it once on her way out the door.

That picture that showed Jesus as a non-conformist; as a person who spoke his mind and followed his heart. A rebel in every way, yet completely void of a rebellious style. And, by most definitions, an outcast to many. A rugged, yet gentle, face with a mouth that spoke calm repose and reassurance, and eyes that not only saw, but reached straight down to one's soul, and hair that looked as if it were highlighted by spun gold.

The similarity between the two images was nearly too ominous, even by Christina's standards. Similar except for one distinct point. The man in the picture may have outwardly appeared as a rebel, yet his actions had been controlled by righteousness. The man standing on the peak before her had also outwardly appeared as a rebel, but his actions had always been controlled by his temper, a temper which gave no credence to the repercussions that came with it or resulted from it.

She continued to watch the man in front of her as he stood perfectly still, completely spellbound by the magical power of the spot where he stood. Then as he finished his own private prayer to Christina's God, a God who had also fathered him, Shane gazed up into the sky to see the most picturesque clouds he had ever seen. Clouds that had spoken to his angel in that exact spot so many times were now sending the guy from hell his own messages.

Messages of love. Messages of forgiveness. Messages of a prosperous future. Messages of his own calling from his Heavenly Father.

She watched as tears slowly made their way down his face. She watched as a lone bird that had been soaring high above was joined by another. She watched the clouds that had been flashing images across the sky, making their own feature presentation as Shane stood in the amphitheater below. She saw Shane's entire expression and appearance change as God accepted his plea of repentance and began the transformation process of a new disciple. A disciple who had been more hated than a tax collector. A disciple whose past would open many doors unknown to other disciples, giving him a special mission.

And then she heard it. The most horrifying sound she had ever heard in her life. A sound that broke right into Shane's concentration. A sound that signaled battle – battle between good and bad, right and wrong, God and Satan. For here stood a warrior who was wanted by both sides. A warrior who had been a leader, victorious in numerous encounters, on one side for many years. A warrior with no prior experience, only long covered-over roots, who stood to be an even greater leader on the opposite side.

Christina sorrowfully watched the disciple fall prey as he succumbed to the messenger who served as his angel from the evils of his past. She saw Shane answer his cell phone to a call that should have never come through, for he was out of transmission range – that was, human transmission. And she knew that as great was the miracle she had just watched in progress, this was a miracle from another source. But she also knew that Shane was the only one who could choose which miracle he wanted to accept.

As she sat there watching his natural calling turn into a struggle of powers, she began to fear the impending answer to her question of just a few minutes ago, the question before the fateful phone call. And then she had one last thought of the similarity, yet the one big difference, in the two men from just a minute ago. She received her own transmission, a message that many would have missed, but one that was clear to Christina because of her closeness to the Almighty. Her own call that told her that both of these men belonged in her life – for all time, for all eternity, no matter which twisted turns her path would take. But something inside the eternal optimist also told her that one of the men would bring her joy, happiness and peace, and hold her close in times of pain brought on by the other man.

At that moment, Christina faced her own battle. Was she willing to take a chance on what would come, or did she want to rid herself of possible heartache and lean solely on the One whom she knew would always love and care for her? As she watched Shane turn toward the car, his own vision interrupted by the call from which he had just hung up, she saw the joy still radiating on his own face. Joy that was brought about by his own foresight, his own knowledge that he truly *was* a child of God, his own ability to know and feel his Father's blessings.

*Yes! YES, YES, YES!!!* her heart and soul chimed in harmony as she read that face. What was the saying? "No pain, no gain." *Yes, that was it!* Even though foreboding pain seemed inevitable, the rewards she stood chance to reap called to her with such a dynamic force that she was unable to ignore them.

Shane stepped back into the vehicle and neither of them uttered a word, but each full of wonder at the other's thoughts. She wondered whether the realization of the phone call that miraculously reached their magical pinnacle – the calling from another source - had hit him. He wondered whether his angel had any idea of the vision he had just encountered – a vision that included Christina, his companion, his helpmate for all time. But what they did know was that for this moment, for this time, for this place, they were bound. Bound by a force so strong that they could not pull loose from it no matter what. *And* bound by a love that was so strong that neither of them *wanted* to leave this time, this place.

They reached for each other as if drawn together by a magnetic force, lunging into such a tight embrace that they felt they could never be pulled apart. Shane covered his lady in kisses, not of passion, but of purity, of divine blessedness. Christina caressed him with such emotion running through her fingertips that he felt a newness in her, also. A longing and an acceptance that had been foreign to him up to this point. And both of them knew that the flame that had ignited exactly twelve weeks ago at a dimly lit corner table, and had kindled exactly ten weeks ago, as an angel – *not* Cupid – shot an arrow through their hearts, now burned wildly, fueled by the source that had brought each of them to the other, and had also cared for each of them individually,

At that moment, a thought ran through each of their minds, a thought that neither shared with the other, but a thought that involved both of them and their acceptance into this relationship. Christina sensed a high she had never achieved from any of her concerts, performances or premieres. Shane reach a high that he had never reached from any of the drugs he had tried. Both of them basked in the aura that kept their hearts soaring up, up, up.

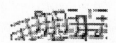

It was Shane that finally broke the silence. "Christina, you were right about this place. You made it sound like it was not even of this world. And after what happened while I was standing out there, I realize that, in a way, it is *not* of this world."

She listened intently, not surprised at all by his comments. They were the same ones she had heard, accompanied by the same expression she had seen on the many faces that had been stricken by the beauty and power of this place. "Shane, do you have *any* idea what happened to you this morning?"

"Yes ... and no." He took Christina's hands into his and held them up in the air between them. "I *do* know that God *does* have a purpose for me. I *do* know that you are a part of that plan. I *do* know that I *never* want to lose you. I *do* know that I love you, and no matter whether I chose you, or He chose you, I want you. I want you now, I want you tomorrow, I want you forever. Christina, I need you. I need you in *everything* that I do."

Christina felt a warmth rushing through her face. Like tears streaming down it, yet it was completely dry. This *was* her man. This *was* the person God had chosen for her. This *was* the person with whom she wanted to share her life, her ups, her downs. This *was* her ultimate reward – to be able to work, plan, laugh, play, and express love *with* someone whom she truly adored.

She leaned her face closer to his, so that their eyes were inseparable. "And you shall have me . . . as long as you want me."

Her words, *and* the meaning behind them, rang loud and clear. For Shane saw in her expression, *and* heard in her voice, that Christina wanted to be his forever, but that she would never stand in his way if he chose another. He had never known love to be that real, that honest, that free. The openness she had just given him spoke to him in a way that no words ever could, and it made him more sure that here *did* sit his own angel, and it made him even more desirous of her, in *every* way.

She broke his train of thought with a kiss before she started the engine. "Now where? I'm starving, so pick out a place for lunch." Christina started to turn towards downtown Waynesville, but Shane directed her to keep driving straight.

"There's a shop just down this road that I want to see. That is, if it's still here." They had only gone a couple of blocks when he pointed to the right. "Turn here. Yep, there it is."

Christina watched as Shane got out and walked into a tattoo shop. *Oh, great! Just what he needs. Another one of those disgusting pictures.* And her mind reflected back to the evening when he was laying on the sofa and she was sitting on the floor beside the sofa, gently massaging his shoulders. She unbuttoned the top button to reach the spots that were still full of tension. As she did, an ink drawing of an ornery old cuss was staring at her. Shane looked at her, as she looked at it. His chest did not move as he held his breath, waiting for a negative response from her.

She never said a word, simply kept rubbing her fingers across his skin, but as she did, the shirt moved in the other direction to reveal another drawing on the other shoulder. Shane knew he had to say something to break the roar of silence that had crawled into their conversation.

"I was afraid for you to see those."

"*Afraid?*" she responded, questioningly surprised. "Shane Sievers *afraid?*"

He looked at her rather sheepishly. She did have a point. Shane had never been afraid of anyone – no man, certainly no woman, and over something as trivial to him as his tattoos. *What is my problem?* Then as he gazed into her watchful eyes, waiting for an explanation, he knew the answer to his own question. *You are, damn it, YOU are!* And as much as he hated to admit it, he loved having her for a problem. "Christina, I was afraid they would turn you off. That you wouldn't like me if you saw them."

Christina burst into laughter. "Shane," she started as his thoughts went off again.

*Wonderful. She NEVER calls you by your name, and on top of that, she's laughing. It's going to be one of those scoldings like when your mom tells you to go sit in your room until your dad gets home!*

Seeing his mind somewhere else, she jerked at his shirt, grabbing his attention. "Shane, you mean to tell me that after all you sat right in this room and told me about your past, all only two weeks after you had met me, now you're afraid that I won't like you simply because of a couple of pictures."

He had to laugh, too. She was right. His fear was pretty ridiculous. But Shane could not give up that easily. He refused to be had by her quick wit this time. "That was before I really got a chance to know you and decide whether I wanted to keep you or not."

"And now you know you do?"

*Damn it. She's STILL one up on me!*

Christina didn't give him time to think of a response. "Just promise me you won't ever get my name tattooed on you."

Shane laughed again. "I won't, baby. At least in a spot where anyone can see it!" Now he was feeling better. He was catching up.

She glared at him, this time without any laughter, and in fact, quite serious eyes. "Shane, please tell me . ."

"No, baby, I do not have any female's names or naked women on my body. Even *I* knew better than that. I guess I always thought, *or hoped*, that one day someone might come along who might take offense at that."

"Thank you! . . . .I think."

*Good. Now I'm no longer behind.*

"Shane, . . . exactly"

Before she could finish her stammered question, Shane was rolling up his shirt sleeve. "Just one." He showed her one last drawing that had lost its wording and its color. "This one was my first one. They're all milestones." And he proceeded to give Christina the history of each. "There is one more that I intend to get," he exclaimed as he watched her eyebrows raise. "It is a scene of a western sunset with the word 'Sundance' over it."

Christina's mouth gaped open. *He really IS my Sundance!*

"I have a cousin out west who is an artist and I've asked him to sketch it out for me so it will be an original. But then, all of my tattoos are originals. I've designed them all."

She eyed him carefully, observing his pride in his tattoos, and thought to herself how she had never been with *anyone* who had those abhorrent pictures on their skin, but on Shane, they looked so apropos. In fact, she sat there staring at them, running her fingers over them, thinking how she loved looking at him – tattoos and all!

But to think that she was parked outside a tattoo shop. Just as her thoughts returned to the present, Shane came bouncing out the front door. "Christina, come in here. I want to show you something. I've found a tattoo I want."

Christina had just caught a glimpse of a guy's Satanic drawing on his arm as he exited the building, so she thought to herself, *I'm sure there is nothing in that joint that I want to see.* But rather than spoil the day, she got out of the Blazer and went in, with Shane dragging her by the hand. And she prayed as they hit the front door that he would change his mind.

When he got back in the shop, someone was standing in front of the sketch he wanted her to see, so Shane continued to look at the other pictures. Christina stood examining the copies all over the walls, trying not to appear shocked or out of place. As she turned the corner and started eyeing another wall, she stopped. Her eyes caught a view of an eagle soaring high above treetops with mountains in the background. She stood there staring in disbelief that the picture she saw in her mind every time she read Psalm 91, or every time she needed to feel God's peace, was hanging on the wall of some tattoo shop. As she caught herself, she realized the music to one of her favorite choir anthems, an arrangement of the same psalm, was playing in her head.

*That's it. That's too much.* She walked over to Shane and grabbed his shirt sleeve, pulling him over to the picture, to which she pointed.

Shane stared at her in disbelief. She caught the shock in his eyes. "What is it? What's the matter?"

299

"Christina, that's the tattoo I want." Shane then looked at her sharply. "*How* did you know?"

She stood there, swallowing, unable to say a word, watching Shane's face. He, seeing the shock in Christina's eyes, shot her the same question. "Now you tell me – what's the matter?"

It was a few seconds before Christina could retrieve her voice from the pit of her stomach. When sound finally escaped her lips again, she explained the significance of the picture to Shane. He walked out the door without a word and lit a cigarette, leaning against a post on the sidewalk. She desperately hoped that she had not offended him, or made him decide against what he wanted on her account. After taking another close look at the sketch, she joined him on the sidewalk. But when she saw him staring into space, with a sallow expression on his face, she became even more concerned.

"Shane, are you okay?"

"No, I'm not. Well, yes, I am. But I'm not sure I like it."

"Would you please try making some sense?"

"Why? Half of the things you do make no sense. No sense whatsoever. It's just that you get some idea or some vision, and you know that God has spoken to you, and that's that. No questions asked."

"Yes, but I stop and look and listen. I take the time to see and hear God speak to me in His own way."

"That's the whole point, Christina. I'm not used to that. More and more lately I feel God's presence all around me. I feel His desires for my life. It is very rare for me to be on your beloved deck without feeling Him reach out to me, to speak to me. This is *very* different. I *do* like it. It's just that . . . well, . . . *God in heaven!*"

Christina looked at him, almost ready to make a remark, but decided against it. Something was really eating at Shane, and she hated it for him. She was sure that it must be unsettling to go through thirty-five years of your life, and then, all of a sudden, strange, seemingly supernatural, occurrences begin happening, more and more often. The wise female also knew that what really flustered the rebel about all of the esoteric experiences was that he couldn't fight what he couldn't see.

Shane tossed the cigarette across the parking lot and grabbed her shoulders. "Christina, when I was standing at the cross just a few minutes ago, I saw scenes, *many scenes*, go across the sky, as if they were being shown on the silver screen by a huge projector. They all included you. All of them except one. It was one that did not include you, and I was falling. An eagle came soaring across the sky and caught me in mid-air. The scene was the same view of the eagle as the one hanging on the wall, you know, over treetops with mountains in the background."

She took Shane's hand and dragged *him* back in the door this time.

"Where are you going? What are you doing?"

"You're going to get that tattoo."

"Oh no, I'm not. That tattoo is two hundred dollars because of all the intricate detail. I already asked."

Christina whipped two crisp new one-hundred dollar bills out of her purse. "Yes, you are. You are obviously meant to have that tattoo."

"Christina, have you lost your mind?"

"Probably so! But there is too much going on here for this to be just coincidental. Go tell the guy you want the tattoo."

Shane returned a couple of minutes later. "He can't get to me for a couple of hours. Let's go eat that lunch you wanted."

"We can't. I'm broke. I just spent my last penny on some picture from in the clouds!"

"Lunch is on me," Shane grinned as he popped her backside. He grabbed her waist as she started to get in the Blazer. "I love you so much, angel. We *are* going to have a wonderful life together."

301

She looked at him, wishing she could change the thoughts in her head. "I hope so, baby. I *really* hope and pray that you are right." But as they stood there in a powerful embrace, God's love running through their bodies, Christina could not help but reflect back on the vision she had seen while they were on the mountain peak. She prayed that when the time came, the eagle would be there to rescue Shane from returning to his past, and that he would recognize it. *Well, at least now he'll have a visual reminder*, she thought, remembering how his tattoos all had a history. *Let's just hope he sees this one everyday – AND its background.*

The lunch was completely void of all the seriousness of the past couple of hours as Christina and Shane were their usual invigoratingly humorous selves. By the time they left the restaurant, they were literally in an uproar, mostly laughing at how opposite the two of them looked, and even more, how odd they must appear as a couple. But they were also amusingly warmed by all the common ground between them, and their ability to give and take, accept, and love unconditionally. They both wished the joy, the peace and the happiness they felt at that moment could last forever, and they were both ready to take that chance.

As Christina turned out of the restaurant, Shane touched her hand lightly. "You *are* going to give me a couple of beers now to help numb all the needles, right. After all, you're the one who insisted that I get this tattoo."

She glanced at him with a raised brow, playing with him. "You'll go to any extreme to have your beer, won't you?" But she knew she was going to allow him his request. Shane had given her a lot, he had given up a lot for her, and at this moment, she felt like he deserved his couple of beers.

It seemed strange that her attitudes and her viewpoints were changing, but not her morals or beliefs. No longer was she turned completely off by his request for one or two beers. She saw that he did not *need* them, but *enjoyed* them, like her with her iced tea. And even in her childhood rearing that contained an addendum to the commandments that read, "Thou shalt not drink," Christina had visited enough of Jesus' stomping grounds to know that the grapes *were* made into wine and not grape juice. And somehow she did not see the technology of those days allowing for non-alcoholic wine, or sparkling cider. Though she was not a drinker, she learned not to condemn him, as long as he did not abuse his beer. He had taught her a lot, as she had him.

When he was with her, he still enjoyed a cold one once in a while, but he did not feel the need to cure his boredom, or wash away his problems. She gave him a variety of other things and ways to take care of his reasons for drinking. And he knew that once he could hold her in his arms every night, he would not even need to feel that long-necked bottle in his hand any longer. He watched her as she pulled into a space in front of the pub. She had even introduced him to the imported beers she had seen and heard about while traveling, and convinced him to sip and savor, not guzzle. *To think this angel who doesn't even touch the stuff, gave ME, who visited bars almost daily for nearly twenty years, an education in beer drinking . . . she IS a walking miracle.*

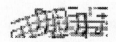

When they arrived back at the tattoo parlor, Shane suddenly wondered what Christina was going to do for the two hours the drawing would take.

"What would you like for me to do?" she asked, giving him the opportunity to ask her to stay or leave.

"I'd really like for you to be here with me. There's something that seems and feels very ceremonial about this tattoo."

She had already sensed, but did not mention, that same aura herself, figuring it would be another of the things Shane had already said made no sense about her. But to think he felt the same awe for what was about to happen truly did make the ordeal of the tattoo seem sanctimonious.

"I'd love to stay. Actually, I'd like to watch, but do you think the guy would let me back there with you, or would I be in the way?"

Shane practically guaranteed Christina that he was *sure* he could persuade the artist to let her in the work area, and within a few seconds was back, leading her by the hand to the back room. The dude was even bringing in a chair for her when they got there.

He positioned Shane in the chair, prepped his left bicep for the procedure, and set about laying out the right size needles and colors of ink. "This is one of the most difficult designs I've ever done," he stated.

"Don't worry," Christina piped up. "I'm sure you'll have no trouble with it at all. I have it on highest authority."

She glanced over at Shane to make sure he was not upset at her for her abruptness. Christina was pleased to see him wink at her.

The shop owner took her remark as an experienced comment, so he kept talking. "You go to tattoo parlors often, do you?" His question drew an outburst of laughter from Shane, who quickly hushed to hear what kind of trip Christina was going to take the poor soul on. He knew she was already in for a good time. And already he knew that this was certainly going to be the most *fun* tattoo he had ever gotten.

"No, actually this is my first time."

"Oh." The guy was still busily working, making small talk all the while. "What do you do?"

"I'm a minister."

The artist looked at her with no change of expression, then scrunched up his nose, squinted up his eyes and did a double take of her. "Aw, hell."

This time Christina and Shane both burst into laughter. Shane was grateful for *two* things: that the guy was still laying out tools instead of working on his arm; *and* that he did not have a mouthful of beer at that particular moment. Otherwise, he would have showered everyone in the room. She was thinking of all the odd comments she had gotten in strange places when she told them of her profession, but this one had just moved its way up the list to her favorite.

"You're kidding. Right?" He was still eyeing the shapely creature in front of him who appeared to belong to the hellion sitting in his chair.

"Why would I kid about a thing like that?"

*The poor old dude is going to be so confused that I'm liable to wind up with a goldfish on my arm!*, Shane reasoned as he sat, continuing to snicker at the conversation.

Still trying to make heads or tails out of the unique female, he decided to change his tactics and ask Shane for some sort of answer. "She your old lady?"

Shane was still rollicking in the chair. He looked over to Christina with eyes that said, "You started this, now get yourself out of it!" That was all the invitation she needed to gladly amuse the gent.

"I'm not his or anybody else's *old* lady. Yes, I *am* a lady, and I *am* his lady, but I refuse to *ever* be anybody's *old* lady, no matter how old I get!" she stated emphatically.

"I didn't mean it like that. It's just . . . Aw, hell."

*There he goes again!* Christina cringed. *He doesn't realize that hell has nothing to do with this tattoo!!*

"Are you two . . . together?" Neither Shane nor Christina answered as he looked back and forth at them. He looked straight at Shane as he muttered, "It's just that you don't look like the sort to be hanging around no female minister."

This time it was Shane's turn. "Would it make you feel any better if I was hanging around a male minister?" Christina buried her head in her hands to keep from appearing too rude.

The confused man finally decided to give up. Shaking his head, he added one last comment. "You two really are something, you know that?" Again, neither Shane nor Christina spoke, but they both knew that his latest words were probably the truest ones that he had ever spoken.

He went to work with his needles, and Christina sat, watching his every movement and the ink as it permanently marked Shane's arm. All the while she was taking notes, making analogies and inspirational notes from which to draw later. It had become her habit to never be caught without pen and paper. The fact that this man, whom she loved so deeply, constantly encouraged her in that direction made her more determined to be a writer, and more determined to give him a life of happiness - *that is, if I have anything to do with it!*

She watched his strength as he sat there completely immobile, never once wincing as the needles buzzed and drew their object. Christina also watched the handiwork of the artist. As she sat there, watching the two of them, and sensing the quietness that had come over the entire shop as they also watched the tattoo progress, it hit Christina. Every mark was too detailed, too perfect. *This man is not drawing this tattoo. There is an even greater Artist in control of those needles*, she realized as she saw and felt the Omnipotent Presence.

Christina could hardly wait to tell Shane, even though she wondered if that would make him uncomfortable, or more concerned about the subject of their earlier conversation. But she was nearly bursting from the excitement, so she was bound to tell him. Besides, she knew he could read her face well enough to know the wheels were turning in her head, and he would *demand* to know what was going on up there.

Both of the men needed a smoke break. She knew this was her chance to inform Shane of her thought, even though she suspected a shocked expression of surprise from him. "Shane," she blurted, when they got outside, "that man is not the one ..."

"I know, Christina. *God* is giving me *this* tattoo. I can feel it on my arm, I can see it in the mirror. This eagle far surpasses the work of any human being. Don't think I am either that blind *or* that stupid."

Christina was so awe-struck that both of them felt the miracle happening in that most unlikely place that she wondered if the shop owner also recognized its greatness. But, she decided against taking him down that road. She did not want to *completely* blow his mind. God *did* need someone's hands to guide to finish this great work that encompassed far beyond being just a work of art.

They returned to the back room of the shop holding hands and laughing. The shopkeeper repositioned Shane in the chair, turned on a personal-sized fan and set back to the business of the tattoo, again starting a conversation.

"So, you're *really* a minister?" he again questioned Christina, looking at her less quizzically this time.

Shane decided he'd better put a stop to this before the guy went completely daffy. He glanced at Christina, signaling her to let him take over. "Yes, she really is a minister."

Christina braced herself for those same two words, but this time he refrained from that choice response. "I didn't mean to be disrespectful before, ma'am. It's just that you don't look like most of the ministers that come in here."

This time it was Christina's turn to be surprised and start the questioning. "You mean you really *do* have ministers come in here?"

307

"Oh, yes, ma'am. Every year at that big convention, or whatever you call it down there."

"We call it the conference. Do they come in and look, or do they get tattoos?"

"They get some of the weirdest tattoos I've got, and in some of the strangest places!"

She decided not to pursue that remark. She was really *not* interested in what he considered weird *or* strange. Christina's next comment came out differently from what she had meant, but she loved the response it got.

"I just never expected this to be a place that attracted men *or* women of God."

"Oh, it is. And believe me, ma'am, they call on God with great regularity when I get 'em in this here chair. And I don't mean like they do in the pulpit, either," and he leaned over to her, "if you know what I mean!"

Christina rolled her eyes at Shane. She was sure she knew exactly what he meant, and she was praying that he would decide *not* to go into anymore graphic detail. Ready to get back to work herself, she started writing in her notebook again.

"You a writer, too?" he asked, still watching her.

She wondered how in the world he was able to do a decent job on Shane's arm and still run his mouth the whole time. But then it hit her that he was only an instrument in this particular instance, so it probably did not matter how attentive he was to his subject.

"Yes, in a way."

"Whatcha writin'?"

"A book." She looked at Shane, wondering whether to continue, as he winked at her, signaling her to go ahead. Christina knew she was going to have the guy baffled again. "It's called *On Eagle's Wings*, and I'm thinking that I'll use that particular tattoo on the cover." The minute the words escaped her lips, she wished that she could retrieve them, knowing full well what the artist's next words would be. She heard them in her head at exact same time they hit the air.

"Aw, hell!"

*At least this time he said it with a little more enthusiasm!*

He asked her about the book, to which she depicted it as simply as possible. The drawing was really beginning to take shape, and she wanted to watch its every line. With each stroke, she felt the chills tingling down her spine. It truly was like watching the Master at work, and she wondered what it must feel like to be Shane, knowing that this was not just any tattoo, being done by any tattoo artist. She gazed at his face to see him beaming at her, with an expression that spoke both pride and devotion, to her *and* the Artist.

"Will I even get to have my name in the book, too?"

"I suspect so, since this is your tattoo shop."

"The name's Dummy Dale. That's Dummy with four m's. D-U-M-M-M-M-Y.

Christina glared at him. *Yep, you're exactly right!*, she thought to herself, nodding her head at him and making a note, both on the pad, *and* mentally.

The shop owner's wife came in just as the tattoo was getting its finishing touches. "That's the best I've ever seen white take on a person," she exclaimed, pointing to the snow-capped mountains.

"Yeah, it really did do good! I've never seen it look like that, either."

Shane and Christina beamed at each other, both fully aware of a wonderful secret, a secret that would remain between only the two of them and the Artist. The drawing truly was awesome and the guy took a photo of it because it had turned out so beautifully. As the couple exited his shop, his wife and he stared at them, wondering what it was about them that they didn't have themselves.

"Who were those people?" the wife asked, in a tone reminiscent of someone watching the masked man ride into the sunset

"You'll never believe this, but she's a minister, who's writing a book and she's going to put a picture of that tattoo on the front cover."

"Aw, hell."

# 20

It came time for the annual celebration to honor her parents'
birthdays, an event which Christina always looked forward to
with great pleasure. But as it turned out this year, Shane had a
legal appointment to clear up two of the major items on his agenda
the next day, and she tried every way possible to figure out a way
to do both. Finally, she called Mr. and Mrs. Cache to ask if she
could bring along a friend, explaining that it would save her a trip
back down and up the mountain if he were allowed to join them.

As the time neared, Christina was more than a little concerned
about the outcome of the visit. A couple of days before the birthday
trip, she called Abigail to see if she was making a mistake by taking
Shane with her.

"It's just that I don't want my parents to get the wrong idea,"
she explained.

"Are you sure that you're not more afraid that they'll get the
*right* idea?" was the comment Christina heard from the other end
of the line.

"I guess you're right, but I don't know what kind of impression
he'll make, or how they'll accept him."

"Christina, you're letting your fears run away with you. How many times have you told Shane to stop stressing, especially when it was about matters over which he had no control? Well, now you're stressing. What happens between them is going to happen and there is nothing you can do to change the outcome. Shane is a good old country boy, full of common sense and down to earth, and your parents, of all people, will sense the genuine concern he has for you."

Christina couldn't help but notice his phone call just as they were about to eat dinner – a phone call that was getting more and more frequent. It bothered her, for she knew who he was calling, yet she had to trust him and let him do what he felt necessary in order to help his friend.

Just as it gave her a thrill to help him, she had to allow him that same ability to help another less fortunate than he. Christina was not known to be a jealous person and she made up her mind that she refused to stoop to that vile trait, no matter how much she loved Shane. She found it most unbecoming, especially in females. Not only that, she had made up her mind long ago that if her man did not love her enough not to be interested in another woman, he was not worth her. Thus, she elected to ignore the call. Besides, it was a joyous event, and she had *no* intention of letting some tramp ruin her blessed day with her parents or their birthdays!

The meal was wonderful, Shane and Mr. Cache talked car repair, and Shane gave Mrs. Cache a tip about replacing a fuse in her microwave that saved her a healthy service charge. Christina took her beau out for a walk through the mountain drives following dinner, and they shared their dreams under the stars, walking arm in arm.

He was a wreck about the next day, but as usual, Christina had her magic effect on him. Shane had gotten to the point that he called her every time he felt pressured, or like he was losing control. It was like, even over the telephone, she possessed a mystical potion which had a calming power over him, a power that allowed him to think before he acted and to make rational decisions.

When they returned, Mrs. Cache had coffee and cake set out in the den. The four of them sat and talked about trivial subjects, yet all of which included Shane into their conversation. He had never been invited to the home of any of his female friends' parents before, so he had also been a little apprehensive about the visit. But he was amazed at the openness with which Christina's parents welcomed him.

Shane also could not help but notice the pride within the older couple of their daughter and her accomplishments in life. The acceptance he saw in their eyes made him jealous of her relationship with her parents, but jealous only to the extent that he was glad for her. He knew that no matter what paths their lives took, he could never begrudge her of that relationship. And he longed to be a part of it.

He awoke to the smell of fresh coffee and bacon. Shane was greeted in the kitchen by Mrs. Cache who already had a cup out waiting for him. She joined him on the huge screened porch overlooking the mountains for a hospitable chat while he got his morning nicotine.

Christina had warned him about her mother. He could still hear her words as he listened to the lady of the house. "She's extremely quiet, and extremely intelligent. She was the valedictorian when she graduated," then chuckling, "claiming it was because she always kept her mouth shut and no one really knew how stupid she was. And when she does talk, it's just like E.F. Hutton – *everyone* listens!" Was this the same woman sitting here making small talk with him?

The few minutes they spent alone before Mr. Cache joined them told him that Christina had been right about the intelligence. But he found the woman to be most pleasant, witty, and more than ready to tell stories of her daughter's happy childhood. His favorite story had been about how the child had only cost six dollars at the time of her birth.

"If I give you the six dollars back, can I keep her?" Shane asked, only half joking.

His reaction told Mrs. Cache everything she needed to know. It was not her imagination that she had seen a renewed sparkle in Christina's eyes, or glow on her face at the dinner table last night. Nor had she overestimated the charm of this plain old country boy that her daughter had chosen to befriend. Christina had not brought a guy home to spend the evening since college. When Mr. Cache stepped over the threshold onto the porch, she nodded to him, alerting him that she had been right in her prediction from the evening before.

Mrs. Cache had already seen the similarity to her own husband in Shane's actions and way of thinking. And she had recognized his similarities to Matt from Christina's prior comments about his troubled past. She saw a cleverness and humor about him that resembled her daughter's favorite cousin, one whom, as a very young child, Christina had vowed to marry when she grew up. Lastly, she saw the attentive affection and the ease of conversation that Christina lost after her first marriage. All of those virtues wrapped into one package was hard to miss as she carefully observed the suitor.

Shane was so keyed up about meeting his son's case worker, Christina feared that even she could not keep him from going off on someone. She had tried to convince him that his attitude would make all the difference in the world, and that he should go in and show them the bright, intelligent Shane Sievers she knew - *not* the one with the reputation of being the "baddest hombre in the county." But she knew he had worn that label much longer than the one of a disciple, and right now, she was afraid the first one fit better.

He had cussed and fumed all the way there from the Cache's, and Christina braced herself for the worst. Not only did she keep trying to convince him about his actions, but she also was trying to convince her own self that no matter what he did, or how he behaved, Shane *was* a creature of God, and she must love him regardless. And as she looked at him, basting in his own stew, she was reminded how very much she did, in fact, love him. *But dear God, I DO NOT like all this garbage going on with him right now, OR the way he is dealing with it.*

They went in the white frame building high atop a hill, via only by a gravel road, and took a seat in the waiting area. She was thankful that before Shane had a chance to get comfortable, *or get stage fright,* the case worker called him back. He introduced his angel to the person he saw as the devil, almost wishing the two of them could duke it out and he and his lady could get the heck out of there, knowing his angel would surely come out on top. But he made up his mind that this was a problem of his own making, and he would deal with it as such. Christina loved the stamina and attitude she saw take over his demeanor as they started down the hall toward the back of the building.

"You do realize, Mr. Sievers, that I cannot really talk to you about confidential matters in front of Ms. Cache."

"You have my permission to say anything in front of her that you would say to me. We intend to be together for a very long time and I have nothing to hide from her."

The case worker examined him with a scrutinizing eye, wondering if he had forgotten all the items she had from his past on her record. However, the look in his eye, combined with his past reputation, affirmed that she should go on and not argue with him.

"Would you be willing to sign a release form verifying that?" she asked, searching Shane's face for any trace of doubt in his decision.

"Absolutely. I'll sign anything you want. And if you need me and cannot get hold of me, you also have my permission to discuss anything regarding me, or my son, with Christina."

Christina could see the apprehension written all over the bureaucrat's face, and she sensed that it came from *not* following her best judgment. But she respected the fact that the woman did not use her power to sway Shane's feelings on the matter, which would have been to no avail, anyway – obviously a fact that she already knew. After all, she had met with Shane on earlier occasions.

As the two of them chatted, Shane answered questions without hesitation, looking the woman across the desk squarely in the eyes. He did not lose his composure the first time, and was careful to leave out his usual colorful language which still escaped from time to time where red-taped bureaucrats were concerned. In fact, Christina loved the woman's reaction to his visit, knowing this was a first for her. The religious counselor could read in the face of the state's counselor her viewpoint of this entire case upon their entrance through the door. And now, the woman was completely baffled at the total change in the man before her.

He had cleaned up extremely well that morning, and as Christina sat watching him, she was enamored by not only his appearance, but even more by his intelligence and his ability to leave this professional, with her degrees hanging all over the wall, wondering where he had come from and what he had used to hit her upside the head. Shane was running circles around the female who had looked down her nose at him on his previous visits.

Christina's favorite part of the meeting was the sideways glances that kept getting tossed in her direction. She knew that given the fact Shane had already implicated her as being actively involved in Shay's life, her lifestyle, her background, and her career were only minutes from being picked apart. The question of how this lowlife had gotten hooked up with her was obviously already playing around in the woman's mind, so she could hardly wait for the startled reaction when her profession was announced. *It'll be almost as good as the one from the tattoo artist!* she chuckled to herself. Her mind was reeled in from its daydreaming as she heard the inquiry turn to include her.

"Just how would you describe your relationship with Ms. Cache?"

"I have been seeing her for over two months now, and in that short period of time, we have grown extremely close."

The woman thumbed back over her records. *Two months. Let's see. When was he in here last? Nearly four months ago.* Her records clearly indicated the mishap from December. She examined him carefully again. *No glassy eyes, no alcohol on his breath, dressed nicely, no vulgarity, no bad attitude, logical well-thought sentences, no dropped vowels or consonants, no slurred speech. Can this really be the same guy?*

Her line of work saw this kind of acting on the part of clientele all the time. But she saw no indication of insincerity in his face, his eyes, his speech or answers.

She scrutinized Christina this time. *Where did this woman come from? What is she doing with the likes of him? What would make her want to spend her time with someone of his background? What's in this for her?* Thoughts of madams or high rollin' drug dealers ran through her mind. *It's either that or she's a miracle worker! There's something here that doesn't meet the eye.* She decided she had spent enough time rambling nicely. It was time to go in for the kill.

"Ms. Cache, exactly what do you do?"

"I'm a Minister of Music and Christian Education," trying not to smile as she watched the woman gulp after nearly choking on her coffee.

"How long have you been in that profession?"

"Thirty years."

"I take it you have credentials to prove that?"

"A degree in Church Music, Music Education, and Christian Education, with graduate courses from three seminaries and a Master's from SMU."

Shane loved the expression on the face of the bureaucrat that was becoming more contorted by the minute.

"Have you any background in working with children?"

"Yes."

"Could you be more specific, please?"

*You asked for it,* mused Christina. "In addition to the children in my weekly choirs, which I have directed for the thirty years, I have led workshops for children all over the U.S. and also in Canada and Mexico. I've taken my choirs to Europe and Australia, written an opera with one of my fourth-grade classes in conjunction with the Metropolitan Opera House in New York . . ."

"Thank you, I believe that will be enough to verify that you have some experience with children."

Shane looked at Christina, winking, and rattling off phrases with his eyes, most of which were unfit to be vocalized in front of the woman casting down judgment upon them. He reached out and took her hand, squeezing it in approval. *Damn, she's good! What a woman!!* Something inside nudged at him to say his own prayer when they got outside – just after he smothered her in kisses!

"Mr. Sievers, how closely do you anticipate Ms. Cache to be in the lives of you and your son?"

"Pretty close! I intend to marry her."

There were no more questions as the woman looked up from her pad and stared into his face, then over at Christina. She made a few more notes, then rose from her seat, signaling that the meeting was adjourned. The case worker reached out her hand first to Christina, then to Shane, and congratulated both of them, wishing them well as they entered a life with Shay and promised a decision in Shane's favor to be rapidly forthcoming.

"I only have to finish up the paperwork. I'll be in touch very shortly."

She walked to the front door with the couple who was holding hands, and watched as they went outside, got in the Blazer and Shane rewarded his angel. As they pulled out of the parking lot, she went back to her desk, sat down, jotted a few sentences, then closed the folder. *Miracle worker has taken over. Case closed.*

There was a major item of agenda to which Shane had been looking forward to all week. He was supposed to go by the attorney's office and sign his divorce papers after he left the case worker. The rebel was already on a high from the successful outcome of the meeting, another occurrence correctly prophesized by Christina. He was learning to trust her more and more. Her advice to him was batting a thousand so far, and it seemed he was getting more hits with each passing day.

The attorney's office was only fifteen minutes away, so they were already there before Shane concluded recounting the complete victory of the meeting he had just left. He gave Christina a quick peck and promised to be right back. Within minutes, he was headed out the front door, and she saw by the look in his eyes that the papers were not ready.

Christina had already wondered if the papers had even been filed, given the track record of Shane's promises from his ex. When he jerked open the door, she knew her gut feeling had been right. There were several explosive sentences of dialogue, which she ignored, letting him vent. After he apologized for using the words that he knew she abhorred, he verified her thought.

"She never even filed the complaint for the divorce?"

"Oh yeah, she filed it alright. She just never came back and paid for it."

"Shane, I can't believe that an attorney went to the trouble to do the paperwork before he even got his money."

"Christina, take a good look around you, honey. You *are* in the butt-crack of the world!"

She glanced at him, amused at his gut-honest analogy. "Maybe so, but still, professional is professional, no matter where you are."

"Baby, haven't you been listening when I told you about all the kangaroo court cases here, and the crooked legal system? Did you think I was lying?"

"No, I just thought you were slightly prejudiced and judgmental."

"Well, think again. The county is full of nothin' but self-servin' dumb-asses."

"And you just happened to be the biggest and baddest one of

them all."

His eyes sliced straight through her. "Christina, I *am not* in the mood for joking. Do you realize how badly I wanted that divorce? For the hell to be over?"

Christina certainly felt empathy for him on that account. What she did not want to tell Shane was that simply because he had a piece of paper in his hand, the hell would not just up and go away. It would take a long healing, *and forgiving*, process – *if* it *ever* happened. She took his hand, expressing her sorrow at being so insensitive at that particular moment.

Shane looked at her blankly. "Let's go."

She felt so bad for him that she could hardly stand it. Here stood another major obstacle in the way of his progress, and although she definitely defied divorce, even though she had been through it twice herself, she knew that in this case, it was not only the best, but the only solution for Shane and Shay.

Christina drove a couple of blocks and made a turn. Shane glanced up to see her wheeling around in a bank parking lot.

"What are you doing?"

"I need a little cash," she bolted frankly. She grabbed several bills as they came spitting out of the ATM machine, and handed them to Shane. "Go inside and get a cashier's check for one-hundred-fifty dollars made payable to the attorney. Make sure it has your name on it for proof that *you* paid for this transaction."

"Christina ..."

"Just do it, and bring me back the change."

Shane sighed deeply, wishing there was another way, but relieved that herein laid his chance to be free and clear once and for all. He came back out with a check in one hand, her change in another, and a little more of a smile than when he had gotten out of the vehicle.

Christina drove back over to the attorney's office and waited outside as Shane went in and took care of business. This time when he got in the Blazer, there was a widespread smile across his face.

"All done?"

"All done," he answered, kissing her lightly on the cheek. "Baby, I love you so much. I don't know what I did to deserve you, but..."

"Don't worry about *how* you got me. Just don't *lose* me."

Christina's words were like a direct order – one which Shane did not know whether was from her or a higher authority. He looked at her for some sort of indication as to the source of her comment, but she kept her eyes on the road.

"Christina, how did you know how much..."

"Been there, done that." He wanted to take back his question as badly as she had her remark minutes earlier. Shane felt a hurt for Christina that her own life had not been more perfect, like the one she had envisioned her entire childhood, as he heard the hurt in her own voice. "As badly as Tom wanted to get rid of me and the kids, I had to even hold his hand and walk him through our divorce. Isn't that a bummer?" she mumbled remorsefully as she pulled up to the red light.

"No, baby, it isn't," he answered sprightly with a huge kiss. "If that moron hadn't been so stupid as to have gotten rid of you, I wouldn't be here right now with the most beautiful creature on the face of the earth!"

"You certainly know how to get to a girl's heart, don't you?" she smiled, the depression from seconds ago disappearing.

"I hope so!" he said, grinning more excitedly now.

Christina had already made plans to surprise him with their own private celebration, but after the way things turned out, she changed her mind, afraid that neither of them was in the mood. But his giddiness and humor changed her fickle female mind again.

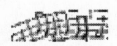

When she made the turn at Little Switzerland, she darted up the hill into the joint where he had brought her only a few weeks before. "I thought you could probably use one just about now."

"Oh, Christina. You *really* are an angel!"

"I *have* been told that on occasion!" she laughed, once again full of glee.

Shane slipped his arm around Christina's waist, feeling her small frame in his hand. He would have given that arm to take her to the motel room above the bar and make her his at that very moment. The feeling inside him was overwhelming, yet at the same time, it tore him apart. For two years, he had known what he was going to do the minute he got his divorce, and now his head was in a spin trying to change gears and regroup.

They headed for their corner table and Shane placed an order for a beer and an iced tea, with potato skins for her and mushrooms for himself. The two of them sat in the corner and laughed until they were doubled over. Luckily, they didn't have the same waitress as before. They were causing even more of a scene this time than they had then.

The day had been a success for many reasons, all ones that Shane prayed for heartily. And now, he was going to get to watch the sunset with his two favorite things, one in each hand. It was all he could do to fight the tears. Tears of joy. Tears of betrayal. Tears of fear for what came next. But the face in front of him signaled his brain that he could do that later, when he was at the Kershaws' all alone. *Alone? I'm never alone anymore. There's always at least two presences with me everywhere I go, even in my sleep.*

When the waitress brought their drinks, Christina picked up her glass and held it toward Shane, who took her cue and picked up his bottle. As their vessels met in the air, she gave the toast.

"To you. To you and Shay." Christina eyed him, wondering whether to continue. "And . . . to us."

The sound of glass clinking in the air did not even stir the attention of the people around them, but to the enchanted couple, it was loud enough to shout Shane's successes of the day to the entire world.

He gazed into Christina's eyes, knowing that he owed the lofty heights to which he had climbed that day to her. "Baby, I would not be here right now without you. Not just physically, but mentally or emotionally. You have been *everything* to me." Shane's pause allowed her to realize that he also regretted the *one* exception to that sharing of their love. Even as they sat there, staring at each other and carrying on one of their conversations without words, she wondered how much longer she could hold onto him without shattering her values, those things which had been sacred to her ever since she could remember. "Christina, I will give you every last penny of that money back."

"Oh, no, you won't!"

"Baby, there's no way I could accept that money from you."

"Listen, dude. You'd better enjoy it. It is the *only* divorce I ever intend to give you!"

He looked at her, evaluating her comment, and wondering whether there was indeed any seriousness in it. "You promise?"

"I do. Twenty-five years or otherwise."

Shane put down his bottle and reached over and kissed his lady. Had he known for sure that she would take that step with him, that step which she had vowed never to take again, and had warned him on numerous occasions not to dare cross with her, he would have made her his forever. Yet, in the back of his mind, promises from the last two years came pounding down on him. Promises that were made before Christina. Promises that he feared, if broken, would shatter the life of another. He decided to retreat from that line of thinking and enjoy the rest of the day.

"Christina, I know you make a lot of concessions for me. I really feel bad about that."

"Stop!" She had rarely put her foot down like that with him, and he knew better than to cross her if she felt the urge to be that emphatic. But Christina also knew him well enough to know that he would listen, especially to reason, and especially if it was from her. "Shane, I am not doing anything here against my wishes. Can you not see that for me, a person who has given my entire life to God, to see Him take a person like you, a product of your own hell, and shape you and mold you, and allow you to stand beside me and make a difference in the life of others . . . can you not see that *I* am the one who is privileged here? To me, it feels like I've been chosen to see a miracle happen right before my very eyes. Yes, I am good for you. I know I'm *very* good for you, just as you are for me. But, baby, this is *your* life. And nothing is happening here that *you* do not want to happen, that *you* are not allowing to happen. I am nothing more than a hand for you to hold. *You* are the one in charge here. *You AND God!*"

She reached out and pulled his sleeve up over the eagle and rubbed her fingers over it. "Shane . . ." Christina looked at him, lost for words, but with an expression that needed no words. The man gazing at her knew everything that she meant to say, and that she felt. It drove down to the core of his soul, and pulled at him like nothing he had ever known.

Shane watched the woman in front of him, a tower of strength, but a person who still needed someone else. She leaned solely on one source for her strength, but he knew that he had pulled much of it out of her – strength that had been sunken like treasure from an abused past. He thought of her as opposed to Carla, a good person who wanted to help others, but was incapable of even helping herself, thereby only becoming frustrated at her own inability to help anyone, especially herself. He thought of himself, who had been in the same boat as Carla, but who, thanks to Christina, had met and faced the challenges of getting himself to the point that he could help others. He thought of Christina, whose ability to help others had taken over her entire life, to the point that when she needed help herself, she shut down and locked herself away, still throwing all of her energies into all of those around her. *And,* he thought of the decision he was going to have to make, and how he was going to handle it, trying to find an easy, *and painless,* way out – *for everyone.*

# 21

The day of the big musical finally arrived. Christina got to the church to find Shane already there, checking all the sets and props, making sure that the scenery was all still in place, and that the luncheon crew had everything under control. There was not one thing left unattended by the time she arrived. He came over to greet her, handed her an iced tea, and give her a quick kiss.

She smiled, knowing that she really had no need to worry. There was something about the rebel's presence that gave her a calm and a security that had been absent, not only from her life, but especially in her work. Her first husband had been supportive of her work, but Tom, who himself was a musician and performer, did nothing but *totally* stress her and everyone else, so she had been left her entire life to find her own way of preparing for performances. And even though she had never seen her church work as a performance, she had always felt it her duty to give her very best to the One who had given her the talent.

Now here was the most unlikely of characters, who not only gave her a feeling of assurance, but checked every detail behind her, reading her mind, and taking care of things, even before she realized she needed them done herself. Christina had notoriously taken great pride in her work, but since Shane had become a part of the picture, she had truly blossomed. People who had been her greatest admirers began to comment to each other, and to her, about the quality of her talent, saying how she had gone beyond the realms of her usual grandeur.

The musical was a great success, the greatest, in fact, that she had ever done. Shane did a superb job, hidden back in the balcony, as he provided the booming voice of God speaking down to Moses. *Not your typical type-casting!*, Christina had ribbed him when she asked him to do the part.

Everyone claimed the best line of the musical came when the guy playing Moses meandered out onto the stage in perfect western fashion, minus one minute detail, however. He had forgotten to bring out his rod at the time it was supposed to become a snake. In his deepest, demanding voice, everyone heard a voice, intended to be God's, rattle the rafters with, "Moses, you need a staff!" The crowd cheered as the Moses character tapped his ten-gallon hat in a salute to Shane, still hidden in the balcony, and scooted offstage to grab the originally designed prop that actually did convert to a snake, thanks to Christina's unlikely sidekick.

People had begun to expect that where one was, so was the other. Shane showed up for every function which involved Christina, and even took her to a couple of his favorite old joints to let the guys see what exactly had taken up his time lately and caused the sudden change in him.

"Man, you don't even look like the same person who was in here three months ago. What's got a holt o' you?"

Shane beamed as he held onto his lady, who smiled up at him. He tightened his grip on her as he pulled Christina in, closer to him, and answered, "An angel. An angel who loved the hell out of me." And with that, he reached down and kissed her forehead, while she squeezed his arm and rested her petite palm on his cheek, as they stared in each other's eyes.

Had it been anyone else, the guys would have ribbed him terribly, or guffawed at the mention of an angel in their hang-out. But they saw from the sincerity in his eyes that Shane spoke the truth, and they were genuinely humbled by the couple's reaction to each other, and the sway as their bodies moved together in complete harmony. This was not the same picture they had seen of him with Carla, or his other female companions. His 'angel' was in a class all by herself, a class out of their league, yet that they respected. The guys immediately accepted Christina into their company, and, as if they sensed her status as a lady, their rough language was suddenly minus the four-letter words, and the topics of their conversation hit a notch higher on the intellectual totem pole. Several of them even wondered if they might be that lucky one day, mentally speculating on how their friend had entered her realm.

When the couple got outside, Christina paused before getting in the car. "Shane, about what you said in there . . ."

Shane looked at Christina, wondering if he had humiliated her in an uncomfortable surrounding. "I didn't embarrass you, did I?"

"No, not at all. But do you realize the impact of what you said?" Shane looked at her, puzzled at first, but suddenly aware of the fact that his friends did not make jokes or give Christina all sorts of tales of his past. She went on with her thoughts, "I *did* love the hell out of you. I really *did* love the very hell right out of you."

He saw a pride in her eyes that he had made that realization on his own. Shane could tell from the expression on her face that she had been aware of that truth for quite some time, but had kept it to herself, waiting to see if his mind could make the analogy for itself.

"Great! And now you're never going to let me live it down, huh?"

"Absolutely not. I'll bet you've never known any one else whose love was strong or solid enough to do that."

Shane looked down into her serious, yet smiling, face, its eyes huge as they questioned him on that point, with her eyebrows raised – an expression she shot at him often these days. He thought about her comment and the look on her face for a few brief moments, then he said in the most serious tone she had ever heard from him, "No, I have not."

At that instance, Shane realized, even more than ever, that she truly did possess a love for him that was incomparable to anything he had ever known. And her expressions of that love not only had an impact on him from her personally, but from her God, too. He sensed the extent to which he had already changed, suddenly feeling that much of the weight that had been on his shoulders, even a month ago, was now gone. But the thing that grabbed at him most was the feeling he had for her, the love that was so unlike what he had for Carla, who he still wrote and talked to every day. It was nothing like he had felt in his first marriage, or for any of the women between them. But, it was a feeling that really began to gnaw at him, making him wonder more and more if he was worthy of his angel, of the love that came from above by being with her, and more than anything, if he could love her in return with that same fervor.

Christina read the worry on his face and said to him simply as they got in the Blazer, "Shane, the love that God has for you has *absolutely nothing* to do with me, or being with me, or you being with someone else. That is a love that God had for you when you were still in your mother's womb," and she could see the distrust in his eyes, knowing his real mother had given him up for adoption at birth, so she finished, "no matter *who* she was, or *what* she was.

He loved *you*, babe." Her rebel looked at her, wanting to believe her, yet still feeling unworthy, and now wondering about his biological mother. "And Shane, God loves your mother just as much as He does you." His eyes were still questioning the words that he had just heard. "If you don't believe me, take His word," and she reached into the back seat for her Bible which she had taken to the hospital earlier in the day, turned to Jeremiah 1:5, and handed him the Book.

Tears formed in his eyes and began to run down his face as he read the verse of scripture, and reread it, several times over. He closed the Bible and handed it back to the unusual creature who sat looking at him. "Christina, I *do* love you. I *really do* love you."

"Yes, Shane, I know you do. And I accept that love, and I *love* knowing that you love me. But the question here is, 'Can you accept and deal with that great a love?'"

With those words, she started the engine and drove home, giving him an entire ride in silence, letting the reverberations of His word and her words reach the farthest depths of Shane's mind and his soul.

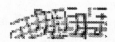

Sleep would not come as the words of Christina's question kept repeating themselves the rest of the evening. Finally, after three restless hours of tossing and turning, he wandered over to Ron's downstairs bookcase and hunted until he found a Bible. Shane thumbed through the pages until he found the passage Christina had shared with him earlier in the day.

*He knew me while I was still in the womb. He had a purpose for my life. I can be that disciple that Christina keeps telling me about.* Shane's mind and conscience were wrestling between setting a good example for one who he knew had no one else, and being true to one who was surrounded by numerous others. As badly as he wanted to be true to his angel, so he also wanted to help Carla before he left her stranded. Shane read the verse several more times as if it held some coded message for which only he held the key.

*If Christina's God loves me as much as she says He does, this can work.* Thirty minutes later, he was sleeping soundly, sure that his vision was heaven sent.

After work the next day, Shane called Carla to ask if he could come over for a short visit. The fretful anticipation of seeing her had rippled through him all day. *This is it,* he had told himself over and over, building his own inner confidence that he could give her a hope – the same hope Christina had offered him. *No,* he could hear his angel's voice, *the hope your Father gave you.*

The huge grin plastered all over his face proved that he had finally caught Christina in a lie, and he could not wait to call her hand on it. *For someone who professes to be unable to sing, she certainly uses her voice a whole lot as an instrument – His instrument, even when she's not physically with me.* He knew his comment would get just as large a grin from her.

When Shane knocked on the door, Carla opened it, handed him a beer, and kissed him before bursting into tears.

"What's wrong, Precious?" he responded, calling her by the pet name he had affectionately given her two years ago.

"I got called in at work today. The old jerk claims I'm not keepin' up like I used to. Says I look hung over all the time. What the hell does he expect? For Christ's sake, I just got outta prison and I haven't got my groove back yet. And on top o' that, now he's makin' me come in at four ev'ry mornin' when he opens the kitchen. How am I supposed to get there at that ungodly hour? My roommate has been droppin' me off on his way to work ev'ryday, and there's no way I can pay a cab fare on my measly pay. It's all I can do to pay for my beer and cigarettes."

Shane noticed that after being with Christina for only three months, his mind mentally skipped over all the colorful adjectives that were a part of Carla's vocabulary. The difference in their speech and mannerisms had never really dawned on him until this very moment. *But then Carla was gone by the time I met Christina. Maybe there is something to that old adage, "Out of sight, out of mind."*

Although Carla had once been a beautiful creature to him, the effect of alcohol was evident in her appearance. He knew what had first attracted him to her, *besides the fact that she could drink as much as me,* was her ability to accept anyone, and let all the bums who had gotten thrown out of their homes stay at her place until they could get back on their feet again. *In a way, like Christina,* he thought, trying to convince himself that there really was not all that much difference between these two women.

"What's the matter? Too good to drink with me anymore?" noting that Shane had set the beer, untouched, on the coffee table.

"No, it's just that . . ." *How am I supposed to explain to this person, who* was *my drinking partner for the past two years, that I have a life outside the bottle now?* But Shane knew that in order to carry out the vision he had seen last night, he had to do exactly that. "I'll have *one,*" he ventured, not wanting to offend her, "then I've gotta go. I'm supposed to be helping a friend do some work on a garage this evening."

Shane didn't bother to share the identity of that friend. *That can come later – AFTER I get Carla through this crisis,* he told himself confidently.

Three beers later, Carla was begging him to hold her, to tell her everything would be alright, like he had done so many times before. "I don't know what I woulda done if you hadn't called me," she whined, her words slurred, in that same voice of desperation that had first pulled him into her drunken web. But Shane knew. She would have lost herself in her bottle, like he had watched her do on so many previous occasions. *And like I had done so many times myself before God gave me my very own angel.* He excused himself, knowing that Christina had a scrumptious meal waiting for him, and a garage whose contents needed to be rearranged to make room for the things she had offered to let him store until he found a place of his own.

Before he left, he offered to get Carla to work for the next few mornings until she could make other arrangements, thinking of how he was only extending the same helping hand Christina had so graciously reached out to him while he was working his way up his self-made cavern.

*God's plan WILL work,* Shane assured himself, backing out of Carla's driveway, proud that he had been able to help someone who really needed him.

# 22

Normally, there was such a rush through Lent, racing straight up to Palm Sunday and then Easter, finally moving into the spring musicals to finish the school year, it was all Christina could do to keep up with herself. But every since that fateful evening that she and Shane had clashed into each other, like two out-of-control meteors, with years of pain and distrust being chiseled away, like sparks flying in every direction to make a colossal meteor shower, time had barely moved for the two of them.

It seemed their Father had given them a world of their own to connect, to learn each other, to share everything within and around them, like Adam and Eve in the Garden of Paradise. But, Christina wondered how much longer Shane could go without listening to the voice of the asp, and taking a bite from the forbidden fruit. As much as she wanted to hold onto him forever, she sensed more and more that the day would come when he could no longer fight off the temptation. She feared that day, and the doom that would become of their love, a love that was meant to be an eternal love. Shane did not have the background of spiritual strength that she did, and she knew *that*, in itself, would prevent him from resisting the evil that was weighing on him heavier and heavier with each passing day.

Carla's interruptions were becoming increasingly more frequent, and Shane was jumping at her every command, not realizing that she was only taking advantage of his generosity. Christina was sure that the poor woman had no idea of the relationship between Shane and herself. She pleaded with him to talk openly and be honest with Carla. But every time he got his courage up, he was beaten down by the giant of her alcoholism and instability. The minister even offered to go with him, but he was so determined that since he had successfully fought off every other avenger in his life, he could beat this one, as well.

Christina's prayers took up more of her days, as she searched for wisdom and guidance in her love for this man whom she had found out actually belonged to another. To her, the love they had shared was so blessed, however, if that *was* the case, why was it threatened by another being. She knew the value of conflict and strife. Perhaps, once the temptress had been overcome, the relationship between she and Shane would be even stronger. She also knew that the temptress was only interested in Shane for the moment. That was obvious by her actions of calling him at all hours of the day and night – only when she wanted something, begging him to come over and take care of her, then throwing him back out, back into the arms of Christina.

With each phone call, Christina could not help but hear the constant yelling and screaming that came from both ends of the phone, as Carla and Shane tried to make the impossible happen – a love that was sanctified from above. Still a gift that neither of them knew how to accept, much less tend and cultivate.

She was not the poor, blind, naive soul that Shane suspected. Christina was wise enough to refuse to be a fool for anyone. During the course of the last four months, she had learned that, for all of his outer shell, his fierce guard which he never let down – except to her – he was the most tender-hearted creature she had ever encountered. It was clear that even though he had grown accustomed to 'having his cake and eating it, too' over the last twenty years, his major problem in the present case was his insatiable desire not to hurt *either* of his women.

His angel begged and pleaded with him, time after time, to face the reality of the situation, and move forward with his life, no matter which direction he chose. She tried to make him see that his aloofness would only hurt everyone, *him the most*, even more in the long run. As badly as she wanted to come out victorious, Christina also wanted his happiness. She loved Shane enough to fight any battle to keep him, *if* that was part of her Divine Plan. But, at the same time, she knew that good things came to those who waited – who waited upon the Lord.

Yes, she indeed wanted Shane Sievers. She wanted him more than anything, to share a life with him. But, she knew that even though it was clear that the Almighty had brought them together, perhaps the timing was not yet right. *And*, perhaps Shane's weak consciousness needed a longer period of growth. For whatever reason, though, Christina pledged to God, and to herself, that she wanted to hold onto him until the time came to cut him loose. Then she knew, that if it was ever meant to be, Shane Sievers would find his way back to her. And, if he did not, then they had never shared love.

So, now that the Clueless rock no longer existed, along with the heinous tortures that had been attached to it, Christina pondered over whether Shane could do the same with the monkey on his own back. Regardless, for her sake, her life had lost a whole set of stresses with the disposal of that rock, ones that had weighted her down for years. And now, with or without Shane, her life would be better for it.

Shane could sense the distance that Carla's calls were placing between himself and his angel. Holding onto his personal vow to never lose his place on Christina's plateau, he knew it was time to come clean with his ex-lover. Besides, this had become the same as a dare to him. He had promised Christina that he *could* accept, and *could* reciprocate the love given to them from a greater being. Now he had to prove his point not only to her, but to himself.

*This is the day!*, he declared emphatically, looking in the mirror as he got ready for work. *I've given Carla as much as I can, and now she's got to depend on her own inner strength.*

Carla had called him again last night, begging him to pick her up after work today. "You've got to come talk to me. I *need* somebody, and you're the one who's *always* been there for me."

Hesitant about going at first, Shane persuaded himself that this was the perfect opportunity to clear the air with Carla once and for all. Even though he was anxious to take this giant step forward, the confession was *not* a chore that Shane relished.

Shane knew the stars were smiling on him when his boss gave him the afternoon off. While the rest of his co-workers took off for the golf course, he headed towards the grease dive where Carla worked. He called Christina to tell her that the bothersome phone calls were about to be history, and to be prepared for a big celebration at dinner. The enthusiasm in her voice made his heart beat a little faster as it gave him an extra dose of confidence.

His instinct told him to wait until he got Carla to her trailer before he broke the news. Shane had no desire to go in, but he felt like he should at least have the decency to look her in the eyes when he told her about the angel who had walked into his life. But before he got a chance to start a conversation, Carla broke out in tears.

"I know you need me as bad as I need you. Take me to your place, baby. I need a break from this old trailer. It doesn't even feel like home anymore. I need to be in a man's arms. I need to feel loved."

There was a slight pause as Shane stood silent in the doorway, his mind fumbling to put together the words that he wanted to come out without offending this woman who had shared two years of his life. *Or hell, as it was*, reminding himself of the difference from what the past few months had been. But as Carla wrapped her arms around him, pulling him closer to her, he felt the desires that had been such a common part of his life for so many years making their way slowly through his body - a body that was fighting everything it felt, trying to overshadow his physical feelings by the mental and emotional ones he shared with Christina.

"You do still love me, don't you?" Carla's words, accompanied by her usual muffled whine, interrupted the tug-of-war going on between his head and his heart.

*This is going to be harder than I thought. I'll take her somewhere that we can have a quiet place when I tell her there is someone else. I'm sure she'll need a shoulder to cry on, so the privacy of Ron's basement will make it easier for her. Besides, my own turf will keep me stronger*, he reasoned, battling with himself rather than with her.

The drive to Ron's was silent as Shane tried to choose the right words to break the news to Carla. In reality, he knew his head was trying to convince his heart that he was not making a mistake by taking her to his current residence.

*Christina allowed me the courtesy of coming over to her place when I finally decided to unload the sins of my past. It wasn't so bad.* Shane knew that if it was alright for Christina, it was alright for him. There was no way she could object to his motive. *Besides, in a couple of hours, this will all be over, I can be a source of*

339

*strength for Carla, and YES, Ms. Christina Cache, I CAN deal with that great love you are able to give me.*

Just before he turned on the street to his temporary apartment, he stopped at the corner convenience store and grabbed a six-pack. *To ease the blow!*, he told himself, getting more and more worried about the oncoming reaction from this woman sitting across the seat from him, knowing it was going to hit more than the proverbial 'fan.' Shane's sense of confidence dwindled as he turned into the driveway. *No, I need all the help I can get*, he decided, patting the bag of bottles beside him and forgetting the first lesson, that one about "from whence my help cometh", that Christina had taught him.

One day in the middle of May, Christina got a call from Ron. They spoke to each other fairly often since she was a frequent visitor of their basement guest. He called to inquire about the female who had been with Shane that afternoon.

"Oh, yes. She's that friend of his that got out of prison a few weeks ago. You know, the one who kept trying to call your house collect. He just took her out for a late lunch and is trying to help her get acclimated to being home. Her roommate apparently changed around her entire trailer while she was gone, and she is having a tough time adjusting."

They chatted briefly, each inquiring about the other's family, and comparing notes from each of their respective jobs. Ron offered Christina some fresh ideas for children's sermons, and she offered him some suggestions for summer programs.

After she hung up the phone, she played the conversation back over again and again in her head. *There was a reason for that call from Ron.* Christina, with her sixth sense, could tell that the *real* message was not in what he had told her, but rather in what he had *not* told her. *Yes, there was most definitely more to that phone call than met my ear!*, she exclaimed to herself, as she saw her worst nightmare coming true before her very eyes.

Christina failed to mention the call to Shane. She knew that he was facing a jail sentence in a couple of weeks, and regardless of what was going on between them personally, she *had* been a mentor to him. He needed her strength to get him through not only the court case, but the impending incarceration.

She was so extremely proud of the fact that he was facing challenges that had haunted him for up to five years. He had earned her support and her friendship, especially now that he was turning himself in and accepting punishment for crimes of his past, just to clear up the record for his son's sake.

Besides, Carla or no Carla, he and Noah had given her the most wonderful birthday in her entire forty-four years. Who else would have been cunning enough to have set off fireworks both to begin and end her special day? And who else could have managed everything he did for her musical? She knew there was no answer for either question, so out of obligation, she made up her mind to be a lady and stick out the next couple of weeks with him. After that, she would have done her duty, and could chalk him up to another major mistake in the life of Christina Cache. But, for the time being, she was, true to tradition, going to take the brunt of the hurt to try to allow someone else to get their life together.

*It's only a couple of weeks. After what I've withstood for the past thirteen years, that will be a breeze. Besides, who can say what may come of this?*, Christina asked herself as she prayed that if there be any way possible, he would one day be hers.

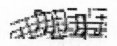

What she did not know was that while she was tending his child during the day, Shane was tending something else, something that was unavailable from Christina. His angel could buy expensive wrestling tickets for his son's Easter basket and lower herself to go to a sports arena to watch the event, she could entertain them, giving both of them opportunities that would have otherwise been impossible for Shane to give his son, she could drive all over the state to provide transportation for the father and son, and she could even move in with Abigail and give up her own home for the two of them, so that they could be together. Yet, she could not give him the one thing he had not been able to do without.

Christina noticed that every time they were anywhere together, his phone continued to ring, most of the time with Shane excusing himself. When she realized that Shane was keeping Carla in the dark about her, she put her foot down, demanding that if she was going to be a part of his life, Carla needed to know about her presence. After all, they were hopefully someday going to work together, regardless of their personal relationship, and Christina wanted his friend to know from the outset exactly how close they were.

The one thing that Shane failed to inform his angel about was the fact that some habits were too hard to break, even for someone as strong and determined as himself. He had been married to a woman who not only let him, but expected him, to go out and have himself a good time in her absence, knowing that she was enjoying the same privilege. In his mind, he argued that he was only going to see Carla when he absolutely had to, still trying to convince himself that he loved his angel, that she was the best thing that had ever happened to him, and that he would wean himself off Carla gradually until he could have all of Christina.

There was only one court case pending. Shane had breezed through all of the others, more than he could count on his fingers, with the judges and district attorneys being so impressed with his obvious change that he had managed to escape any jail time, which to date, could have amounted to at least eight years.

But his last case was assured to get him some time. "Up to two years," he had confided to Christina when she cornered him, demanding an answer.

She had yet to mention Ron's call, *or* her intuition that was admonishing her conscience daily for allowing his betrayal. There was no point in adding salt to a wound at the time being. Besides, as usual, she was the strong one who always got the duty of holding everybody else up.

Christina was the only woman who had ever "kicked his ass," as Shane put it, on the one time he had allowed himself to get into a drunken frenzy, feeling he had let Carla down by not being at a hearing with her – the first he had missed in their nearly two years together. The angel's threat to walk completely out of his life "if you *ever* pull that stunt again" grabbed his attention enough that he promised her, *and himself*, that it was a one-time slip into the past.

She had felt so bad that he sensed such a deep devotion to a friend in need, Christina forgave his drunken behavior, and went over to sober him up. However, he did not get by without a good, swift kick in the rear, along with the words of her reprimand.

"You'd better enjoy that," Shane had told her. "You'll never get the chance again!"

"I'd better not, or you'll never get the chance to enjoy my company again!"

Shane could not believe that, even in his inebriated state, she still was not afraid to face him, give him "what for" and stand up for herself, then brag about it. As mad as it made him, he couldn't help but respect Christina's raw, gutsy disposition. He questioned her knowledge of how to take care of his condition the next morning.

"Do you not think that Sundance had Etta stick around for some useful purpose? She knew to give him a 'hair of the dog' when he had too much!"

He immediately dropped the subject, knowing that no matter which turn he took, she would win that round hands-down. Shane's best option was to let it slip from both their memories as quickly as possible.

Christina did not have the nerve to tell Shane that as soon as his jail term was up, he would not get another kicking, but he *would* get a "Dear John" letter. His incarceration would give him a chance to start anew, and she was determined that it would be without her. She refused to play second fiddle to anyone, *especially a low-life piece of trailer trash* - a judgmental thought she regretted having made as soon as it ran its ugly path across her brain.

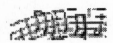

The hearing came, and Shane was given two weeks instead of two years. He called Christina everyday, and begged her to come and see him since she could get in any time with her status as a minister. The inmate grabbed her shoulders, pulled her to the bars, and planted a kiss on her.

"I'll bet that's the first time you've ever been loved inside out," Christina teased.

"You've loved the hell out of me. Why shouldn't you love me inside out?"

They both laughed and enjoyed the visit immensely. Shane introduced his woman to the other inmates in his block, proud of her poise and beauty, and prestigious position, although he never admitted the last detail to her. The guys all commented on the cards she had sent to him, verbally wishing they had a woman that thoughtful. Christina drove across the street to the drugstore and bought cards for each of the inmates, taking them to the local post office so that all the guys would get mail the following day.

She left, hating what would happen in the next two weeks. The attraction between them still could not be denied, and it tore at Christina's heart to think that she was going to have to end their relationship. Shane *was* the love of her life.

*Wouldn't it be just my luck to pick a player that's already on another team?*

Shane had tried his best to be faithful to Christina, but he had found Carla before, and they had shared their addictions with each other - Shane with his drugs, and Carla with her booze. They thrived on each other's company, for one was as out of control as the other. The problem was, for both of them, that their additions were so overbearingly strong, that they mistook their love for their habits as love of each other, especially while satisfying their addictions of the flesh.

When he got home, after Christina picked him up at the jailhouse, she packed Shane's things that he had stored in her garage, and told him to go to his mistress. Shane did not want to leave her, yet he knew that Carla was struggling with holding herself together, and he felt responsible for helping her get to the point to which his angel had brought him. What Shane failed to see was that as he was turning more to Carla's aid, so were his denied habits.

He continued to call Christina and go by to check on her

everyday. She could see the alcohol and the stress of the lifestyle back on his face and in his eyes. It bothered her, a fact she did not keep from him. With the same honesty on which they had built their relationship, she continued to tell him exactly what she thought. Shane listened to her advice, and wanted desperately to follow it, still fighting with his conscience over what was the right thing to do.

Shane refused to let his angel get away. In his mind, he simply had some unfinished business from the past, some chores that still needed to be done. One afternoon, he even dropped by Christina's house with a CD of a song with that same message, asking her to be patient with him, and continue to love him as he did her. The female minister looked at him, wondering how ridiculously stupid he thought she could be. Yet, as he backed out the driveway and headed down the street, she made a personal promise to herself that she *would* have him one day when his chores actually were done. But, *at the same time*, she vowed that would only happen if she had not already gotten to the finish line with someone who was the man she had dreamed of her entire life – a man who believed in her fully, and in whom she believed and trusted with all her being. That picture of a man no longer fit Shane's image, changed drastically from the man she had met five months ago.

Her heart still yearned for him, even though Christina tried to throw everything about Shane out of her life. She threw herself into her work, her writing, her sons – anything to try to avoid his memory, but to no avail.

Abigail and Noah both saw through the facade she built to cover her thoughts and emotions. Others simply thought her elusiveness came from all the trouble she was going through with Matt, Tom, and the fact of being a moody musician – especially a female one who had passed the age of forty.

In spite of her continued efforts to rid her life of him, and force his hand to go back to Carla once and for all, Shane still spent several hours a day with Christina, and continued to call her throughout each day, needing her magic mental potion that helped him keep his anger and bitterness, and especially his aberrant temper that went with them, under control. Christina wanted to help him, and she knew why, but she forced herself to accept that he was her job – *only her job* – from here on out. Her heart would no longer rule her actions, but only her head and her call to her profession.

That realization made her think of both Shane's first wife, and Carla, each in their own personal scenarios. For years, neither of them had been nothing more than a man's plaything. They had never expected enough of themselves to make a man give up everything for them, so why should the men in their lives. Of course, their men were going to do nothing more than was expected of them. That was only human nature. And so, in a sense, their degrading moral situations were *their* calls to their hobbies.

Christina looked at her background and upcoming as compared to theirs, and her educational level, as well. She had been blessed with gifts that neither of them had. Her opportunities had afforded her the chance to be somebody, a lady, a servant to mankind, but in a very different way from which they served mankind.

Yet, who was she to judge them, to downgrade them. They *were* what they were, just as she was. And the situation *was* Shane's bed. *Literally.* He had made it and now he would have to lie in it. In it, without Christina, and all she had to offer. The problem was, she knew that ultimately, it was his loss. *But, why do I have to be the one who feels so lost now?*

Shane, who had not completely conquered the infamous addict mentality, still had no idea what his association with Carla was doing to him. His work had suffered, his child was losing out on a decent future, and his own quality of life was diving straight back into the mire of the past. He was struggling to be strong, yet he was still not equipped with all he needed to have his own life in order, much less take in someone else and their multitude of problems. The rebel had neither the experience, nor the resources, for that astronomical undertaking. And the desire, which accounted for much, to care solely for his former lover was not really there, either.

What was there, however, for both Shane and Carla, was an obsession – one that was evil and demeaning to them – individually, and as a couple. One that was tearing them both apart inside. One that was leaving each of them feeling unfulfilled. One that was built on screaming and yelling. One that was trying to force something that wasn't really there. Something from above. Something that Shane had tasted and longed for in his life. *Yet*, something that God only gave as He saw fit.

After Ron's phone call last month, Christina had purchased a city map and found Carla's street. Her quick sense of memorization had recalled the address from the first time she accompanied Shane to the courthouse to face one of his many past offenses. She could not believe that the trailer park was not even five miles away from her own house.

His angel decided to make it easy for him. Christina did not want him to be placed in an awkward, or an uncomfortable situation, even though she knew Shane deserved everything he got. Perhaps she was being even more of an enabler by not forcing him to be completely upfront or honest with Carla. But the fact of the matter was, it was over, she knew it was over, and he was going to have to face for himself that it was over – a *slight* detail he had not taken care of, as of yet.

She knew that he would be there, that he had moved in with his lover, but the horrendous ripples of pain still ran through

Christina as she passed by Carla's trailer and saw Shane's car parked beside it. Every bone in her body yelled at her to march right up to the door, confront him, and blow his little scam. But she had to leave him with some sense of dignity.

Christina quickly pulled the mounted bear head – one of his prized possessions that had made its way to her house – from the hatch, leaned it up against Shane's car door, and tied the "Get Lost" letter around its neck. When he came out the next morning to go to work, he would get the shock of his life, but he would know that the truth was out in the open and there would be no point in him making excuses or trying to lie or deceive anyone any longer.

As badly as she hated that it had come to this, she was, quite frankly, extremely proud of herself. She was surviving, she was laughing, she was . . . *Christina, who are you trying to fool? Your heart is breaking.* The only way the servant of God knew how to get through this was to look to Him for comfort, to pour out continual prayers. Prayers for herself, prayers for Shane, *and yes,* even prayers for Carla.

She had called Abigail before her trip to the trailer park, and Paul insisted that Christina come to their house when she got back. He was worried about her safety, going into such a rough crime area so late at night (or early in the morning, as the case was), but more than that, he was concerned about her emotional well-being.

The psychology major had seen the mounting love between the couple during the past five months. But Paul, who had gotten Shane a job in his warehouse, had also seen the number of phone calls the two-timer got at work each day, and the number of afternoons he had taken off to be with Carla. He had desperately wanted to warn Christina of what was going on, afraid that she was unaware of the situation brewing between her rebel and his former lover, but decided he could not be the one to tear her world apart, knowing that he and Abigail would be there if, and when,

349

the need arose.

Christina used her key to get in the Howell's house, not wanting to get them out of bed. She pranced right into the master bedroom and plopped up squarely in the middle of the couple she had come to visit, rattling off all the details of her excursion like an excited young child who had just seen all the surprises left under the Christmas tree by Santa. Paul realized, as he lay there in bewilderment, watching and listening to her, that his son's godmother was going to make it through yet another crisis. Their guest had both him and Abigail rollicking in laughter as she spilled out her reaction to the forlorn love she had just left.

Paul had known her intimately enough through her close sisterhood to his wife to understand that Christina dealt with her pain through laughter. *The best medicine in the world*, he thought as he recalled the quote from numerous college courses, and as he watched her prove its validity.

The threesome talked for more than an hour, with Paul shaking his head at Christina most of the time. He had grown to know better than to listen to her in disbelief, but rather, in amazement at her ability to shake off her hurt. Most people would have harbored bitterness and anger, destroying them and making their period of grief last longer. But this woman, this creature whom few understood, breezed through life with an affection for all its offerings, so that she did not miss anything that God tossed at her. *For better or worse!*, he mused, as he continued to listen to her.

Abigail asked if Christina, who was providing them with a wealth of entertainment, would like to stay the rest of the night, still concerned that her mood might change drastically if she were alone.

"No. I need to go home. Besides, I'm still not sure that I may not go camp out and watch Shane's surprise when he faces the bear later this morning."

As much as they both wished she was kidding, Paul and Abigail knew quite well that it would be like Christina to do exactly that, and if she so chose, there was nothing they could do to change her mind. They said their good-byes, and the couple bid their guest to be cautious, whatever she did.

Assuring them she would, Christina went home, and lay awake most of the morning, still thinking of going to see Shane's reaction for herself. However, she knew that he really *did* love her in his own way, and she respected even that small amount of love enough not to put him through the humiliation of facing her when he was hit with the truth. She suspected that his morning would be difficult enough, and she did not want to add to his pain.

In fact, she felt terribly sorry for him. Even though he would get the prize he wanted, he would miss out on the real prize – the one that could offer him true happiness and eternal bliss. The pity for what he had just lost hurt her much deeper than her own loss of the one man she had ever loved.

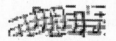

Wanting to be gone when Shane came to collect the rest of his belongings, Christina planned a full day of running errands. The first item on her agenda was to take Noah to get his driver's permit. They celebrated royally for lunch, laughing and joking at everything that came to mind. She was determined that Noah would not see any pain or disappointment in her.

By the time they finally returned home, Christina knew she had to get away, or literally go out of her mind. Her week's responsibilities at church were over after the Bible School ended yesterday. And she felt like the world's biggest fool for watching Shay all week while Shane had spent his time with Carla. Had she not just recently vowed that *no one* would ever abuse her again? If this was not abuse, what was it? There was no doubt in her mind that it was most definitely time, *NO! long overdue*, to excuse herself from this situation.

She could not believe that he took Shay to jail in the pouring rain two evenings ago to get Carla. Rain and wind that were so bad that it ripped his umbrella completely to shreds. This was for a slut who showed up drunk for her probation meeting and was hauled straight back to jail.

And then yesterday, she forced Shane to make Carla keep Shay after Bible School was over. When she talked to Shay today, she found out that they had played poker for peanuts. What a wonderful, enriching and educational thing for a ten-year-old, especially one that bright, and who followed in his dad's footsteps so closely. *They've probably got him tending bar as they sit and get blitzed.* Christina's ramblings were making her feel more and more like a total fool as she continued to scrutinize herself.

To top it all off, Christina's suspicion was confirmed when she found out that Shane had asked Carla to move away with him and get married. She was flabbergasted at her own stupidity. Stupidity that arose from trusting someone when she had promised not to ever do that again.

All this time, she had thought he loved her. That he *really* loved her. They had planned a future together. They had planned to work together helping others not to have to go through, or at least, how to deal with, all of the hurt they had endured. They had planned to get her books written and published. So many plans. So many goals. All gone now, like a bottle that had washed out to sea.

Yet, she agreed to keep Shay again this afternoon because Carla had to meet her probation officer to get set up on some new type of addiction program. But the more she thought about it, the madder she became. Christina called Shane to tell him that she was taking Shay over to Carla's because she had a life of her own, and she intended to enjoy it with her *own* son. She had hit her boiling point and she really did not want anyone to see her explode, so she was trying to get out of town gracefully before Noah or Shay saw her growing animosity.

As she was packing up the last of Shane's things, he rang the doorbell. He took no chance of a confrontation between his two women, considering Carla still had no idea what had been going on between her man and Christina. *If this frightened two-timer has gone to the trouble to get off work, take Shay to Carla's, and go back to work, he really IS afraid I'll blow his cover.*

That action, in itself, was a slap in the face to Christina. She had finally been hit upside the head with the fact that she had been a *total* fool. *It is quite alright for MY heart to break, but there's NO WAY Carla is going to have to deal with this love triangle.* Her temper got the best of her as she pushed Shane to turn on her, to say that he didn't care about her, that their love had meant nothing to him, or that there had never even been a love between them.

But he only retreated quietly to his car, slowly leading Shay, taking in every harsh word that this woman, who had been his angel, spit out at him. Shane did not have the nerve to tell her that she was all wrong. That he still *did* love her, that *she* was strong enough to move on, whereas Carla was not, that he would *never* be able to completely leave her, and that *his* heart was also breaking, knowing how he must have destroyed her to make her behave in this manner.

# 23

The need to get away was literally tearing Christina apart. She knew that if she did not get out of *their* setting, the increasingly overwhelming feeling inside would completely overtake her – physically, mentally, *and* emotionally.

*Thank God, Noah got his driver's permit this afternoon. Getting him out of here will be no problem. I won't even need an explanation.* Christina was in no mood to talk about the emotions running loose in her at the moment. She was even apprehensive about saying much of anything at all to Noah since he knew how to read her so well.

Christina had just sent Shane packing with Shay, and all the child's belongings, along with strict instructions to go away, *and stay away*. She knew that no matter how badly she wished for that at the moment, she would probably feel much differently once she had gotten away, and had time to comprehend everything that had happened to her within the past five months.

Regardless, at the moment, there was only one thing on Christina's mind, and that was to make a quick escape. The thought of where to go never even crossed her mind. There had been so

354

much garbage going on, as of late, with Matt, and her job, that she was long overdue for a visit to her parent's house. She wanted them to see her happy, out from underneath the encumbrance of everything going on all around her. The last few calls and visits had been strained, accompanied by a shaky, tearful voice. It was time for them to see that she, the strong-willed survivor, was going to make it through this one, too - on her feet and laughing, as usual.

*Yeah, that's a great thought. And how do you expect to pull THAT one off, Christina? Even you're not that good of an actress, and you CERTAINLY aren't that adept at lying!*

No matter, she was going, and the sooner, the better. She rushed about, throwing a few items in an overnight bag, as she implored Noah to do the same. Christina's thoughts meandered back to his words of an hour earlier when he had reprimanded his mom for her harsh comments to Shane.

"Mom, what has gotten into you? I've never heard you speak to *anyone* like that. I know I have no idea what's going on between you and Shane, but whatever it is, he didn't deserve that. You're the one who is always saying, 'Remember, others are made in God's image, also.' So here you are, crucifying him, the one person who has meant more to you than anyone else. The one man who has loved you more than either of your two husbands, and the one man you love. Mom, I've watched that love. I've heard you tell both Shay and me that when we one day find a mate, you hope and pray that we will find that kind of love. You and Shane may go your separate ways, but the love between the two of you will never die. I'm *sure* of that."

She had run into the house, burst into tears and thrown herself across the bed in the huge master suite. The bed that was never to be shared with him. The bed that proved to be the difference between she and Carla. The bed where she had dreamed of him nightly. The bed that she had hoped would one day be theirs. The bed where she had learned to take naps to forget him with another woman. The bed that now became her solace as she tried desperately to forget him running into another's arms, covering her with kisses – the kisses that should have been hers. The bed wet from the gush of her tears.

Her thoughts wandered madly at first, then slowed with each tear until she finally fell prey to a sleep that allowed her brain to quit the race it was having with itself. Although it proved to be only a catnap, the release that Christina got from that short period of solitude was enough to get her out of her slump to the point that she could move forward.

When she awoke, her mind was still flooded with thoughts of him and another, but Christina was determined to beat her brain at this game. After all, Shane was only a human, and her strength came from a much stronger source.

Noah rounded the circular hall with his bag. "You ready, Mom? I'll be glad to take your things to the car."

She wiped the traces of mascara away, not wanting him to see how many tears had escaped. The son who always made her feel better walked into her room and gave her a much needed hug. "Mom, I'm really sorry about all the fuss I made. I don't know, and I don't want to know, what's going on between you and Shane. It's just that I know you, and I hated to see you say something that you'd regret for years to come."

Christina hugged Noah this time. "Forget it, hon. You were right. I really *don't* know what got into me." She stopped, thinking about the force that was controlling Shane's movements right now – the same force that was creeping its ugly way into her life and her direction. "Yes, I do." The mother, usually full of strength and wisdom, was taking just enough of a pause to compose herself, and find the right words. "Noah, sometimes we get so caught up in the situation around us that we lose all rationality. That is a very jeopardous habit to get into, unless you rely on a power greater than yourself to always guide your path. No matter how strong you are, that is sometimes a *very* difficult task. I was so busy being selfish that I didn't stop to think about Shane's happiness, nor what I really wanted for him. He is the *only* person who can make decisions for himself and his future. Those decisions may not lead him down the path that God has planned for him, but that is his problem to deal with, not mine. I have enough of my *own* problems without trying to cope with his, too. I was trying to control a situation over which I was not the captain."

The son, who possessed his mother's wisdom, listened tentatively until her words stopped. He nodded at her, letting Christina know that he completely understood, and that he accepted her attempted apology, even though it was offered to the wrong person. As he started out her door, she called to him one last time. "Noah, there is a saying that I saw posted at the hospital not long ago. It read, 'We cannot control the wind, but we can control the direction of our sails.' I hope we can both remember those words. They contain a lot of wisdom."

Noah smiled and nodded again at Christina. She was one in a million. "C'mon, Mom. We need to get out of here before Charlotte's Friday afternoon rush hour. I'd hate for you to have a stroke on Brookshire, trying to get on the interstate."

She laughed. How many times had she dreaded riding with him, fearing the worst from a young teenage driver? Now she had not a care in the world, as she looked forward to being chauffeured, giving her mind a break from the weight of the past few weeks.

They got in the car and Noah turned on the radio, which happened to be on a country station, traces of days gone by. He heard his mom give a half laugh, half sigh as she heard the words, "I wish you could have turned my head and left my heart alone." The catty female part of Christina sighed and wished that she could send Shane an autographed copy of the words. But the minister part of her laughed and told her conscience to let it go.

The ride to her parents' mountain home provided a time for conversation that both Noah and Christina needed. It had been a long time since they had been able to enjoy each other's company without interruption, and they both savored the privacy. They had already crossed the state line before Noah warned his mother that he was not allowed to drive in South Carolina on a permit.

"I don't believe this, Mom. I haven't even had my permit for six hours, and you've already got me breaking the law."

Christina, the one who always followed the rules, (*well, almost!*) had turned her fifteen-year-old into a criminal. "I'm sorry, babe. I forgot to tell you to take the exit a few miles back." She did a quick scan of the summer weekend traffic and decided it would be safer to let him continue at the wheel than to try to pull onto the shoulder and change drivers. "Take the next exit, and we'll be back in North Carolina in no time."

"Sure thing. What was that you said about changing the direction of our sails?"

"Yeah, well, just don't ever let it happen again!" Noah and Christina both laughed, hoping the Controller of the Wind would pull them out of this one.

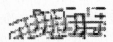

As soon as the greetings were over at her parents' home, Christina went for a long, relaxing walk. She still felt so lost, so helpless. *Helpless* – the word was controlling her. For months, she had been a factor in Shane's life, a major factor. Now it was as if he didn't even know she existed, or so it seemed to her. All the work, all the time, all the effort – *all* down the drain.

358

*Stop it! STOP IT!! Christina, leave it. He isn't worth it. That woman CERTAINLY is not worth it.* And then a strange wave swept through her as she realized that Shane and Carla were both just as worthy of love as she was. She was extremely fortunate in that she had literally hundreds of friends. Friends that she could call, and that would drop everything to come and help her, to hold her, to comfort her, to pray with her, at any given instant. *What did* they *have?*

The pity that took over Christina's thoughts banished all traces of anger and bitterness that had controlled her earlier in the day. She realized that being the survivor she was, she still had a life. A life that she would take and run with, whereas Shane and Carla were going to be stuck in a neutral zone, holding each other back, *at least for the time being.*

Christina felt an increased sense of revitalization with each step she took. She was suddenly saddened that Shane had never succumbed to going on long walks with her. Walks that cleared one's mind. Walks that threw stress and anxiety out the window. Walks that provided the quiet and solitude in which one could listen for God. Walks that made a person one with nature. Walks that healed many wounds. No wonder walks were renowned as one of the greatest exercises known to man. For a long walk truly *did* exercise *all* of a person's being.

By the time Christina had made her way up and down all the surrounding mountainous drives, she felt like a person in control of her own life again. She had no idea how long she had been gone, but she knew it was long enough to get a major attitude adjustment. In fact, her life once again had a new direction. The recent musical about Moses had allowed her to see many parallels between that ancient patriarch and Shane, as she saw inside her rebel, and all his attributes and possibilities. But now, it was she who had been to the mountaintop with God, *literally*, and come back down with the message that she was to leave her past behind and move to the mountaintop – only this time it was *not* the *proverbial* mountaintop.

She had been sensing that redirection for a couple of months, but she had not shared it with anyone. *Anyone besides Shane.* Now that she had sought God's guidance and listened, *really listened*, she knew that the feelings she had perceived over the past few weeks were real. Christina knew herself well enough to know that her mind would be running away with thoughts for the future if she was not careful. But for once, she listened to the common-sense side of her brain that told her to get a good night's rest, *not like it hasn't been quite a day!*, and let tomorrow be the fresh start of a new chapter in her life.

Noah heard his mom's footsteps, and excused himself to go check on her. "Mom, are you alright?"

"Noah, I couldn't be better!" The change of mood showed all over Christina's face. She saw, once again, that it was impossible for her to hold anything back from Noah. He was so in tune with her thoughts and emotions that it was obvious he had seen through her earlier mask. Worried that her parents might have had the same perception, she asked, "Do you think Mama and Daddy know what's going on?"

"Who knows? Even if they did, they wouldn't ask you about it unless you volunteered." Christina knew her son was right. Although she was extremely close to her parents, she did not sit and disclose everything with them the way she and Noah did. *The difference in the generations,* she reckoned to herself.

She proceeded to tell Noah about what she had felt and heard in her heart during the walk. Her mind was made up. Christina, as usual, was going to follow the voice she had heard and put her house on the market as soon as she got back home.

"Noah, be honest with me." She knew that was an unnecessary command. Her son had *always* been honest with her – sometimes *too* honest. "Do you think I have *completely* lost my mind?"

360

He looked her dead in the eye, not even taking any time to think about his response. "No." Noah carefully surveyed his mother's face. "But if you have, it's in a good way!"

They both laughed as Noah reached over and embraced Christina. He had seen the writing on the wall for a long time, and wondered how long it was going to take his mother to face the reality of picking up and moving. Her greatest challenge was going to be leaving him, knowing he would not want to leave his high school and all his friends. In the back of his mind, the intuitive son began to mentally prepare himself for the challenge of helping her get beyond that obstacle.

As a perfect ending to their day together, the two knelt in prayer as Noah took his mother's arm and guided her to the floor with him. Christina had never felt so humbled in all her life. She became overwhelmed with such emotion that she could not even speak to God. But she knew inside there was no need for words. He knew every thought and every concern that existed within her being. *Just as He knew my prayer, a prayer that I did not even pray, or was even aware of, for a solace in time of need. A solace that brought healing. A solace that gave me strength. A solace that gave new meaning to life. . . A solace . . . named Shane Sievers.*

# 24

It had been quite some time since Christina had awakened with the vibrancy she felt the next morning. There was still the same longing in her heart that had been there for weeks. As many weeks, in fact, as she had known Shane. But there was a difference in her this morning. She sensed the overhaul that her system had experienced last night. Today, she was ready to face anything He threw at her, and she knew from the evening before, that there was plenty more where that came from.

She was up and out the door before Noah awoke, sprinting up and down the same paths she had traveled the night before. Christina could already feel the presence that was descending itself upon her. *Yes, Lord, I'm ready. Let the festivities begin.* To her, it was a day of celebration. There was something definitely going on in her life, a lunge forward that she had not experienced up to this point. And whatever it was, she could tell that she liked it – *immensely!*

By the time she got back, her mom had breakfast waiting for her on the screened porch overlooking the brook and the mountain. Almost afraid to tell her mother about her upcoming change, for fear Mrs. Cache would think she had gone off the deep end,

Christina decided there was no way to break the news but to dive right into it.

"Momma, I know you and Daddy have never stood in the way of anything I did. And not only that, you supported me fully in whatever I did, even when I made grave mistakes. I never doubted your love, or your faith in me. I have to tell you something, and I pray you will be able to accept *it* in the same manner. I've never been known for taking the easy way out. I guess it's the continual challenge that keeps me going. For whatever reason, this is no exception. You've taught me that, no matter what, I should always place my faith and trust in God, and there have been many times in my adult life when it was just me and Him out there, and I sometimes felt like we were up against the whole world. But not once was I afraid. I was never even apprehensive. However, I *was* always ready to face the battle. I've always invited the challenge of having the odds against me. It made the victory sweeter."

"For a good while now, I've been feeling out of place, like I just didn't belong amongst my friends any longer. Whenever I'm around them, it doesn't feel right. It's not them, it's completely me. My life seems to be taking a turn, and I'm not exactly sure where I'm going, but I do know that I'm in a rut where I am. During my walk last night, I felt God's will for me to leave, to go to the mountains. I have been feeling that urge for a few months, but I wanted to make sure it was His will and not mine."

"You know that I have always wanted to reach out to people in a different way, and I perceive that is the direction in which I am going. You also know that I have had these books flowing out of my fingers for a few years now. I feel confident that I *must* follow my dream. I *must* go out there and give it all I've got. And, most of all, I feel like I'm being pulled to that end by a power greater than myself. Mom, I *have* to do this. If I don't, I'll regret it for the rest of my life. So . . . I'm selling my house as soon as I get back home, and following the path I see laid out in front of me."

363

Mrs. Cache, the woman of few words, had seen her daughter face every challenge she had ever been dealt, and she knew the reason Christina had seen them through was precisely her deep faith. The wise woman had also watched the struggle going on within her daughter over the past few years, and she had seen it all come to a head during the last several months. She also knew there was a much deeper problem than met the eye.

"Christina, you're the *only* one who can know what is in your heart, and what is right for you. We have raised you to be able to take care of yourself, and to make it on your own. You are a strong person, and you can do whatever you set your mind to."

The daughter didn't make a sound. Christina only sat there, staring out across the beauty that stretched out in front of her. Thoughts were racing through her head, and she knew she must spend the day listening, lest she miss further instructions from her Father. She remembered visiting a place right after her parents moved to the mountains, as they were giving her the grand tour. That was where she must go. She told her dad, and within minutes, she was standing atop a rock, overlooking miles and miles of nature's splendor.

Noah came from out of nowhere and grabbed her. "Mom, come here. I've *got* to show you something."

She followed her son's footsteps, which wandered down a path so narrow and steep that Christina wondered if she was going to slip over the side of the mountain. Noah stopped and held out his hand. Her eyes turned to find a cave – small, yet a large enough cut-out in the rock for her and her adventurous son to sprawl out and enjoy its comfort and warmth.

"How did you find this?" she quizzed Noah.

"I just went roaming, you know, like any typical fifteen-year-old guy, and found this covered path. When I saw this indention in the rocks, I knew you would love it."

The indention proved to be rocks that had fallen at some point long ago and made a natural cover over a flat place that jutted out on the mountain.

"I can't believe people aren't swarming all around this place. It is awesome!"

"It also has *Christina Cache* written all over it," Noah chuckled, realizing he had just played a role in what was yet another blessing that spoke to his mom.

"Oh, Noah," Christina shrieked, brought to tears by his sensitivity.

Christina immediately sat down and took out a small tablet and began jotting notes. Her son watched briefly, shaking his head. Once again, he had been privy to his mom's fate. *Only this time, it's pretty cool!,* he thought, as he went on another exploring expedition.

As words filled the tiny pages, Christina literally *felt* God's richness pouring all over her. She stopped writing and stared into the vastness that stretched out in front of her. It felt as if her "halo," as Shane called it, had a new luster. She felt no burdens, and Shane was absent from her thoughts. The idea of being homeless was even intriguing.

The pad in her hand caught her attention. She flipped back through page after page of notes. Notes taken all over the world. Notes about all types of people. Notes about all kinds of experiences. And it was as if she could hear His voice, *"Christina ... Christina..."* The ecstasy of knowing her destiny was bouncing throughout her entire being, like electrical charges, or shockwaves. Her hand was drumming the pen against her knee in an uncontrollable rhythm. It was perfectly clear to Christina what she was supposed to be doing, and she knew exactly where she was to go to start.

Noah walked back into the cave, expecting to see tears streaming down Christina's face, given her sentimental nature. But instead, he beheld her face, radiant with a glow, a smile, and true contentment, combined with a gaze of awe, that reminded him of Moses after seeing and hearing the burning bush. *My God. She really HAS been to the mountaintop!* The mesmerized son could not speak, afraid that he would interrupt the sanctity and the sovereignty of the moment. He truly had shared in her blessedness, and he, too, sensed that this was only the beginning of a full day of her amazing experiences.

When she finally moved, her words did not surprise her son. "Noah, I'm going to quit my job and turn all of these notes into books. All of those ideas in the computer are finally going to happen."

"Well, it's about time!" Noah was ecstatic for his mom. He knew she no longer belonged where she was, and that it was time for her to move onto greater things, *and a more fulfilling life.* Not wanting this high to turn into a binge of tears, he added a phrase about which he always teased her. "Besides, you have too many episodes of 'explosive diarrhea of the mind' not to do *something* worthwhile with all those words!"

She wrapped her arm around Noah, hugging him with all her might, as she recalled the first time he had said those words to her. *Has it really been four years? He's right. The time really has come!*

They rushed back to pack their belongings and get started on their new venture. Mr. and Mrs. Cache could see the lack of stress in their daughter's face. She hugged them good-bye and told them of her plans.

"I do hope that I haven't lost my mind," Christina said, almost apologetically, figuring they were probably skeptical about her giving up a good job and moving out of a house she loved.

"No," replied her mother. "Sometimes peace of mind is worth more than other things." The daughter realized that her parents were behind her all the way, which added to the relief that she felt over the monumental decision to let go of all the material things in her life.

"You really *don't* have to worry about me. I don't feel crazy at all. In fact, for the first time in years, I actually feel like I've got my head on straight." The peacefulness on Christina's face said more to her parents than the words she had just uttered, and they knew she was right in her statement.

As Noah drove onto the parkway, Christina settled back for a day of meditation and relaxation. Having felt numbed much of the time lately, she had gotten her feeling back that day. She let her healing thoughts take control as she watched the curving highway stretch out in front of them, revealing peaks and valleys that could only be seen from the vantage point of the Blue Ridge Parkway.

She had finally grasped what a great impact Shane had on her. *If it hadn't been for him, I wouldn't be ready to take this giant step.* He had taught her so much, even amongst all the lies and deception. Christina knew she had to reap the good, which had tremendously outweighed the bad. *He has been rewarded greatly for his contribution, and I have paid dearly for the lesson.* However, most of it had been fun and enjoyable. She had to be appreciative for what there had been, and not worry about what there had not been.

Christina knew that from now on, her lifelong friends would be few, but Shane would rank right up there with Abigail. Her circle would include her parents, and her sons. *That is, if Matt wants to be a part of us*, knowing he was still moving as far in an opposite direction as he could.

Just then, Christina's cell phone rang. Her heart stopped, praying that Shane would not interfere with her newly found peace of mind. To her delight, however, it was Matt's voice that spoke. He sounded terrific, especially for Matt, and was full of plans for getting his life in order.

"I can't wait to see you, Mom. We have so much to talk about. And this is one time you'll actually be *glad* to sit and listen to me. I love you. Tell Noah I said 'hello' and not to get too many speeding tickets before he gets you home."

She hung up the phone. *Was Matt's call an omen that I should get on with the program and he will fall in line? I assume so,* she mused as she looked up at the cloudless blue sky, knowing her Father was looking down on her.

Noah continued to drive for a couple of hours before Christina finally told him to take an exit. He had no idea where they were going, but he was following her plan, just as she was following the plan from above.

It had been imperative that she go to Little Switzerland the minute she left her cave. *Funny that I was afraid I would be depressed, since this is the first place Shane took me, where we sat at this same corner table and watched that spectacular sunset. What a mesmerizing experience it was! We spent our first three weekends together in the mountains, staring into each other's eyes, exploring each other's minds, searching the depths of each other's souls. Yet, here I sit, eating on the same deck with Noah, mentally outlining a beautiful love story in this setting, without even thinking about Shane.*

She envisioned a couple, the love and trust they felt, and the experiences they shared, yet Christina was able to totally step out of it and still write it from her heart. *It really happened, yet it was fictional, and oh, what a beautiful love story. The most beautiful I have ever heard.*

Christina pulled out her writing tablet and began throwing words on the paper as fast as her hand could move the pen. Knowing Noah had a paperback in the car, she suggested that he read as she wrote, not wanting him to be bored.

"If I read that much, I'll be a genius. Not that I'm not *already* a genius!" Noah joked with her.

"Do I write *that* much?"

The look on Noah's face answered the question. Christina knew she had never been at a loss for words when she sat to write, but she had no idea that it was obvious to everyone else. "Don't worry about me, Mom. Seeing you this happy and together right now is enough to keep me occupied. Besides, I know that you'll write until you're so tired that you will have no choice but to let me drive home."

She smiled, thinking of the winding curves that lay ahead of them on the way home. Yet, he had done a fine job of getting her to Little Switzerland via the Parkway. And compared to the way Noah had dealt with the curves that had been hurled into their lives, getting her down that mountain would be a breeze.

Christina reflected back over the situation of the past few months, and how incredibly fast she had begun the healing process. She had spent the night before with the most wonderful friend and confidant she'd ever had, and knew that in the long haul, He was all she needed. He had allowed her to grow into the person she was – strong, secure, proud, humble, and loving – and excited about starting a new journey. Although it was going to be a total overhaul, it had generated out of forty-four years of experience.

Funny. It started here, now it was ending here. It seemed the perfect ending. Christina was actually able to go for several minutes at a time without thinking of Shane – or Shane with Carla – a major accomplishment from the last few weeks.

Thinking of him loving Carla the way he did made Christina realize what a big heart Shane really had, considering her physical handicap, added to several maladies. As the minister had recognized ever since she had known him, he needed to feel he could take care of someone, too. Christina had seen that she was too strong and too much for him. Her independence and power of will made it difficult for him to feel she could ever need him the way Carla did. She knew that Shane could truly feel like the caretaker in her eyes and could take her places, instead of the way it had been in their case. Every man's ego thrived on that, and she needed to understand that in order for him to be the responsible being he needed to envision of himself, Shane *must* have that.

She felt no pain, hurt, or betrayal from Shane right now. Christina prayed that her present emotional state would continue once she returned home and found herself in the setting where it had all taken place. For the moment, though, she was pretty confident that it would. Had she not just told Noah that this was the best she had felt in quite a while?

Noah had eaten chicken tenders, mozzarella sticks and a huge cheeseburger, washed down by three Mountain Dews, and was playing the juke box and the pinball machine, and had not uttered even one complaint. He seemed to understand that his mother needed the time, that she deserved a life, too, and that they were sharing a special mom-and-son thing.

*It's super being Noah's mom. He's such a cool kid.*

When Noah scooted back over to the table for a brief moment, grabbing a sip of soda, she asked him how he was able to occupy himself on such a gorgeous late summer afternoon, just for her benefit. He looked at his mom's loving face and said in his usual ironic manner, "I'm just a cool kid."

Christina gave him a glare, urging a serious response. "It's just that I don't get upset easily, Mom. I take things as they come." The astute son saw the sentimental look spreading over her face, so he quickly added, "How else could I survive in this family?"

She flashed that "get outta here" smile at him, sending him back to the pinball machine. He gave her a hug as he left, and stated simply, "We *do* have a unique relationship." Noah started to walk away, with the coda, "I love you, Mom."

Christina put the pad down long enough to watch him pull back the spring rod and shoot the first ball. Six months ago, she would have never entered a place like this, much less have brought Noah. Now she wasn't at all afraid of the characters whom she might see. And all of the glasses and bottles clanging, the loud talk, the banging of the pinball machine, and the wails coming from the jukebox didn't even faze her. She heard all of it, but it was lost somewhere in the background.

All that had her attention was the gorgeous setting that God had painted out in front of her, and the story inside her heart that was pouring itself out on paper. *What a life!* Christina was so happy and content at that exact moment that she could care less if she ever saw, or heard from, *anyone* again. She was in her own world of perfect tranquility.

She was aware that she had to go home and endure a grueling morning the following day, and she wondered whether Shane would call her, as was his normal routine, but right then, none of it mattered. Sitting there, watching Noah be so content with who he was, and throwing herself into being his mom, *was* her reality. It *was* Christina Cache, the final reward for which she had lived and worked, and it was *all* she needed. As far as she was concerned, the stress-free, laid-back relaxation that had transcended upon her was hers from now on. She took another glance over her shoulder, again looking at Noah, then peered out over the mountains that flaunted a flawless summer sky. *How fortunate and blessed I am!*

Noah peeked over his shoulder and looked at his mom out on the deck. He was surprised that he actually liked half of the songs on the jukebox. The joint really was a low-life place, a far stretch from Christina's usual hang-outs. Most of the places in Little Switzerland appealed to a higher class of clientele, more to her liking, but he realized that she had to come there to settle a record, to say her good-byes. Seeing the strength with which his mom dealt with her problems made him proud to be her son. In all reality, it was *her* who was the coolest. Noah prayed he had inherited those genes so that when he was a dad, his kids would love and admire him as much as he did her.

Christina closely watched Noah, trying not to let him see that she was reliving their past in her mind. She had been ruefully concerned about how she had neglected him when he was young, busy trying to be the attentive wife to Tom, who demanded all her time. But as she followed his steps with her stare, the guilty mother tossed an albatross from around her neck as she realized that the two of them possessed a bond that was a rarity between most moms and their teenage kids.

Her thoughts turned back to the present as she decided that she would not even have to rent an apartment or a motel room. She could write sitting right where she was and find a place to hide away in the Blazer on nights when she was not staying in the family's house in the country.

Looking out over the deck, still admiring the view, a spontaneous idea wriggled its way through Christina's mind. *Maybe I'll even learn to drink Michelob Light.* She looked at the people sitting behind her, wasting away into oblivion. *Or maybe not!* There was far too much work to do in the coming months, and incomparable scenery to enjoy, not to be in total control of herself. *I've lived this long without addictive habits. There's no point in starting them now.*

There was only one Man on Christina's mind, the only one she needed to be thinking of, the only one who had *never* let her down. He had led her to this spot the first time, and He had led her there now. Shane had been merely an instrument, a part of His plan.

Looking back on the past few months, they had been so awesome that they were beyond words, even for her. She had watched a miracle happen, *two miracles actually*, and she was happy again for the first time in years.

*Yes, I will truly miss Shane, but he's done his work; he has taken care of me unknowingly, and now I'm able to go on with my journey, with or without him. And I am actually excited about it.*

Christina had known for years that she was to move in a different direction. She had prayed daily that she would find the path she was to follow, a path that would allow her to reach out to people outside the four walls of the church building, and as of that morning, she had gotten her answer. Her professors at SMU had encouraged her to write four years ago, but that morning, after boxes of notes on legal pads, she had gotten her own personal message. She was to write, and she was to begin on that very day. And she had already begun to follow that order. Words were flying from her pen, and the pad was filling up, one page after another. *No more days of scribbling notes. The real books are now underway!*

*Today IS the first day of the rest of my life. July 11th – only one day so far, but it has been going uphill ever since it started. I know it won't always be this way, but what a way for life to begin! Abigail is right. I CAN have it all – I do right now. It's just a matter of realizing it and accepting it. From here on, it is going to be Higher Ground.*

She finished up her journaling and looked out across the view in front of her, thinking still of her future and how she had started down a new path, one that would lead her toward that *Higher Ground*, as of that very day. There was a small, lone bird, floating, simply floating on air, so carefree, enjoying its limitless freedom. Christina could not help but notice the similarity between her own life and the symbolism of that bird. *Another omen from the Father?* She decided so.

But then, she *was* the queen of analogies. *There is no way I can get through this experience without some sort of symbolism,* she thought as she jotted down a note about the bird. Then it hit Christina just how long it had been since she had analyzed anything. The symbols simply had not been there, they had not caught her attention or spoken to her.

Christina looked up at the bird again, still floating right out in front of her as if relaying God's private "for your eyes only" message. Her 1-800 line was back in service, and her Father was once again standing right along beside her. *Like He was the one who went anywhere!* The story *had* ended the same way it had begun, but so much had taken place in the middle. A whole new life, yet the same person, with the same values.

Noah had played three songs on the jukebox, the last one being *I Heard It Through the Grapevine.* The music was so energetic, and had such a driving rhythm, that it automatically raised what few of Christina's spirits that were still feeling down in the dumps. *My son and his perfect timing! I must tell Noah that he's done it again. Just as I finish up my writing here, he plays this song and reminds me that I indeed HAVE heard it through the grapevine – God's grapevine. My analytical sense is truly back.*

Her son came back over to the table just in time to hear his mother spout off, "How perfect. I *did* hear it through the grapevine - God's direct, 1-800-WATS line."

"Mom, you're too much. You should write a book with that song title about that direct WATS line of yours!"

Christina threw her hand up and gave him a high five.

"Are you really going to, Mom?"

Nodding her head yes, Christina's pen began to pour out words non-stop again. Noah grinned and turned around, heading back over to the jukebox to listen to his selection. He walked back to the table one last time as the song ended to check on her. She was packing up her tablet and pen. *She truly is amazing. My mom is so incredibly talented and so awesomely in touch with everything around her that it's hard to believe she is only human sometimes.*

She gazed proudly at her son, thinking of the inspiration he had just given her, which he did quite often – practically every time they were together. Christina was glad he had been along to share the day with her. It made it all the more special. She glanced into his youthful blue eyes, which were beaming with pride back at her, as she thought dreamily, *What a day! What a life!! What a perfect ending!!!*

"We have certainly seized the day, haven't we?" Christina asked, at the same time thanking her Maker of the Stars for the blessing of her sons and parents.

"Most definitely," Noah replied, holding out his elbow to escort her out the door and to the parking lot, treating her like the highly respectable lady that she seemed to him.

He opened her door and took a deep bow, waving his arm out in front of him to signal his mother to get in the car. Christina laughed at Noah's antics, appreciative of his sense of humor, but more for his desire to make her feel better, wanting her to forget all the pain that accompanied the situation of the past few months. Before she got in the car and allowed her loving son to chauffer her home, she took one long, last look at the spectacle in front of her.

Somewhere out there, over the side of those mountains, lay thirteen years of hell, chunked into hundreds of pieces – all pieces gone from Christina's life. She started to chuckle, then her face settled into a broad smile, as she sipped on her iced tea, still staring out over the incomparable view that Shane had introduced to her.

*Life is great. I have nothing, yet everything I need. I am ready to board my train (and leave the station this time!) – by myself – but a whole and complete person. Love lifted me!*

# LOVE LIFTED ME

*I was sinking deep in sin,*
*far from the peaceful shore,*
*Very deeply stained within,*
*sinking to rise no more;*
*But the Master of the Sea*
*heard my despairing cry,*
*From the waters lifted me,*
*NOW SAFE AM I.*

*Love Lifted Me!  Love Lifted Me!*
*When Nothing Else Could Help,*
*LOVE LIFTED ME.*

*All my heart to Him I give,*
*ever to Him I'll cling,*
*In His blessed presence live,*
*ever His praises sing.*
*Love so mighty and so true*
*merits my soul's best songs;*
*Faithful, loving service, too,*
*TO HIM BELONGS.*

*Love Lifted Me!  Love Lifted Me!*
*When Nothing Else Could Help,*
*LOVE LIFTED ME.*

- - James Howe

# COMING SUMMER, 2002
## *HIGHER GROUND*

In the second volume of The Eagle's Wings trilogy, Christina Cache, because of a recent and strange friendship with the most unlikely of soul mates, dares to take the leap to reach her own higher ground when she follows her calling. Ever willing and anxious to face a challenge, she finds herself with a new home and a new career, but virtually has to start from ground zero with both. Hard work, faith and perseverance pay off as she climbs the peak in search of her *HIGHER GROUND*.

**Reserve your copy of the second book in The Eagle's Wings trilogy, *Higher Ground*, by mailing the form below, or you may contact CRM by toll-free phone, Fax, or e-mail.**

———————————

## ADVANCE ORDER FORM

**Book Title** _____

**Name** _____

**Address** _____

**Phone number** _____

**e-mail address** _____

(Send to)
### CRM
**P.O. Box 367, Paw Creek, NC 28130**
**1-866-CRM-BOOK**
**FAX – 704-391-1698**
**www.ciridmus.com**

# COMING FOR MOTHER'S DAY, 2002
## *IN THE GARDEN*

Rosemary sat on a bench amidst the flowers of the hospital's garden reading the Mother's Day card one last time before she sealed the envelope. It was not the first time she and her mother had spent this special day in this surrounding. However, the last time, forty-seven years ago, was the day that Rosemary was born.

Of course the woman sitting on the bench had no recollection of that day. But she had heard all the stories, both good and bad, of the events that occurred. She had also heard how she should have died, how the nurses told the doctor, "that baby will *never* make it". But God had seen fit to work a miracle on that day, to allow a mother to hold onto her blessed child.

Now, two days after Cheree had been diagnosed with a huge malignancy, and was upstairs undergoing a blood transfusion just to be able to make it until the surgery on Monday, Rosemary prayed that God would once again use this setting to work another Mother's Day miracle. Only this time, she was hoping that He would allow the child to hold onto her blessed mother.

As she finished her prayer, a vision came to her of another prayer once prayed in a garden – a vision of a lone, solitary man, bending beneath the olive trees, also not wanting to drink from the cup. *God grant me the serenity to accept the things I cannot change*, Rosemary whispered as she stood to take the card to her mother.

**In the Garden, a novella ideal for Mother's Day, is filled with memories of a daughter and her mother, all tales that revolve around a garden. More than flowers or vegetables are grown in that garden, as unfolds in words, of the nurturing love of a mother to her child.**

# About the Author

Catherine Ritch Guess, also a published composer, is currently working on a recording to go with each of her book titles. When she is not making music, she can be found either in the Blue Ridge Mountains of North Carolina or the deserts of Arizona writing a fourth volume to follow her Eagle's Wings Trilogy. A mother of three sons, she and her husband, Glenn, live in Charlotte, North Carolina.